Bless You

Barbara E. Heintz

Pinkhoneysuckle

Authorization Code
0246y A
0246 4A

Trans ID
566271914

contest @ community . com

Barbara Everett Heintz
Robert V. Everett - CONTRIBUTING AUTHOR
Rebekah Leah Heintz - ASSOCIATE EDITOR

Attn. Nicole Thanks.
F + W Media Inc.
10151 Carver Rd.
Blu. Ash, OH
24242

Robert V. Everett, Contributing Author and Photo Consultant
Rebekah Leah Heintz, Associate Editor

ISBN: 1461188202
ISBN 13: 978-1461188209
Library of Congress Control Number: 2011908182
CreateSpace, North Charleston, South Carolina

Pink Honeysuckle began long before my birth. The hidden Americans. Appalachian people would come from the highlands of Scotland where they would bring spirits of independence, self rule, and a society who first chose to stay apart, even into the 20th century. They kept the old ways and maintained a culture and identity not always welcomed by outsiders who wanted in. Child abuse and the battering of women, along with sexual molestation were justified using the Bible, without the gift of love as part of the teaching. Codes of silence protected the perpetrators, since fear was a constant companion. The United States government would not acknowledge our suffering and we children were worked as adults. Keeping the secrets of one's world was the earliest messages the weaker among us learned. Even babies would learn not to cry, for one wished not to bring attention to the needs of so many. We are the hillbillies, the crackers, the holy rollers, and the rednecks. To leave such a world behind, the brutality, the shame, and the brokenness begins my story, and my life is simply a mirror of so many others. Blessings to the angels who kept appearing when I would fall; "Oh Glory;" when I would fall. Barbara Everett Heintz

THE DEDICATION OF MY BOOK

There are too many friends, loved ones, teachers, and angels who have crossed my path to even begin some long letter of thanks. You know who you are. From Pisgah, Alabama to Franklin County, Tennessee; in Washington, D.C., Cincinnati, and San Francisco, I have to thank everyone for the help and for the encouragement to write this book. I could not get the names on dozens of pages, so I have to narrow this down some way.

Thanks to Frank, my husband, and to the children, especially Mary and Jacob, who have spent days doing the computer work. I thank Rebekah, my daughter-in-law, who set up my blog and helped whenever and wherever she could. I thank the groups I have written with, my friends, Joe Folger, and Shirley Keith, The Cincinnati Woman's Club Group, Namad who made me keep reading when tears made me blind to what I had written, to Mrs. Betty Thompson of CWC who brought me in to Namad, Mrs. Ellen Sewell and to Melanie Hunt who have cheered me on all of these years. To Roberta Ley, Fr. David Robisch, and The Prayer Group of St. Mary's who kept me hanging on. I thank with great love my brother, Robert Van Everett, for writing his exquisite prologue for me. Lastly, blessings to the other brothers and sisters and to the souls of our parents, Amos and Thelma Everett; I am nothing without the roads we walked together. And for the children of the Appalachian Trail from the mountains to the valleys below—my thanks is beyond measure.

To nurses everywhere, to my sweet friend, Bernie, who taught me about rescue and love. Special mention to: Matthew, Karen and Sammy; Isaac, Erica, Isabella and Rivven; Jacob, Rebekah, Frankie and Gabriel, and to Mary and Kevin. God bless my Catherine with love excelling; perhaps you will understand me a little better from the road on which I traveled. To Marilyn and E. P. Harris, and all the old friends of Clifton, Blue Ash, Hyde

Park and Anderson Township, especially Dr. and Mrs. Stephen Blatt, for we have been together through the best and the worst of times.

Contributing Writer, Robert .V. Everett; Contributing Editor, Rebekah Leah Heintz; Photographs – courtesy of Robert V. Everett, arranged by Mary and Kevin Howell

Disclaimer

This is a work of fiction with some effort to keep dates and times of national events and other significant information close to accuracy. It reflects the life of the author through her personal experiences, and some names may sound familiar that are used, but they too are to be noted as fictional. The writer's thoughts, opinions, and memories are as she remembers, and familiar-sounding names and events are her interpretation of what seemed to have relevance to her life. Truth may resemble reality, but this truth reflects the author's vision, and names of people and places are coincidental in how they relate to the story. Much attention has been given to the details of historical events, times, places, and characters; they are to be considered to be subjective for the benefit of writing this Appalachian tale. The author does wish to open thoughts to the plight of the citizens of Appalachian heritage at the expense of portraying significant events within her own life and hers alone. Each person must seek his or her own reality and it is felt by the writer that what actually happened during her lifetime might give others the opportunity to speak regarding similar life histories and events.

Introduction By Author

I began this novel about eighteen months ago, though the story started in me from the day I first went to school. I was five years old and terrified of everything from the yellow school bus, to the teacher who had the wooden paddle and showed it so willingly on the first day. Something deep within began to stir as early as that time as I saw a lot of other children for the first time in my life, and I noted early on that there were a few children who seemed to live lives where there was so little fear. They came to school with fresh, new and clean clothes, and their mothers could come to school and to help them if they were having problems. It was my early experience with what would become known to me as a "Hierarchy of Well Being" as later I grew to understand human class structures.

There were about four recognizable groups from my earliest days after having been born on the southern-most tip of Appalachia, and it began with this. First, the people who had some wealth. Then there were some families who were just alright, as were a lot of my neighbors. Third were families who had virtually nothing, but they endeavored to stay clean, and parents tried to provide even though they were unable to because of bad luck, lack of support from extended family, or both. At the very bottom were the children who came to school dirty and who had homes that were so filthy and marginal that they were fully ignored and detached from other people. My mother and father, hard as they tried, fell somewhere in the third group, and if I tried hard enough I could always find someone worse off than me. All of us in the latter two groups had no medical or dental care, and the clothes we wore were somehow handed down from higher places. Group three made an effort to prepare for when the cold came and had minimal rations to get through the winter months, but the mothers and fathers got us through on what little could be canned, sewed from flour sacks, and whatever was forageable, and when that was used up we got by on dried beans and potatoes and sometimes one or the other. Children in the fourth realm might be getting a little assistance, but usually it went toward the parents' alcohol and cigarettes, and the parents wallowed in filth while the poor children just scraped up whatever they could, and I mean that.

There were no rescue groups in our world, and toys were homemade if at all, but the farm chores took care of most of the longings for that luxury, and our poor mother could not bear to see us waste time on books, so we treasured our school books as our communication with another life. Most children that were at the bottom-most rung of society had given up on school before they had even begun, and school books might become their toilet paper. Things were so hopeless among the poorest, and for those children, their next generations were apt to be even worse off to the point the best thing that could happen would be removal from the home if the county nurse saw fit to turn the family in to the state. It did not happen as often as it should have, and the care facilities were more like penal institutions. I wanted to be adopted, and I did not even believe that I was born into my circumstances, but it would prove to be true that we were the, "clean" poor. We were slaves within the hierarchy of our own families, because Mama and Daddy thought that a day's work might earn an ounce of care, so we worked from the earliest ages. By age five, one was pulling a cotton sack come October.

We did plant a garden, usually had a milk cow or two, and Mama had some chickens, so spring and summer were filled with work and some hope. We were hired out for as little as two dollars per hour to pick one hundred pounds of cotton, and some relatives would endeavor not to pay us because we were kin, but I tell you that cotton picking in our area until about 1960 would get you a pair of shoes and a dress for school, so school let out for us for three weeks around October every year because kids were not going to be attending anyway. Cotton season might mean pairs of shoes, but of most importance, it had to pay back enough for next season's crop.

After that it was time to strip tobacco which meant that we graded the leaves that Daddy and the boys had hung in the barn to cure, but for that there was no hiring out, but a tobacco check could pay the light bills, maybe. I do not know what the poorest of the poor did in these months, but usually they had the same clothes on they wore every day before school let out.

Celebrations were altogether unknown, though we went to church and we knew about Christmas. A basket of apples and oranges were a pot of gold at Christmas if Daddy had enough left over from the tobacco check to cover that, but I did not know that people had Thanksgiving dinners until I was about ten years old, because that was the time of the year to pull the cotton bolls which were virtually worthless but for a few dollars. They were the trash cotton forced out of the bolls at the end of the season. We picked them until our hands were freezing and Daddy finally said, "Let's go home." I cannot speak for the others, but when I heard those words I would cry tears of joy just to sit around the one wood stove we had to heat a house which had a tin roof that did not leak when Daddy had the money to keep it repaired. Winters were so abysmal that I have almost erased how we got through them, for the cows go dry, and the hens stop laying. All that was pleasant was to finally get in bed with several family members under as many quilts as Mama had left from long-ago quilting with the grandmothers.

We knew of no such places as The Salvation Army, St. Vincent de Paul, or any help organizations. They did not come to us, the hidden children mainly white but with a few blacks who had not gone North, but a rare and kind soul would remember us if they were throwing away something. When I speak of "us," I mean all of the back-road Appalachian mountain and valley kids, for this story is way beyond me, and I can say that most people are not even aware that we ever existed. President Eisenhower had saved Europe, and the bomb had ended Japan's aggression, and there was a plan to rebuild Europe and the lost cities of World War II, and you have been told all about the good old days of the 40s, 50s, and 60s; but you have not been told about us, because no one knew that we existed. It was usually better for those who had not to let the world know about us "Have Nots" right here in the United States of America in the modern twentieth century. You had children living in crude nineteenth-century life's ways and dwellings. In some cases the slaves of the Civil War got more than we did because the rich at least threw things out.

There was not much to be thrown out to us. In our defense, all of us in group three, the "clean" people without, did know about self sufficiency. Such things as canning, sewing, cooking, cleaning, and we were brought up churched, so we knew about morals, and in school and at home we were taught manners to get by on, but that, too, would fade away as give-away programs offered free money not to farm your land. Folks like mine, at least, showed us survival techniques, but as the twentieth century progressed, drugs came to the country. The new attitude of those with the little money and clout seemed to be that poverty meant stupidity, "So let us kill ourselves off" with the new prohibition. If people thought moonshine destroyed communities, then they are thoroughly confused, for it was tainted tap water compared to the ravages of crack and meth in our Appalachian country areas and especially in the little towns—but that is not mine to discuss, for, like all people fear keeps the victims addicted and the suppliers well off, and we cannot do anything about this. We country-bred know when to shut up, and here we draw the line, for we've always been invisible to the rest of the country, and even we must put on blindfolds for those demons are beyond our ability to repair.

The dirty and poor can now lose their teeth even earlier, and the hillbilly jokes can roll like thunder, because America has not owned up to the responsibility it has to the children of Appalachia and to the new generation of parents who throw up their hands now that their elders have passed on. They died off without leaving their fervor for living off what hard work and the good earth could provide. How do we even begin to help people rise up without motivation to plant food, to share community resources, but most of all to help Appalachian poor to know their own strengths and heritage. Politicians do not care or see, and they never have, for you can buy a vote with a lie and a coca-cola, so why waste your time among the poor? From the southern-most tip of Appalachia straight through to the coal mines and the rocky cliffs of Maine—why bother with a bunch of people who can be bought for so little?

Welfare was thrown at the problem, so some sat down and forgot how autonomy felt. Next the skills and dignity collapsed for even families who once forbade such insult. When pride of making one's own way is lost, what is left to take from the empty soul?

I will face condemnation for telling you my story and I will not tell you what is truth and what is fiction, but I will leave you chilled, or so I hope. There are children without as there always have been, and while you are angry about all of that I want you to know that we were the original organic farmers. We made your clothes, your hats, and your shoes, and we had know-how. Bring these things back home to our people, and please help bridge the gap for all poor people and as Dr. King told you: "That is black and white together." Poverty is the most colorblind neighbor in existence because the face is not pretty, and this is your country, our proud country where the wealth is simply now even taking out the middle class, so it is to be feared. Who will be the next bastion of poverty? Who will fall next? And if you want to see what happens, just drive the back roads where small farms were a way of life.

I am not out to show how smart I am or how clever were my friends and family, but I am out to stand up with Moses, Martin, and John in telling you that we've got some fixing to do in our country, and it is time to open your eyes from Hollywood to the United States capital of Washington, D. C., and to help your own poor. If you cannot do this, then I invite you to the water with me, for we are dirty now. We have sins of arrogance to wash away, and I am tired; I am tired of the denial that the poor people of America are not worth the dollars and your time. The river runs and there are souls to save, bodies to wash, and brows to be dried clean of the degradation, so come to this water and this time may we all go together not someday, but now.

Barbara Everett Heintz

About The Prologue With Loving Thanks To My Gracious Brother

Prologue by Author's Older Brother: Robert Van Everett - Recollections of life are tender and troublesome, but, most importantly, this is a truthful account where many male children were expected to do farm work just as the men of Appalachian did, for most fathers raised their sons under the same pressures of fathers before. The expectations became so intense and intolerable that my brother would have to leave us at an early age, and we were unable to be together for many years as he explains in this prologue. He does not tell you that he is brilliant or that he was a self-taught machinist who worked with equipment far beyond the scope of what others could have learned even to the extent of helping make large ship anchors and other such mechanisms which would require college mathematics and engineering training in normal circumstances. It all began with a troubled Appalachian life and the abiding will which is ours to survive in a world which failed to acknowledge that we existed beyond the labor we were born to. With heavy heart and great love, we introduce Robert Van Everett's story: A Prologue to Pinkhoneysuckle.

My Memories

By

Robert V Everett

This will be the story of my life. I will start back as far as I can remember until, when I went North, and I will be jumping around as I recall different things that happened in my life. One of my first memories was when my mother worked in the cotton mills in Rossville, Georgia.

She took me with her to stay with what I believe to be one of my father's aunts. My older brother had to stay home and my father was to take care of him. His aunt had a maid and part of her job was to watch me. Did I ever give her a hard time. She was a black woman. I didn't know any better so I just called her the "N" word. For some reason I was always getting into the salt. One day she caught me climbing the kitchen cabinet trying to get into the salt. I was so mad at her I told her I was going to get all those colored folks after her. Her name was Sara Jane. She must have been a very clean woman as I remember I think she took a bath about two o'clock every day. We would take the bus home every so often. I don't know exactly how long my mother worked in the cotton mills. She must have stopped when she became pregnant with my oldest sister.

We lived near the foot of a large hill. The road was very bad—you could not get over it after a rain. After my sister Violet was born the doctor had to walk down the big hill to our house. On the way to the house he passed me playing in a mud hole by the road. He said to me, "What do you think of your new sister?" I said, "Take her back."

The road was so bad the first two to three years I was in school my brother and I walked the five miles. He had been in school for six years already so he must have done a lot of walking. If we took a shortcut across the woods about a mile and a half to this family's house there was a bus stop. For some reason we couldn't get along with them, so we walked. Philips was the name of the family. More about them later.

I was never very good at school, as I failed the first grade. At the end of my first year in school, I could not spell my name. After, I took my report card home showing that I had failed. By the end of that day I could spell and write my name. The reason I learned was my mother whipped me so much I didn't dare not to learn. I learned to tie my shoes the same way. Her method of teaching was beat the crap out of you till you learned how.

I was born April 16, 1940, to a poor dirt farmer on Sand Mountain in the northeast corner of Alabama. It was a small community called Rosalie. There were two grocery stores—one was Rob Garren's and the other was Bowman's. You shop at one one year, the other the next.

I remember the old three-room mountain house. It had an old plank floor with cracks you could see the ground through. It had a large rock fireplace with a wood shingle roof. There was an old log barn and a chicken house. Over the years they put a tin roof on the house and new floors and siding. They tore out the old rock fireplace, built a brick chimney, and put in a wood-burning stove. We also got electricity. With all the improvements they made in the old house, my father would never build an outhouse. My mother fixed her up a place in the old hen house. For the rest of us, it was any place you could find to hide. Going to the bathroom before going to bed meant taking a leak off the front porch.

Scottsboro was twenty-six miles away and the nearest town. If we got there once a year it was something to talk about for the next month.

I remember like yesterday the day I got put to work. I must have been an old man about seven years of age. Not far from the house was a big blackberry patch that my father had decided to clean up that winter. In the summer it was always full of rattlesnakes. Anyway, it was a cold frosty morning and I had already gone out to play. My older brother and father were walking down the road by the house when my father stopped to look at me. They had the old crosscut saw, ax, and sledgehammer. The third time he stopped and looked at me he said, "Boy, you might as well come on and learn how to do something." I didn't play much anymore after that. I worked that whole winter helping clean out that old blackberry patch.

From that time on it was filling up fertilizers, chopping cotton, hoeing cotton, picking cotton, milking cows, or any other kind of work that a kid could do. My father was a very difficult person to work with. If you could not keep up, he did what is called putting a little pep in your step. Which meant a hickory limb across your backside.

In my early school years we would carry a gallon of milk to school every day for which we would get paid twenty-five cents. Lunch in the old cafeteria was five cents. It paid for a lunch and mother always had fifteen cents left to save. My brother and I would walk to one of the old grocery stores on Saturdays; we would carry eggs and chickens to trade for staples such as coffee, sugar, flour, meal, lard, and other necessities. After my brother went into the Navy it left me to do it all. Mother didn't understand how hard it was to do by yourself.

Getting back to the Philips family. Bob was the father's name. I did not know their father very well, but I understand he was a mean man. The oldest boy as a young teenager committed suicide. We all went to his funeral. That was the only time I ever remembered seeing his father. Sometime after that I don't know how but they were having a birthday party for one of the other kids. I talked my mother into letting me go. Everything went well until the middle of the afternoon. I don't know what went wrong but the mother sicced all the other kids on me. I got loose from them and ran to the top of the hill where there were plenty of rocks. I could throw the rocks downhill and dare them to come get me, calling them son of a bitches the whole time. One of girls was in my class in school. As I remember she was a very smart girl. Anyway that was my last time at the Philips home. I don't know how mean the father Bob Philips was but he was not the meanest man I ever knew.

The meanest man I ever knew was our neighbor by the name of Belt Currie. He was a drunk that was horribly brutal to his children. I don't know how the other men in the community let him get by with what he did. A couple of things I remember well about him include the time he beat his second boy with baling wire so bad he couldn't walk for a week. Another time one with of his boys a year younger than I, Belt was calling him from the other side of a cotton field. The boy was going to him in a dead run when he fell and put a cotton stalk into the roof of his mouth. He was hurt so bad he was going to need a doctor. Belt beat the hell out of him because he was going to have to take him to the doctor. That boy was later killed in Vietnam. Belt was also a moonshiner that made whiskey for a judge who owned the farm he lived on. The judge owned about four farms together and lived in Scottsboro, Alabama. He was always sending supplies out to the farms, but more than anything he was having the moonshine picked up. One day he sent a flatbed truck loaded with stuff with two colored men. They would not get out the truck until the other man arrived. At that time colored people were not welcome on that mountain. Anyway I didn't see more than two colored people a year. I heard about the truck waiting for the other man to come, so I took off over there. I wanted to see what those black folks looked like. And naturally I called them the "N" word, the only word people knew back then.

My best friend in school was Royce Garren. During the school year, I was able to spend a couple of nights with him, and he would also spend a couple of nights with me. We didn't live all that far away from each other, but it was far enough that we did not see each other in the summertime. The last time I saw Royce I had gone to the mountain to visit my first cousin Gladstone. We were driving down the road with another friend of ours when we saw a tall skinny fellow walking on the side of the road. Gladstone recognized him so we stopped. I got out and went to talk to him. He was so drunk and did not remember me. That was the last time I saw Royce. I understand he passed away a few years after that. The other friend that was in a car with us was Buddy Hendricks. He got some sort of cancer and passed away the year after he graduated high school.

I was seven years of age when my grandfather Everett passed away. The many stories I heard about him were not very good. He was a mean man that abused his children and beat my grandmother on a regular basis. They were divorced at the time of his death. In his last days he lived with an uncle of mine. For several years, he lived with one or the other of his children. One of my memories of him was a cold winter day when we went to my uncle's house to visit him. A neighborhood bull shitter, Bob Cox and another man, had him up trying to dance in the bed. Bob had his nose in everything going on in the community. The day of my grandfather's funeral it was horribly cold. The night before we had four inches of snow, it rained on top of it, and froze. Just getting to the top of the big hill was a challenge. His sons had to dig his grave and act as pall bearers. My first cousin and I sat together at his funeral, and we had made up our minds not to cry. At seven years of age I still remember the preacher. He was saying what a good man my grandfather was and how loved he was in the community. I guess the preacher was a good old man that didn't know Grandaddy. I couldn't help but think of the lies he was telling about Grandaddy. Outside of family there were not more than three to four people that attended the funeral.

In the early 1900s the government opened up the mountain to homesteads. The farms were laid out in forty-acre tracts. My grandfather got one of those farms. Over time he purchased three or four more of those little farms. He had one of the better farms on the mountain. My one aunt still lives on one of the eighty-acre farms. Most of the farms had twenty or less arable acres. Just before I was born my mother and father purchased one of these farms. Me and three of my sisters were born on that little farm: Rose, Violet, and Barbara. My brother Neil was almost grown when my sister Barbara was born. She would have been the baby when he went into the Navy.

Some things you could always count on. Our small farm did not have enough tenable acres to make a living. Every year our father would rent more land than we could handle. One year he rented ten acres of cotton on top of the five acres we already had on our little farm. This was more than we could handle. We worked like slaves that year. In order to save time my mother would carry our dinner to the field and stay and work the rest of the day. Another time he rented several acres of land for corn. He had rented the corn land from Bob Cox; as I remember the corn looked pretty good. I was with him late one day when he and Bob were looking at the corn. Bob said to him, "When are we going to get some hogs and let them start knocking the corn down?" My father said, "I don't think so. I need the corn."

Anyway a short time later Bob's hogs got into the corn patch. My father saved what he could of the corn. Another time he rented ten or fifteen acres of cotton. He had to hire cotton pickers to help us gather the crop. There was never any money left over for anything. After paying the fertilizer bill, the rent, the cotton pickers, and the grocery bill, it was all gone. Every year it was the same thing—after the last of the crop was taken off and sold Mama would be waiting on him to come home and see how much they had made. Then the fight started, there were things she needed and wanted, but no money. He would tell her the fertilizer bill and rent had taken all the money. She would start hollering about the fertilizer bill and being overcharged at the grocery store. She would be hollering that her father never used fertilizer or very little and still made a good crop. Which was true; her father farmed virgin bottom-land. He would tell her to shut up before he slapped the shit out of her, but she would keep going on and on and get a good beating. He would beat her at least twice a year, sometimes more. The only way we ever had money to buy school clothes or shoes was when we were able to pick cotton for someone else.

One of the worst beatings I remember her getting was on a summer day at dinnertime. He had just come to the house for dinner when a man with a flatbed truck with sideboards drove up. On the back of the truck he had two small heifer calves that didn't look like they would make it to sundown. We had a half-grown bull calf that had been hand raised; and he was beautiful. The man wanted to know what kind of trade my father would make. The man should have been paying my father a difference. But my father asked him how much boot he would take, meaning how much money he would charge my father to trade. My mother had sent me to tell him several times to ask him not to trade. The last time she sent me he told me if I said anything else he was going to bust my ass. Anyway the man told him thirty dollars. So they made the trade.

After the man left my father almost running came to the house in a rage. He started beating and kicking her. He slapped her across the face and broke her glasses. I don't know if she had been holding the baby or not. Anyway he hit her between the eyes with his fist. She went falling backward dropping the baby. He caught her before she hit the floor. The baby was Barbara. What he had done was knock her out. Needless to say dinner wasn't very good that day. Getting back to mom's glasses, it didn't make any difference if she was wearing them or not. He broke them several times slapping her across the face. A short footnote to add to the above: things got worse after our move to Tennessee. More on that later.

I always hated planting time when it was just me, my father, and brother doing it. Fertilizer came in 100-pound cloth bags that you tried to be careful and not damage. For mother would take these bags, wash them, and make shirts for us after she dyed them. There was a way to unravel the string to open them and not do damage. You would keep the string and later on wind it up tight into a ball to play with. Anyway he would have this big wooden box to mix the fertilizer in. He would put this big box in the middle of the edge of the field. He would help you with mixing the first batch with a hoe. After that you are expected to wrestle the 100-pound bags into the box and keep enough fertilizer mixed to keep the distributor running. The way you did this, you had a five-gallon water bucket full of fertilizer that you would meet the distributor in the middle of the field on its return trip every time. My brother would run the one row distributor, and my father would run the one row planter. When you first started you could keep up pretty good. As planting continued they would be getting further and further away from you. You were expected to pour the five gallons of fertilizer into the hopper yourself. No easy task for someone under ten years of age. My brother would help me get the fertilizer into the hopper and tell me to try harder for my father did not want the mules to stop. Planting cotton one time, they got so far away I couldn't keep up. My father stopped his mule at the end of the field and cut a skinny long limb that he lashed me with two or three times to make me try harder to keep up. We had the field almost planted at that time. When my father and his brothers worked together during planting season it was much easier.

A family by the name of Barrentine lived not far from the top of the big hill. They had one son named Jim. He was a mean child that grew up to be a mean man. Jim was a privileged child that had what the other children in the community could only dream about. He had the little red wagon, cap guns, bicycle, tricycle—you name it, Jim had it. It was his bicycle I learned to ride. Jim had an Uncle Jack that he worshiped and wanted to be just like. Jack was married nine times. The last I heard of him he had just remarried his first wife. Jim would be married five times himself. He once shot me in the back of the leg with a BB gun just to see if it hurt. It did hurt when I got through putting knots on his head. His father Mr. Hud Barrentine and my father worked together sometimes.

My father and Mr. Hud were working together one day shoveling corn into the crib. Near lunchtime my father called me. He wanted me to walk to the mailbox and check the mail. It was about one and a half to two miles to the mailbox. You had to go up the big hill. Jim tagged along with me. When we got to the top of the big hill, an old man and woman were cutting their winter wood and on the way back from the mailbox they had gone to lunch. We thought how funny it would be to see that old man carry those big sticks of wood back up the hill. So we rolled a few sticks of wood off the hill. It was fun to see those big sticks of wood tumbling down the hill. The fun didn't last very long. We had just got to the house, looked up the road, and here the old man comes. I didn't know anyone could walk that fast. He didn't come to the house, he took a shortcut across the pasture to where my father and Mr. Hud were working. He had a talk with my father; he was mad. My father kicked my ass one time, and then he kicked it again. Next he took me and Jim to carry the wood back up the hill. There was no way I could ever carry those big sticks of wood up that hill, so my father kicked my ass one more time and carried about three sticks of wood himself. I think he also thought it was funny, because I could see a grin on his face.

Another time he sent me to the mailbox and I had my three dogs. I didn't want them to go with me, because Bob Cox had got what they called a bear dog. I was afraid of what he might do to my dogs. Anyway I hadn't gotten very far from the top of the big hill. I turned around to see my dogs following me. I tried to chase them back home but it was too late. I heard the big old bear dog bark. Here he came on a dead run. Two of my dogs were little black fist, one had a bobtail and looked like a little bulldog, and the other had long orange-colored hair. He was part collie and hound mix. The bear dog went straight for my dogs. I was scared to death. I didn't know what to do. The fight didn't last very long.

The next thing I knew the orange dog was under the bear dog's neck, one of the little black dogs was biting his butt, and the other little black dog was riding him like a cowboy when the old bear dog went underneath the house. I didn't worry about my dogs anymore. When we would walk up the road, the old bear dog would run and hide. I would just smile and hope he would come out. The way I got the orange-colored dog was when I was small my mother and father had this beautiful collie dog. She had a litter of puppies by the hound. They needed money badly so they sold her. They kept two of the pups. The orange dog we named him Judge the other Jack. Jack was lazy and spent his time sleeping in the little road by the house. But he was a good guard dog. No one came to the house without getting past Jack first. The orange dog or Judge, was a hunting dog, and when he heard the fox hounds in the woods he was gone. He would be gone weeks at a time. Jack came up missing. I didn't know what had happened to him. Some time went by, and one of my uncles said he found Jack's remains. Said someone had killed Jack. I didn't know why someone would do that. Over a period of time I came to believe my father was the one that killed Jack. I have good reason to believe he was the one. For over time he killed dogs and cats I had.

More about the dogs. Their names were Lum, Abner, and Judge. My father was tired of Judge being gone all the time. In Scottsboro, Alabama, they had a day every month they called first Monday. On that day the old farmers would gather in town and trade everything from soup to nuts. Anyway my father gave Judge to an old farmer that was going to first Monday. He took Judge to town and traded him for a turning plow. Thursday morning Judge was back in our front yard. Not long after that an uncle was visiting from Tennessee; his name was Joe. He liked to hunt so my father gave Judge to him. They put a rope on him and put him in the truck of the car, leaving it open enough for him to have air to breathe. Anyway it was dark when my uncle arrived home. He pulled his car into the hallway of a barn with the intent of getting Judge out and tying him up. Judge got loose from him and ran. A week later he was back home again. He was very sore and didn't get around very good for a week after that. In both cases he would have had to cross the Tennessee River and climb the mountain. Judge never left home after that. He made the move to Tennessee with us.

The first car my parents owned they bought from my uncle Homer Bain. He had bought the car after the war and couldn't pay for it. They used money they got for the sale of land my grandfather had given my father that he had won in a poker game. The car just sat most of the time, no gas money. My father never learned to be a good driver. He never understood down-shifting to keep the car going. He never learned how to get the car to the top of the big hill. When we would start up the big hill he would get so far and stop and then my brother would need to jump out of the car and put a rock under the rear wheel. He would need to do this three to four times to get the car to the top of the big hill. He almost burned the car up several times trying to climb the mountain. He would never have any speed at the foot of the mountain and would need to shift down soon after starting up the mountain. Climbing the mountain in low gear took a lot of time and was very hard on the car. It would overheat almost every time.

Watkins is a sales business where you took from door to door spices, drink mixes, cough syrup and home remedies. After my grandfather passed away and my father got his inheritance, he went into the Watkins business for a year. Not to get ahead of myself, but they had one big fight over my grandfather's will. They almost lost everything in probate. There were two reasons for the big fight. Reason number one was that the last six months my grandfather lived, he lived with an uncle and aunt. My aunt thought because of this, they were entitled to everything. She and my mother had a big fight and didn't talk for years after that. The other reason was that he had left my Uncle Weaver one dollar. Uncle Weaver was not going to stand for that at all. The reason he left Uncle Weaver one dollar was that one morning my grandfather was in the process of giving grandmother a good early-morning whipping. Uncle Weaver still lived at home and was getting out of bed when it started. "Hearing his Mama's cries, he gave the old man a taste of his own medicine, and he beat the crap out of him." He said In the end they all got equal shares, some getting land, others money. My father used his share to go into the Watkins business. He bought an old jeep to get around the Mountain. Business was good; he sold plenty of stuff. The only problem was he did everything on credit. In a year's time he was broke and had to start back farming. His favorite saying before he went broke was "I know that old boy, for I went to school with him, and he's good for the money." He never collected anything. The calves I talked about earlier was the trade my father made. One grew up to be a little brindle cow that was one of the best we ever had. The other one, a skinny red cow that was never any good. We still moved both to Tennessee with us. The car I talked about was a 1941 Chevrolet Bel Air.

I could tell more stories about my Uncle Weaver. Like the time he cut up all my watermelons, about his old cars, and being the only one that could drive a tractor. And he could not pronounce the letter *T*, all his *T*'s were *F*'s so you can imagine what it sounded like when he used to say truck. My father, Uncle Weaver, and Eugene grew up to be like their father. My Uncle Elva, Homer, and Ira grew up to be kind and gentle men, more like their mother.

My grandmother would have this big dinner every year that the whole community would come to sometime during the day. At this one dinner, I was in the front yard with all my cousins when a young man rode up on his horse. He tied the horse to a tree beside the road and went in to eat. We were all looking the horse over. I was going to show how brave I was. I got a stick and hit the horse across his rear end. The horse kicked, catching me on the thigh and lifting me off the ground sending me across the road. My uncles made him take the horse away. I was sick the rest of the day and limped home. Mother found out what I had done and gave me a whipping.

My father had a set of hand tools to cut our hair. Did I ever hate getting a haircut. You dare not to move, even if you set very still. If he made a mistake, he would bounce the clippers off the top of your head. It would be your fault that he put a gap in your hair. Getting the clippers bounced off your head hurt like hell. As soon as I was old enough I always tried to have the twenty-five cents it would cost to get a haircut. Every Saturday there would be a man cutting hair in the back of Rob Garren's old store.

The worst beating I think any of us ever got was my brother. My father had gotten two large peppermint sticks of candy. He had put them in one of the old kitchen cabinets. One day he decided that we would eat one of them. We all sat at the old kitchen table waiting for him to cut one of them. When he got them out my brother had already taken a piece of one of them. My father went into a rage. He grabbed a razor strop and started beating my brother. A razor strop is made to hang on a wall with the handle you would grab to sharpen a razor. The handle was very hard. The way my father was holding the razor strap, the handle was also hitting my brother. He broke the razor strap in half on him he beat him so bad. My mother was in a chair holding the baby and crying.

She was saying, "Amos, that's enough, please don't hit him anymore." The more she would plead with him the more he would whip him. If she had said anymore she would have gotten a beating, too. No one should have to take a beating like that. And all because of a piece of candy. I asked my mother about that several times and she said, "Well, I did tell him to stop." If I had been her I would have had to take a beating myself for I would have to stop it.

We were sitting on the front porch some time after that, and she was telling my father about some woman she had talked to who'd said her children were her own flesh and blood and to beat them was like beating yourself. I think the point she tried to make was she was hoping he wouldn't beat us anymore. My sister Violet was a small little girl. She was on the front porch at that time.

Mother said to him, "I don't think Violet could ever take a hard whipping." That was the wrong thing to say to him. He started looking for a reason to whip Violet. For no reason he slapped her across her butt.

Kids on the mountain almost never went to a doctor. They got a nurse to live on the mountain. Rose and Violet were so very sick with the flu. My brother was old enough to drive, so he drove us to the nurse. It was a cold day. She was on the porch getting firewood when we drove up.

I looked at her and said what I had heard my father say: "My, she has a big ass." My mother backhanded me so hard I wound up in the back window of the car. I couldn't understand what I had done wrong.

One more thing about my father, he had a sun stroke once and spent about six months in the hospital. One time my mother would tell me he had a nervous breakdown, the next time it would be the sun stroke. Anyway he had shock treatments along with other types of treatments. The day it happened, he and my uncles had been working in the hay. That day it was very hot, and something happened to him. I can still see them tying him to a stretcher and carrying him over the road.

About two years before we moved to Tennessee, my Uncle Joe married this woman, Doris Reeves. I thought it was great at the time; later on it would turn out not to be a good thing. They became very frequent visitors, especially her. I would look forward to them coming for we would get to go somewhere occasionally.

My brother graduated high school in the spring of 1951. He was sixteen years old at the time. He joined the Navy and had to wait until he turned seventeen to leave. My life was about to change, I just didn't know how much. Things that we did together, I was going to be doing all by myself. I didn't know how much I had depended upon him. The milking, feeding, putting the animals away for the night, all became my job. I learned to milk the same way I learned to spell my name, with her beating me on the top of the head. Neither one of them wanted to do the evening work. You also had to get in the firewood, kindling, and stove wood for cooking. You also got to make the Saturday trip to one of the old grocery stores. I had to carry as much to the store and bring back as much as the two of us had done together. On this one trip to the store I had so much stuff to bring back, the only way I could do it was carry part of the stuff down the road and go back and get the rest. I did this for the five miles home. My mother's reply to me was that she didn't know it was going to be that hard, but that's the way we always did it, the hard way.

That fall was no different than any other: we didn't make anything and they had their annual fall feud. She also found out she was pregnant with my brother James. She did not want to have any more babies. So on one of her visits Doris got her something to take to terminate the pregnancy. After taking it mother only became very sick.

My parents would go two or three weeks without talking to each other whenever they had one of their feuds. It was a cold fall day and they were in the middle of one of their feuds. I was in a cotton field with her; he had been gone all day. He came to the cotton field and told her he had a chance to sell the little farm. He wanted to know what she thought about selling out and maybe moving to Tennessee. He didn't need to ask her twice. She was ready to go. It was a chance for her to live near her family. They wrote to my uncle to keep an eye out for a farm. Shortly after that they made a trip to Tennessee. He found what he said was the perfect farm for us. It was a hillside farm with approximately eighty-six acres. I stayed behind to care for the farm animals while they were gone. Anyway they bought the farm and preparations were made to move.

When someone would ask my mother about the house she would say it had wallpaper and an outhouse. When someone would ask him about the farm he would say it had a good barn. I was in the middle of my fifth grade in school when we made the move. He made several trips to Tennessee moving farm equipment, cutting firewood, and other things. Three days before the actual move the farm animals were taken. I went with him to take care of the animals until they arrived. I still had not seen the farm. For some reason I was dropped off at the house of one of my uncle's and would not see the farm until late that evening. He and I would go to the farm to take care of the animals about sundown. I looked at that place and thought, "My God, they must have been blind."

It was about sundown the evening I went to the farm with my uncle to take care of the animals. I could not believe what I was seeing. The house was about one and a half miles from the gravel road. We parked and walked because he was afraid we might get stuck. The old road was a dirt road with deep ruts. No electricity, no well, and the only water was a cistern that was in need of repair. Old split rail fences everywhere. That would be the first order of business, to make a fence to keep the cattle in. The old house was not like anything I had been told. Anyway three days later the whole family arrived. My mother was in a dream world that would be short-lived. She was now going to be living near her brothers, sisters, and mother. I was told that my grandmother came to our house one time, but I don't remember it. The aunts never came, the uncles only a few times. The only ones to come on a regular basis were my Uncle Joe and Doris. When we made the move we had plenty of corn, hay, and canned goods. That would be the last time for that. Talking about my mother living in a dream, it would take my father less than a year to find out you could not make a living on a hillside farm.

The day the family arrived in Tennessee, I was picking cotton at my grandfather's farm when the truck went over the road with the family. My uncle and I went to help and unload everything. My mother was so happy. Anyway after everything was unloaded, I went back to my grandfather's to finish the day. Late that day I was walking home, and I knew the way walking the road. I was about halfway when this old man stopped me and wanted to know who I was and where I lived. I told him, and he told me about a shortcut to get home. I thought the shortcut was a good idea so I took it. I got lost and had no idea where I was. I walked and walked. I ran. I was scared to death. It was well after dark when I made my way to a house. I was crying and told them who I was. I was trying to tell them where I lived. They didn't know but they knew where the old store was. I knew the way from there. They drove me home. When we got there they had already organized a search party to look for me. Mr. Bain, the old man that had told me about the shortcut, my father raised hell with him.

A couple of days after that I went to the little school at the crossroads to enroll. I was in the fifth grade, and my sister Rose was in the first grade. I couldn't believe the little school. Two teachers for eight grades. The teacher I had, Mrs. Vera Mason, was a hard-working woman but no teacher can teach four grades as they should be taught. I got very little out of school after that. I had been doing pretty well in school until the move, but it was all downhill after that. It had to be the first week we were in school and it was cold and rainy. Mother had given me a list of stuff she needed from the grocery store. After school my sister and I went to the store to get what she wanted. It was raining, it was cold, and we had about three and a half miles to walk. It had already gotten dark. I was doing everything I could to keep things dry. Things started to get wet so I took my coat off to wrap them up. Bags had started to fall apart when my father drove over the road in the old Jeep to pick us up. He asked us why the hell we went to the store and we answered. She said we needed everything we got because we were out of everything.

There were so many split rails from the old fencing that we used them for firewood. As I said before, the first order of business was to build a pasture fence to keep the cattle in. I had to help my father with the barb wire. I didn't know how heavy a roll of barb wire is. The idea to unroll a roll of wire was to put a stick through the center of the spool, and one man at each end would carry the spool until the wire had been unrolled. My father was a strong man and expected me to keep up with him. I would get shoved into a ditch, trees, or anything that got in the way. I was expected to keep going regardless. There were always three ways to do things. The right way, the wrong way, and my father's way, which was the hardest of all.

Have you ever seen a mule smile? I have. At one time there were wild chestnuts that grew in this area. They were a tall straight tree about the size of a light pole. On one big hill on the old farm there were probably two or three dozen such trees. They were tall, straight, and hard. Perfect for making fence post. The trees had been dead for years but were in great shape. I have never seen a wild chestnut alive. Anyway, we cut them and sawed them up for fence post. One Saturday at dinner he said to me, while you were at school I dug all of the holes for the fence. We might as well get the post and start putting them out. We had the mules hooked to the wagon and got to the top of the big hill. He looked down the hill and said damn. For some reason he had two stacks of the post at the very bottom of the hill. I don't know why he took everything down hill. There was no way to get the wagon down the hill. We were going to have to carry them up ourselves. He said to me you get the small ones, and I will get the large ones. They all looked pretty much the same size to me. Anyway every time we got to the top of the hill with a post, the mules would turn their head and smile. It took us the rest of the day to carry all the posts up the hill.

After the pasture fence was built, he spent the rest of the winter cleaning off a ten-acre hillside we would plant in corn in the spring. My uncle, father, and myself planted corn on that hill in the spring. I can never forget the day my brother James was born. We had been cleaning up a small piece of ground and doing what they call burning a tobacco bed. It was getting late we had two big stacks of brush. He told me to get a hot chunk out of the one that was burning and start a fire in the other stack. I didn't have anything to move the chunk and got a burn. He had the pitchfork which would have been ideal. He hit me with the handle two or three times and said, "It's about time you learn to do something right. You could have asked for the pitchfork." Where I had been hit hurt like hell. I went to the house and told my mother what had happened, she said to me, "Son, there's nothing I can do for you. All I know is I'm going to have this baby tonight."

In the spring, my uncle, father, and I planted that hillside in corn, and we also planted five acres of cotton. I don't remember what we did with the rest of the farmland. Anyway, the corn and cotton we had planted had came up along with the tobacco we had set out. It was all looking pretty good. When everything was two or three inches high we had a hailstorm. After the storm was over there were only stems left. Everything had to be replanted. We didn't make anything on the replant. The hail beat the roof off most of the house. I went to bed that night looking at the stars between the cracks. He had to put a new tin roof on most of the house. I think this is where they ran out of money from the sale of the old farm. Besides that, he didn't do a very good job with the new roof because it always leaked. They sold the timber to try and make the land payment but still didn't have enough money to make the payment. He and I spent the winter cutting stave bolts. Still not enough money to make the payment.

My uncle was over one day, and I didn't know what was going on. I found out about two weeks after that my father had tried to borrow money from him. When my uncle left I was to ride with him to the store to bring something back. When I got back home he had beat the hell out of her for sticking her nose in his business. That was the beginning of what was to become a weekly affair. Things really went downhill after that. The time I lived on that farm we did not raise one good crop. No corn in the crib, no hay in the loft for the cattle. We didn't have much of a garden either. Mother was wanting us to move, but he wouldn't hear of it. In the fall of the second year, he refinanced the farm. He had got a loan from John Fandricks. He bought a herd of milk cows—we were going into the milking business. My father didn't know a good milk cow from a billy goat. They lost money every day that they fed the cows. He paid two hundred dollars each for those cows. A year later you could have bought the best one for a hundred. Things got so bad we barely had enough to eat. We could talk all day about the fighting, the beatings. I think you get the picture. Anyway, the last fall before he had to go north, they needed five hundred dollars to save the farm. The timber was gone, no money to made from milking, and a bad crop. If they didn't get five hundred dollars soon we were going to be without a place to live.

So much happened in those three years more or less, I don't know where to begin. I had come to think my father was the meanest man in the world. It would be years after that I would understand it was a two-way street. He was very physical. She was all mouth. She must have liked getting beat up for she would do anything to try and get her way. One of the reasons I thought he was such a mean man was that my dogs Abner and Judge came up missing. I looked and looked for them until one day she told me don't you know your father killed them. She was determined to sellout, let the old farm go, and become renters—anything to move off of that road. He was just as determined to try and save the farm. He tried a little of everything but nothing worked.

For a while he did what is called trading work. In trading work you would work two or three days for someone to get them to help you do something you couldn't do by yourself. My mother didn't like that, for he would be gone a lot of the time. She said he could stay at home we could do everything ourselves. By trading work he was able to get some things done we couldn't do ourselves such as baling hay, cutting tobacco, jobs that you had to have help with. Sometimes he would give two or three days work to get one day in return. She could in return put up such a fuss that pretty soon no one wanted to work with him anymore. She managed to get the whole community involved. The neighbors knew more about us than we knew ourselves. The more she would do these things the harder it made it on the rest of us. And I was the one that had to work with him. I would get it from both sides. From him, because I could not do everything he wanted, and from her when she was mad at him.

One time he got to be a deputy for a short time. She got him fired from that job, said he needed to be at home. We could have really used the money. She got all the neighbors to help her with that one. One evening just after dark she had it in for him and took it out on me. I don't remember why she was going to whip me but I wouldn't let her. He was working in an old barn beside the road that we hadn't torn down yet. I went to him and I told him I know what you can do to me and told him what happened. For I knew he wouldn't get into the door until she would be telling him. All he said to me was you know how she can be sometimes. Things got so bad we had parched corn for supper. We had become a joke in the community. I have little use for those neighbors today. My uncles and aunts who could've helped did nothing. My grandparents were both still living at the time; we got nothing from them. I had to work with him in the woods. One time for some reason I think he tried to get me hurt or worse. In fact I am sure of it. Some way or the other, my sisters and brothers all became successful. As for the neighbors the ones that have not passed away are still there. Not all the neighbors were bad. There are two families I still see. The Hannahs and Luttrells were good neighbors. There is no man I have more respect for than Jeff Luttrell.

It was late fall and they needed the five hundred dollars to save the farm. There was no way to get it. My uncle Joe had already gone up north and came for a visit. He told my father he was sure he would be able to get a job. My father left to go north with him. He did get a job at the brickyards, and in some ways things began to improve for the rest of the family. For me the workload had just been doubled.

Not only was I to go to school, I had to keep up with what he'd done. Like getting in the firewood for the winter, making a small crop in the spring, and taking care of the livestock. It was more than I could do. I would be in the field plowing when the school bus went by. I was down to going to school two or three days a week. This one day when I was going to school, I overslept. I asked mother, "Why didn't you wake me up?" Her reply was you're not going to amount to anything anyway.

When I went to school that year she had money to give me for lunch money, but would not. I would go the entire day without eating. I turned fifteen in April of that year and had had enough. I started making plans to run away. That fall I had finished with the crop, and he had came home for a week for she was to have surgery. I told him I was going to quit school and go back north with him. She was not going to hear of it. He told her to let it go, you'll know where he is. He knew I was going to be gone one way or the other. So I went north, lied about my age, and got a job.

Robert V Everett

Rovert V. Everett- Chicago

Mother with baby Robert V. Everett

Chapter One

I am remembering my father on this anniversary of his death, for though it was very long ago, he goes with me everywhere. I talk with him, but even in his lifetime he was a man of few words, so I am content with the whispers within my heart which tell me "Now girl, you can tell them our story now."

He knows that Mama has left us, too, and I believe that they are together. Mom could not take care of herself when she was alive, so Dad had to take her hand and lead her back to the mountain where they were married. She would have felt safe going there, seeing Dad all fresh and new as he was the day they gathered long ago to be married on that same rock formation in 1933, and from that southern tip of the Appalachian mountains they could soar to heaven together.

Daddy's name was Amos, so I was not surprised to read in the book of Amos from the Old Testament that the dour Amos of the Bible had ended his prophecies with the Lord saying that the juice of grapes would drip down the mountains and all the hills would run with it, and the testament continued, "Plant vineyards and drink the wine; Set out gardens and eat the fruit." The new Israel would be rebuilt, and in Mom and Dad's case they'd enter heaven there, for that's about all either of them asked for: food aplenty and to end their lives in the vineyards of the Lord of which they sang as Sunday hymns until their voices ended and the sun set on lives that we protected like marauders hiding swords.

So, Daddy, I will try hard to tell it well. Go on to the new Israel, the one only visible to the dead and keep Mama very close. She's still going to need you to breathe the freedom from earthly fears that stifled her; you were her rock over sixty-five long years, yes—forever your mountain baby that bore us. Walk her to the light and gather the pink honeysuckles together and be blinded by the afternoon light that flashes rainbows over the face of God. Just whisper to me again, for I may lose words especially since some do not believe a word of the grace that was written in a holy book, much less in a God. I'm not going to try to convince them of anything, but I'm going to take them to our place, and rock their very inner spirits with details that are disturbing.

I will go so far as to say that I've got to metaphorically disrobe myself at times, tear at the comfort levels people have made at the expense of poor Appalachian families with the candor of vultures swooping down on us as if we were the fair game left over from old social dictates that fail, to this day, to accept the truth that goes along with the theory of white trash versus pearls, the shining, decent pearls of folks untouched, for the shell around them is so protective. I'm going to sing a little, shout a little, and by the end of this story somebody's going to hear the voice from the valley and all the way to the mountain-top. The new garments that cover some people's nakedness may not feel so silky by some, and if they itch from the acridness of their pretense, then and only then will I have told the truth as it needs to have been told long ago; so help me, Daddy, for here I begin.

There seems to be three days for all souls to resume their flight, but on the seventy-degree Tennessee day when we laid Dad to rest, a great wind came up, and the storm clouds began to gather in the sunlit sky. We almost felt a stirring that seemed ethereal when a great hawk went over his grave and soared straight up into the air as far as the eye could see, just like the rocket that had headed to the moon about forty years earlier. Then as days passed a family of hawks took nest just over the fence from the mortal's grave, as if to shelter a new hatchling that had risen from my father's soul. Hawks know secrets of the living and of the dead and hold majestic rank in Native-American folklore and spirituality, so something special was happening and would continue to happen through the years as the hawks would reappear.

I believe that Father became a holy man and that his return to earth was part testament to the signs and wonders that he taught us from the moment of our birth. I know that the earth has a scent like the perfect perfume. Most of us could smell rain way before it began to fall, and at any season's changing, something would begin to stir within us to ready us for the impending change. It is time to haul wood, children; get the mules, for the winter will be long. Turn the earth and plant today would not have to be said, for the need came just like the need to drink water or to hide among the tall pines when danger felt near. We learned to listen to the woods; the venomous snakes rarely came within our paths. They, just like the devil, crawled in hiding hoping that one day our awareness of their presence would let us down, for all demons must hide if a holy man's offspring walks by. They have their own awareness that they will be trampled to death if they dare attack. The laws of ages endure, and the ground continues to shelter evil until the forces of goodness return. Three days—that's the most it takes for angels to reappear. We are given Easter bodies and sacred minds by those who came before us. God in us sometimes cares to come back around, for we are all the wings of one great hawk that reappears on a day of the dead so the living may continue.

Yes, this is my real birthday, and I want to give you one gift from me—that sacred moment when precious memories such as these reappear. Were you here, I would sing to you the sweet hymn of assurance that they surely will, surely they will. They will wait for us, their children, to celebrate in The New Jerusalem together.

Chapter Two

It is time for me to take you to a place where we'll meet the little girl that I was. I have found that after a significant one leaves you behind that it is an opportunity, if not an imperative, to look at one's own life and to circle, circle—to dance in the circle and to look at who you are and where you are and where you've been. I must let my daddy and mama rest now and go deeply into the 1950s when agrarian families such as mine would see an end was coming to the world as they knew it. The farms were about to disappear, and a Republican president who came back from the war as a hero would, along with his marginal understanding of the mainly agrarian population of the United States, bask in the glory of a great victory in Europe. He brought in a cabinet that was filled with pompous and zealous arbiters of newly found wealth who would destroy an ordinary person's ability to make a living on the land. After all, he was a great general and it would be among the last great wars where American soldiers could come home victorious over an evil that had to be crushed. The population needed to wave flags and to cheer on the living and to give homage to the glorious dead, and patriotism burst out all over the country as it needed to. Those who were unable to fight the war or to profit off the factories that were springing up like poppies to make cars for the returning boys who were left to cheer victory, but then to wonder where their family's next meal would come from.

Most men, like Dad, who wanted to fight but had to stay on the home front would bend their heads in shame, as if they had done nothing but to sit on their sorry asses while the real boys came marching home. But then, an ugly problem would begin to come to light for all farm men, heroes or not. Their land would no longer really be theirs to plant, and farm subsidies and GI bills would not keep food on their tables. Women would stop bringing home salaries, as the factories that supplied the war effort closed and the big baby boom became a woman's main focus again. Washington was becoming the disaster and not the help. Many of the boys and men who came back would have great war stories, but many would also have developed such a taste for alcohol and violence that women and kids, country and city, were seeing a new reality of brutality toward them they had never expected to endure.

Men had been trained in violence, and the dirty little secret that violence was not left behind on the battlefield would become daunting. The automobile and steel industries called fathers to the north. And women and children would be left, once more, to run farms and the table provider became a weekend visitor. A new round of alcoholics would emerge as lonely men endeavored to stay sane in the harsh winters of the northern cites and as they tried to suffer in silence to send a check home now and again to pay farm mortgages taken out when things had been left up to them as farm men and decision-makers. Some would move their families, but few were alright in the big cities where they did not understand city ways or how to find resources for their children. Valor began to be replaced as folks who left the farms and those left behind became the new "white trash," and the farm folk took over the title of "hillbilly." Johnny marched home, and thc band stopped playing. The great divide had come, and pompous me who had a little money would become the new aggressors as the guns were laid down and the financial elite of America would see that Johnny boy and the farm hands never got uppity again. Our family was among the prey, along with so many others. All of us were ready to become the new servant class.

This was true for both white families and black families. It would hardly be an afterthought until the 1960s brought in the knowledge that people together could have a voice and Washington D.C. might have to take a second look at all hidden people who remained silent, because heroism didn't mean a thing unless the people decided that their march and their vote counted.

As a child I was just one of eight "mouths to feed." I was a mouth in a ragged dress, but I could find happy places. All children dreamed, and little neighbors and I would walk a mile or so to get what the daddies could send home, and we would play. Agatha, a friend of mine, and I would crouch and almost eat our mud pies on rainy days, and we could talk about the last night's supper.

"Yes, we had hamburgers and beans at our house, and you had what?"

"Well we ate cakes and cookies, and after that we had potato cakes and bananas!"

One-ups-manship became the sport of many in our community. Yes, we made up all kinds of nice stuff. The truth was that we'd almost cried the night before, either or both of us, for there was rarely enough for anybody. How could one say that they'd had nasty boiled possum and bread, for that was all one's Dad could shoot before he had to take off north again. We'd try to choke down what we could as the nasty possum skins rubbed against each other on the line still dripping with a little blood and stinking. They'd flap around like proud beavers rubbing against each other with that odor of dead meat, then old Abner and Butch, our dogs, would find the pelts and start fighting over them, pulling the hair and stretching the sinews, barking as if they'd made a big kill. They'd suck the blood and skin leaving something that looked like a bird's nest, a nasty sight. But because it was just old possum skins Dad would never ask what had happened to the remains. I missed Agatha if I couldn't walk to the mailbox, for she'd let me boss her around some.

"Alright, Gather, this time you're gonna be the horse." Agatha could be the horse, and I was going to be Dale Evans. "What do you mean, you stupid horse? You ain't gonna eat this bale of hay I just pulled up for you? You are a sorry old nag, and my grandma would tell you to kiss her ass. Whoa girl, and I mean whoa. Agatha, I'll be the horse next time, and I'll eat the grass cause you seem mighty ungrateful. Did you wear your drawers today, Gather, for I ain't wantin' for the mailman to come and see where the sun ain't gonna shine. I got my pink ones on today, but they're gettin' pretty dirty. Do you know that we are about due a catalogue, horsey? I think we might be gettin' some cowgirl hats and some cowhide boots, for the checks a comin' too. We're about to get rich, so I think we can stop playin' for today. Then we can dig ourselves an oil well and get as rich as Bill Crouch's store. We can play something else for a few minutes, I guess."

Ring around the rosy was about the last game we'd get to play, and we'd hear the mail car coming. The days we got to play were pretty hot, and sometimes we'd have to wear our sun bonnets made by our mamas. Ashes and roses, ashes and roses, and red hot sun; some old stray dog begging for a handout; blackberry briars and a ripe berry or two. We are in our own world, a day like most others. Circle to your left and circle to the right and two little girls dancing in the sunshine. That was what white trash looked like. Can you see our faces?

Chapter Three

I was only five years old at the most when I ventured over our road at the end of nowhere to the blacktopped highway that came and ended at another place that most folks had never heard of. Daddy was working in his blacksmith shed which came with our property, and I just could not resist the white-graveled road's call to walk on and on. I could look back at our faux red brick tarpapered covered house, and the sun was out glistening and washed by morning sun and dewdrops. I passed Dad's field of green alfalfa blowing softly with each tiny breath of wind, and as I passed the garden gate the huge field of red clover came into view as I crossed over the first knoll which would call me on.

It is a portrait in my heart to this day: red crimson clover waving to and fro. I stopped to break a twig off and taste the sweet nectar. I sucked on these honey-tasting twigs as I walked on and could see before me whatever Mr. Mason had planted on the adjoining field. It was usually cotton which was also in bloom. The cotton blossoms were white touched by pink kisses where the cotton boll would form, and this against all the crimson, the shades of green, and the sunlit skies linger like an impressionist painting in my heart and I will remember it for as long as I live and can perceive beauty.

My feet felt just right on the new white-graveled path, as I walked along that late springtime day. Cars and work horses, the new tractors, had left two ruts where you could walk and pretend that they were sidewalks taking you along to the next place of somewhere wonderful. The wonderful was also the sweet perfume of wild roses which grew on every other fence post, and they remained until the frost. I have rarely come across roses since then that had that alluring scent which caused one to walk on and on, because you could not get enough of it. Maybe it was a sign of the blessed virgin that someday and somehow all of the sorrows which would interrupt our lives would pass away and leave a memory like a photograph within our minds that could ease the pain of a future none of us could comprehend beyond the hours of the small places and things like crimson clover and wild roses, these things that made the perfect moments of our youth wonderful beyond our heart's measure.

I go to that day and those places again and again when I am broken, and I find it to be a healing place where everything ugly can fade away and I can rest in that memory.

Mama appeared angry when I told her how I had been walking to the highway, as we called our roads from nowhere to what people from the outside world would consider to be another nowhere. She promised that the next time I did this without telling her I'd get a good whipping, for you never knew if some old man might be out there, and she did not explain further what that meant. So to me it meant little at the time, and later in my life her warning would come back to me like a sword that would pierce me as if blood were dripping from my every pore, like marrow sucked from a dead animal's bones. I told her that Daddy was in his shed shoeing mules and that he had seen me, but she took no consolation and put me to ironing Dad's socks and handkerchiefs as if this were real work. Mother was a master of making work, for she knew that everything that she taught her daughters to do would be one more chore she could turn over to us. So at age five I mastered ironing socks.

Later in the day I would hear her shriek, "Somebody left that cattle gate open, and the cows are in the clover gorging themselves. They're going to explode, so go get your daddy and get help before they explode!"

I ran like crazy to get Daddy and the men hanging around their mules, for exploding meant to me that if I didn't get there fast enough, those old cows were going to be blown to bits like an A-bomb with no fallout shelter in sight. All I could think of were cow intestines and excrement and an old bull's horn sticking into one of our backs like an arrow flung with nuclear force. We were verging on death by cowhide.

Many years later, I would learn that cows can be really stupid, and crimson clover is like cow cocaine. It is so sweet that they eat and eat until their stomachs perforate and without veterinary intervention they die a painful and horrible death, but to my mind then mama said they would explode, and what she said, I took literally and without questioning that a cow apocalypse was about to occur. Fortunately Daddy and a few helpers rounded them up and sent them to the pasture again. Mayhem was avoided because I had run for all of our lives like the wind to get help.

Chapter Four

Mother, I've been avoiding the thought of bringing you into my story out of my shame, and even out of my sorrow that you are gone. Your death, but mainly your life, I have re-evaluated out of need, out of compassion, and as a way to find some tribute to you. You would be there after my first foray to the highway, and as I came home, I'd try to decide if you were going to be there to scold me with a switch to my limbs or if you would spare me this time and give me a chore instead. Fortunately for me, you chose that I should help you break the washtub of Kentucky wonders, a green bean that had become your favorite to can. I do not want to go into your madness now, Mother, for I want the ones coming along with me on this journey to understand how beautiful you were and how unaccomplished I was in recognizing you as such.

Mom was about forty when I could even begin to recognize her features, and it began at a Lexie Crossroads ice cream social, which was supposed to be for the benefit of the little school, though later I'd realize that it was the principal's way of lining her own pockets and of taking all that the local farmers could give. It was at such an event that an old friend, Jean Walker, would amaze me by saying, "Is that your mama? She's so beautiful." Rarely does a child see a parent as beautiful, but I looked at Mother, really looked at her, that evening, and I was very proud of her.

Her skin was like a porcelain doll's, and her eyes were as blue as Mediterranean waters. She was about medium in height, and as always, she had a baby in her arms. She would always have on a plain house dress with some print of flowers, and she had a voluptuousness about her. Her dresses could never cover her breasts, nor could any occasion blur the sadness that dwelled in the twinkle of her very large and round eyes. To her, she was some miserable wretch in a crowd of people where she wanted to find enjoyment and companionship, but she was too fearful to be just another mother. Mom, like me, tended to feel warm, and Daddy, among his few lonesome love letters to her, would comment on the pleasure of the softness of her body. She had a coal-black hair into her midyears that had natural curl which would have been envied by Hollywood sorts, and it had a natural bounce and sheen that would only disappear when Mom discovered the boxed horrible new permanent waves.

Her scent was of a working woman, perspiration covered with a little bar soap scrub in the morning, but there was something about being around her that made one want to lean more closely when she had time only to push you away. Her energies were so sapped from all the childbirth, farm labor, and abuse from everyone—her own mother, Dad, and the thyroid disease which required removal of her thyroid gland. No one gave her thyroid replacement therapy; they let her suffer, and we would all come to see a madness from this beautiful human being, which would tear us again and again until we began to grow up a little and to remember her beautiful smile that was so rarely seen.

As young as I was, I could not get over that one by one, my mother's beautiful white teeth were pulled, partially at her request. In her way of thinking, dentures brought her closer to old age, and if one was old, then they might find some kindness somewhere. Thus early on I would see my mother destroy her pretty womanhood and trade it for old age just in case it would ease some of her pain. Mother's beauty passed much too soon in this way, and yet she'd find that it was all for naught.

On the days she was not depressed, she might make her teacakes for us, if the hens were laying. She'd use a basic biscuit dough, add a cup and a half or so of sugar, some vanilla flavoring—Watkins, of course—then she'd make it a little more moist with the beaten eggs, one or two, depending on how horny the rooster had been. She would then knead the dough, roll it out to about two-pie crust thickness, and cut it with a floured snuff glass before baking in an oven that might have been 350 degrees had she a thermometer. It was a very good day if Mama could make her teacakes. It meant that she was happy for a little while, and to see her happy was like a gift unwrapped on a most exceptional day. I wish so much now that I would have told her that Jean Walker opened my eyes to her physical beauty. It would take years before the beauty of her soul would shine through, but I want you to know this: If there was one human on the face of the earth who asked for her last worn down pair of shoes; they'd go walking in hers. I hope you see her in your dreams and that she holds you close to her warm body before the day breaks.

Chapter Five

My thoughts sometimes come like butterfly wings trying to navigate through a storm, all at once, and I sometimes do not want to share them with you or with anyone, for all will be asking the obvious: "Did that really happen?"

I cannot speak for the brothers and sisters, either the four that came before me or for the three that would come after me. I only see a little girl, and I'm fairly certain that it is me. I have realized for a long time that not everyone views things the way I do, the flickering images that are stuck within my frontal lobe until someone performs the ancient lobotomy, which would take the feelings away and leave a shell without the small girl who could wander after a day's chores, when Mama would release her for a little while. It had to be a good day for her unpredictable heart to give us such a wonderful freedom to venture into the mercy of the land around us, and most of these days came in the springtime and the early summer when the daylight was longer and Mother could rest on our big porch watching as if someone was going to come over the road as a sweet relief from her aloneness and silent suffering.

If her eyes looked easy and she was not perplexed by one of us, then I especially liked to go and look at the blooms in early grasses just turned green on the hill outside the old home place. There were acres of tiny baby blue flowers that the locals called "pissy bed" and there were violets as dark as squid ink and beautiful against the green grass with little baby dandelions, yellow like the sun and too early to be torched by the heat into fragments that we would blow on as if we were sending wonderful wafts of clouds to a good friend. Nearer the woods and in damp places, there would be ferns with tiny white blossoms and moss growing on the trees where the mushrooms grew as if for a wonderful supper for forest creatures. I always wanted to eat them, but I had been told that they would kill you faster than a rattlesnake's bite, so a natural resistance developed to look and hunger for the fluffy white morsels, which I considered to be nature's homemade marshmallows.

It was such a relief to have blue sky, the touch of blue on the hills, and to occasionally get to see blue water if we went to Sand Mountain from where we had come. There the Tennessee River was wide and blue when we crossed the bridge that would welcome us back to Alabama and Dad's family. Oh, I so liked blue then, from wherever it came, and I felt that when I got old enough to ask Aunt Martha if I could borrow one of her Sunday hats, I'd ask for the white one that looked as if it were woven and that was adorned with the loveliest plastic blue flowers that money could buy. Aunt Martha became crazy as a loon, but she was never in church without her hats, so I expected that the hats were probably what kept her sane for as long as she was before becoming the nitwit she developed into at an early old age.

There was a time though when my favorite color would cease to have the same meaning as flowers and springtime gifts. It happened during one of Mama's disappearing times. I would not have been told why Mama had to go to the hospital nor would I know about pregnancies or who delivered those kids other than the stork that visited most houses around us one day or the other and left a family with a new baby. One day in early spring when I was about six was a disappearing time for Mama, only there was no stork that showed up at our door.

My mother came home in an ambulance, and I remember that we were all very quiet. We were not acquainted with people that came home in ambulances, and next thing I knew, they were rolling my mother in to our house, and her eyes looked vacant, and she said hardly a word. I heard that she needed to go to the toilet, but they would not let her get up. I remember something about newspapers being placed under Mama because she was said to be too weak to get up, and somehow this most modest of women with men in the room had to use the newspaper for a bowel movement, and though they said, "You're alright, Mrs. Everett" in a soothing tone, I could see her with small tears tracing down the side of her face, and the vacant stare, and the lack of words hung over her as if she were lost in some distant cave and couldn't get out.

Her embarrassment would be disturbed by the words, "Oh Lord, he's turning blue again." Only then did I somehow watch them place her in bed with the new baby, and he was blue, almost the blue of violets, and I cried. I didn't want any old blue baby, and they just wouldn't shut up.

"Yep, they said he turned blue at the hospital, too. Yes sir something must be wrong, but he's breathing."

I didn't want Mama's blue baby, and I didn't want her on newspapers. My heart was broken, even for Mom, because the stork left pink babies, and somebody might even bring a present to a pretty pink baby, but for Mother, I don't even recall her own mama coming to help. All Mother got from her was some nasty message about how she shouldn't be adding more kids to the bunch, and people who were curious coming in seeing this newborn little freak, as they thought of him, hoping that he'd turn blue for them to go home and yap about.

Fortunately, he would pink up, and Mama had a little boy whose name would be James Amos after her father and mine. I do not know the number of times that I had to run over the road over the next months when James would turn almost black to get help for him. I'd get one of the kind Hannah boys, and they'd bring a truck ready to go. Sometimes I was almost disappointed that he wasn't dead, for death seemed to be a scent in our household from the time my brother came home. Had it not been for Aunt Dorothy coming to help out and Aunt Doris Reeves coming to take brother to a hospital in Nashville run by the Shriners, I think Mama would have died of a broken heart.

Our lives were changed forever by that little brother, and not always for the better. We were told that he wouldn't live past the age of ten, but as I write he is still alive and with a family of angels that are a part of a "Tennessee Cares" program. He outlived both parents and has watched two families of children grow up, and like the rest of us he is getting older, but he lives still turning blue and scaring the wits out of those who witness his seizures over and over.

I tell mama that he's in good hands, and she knew that before she died some years back. She was able to say in truth that James was in the finest home he'd ever had. When he meets Mom and Dad in heaven, the first thing he'll do is hug Mama and ask her for a comb. He hid thousands of combs in his lifetime and still does. He's then going to give his big toothless smile and ask Dad, "You going to fix that sewing machine, Anus?" He always called poor Dad "Anus," and as years went along Dad couldn't help but to give a wry smile.

Aunt Doris helped Dad give Mama emphysema by smoking one cigarette after the other, and the last I ever heard about her was that she'd died a heroin addict in Chicago. Maybe she did or maybe she just died because her time had come. I am certain though that she was an angel to us when it came down to it, and my last memory of her was setting stark naked on her weathered old back porch, sponging her feet in a wash pan and smoking a cigarette, just before she divorced my uncle Joe, mother's middle brother. There she sat, breasts, butt, legs, all naked, and she told me good morning before I left for school. Isn't it quaint how angels can appear in such amazing disarray? I loved her, and I came to love my brother, the blue baby who came home so unannounced.

Chapter Six

With this as the seventh time I've sat down to write and today being Sunday, it seems a natural thought that I should take you back to the weather-worn old school building where my family went to church and where my mother and father would find comfort throughout their lifetimes: The Lexie Church of Christ. We started being prepared for church on what a lot of country preachers called Saturday night "The Devil's Night." Late into Saturday afternoon and well into the evening, the house would have been cleaned, kids would be scrubbed in the old galvanized wash tub until we reeked of Ivory pureness, and if we didn't have regular bar soap, then we might get washed in Tide or whatever washing substance was known to remove a week's worth of dirt, and then came the dreaded hair setting. I remember going from bobby pins to wire mesh curlers, and the humongous effort that it took to sleep on hardware throughout the night.

My sister Violet had hair like Mama's, all natural curl, but the rest of the girls got hardwired to produce the desired appearance of curls. I longed to have my friend Joan's Suave cream and her Aqua Net hair spray, for I was convinced these beauty products would make my hair curl for a week. As it was, Violet was left with the task of trying to turn us in to Shirley Temple who was still remembered fondly by our mother and who would also become beloved to all of us after we were introduced to television. No matter what sister did though, my hair endeavored to go back into its straight-as-a-stick mode, much to her distress. I could not look at myself in the mirror, for I had a lazy eye that wandered in, and I just looked ordinary, certainly nothing like Annette Funnicello. She was who I would have kissed a frog to turn in to.

Dinner was cooked if Mama was feeling well or sometimes Mrs. Hannah or Mrs. Mason would ask us to come to eat after church. They seemed to know when Mama was down and out and once Mrs. Hannah gave her secret away as to how when she looked at me straight as an arrow and said, "I can hear you little kids when I'm out on the hill. I know what goes on." I never let our mother know that people listened to her yell and that they could hear her children's cries when the switch or razor strop was being used often, for then she wouldn't have let us go anywhere and being nowhere in the first place that was a thought worse than death.

There was time to enjoy conversation with mainly grownups before church and time for Sunday school where we might get lucky and be given a pretty Sunday school card. The Baptist church up the hill was the best place to get such cards. Theirs so often featured Jesus and all the angels stretched in someone's artistic rendering of what heaven would look like, and the artist seemed mighty fond of Jesus sitting around with folks who were all white, did no work, and often were sharing a big bowl of lettuce and white grapes. That worried me, for I'd really have preferred to see a big bologna sandwich and coconut cake being passed around. My mother had a way of using only wilted lettuce, which was created by pouring drippings from her lard can as a seasoning on the greens. I considered it to be sorry eating and was glad when summer brought in real vegetables. We did not go to the Baptist church, for apparently each church thought folks from the other church were misinformed about what the church should be called and what the rules should be insofar as what was considered to be sin. I only knew the Baptists used a piano at that building, and our church elders believed that the New Testament did not condone instrumental music, or dancing, and we were "The Church of Christ." The church.

Next came the preaching and the Lord's supper and then there was the invitation to come up and to be saved. This meant full immersion at Bean's Creek or maybe the Elk River until some of the churches started loaning out baptisteries they'd been able to build. I was scared to death of water snakes, as well as being buried in water, so I held baptism off until miraculously I knew you could go to one of the nicer churches and get dunked by our preacher there. Also, Mama had a way of deciding when it was time to get saved, and if you did not go when she said so, then you were in trouble again.

Daddy would embarrass us by sitting in the car, for from his own father he had little use for religion until one day around the age of sixty something happened—which he would never reveal to us—as he ploughed a hill close to the home place. From that point on, he would become a church elder and give all the money and time he could spare to build the new church at Lexie Crossroads. Some believe he was saved from a tractor turnover, but I know my dad and that wasn't reason enough to get saved. I think he had divine intervention, for you must consider that his own father was by the end of his life mostly atheist. In fact, Grandpa Everett and Great-Uncle Louie Mullins supposedly made alcohol money by going out and preaching on some stump, a tent meeting, you might call it. They'd mock every hell-raising sermon they'd ever heard, take up a collection, get some change, and hit the nearest moonshine still, according to family folklore. Whether it is true seems irrelevant now, but I know Grandpa suffered death from pneumonia, probably because he was always walking up and down the road half-drunk or worse, even in the pouring rain.

When you spend three hours in a hot or freezing church building all your younger days, Sunday after Sunday, with the main topic being the coming apocalypse, it does leave an impression on you. There were Sunday night and Wednesday evening services, and just in case you missed your warning about your soul's damnation were you not saved, there were weeks of revival services all across the community, so you learned to cope as a child. I pretty much memorized the hymnal, and we had bible verses to study to learn how to tell people about evil, chapter and verse how they might find the salvation we were hoping for when the nuclear explosion blew us to kingdom come. We even had to watch *Know Your Bible* for pleasure if it was being aired on Sunday television. We watched Billy Graham and Oral Roberts, and Mama tried to get James saved and cured by shoving James up to the TV set when Reverend Roberts was having healing sessions. She even wrote the man, and she was disillusioned when all she got back was a request for money and some pretty pictures of happy folks throwing down their crutches.

Now you know what it was like to be a Bible-belt child and a New Testament Christian. After all the religious education, my sisters and I as adults would decide that we needed something more. Our conclusion was to look into Catholicism and were we ever surprised, to find that cradle Catholics did not take us to some secret and dark room where we were going to get some secret code which had been hidden from us. We already knew the "Lord's Prayer and about the last supper, but we did not know that what those folks called a Mass, we called it "The Lord's Supper, and when they began Bible study with a bible which looked like our own, then we were able to take a refreshing breath, for I cannot speak to how Rose and Violet felt, but I feared that I was going to be snowed by an old man in Rome, some pictures, some roll of film.

We would never stop loving our church home, and we never would forget all of the honey suckle mornings from the sweet faces of those who gather around us at Lexie Crossroads Church of Christ, and the experience of seeing home folks singing the songs of our woodland church. "Peace In The Valley," sung from the hearts of all who would gather took us away from the fields and away from the troubles at home. Every now and then I lose myself in those Sunday mornings, and I am so happy there where our faith journeys began.

The concept of theology began to take shape within our brains. We began to think that maybe interpretation of the word alone was not all that was needed. We would learn that Martin Luther and John Calvin really tore the cloth out from under the one faith principals by their denouncements of a central religious community which had its origins based on the lineage from Jesus beloved Peter to whom was given the commandment to carry on the church Christ had begun. We let a lot of good folks down when we made our decisions to accept Catholicism; and it makes us sad, for hurt was never our intent. Our side is not easily explained. I think I should clarify to old friends and loved ones that we have always remained a part of them. We know there is little way to understand another's beliefs; But even with our new take on things; We are always Church Home Girls. Sweet Elders; You gave us the foundation, and not anyone else.

The wonderful people of the southern churches know all the names they are called—Religious Fanatics, Bible Thumpers, Holy Rollers, and the newest and most tiring sobriquet, Right-Wing Extremists—and they deal with it. They might have a few names for name-callers, but they are usually too polite to verbalize them. I can guarantee you that, though I am not a fundamentalist regarding word, most of these folks can quote scripture and verse to nullify much of what an outsider brings to them. They do know the word as they interpret it, and, no, they are not always good listeners. They don't get tradition and revelation as given to us by the saints, but you are not going to win a Bible conversation with them. Bible Christians do not go for mystery, mystics and studied theologies. We were taught that you needed one book, The New Testament, and from one house of worship one may encounter somewhat different versions of what a particular reading and verse may hold as truth, and many denominations have been formed as a result of such interpretation from the most debated work through out the birth of ministry.

They will give you their last morsel of bread, the clothes off their backs, and a place to rest your weary soul even if you're a deranged bum, as long as they can offer service. I love them, and I always will, for they are and were my friends, neighbors, and family. Always I know that I can share their table, and they will fill me with strength I left behind. They might discuss that I was there, and they might be disappointed that I will not return to the old home church as a member. But they will be there throughout my lifetime, and they know I'm a daughter of their roots. If there is one thing that I would like to share with them other than my love, then it is this. My beloved old friends, Jesus was a Jew, and he had a Jewish mother, so his skin was probably olive, his hair was likely long and black, and he did drink wine—not Welch's grape juice. He just didn't drink so much of it, perhaps, but the first miracle was the making of water in to wine at a wedding at Cana along with dividing loaves and fishes. He, too, thought that people should find a time of celebration and highly contributed to such. He wasn't blond with curly locks like a Nordic child, and if I have anything to say about it, I'll keep the grapes, but when we all get to heaven do you think we could ask for some San Francisco French bread and maybe a stick of salami?

After Sundays, the week simply began all over again, and I had learned a new scripture or I had to pray much harder, for I could never be certain that I'd gone to the right church that day, especially when adults could get in such hair-raising arguments over the meaning of scripture. The divisions which came with American religious leaders of the earlier history of our country left so much to discuss and so few ways to resolve the divisions.

During the period of Reformation, Martin Luther, particularly, and John Calvin were trying to get at a truth that did not involve edicts out of Rome from a very political and wealthy church hierarchy. They did not know that in the new world people like Roger Williams, who began the first of the Baptist Churches of America; John and Charles Wesley who, along with George Whitefield, started the Methodist community of churches; much less the Pentecostal Churches that started out in England in the early twentieth century would evolve into the countless denominations we have today. Joseph Campbell was preaching the foundation of the modern Churches of Christ in the backwoods in the nineteenth century, though much of his teaching was merely a stricter version of Presbyterianism or the United Church of Christ. It became another separate religion called "The Church of Christ" that my parents drifted to, and where we all belonged.

Theology seemed to be much more complex than we had ever dreamt. We were comfortable with the sacraments that were handed from generation to generation until Henry the Eighth decided he had to find a way to legalize divorce. Catholicism seemed to suit us.

Dear friends, this is what I believe to be true, but I want to say upfront that the churches established after the Protestant Reformation had a body of believers second to none. I look upon the faith of my father's as the foundation of this country called The United States of America. Catholics were not always welcome here, for they were viewed as idol worshippers and as treating Mary on the same dais as Christ himself. We ask things of Mary, but our prayers are to Father God, His Son, Jesus, and to The Holy Spirit. We are not a whole lot different and not that far apart from most mainstream Protestants.

I'd like for children to see the Roman Coliseum where Christians were used as fodder for the amusement of the masses and were killed by lions. I would like to see any of us go from the road in Damascus where Paul received the Christ and stopped his persecutions of early Christians and try to imagine how many miles his feet walked and his writings on pages of parchment traveled. How many could walk away thinking that they could accomplish such a feat of spreading a word that has lasted over 2,000 years much less the 5,000-plus years of Judaica? Not one of us could even imagine how such communication was possible much less still exist in the form of churches doing their best to show a way to life after death. We have inherited a great tradition, and it is ours to share. Call me a Bible Belt Diva if you must.

"Come Home, Come Home" are words from that old hymnal that I mentioned. I feel the sorriest for the nonbelievers who cannot imagine this wonderful message of being able to come home, for when we are tired, that is where we seem to find our comfort. All of us look for homecomings every day, that moment when we feel something larger and warmer than anything material or erotic in nature can offer. We just want to be fed, and sometimes the hungriest of parts is our very own spirit. That is what I get from church, and I thank the Bible-belt churches for instilling such hunger and such nourishment that can be consoling and as easy to receive as simply listening to nothing more than my own heart beating the sound of welcome.

Chapter Seven

I need to call on the spirits to help me recollect my Appalachian valley grandmothers, for they are of short life in the memory book of life's table. My paternal grandmother once held me in her arms as we sat in a straight-backed cane chair, held me close to her, and she called me "my girl" ever so tenderly. I was probably about four or five, but I remember having my finger in my mouth and sucking on it as she held me warmly and close. I could smell on her a musty scent of earth and something like an aging stack of winter wood, too wet for the fire. No one ever called me their little girl, so I have carried her words in my heart like rubies. I think that I was special to her because my mother had given me Grannie Everett's full name of Barbara Ellen, but for whatever reason to feel so loved by somebody then made me feel as if I was worthy of any blessing that came to us on that day. She gave me my very first taste of bologna; never had I had something so delicious. I looked up at her, and I remember her faint smile. Before I remember seeing her again, she died and joined the wood and earth from the cancer that had been hurting her long before she was taken for any treatment.

I have heard that she was considered educated enough to be a teacher and that the man she married was not the mean man my grandfather became. She finally wound up living across the road from him. She lived with one son who would own part of her land for giving her a home and her husband lived about a half mile across the road with a similar arrangement. In those days one did not divorce, but she was smart enough to get away from her husband who had lost touch with reality as the years passed by. Some said that he was self-medicating for an oral gum disease which went to the bones holding his teeth. He was known to beat my dad and the other boys to a pulp from the time my father could remember, and each of his sons had a speech impediment. Usually they spoke face-down and very quietly as if a severe master was standing over them. I think the master was the ghost of their father.

Grandmother got away, and all four of her sons who entered WWII would return home to farm on Sand Mountain. My father was denied entrance to the service because of needing to care for a growing family and his flat feet. Grandma's daughters and sons would remain close to the Alabama homestead for the most part, and perhaps Dad made an error in choice by moving us to Tennessee, but Mom thought life would be so much better if she was closer to her mother and sisters.

I see Granny Everett's pictures now, and I wonder how our life would have differed had she not died too soon and could have had some input to our lives in Tennessee. Would Dad have checked his anger for his mother's sake when his world began to crumble? Did she want us to come back to the mountain as her little girls and boys who had gone away? I know there are no answers, but the words "my girl" remain and sustain me unto this day. I lean closer in to her sweet arms, one of the kindest places I ever rested.

My Grandmother Hood was among the oldest women I've ever known, especially considering that I was just twelve years old when she died. That woman lived very hard, and she gave so much of her life to caring for her own mother and father until their death and caring for her sister, Aunt Sissy, who had the mind of a four-year-old, even into her old age. Sissy had been stricken with meningitis as a toddler and was mentally handicapped and had not been taught much self-care. By the time my grandmother was in her mid-fifties, she was seeing to her mother, her father, her sister, and oftentimes her hung-over husband. She made sure they were clean, dressed, and fed, and most of this began before the sun rose over her beautiful farmland. Then she began a day's work, which included housecleaning, canning, and caring for her prized flock of hens that blessed her with a small income of her own.

She was clever, a supreme country cook, a well spoken, and poised person who accepted that family, cared for family—that is, except when it came to my mother and her children. She was known to be a Christian of

Primitive Baptist faith, something she became after her eldest son entered the war. She had four sons who would serve in European or the Pacific portion of the war. All of her sons would return home, and all but one of the four would suffer from alcoholism in one form or the other. They came home with an attitude toward the home-front men who were not in the same category as the brotherhood that developed among those who fought in WWII. People like my father were good for servitude, and their children, all of us, were subjected to the same kind of treatment. Children of the homecoming soldiers were generally beneficiaries of some kind of GI benefits in the form of money or just the fact that their parents had served. Their families had the benefit of fathers trained to do something besides farming. Granny was proud of her boys and saw the heroism in each of them.

One of their newfound skills was, unfortunately, how to make home-brewed liquor, even if it was just from stale bread or potatoes. And if they couldn't make alcohol, then they still had a little money to buy some. I swear that if one had all my uncles and my Grandfather Hood in the same room, it was probably dangerous to light a match, for the alcohol vapor coming off their very breath was enough to cause an explosion of some kind. Or it could have served as the old ether method of putting folks to sleep. It is no wonder that even now there is a widely held view within the communities of faith and in regular households, that one cannot pick up that first drink, for everyone remembers the men who could not stop with recreational or social drinking. What people forget is that most of these men were trying to forget what it was like to have gone to hell and to have come back to their old lives. Most were kids when they left, stuck in overalls and trading farm ploughs for the fears and devastation of the front lines of war. Too many turned to the drink they'd experienced as comfort in and after battle to try to block out the reality of war. The warmth from bottle replaced the comfort of war rations and brotherhood. The boys of Appalachia were natural hunters and the first to accept the call as volunteers, but they were the last to be willing to admit the damage stress and fear had left within them. They had no idea that their chosen mode of home brew comfort would kill what was left of the innocence of their lost youth, just more slowly.

It seemed to me as if we were unrelated to this woman we called "Granny Hood." For most of the time we were near her, even as children, we could see the scowl that would come over her face—something between a face that had just bitten into a sour lemon and the look of someone who'd just had really bad news told to them. I would later come to realize that the bad news was that we had just walked in to her home, and the very nearness to our mother made her cringe even though she endeavored to control every aspect of Mother's life.

I would learn many things about Granny as the years passed, that she had hidden love letters from a valley boy who adored Mom because she had decided that my mama should marry our father. I knew that Grandma Hood had married my Grandfather Hood when she was only a girl of fourteen years of age, but I did not know that she'd had a child within that first year—a daughter whom she'd given the name of Ruby—until my mother in her seventies decided she wanted to see her sister's gravestone. Ruby would have been older than Mom, and how different our lives might have been had she lived. No one needed an older sister more than our mother.

Grandma never mentioned her dead child or even that it had been named and buried. No one knew why Ruby died, but Mama conjectured that it was because Granny was simply too young and that she had labored long and hard and without experienced help to bring this first child into the world. Great-Grandmother Varner had been with her daughter to witness the agony and the loss. Granny would almost immediately have two strapping sons, Robert and Ralph, and then she would have our pretty little mother with the Varner eyes of blue and the coal-black curly hair which is captured in only one picture.

Our mother would become Granny's physical and verbal whipping post as other children came along and as the years led her through all the changes a young girl goes through in a valley which the TVA would finally flood, ,leading Granny, her husband, and her parents to Franklin County out of Raccoon Valley. Whatever her reasons were, it became apparent to us, even as very young children, that a good day for Granny was when she had succeeded in causing as much pain to our mother as humanly possible. She would try to keep conflict going between mother and her brothers and sisters, and then, worst of all, between Mama and her own children. But like the child always ready for a beating even into her forties, Mom would go back to Grandma's searching for the lost love that would never come. We would go almost every Saturday night when Dad had time off and drop in on holidays like Christmas.

The most prophetic thing I ever heard my Grandmother say was this: "All one does before Christmas is cook, cook, cook. Then you eat, eat, eat, and after that you shit, shit, shit." That statement came after she gave each one of us a Christmas pair of panties, or if we were lucky she might give us two. Then she would go on to describe how thrilled the other grandchildren were with their new toys, cowboy and cowgirl outfits, and whatever wonderful clothes she had provided them with, looking at us and waiting for a response. We always did the same thing—we hugged her and thanked her for our present and sometimes hide tears if the presents were just more than we could bear. Mama would get a pair of panties, too, and never say a word about what our Christmas had been like.

When I got old enough, I came to understand my role at Grandmother's. My Uncle Ralph would pick me up, take me the twelve miles over the road, and Granny would hand me a dust rag and sit me under the kitchen table. I was to dust anything I could reach, table legs, the sitting bench under the picture of The Lord's Supper, as well as all of the chairs before the company came. Generally I was dutiful, but one time, while I was under the table at Christmas time Uncle Joe came home. I heard Joe and Granny talking about my mother and "the bunch," meaning my brothers and sisters.

"Yeah, they're coming over, so I guess they'll be expecting something to eat. All they do is come over here if they want something. I guess she's been spreadin' her legs again," Grandmother said as if she were an official birth control specialist. "And they're bringing that idiot, too."

That did it. I knew that they were talking about my baby brother, James, so I told them, "You can't talk about my family that way, and James ain't no idiot. He's a sick boy, and if you keep talking, then I'm going to tell my daddy and mama on you."

Through the years, from somewhere deep within, I would find this fire in my body that had to burn into people, and after both of them threatened me with a whipping, called me a little tale carrier, and gave me more evil looks, I went back to dusting. Those grown-ups knew they'd been caught.

Granny fed our family a dinner that we never had at home: ham and turkey, vegetables, fruit, and coconut cakes and clever Auntie Carol's Yule log. It was questionable whether God should have wasted skin on Granny Hood. She scowled and complained about Sissy and Granddad Varner's lazy asses, but that day I shut her mouth when it came to my folks—only for a day, but not one word came out of her or Joe's mouth about what had just happened.

Mama was pathetic. She came in like a little child yelling, "Christmas gift, Christmas gift." It was one of those old Appalachian mountain and valley holdovers from her youth, but she was always trying to reach her mother somehow and to feel the love that was lost when the blue-eyed little girl became old enough to leave home and marry one late autumn day in 1933. Never do I take for granted that a little child will not understand the inflections in my voice or the unkind words I tried to hide from, for I've been in that place, under a table a long time ago.

The last summer of Granny Hood's life would be the year my sister Rose graduated from high school, and Granny showed some rare emotion as her eldest granddaughter left for her new government job in Washington D.C. Our family had become the regular field hands at the Hood farm, and when Uncle Ralph drove up, we all knew that either one of the uncles needed field work or that Granny needed house help. It was as if we were marked with some sign that said, "Use Us." No matter the situation on our own farm, with Dad away for so many years, we headed to the truck to see which field we would be working in, or if Granny was canning, cooking for field hands, or worse: hog-killing and butchering time. Mama could not tell her parents no and she stayed behind with the smaller children.

But one weekend I was sent to Granny's alone to do the housework, and Grandma seemed to take a little more care in how she dealt with me.

She and I gathered eggs, had a good supper and she showed me all of her treasures back in the room where only special guests were usually allowed. She opened her cedar chest which contained very little. There were a lot of programs from funerals, death notices of her parents, a King James Bible, and a few quilts along with her most prized possession, the tassel from her youngest son's graduation from medical school which she and Granddad helped achieve by providing their family with food and such. It had mainly happened, though, because my uncle had the desire to go, and the older brothers were willing to help. I loved the cedar smell, and I looked around at her nice couch and at the room which she prized. She did not tell me a lot about the other grandkids, but she gave me some ice cream Sunday night before she put me in the bed her dad used (the thought of his ghost petrified me). The next day, I got ready to walk up the road from her house to school.

Before I left, though, she was holding her head, and she said the oddest thing. She said, "No matter what you kids ever hear from the others, I just want you to know that I do love you all." She had tears running down her face this time, something I'd never seen. She handed me a dollar which I took gratefully, for it meant I could have school lunch for a week without worry. As I walked over the road I knew that I had seen her for the last time as a living functioning woman and I knew that she was going to die very soon. The whispers come from over my shoulders, those whispers that I attribute to angels, and I wanted to feel sad, but something deep within my heart just kept seeing my own mother's tears and all of the years of despicable behavior that Granny had shown toward her and the bad words about our family that would slip out. As much as I wanted to accept her contrition, I was finding it very hard to believe that she loved any of us ever.

Within a couple of weeks she had a cerebral vascular bleed from which she would not recover. We would all see her at the old Winchester County hospital, but she was basically gone. Mama got the call that she had died in the night.

Mama cried and cried and I heard this wicked voice come from my mouth asking, "Why on earth are you crying?"

She answered, "My Mammy died, you stupid thing," and once more I wanted to feel sad for Grandma, but mostly for Mama, but the sadness would not come. Maybe it was my age and the arrogance that comes with it, but I could not understand how Mother could cry for this person who had been so cruel to her. But we would all shed tears at Granny's funeral, and the preacher would say such nice things about the bride and mother that had been Grandmother Hood.

Years change all things, and as I grew older, I knew that Mother was weeping for the mother that might have been. She was crying for the lost years and for the lack of understanding since the time she'd left home at age sixteen; she was never to be her mother's daughter again. The girl who climbed the mountain to meet my father in marriage never really left that valley, and that young woman struggled to go home every time we visited. With her own children as a sacrifice, she wanted to be Granny's special girl in a sunbonnet. With all my heart, I hope that Grandmother was waiting for Mama on the other side and that they could walk back to the valley together, place some tiny flowers on Ruby's aging headstone, and maybe laugh about Granny's Christmas wisdom. I take some comfort in thinking that I can accept the contrition of my Grandma's last words to me, if my forgiveness soothes Mama's abiding spirit with the knowledge that if only once, Grandma was able to ease her pain by speaking words which needed to be said, that she loved us. Somehow that has to be enough.

Chapter Eight

Listen to the sound of the stately pines swaying in the breeze, for today it is springtime. Tomorrow the bird's nest will be filled with new life and chirps of early birth. The season is changing before my eyes with the glorious melodic sound of the young girl beginning to bloom like the flowers, to leave one path behind, and to walk, like a silent cloud, into the next unknown. Come with me, my friends, and like the mist we will go into a new morning while the mountain laurel still blooms and our fears will be left behind as they disappear with the dewdrops that we walked on only hours ago. I would like to call the four winds to bid you welcome to the stories and places which cannot be buried unless they go unheard. I will have no bitterness for the new day if you continue to brush beside the silent cloud where I must hide sometimes. From that hiding place I am going to tell you more, but for now, I want to hear only the rushes of the pine on springtime air. The story moves on, and I will awaken you one morning soon with news you would not expect from my cloud and from me.

Man and woman are born of water. It seems they so often want to return to the water and thus I think we should leave dying and aloneness for a while and go to the water. One Sunday afternoon we went deep into the hollows to see our old friends the Picketts who lived by a creek. There was a shallow place there, just perfect for people to go wading, though mother always forbade such closeness to water. "You might drown" became as stuck in my mind as much as the warning that if you stuck your hand under a rotten log in dead summer, there was a mighty good chance that a copperhead might just be cooling on his belly waiting for some fool to come along and get a grand old nick by poisonous fangs. After so many warnings, no matter how many swimming lessons I had, that water always has some magical power of hauling you under. Thus I am a lousy swimmer.

All that aside, this was a most glorious Sunday, and some church brought in folks for baptizing. We got to watch this act of sanctification from our viewing gallery on Mr. and Mrs. Pickett's porch. Somehow it seems that even if you're not a Christian, it would still be a glorious thing to be baptized, with people glued to that moment when you are placed in the fine white garment for your newness of life; and the people would be singing a hymn, so sweetly as you lay your burdens down and the old self that was you is lowered into the water as sunlight blinds your sight and while little fishes and shore birds are swarming, as your body is lowered by a minister, while a chorus of Hallelujahs and The Great Amen rise up from the current, like God is talking to you. Then, splash. You are born again to be a new person.

That is the way things are supposed to go, but not for my Daddy's Uncle Tom, who, according to family history, was brought to church drunk at the age of ninety-nine. He had decided that baptism should precede the grim reaper. So the story is told that the minister went ahead and baptized him in spite of his intoxication, figuring that there would never be another chance. This is not a recommendation for those who are putting off such a spiritual event, for this uncle had survived every battle of the Civil War from the southern coast to Gettysburg and had come home. His ninety-nine years of waiting for the moment of renewing his faith may be just a few more years than most can count on.

Sunday afternoons became a time for my folks to go visiting. My father's job in Chicago was over as the company had closed. He was back from making bricks in Chicago, to farming a little, and then along came one of the angels I've told you about who just somehow appeared and changed my life. Mr. Limbaugh, who lived near Lexie Church of Christ, knew that my family was hurting, and he helped my dad get a job with the county as a maintenance man for all of the schools of Franklin County, Tennessee. Maintenance was hardly the name for it, considering that these men did the heating, plumbing, electrical, roofing, and even built schools from the ground up. It gave Dad a great sense of pride to bring home a paycheck, drive a county truck, and live well enough that he and Mama could shop at Hill's Grocery like normal folks.

One Sunday after visiting Mr. Limbaugh, they did something most unusual for folks around our area. There was a black family who lived off the highway a few miles away, and out of the blue Mama and Dad decided to drop in on them as if this was in the regular course of things white folks did in the early 1960s when Dr. King was preaching that the time had come to reach out as brothers and sisters rich or poor, black or white, and start building a better world together. The poor blacks were still called the N-word around our parts, and I wasn't certain what my parents were getting into.

On Palm Sundays, for example, we got two small newspapers, one was from the Jehovah's Witnesses and the other was a note about white supremacy that included pictures of nooses and warned of burning down the, "N -Lover's" homes, guaranteeing that was the way to create a superior race. The Jehovah's Witness paper was a lot more beautiful, but it scared me to death, because it guaranteed that we were in end times, and that even if you had been saved, that was not a promise that you would get in to heaven. Sometimes one of the charities would also have something asking for money for the Shrine Hospital, and that one our Mama said was the only thing that wasn't a bunch of trash.

I read everything though, and I was scared for my parents and for us visiting these people of color. Mama came home and said that it had been right nice and that they had been treated like real people in the black people's house, almost as if they had been expecting company. She said that they were pretty much like us and they even shared some bread and jam not to mention some delightful iced tea. Dad just listened and shook his head and nodded showing understanding to Mama's report, and I felt dismayed. I don't know what I expected, but I'll tell you another secret about southern poor. A whole lot of us thought there was something wrong with wanting to hang black people, and I kept my mouth shut when the white boys started talking about what all evil they were going to do when the black folks got to come to our school. Mom and Dad did not speak to their daughters, at least, about any inferior race.

We were told that you showed respect to whomever you were with and not act like the bunch of hoodlums that used to point at me with my crossed eyes as I walked past the dime store with my little retarded brother James. We knew what it was to be on the receiving end of hurtful words that dealt with color, physical disability, and not having a decent garment to wear to Winchester. I couldn't have been more than nine years old when some truly disabled and inbred people came down from Keith Springs Mountain and kept pointing at James and me when we went into the local town of Winchester.

I said these words: "If you've got nothing better to do than make fun of my little brother and me, then I think you are stupid," and using something Daddy might have said, I continued, "Besides, if you don't cut it out I'm gonna knock what teeth you have left out and kick your asses clear over to the courthouse." The courthouse was across the street and there would be other times I'd defend my brother and myself, but strangely even though there were about five grown ignorant people together that day that group moved along as if I could have done some real damage. Maybe they just knew a daddy wasn't too far behind us.

I don't know that Mother and Dad went back much to the black couple's house. The south was dangerous then and the folks they visited never came to see us. I just like to think that Mama and Daddy had grown some by then to know that we were pretty much the same as the people up the road. They knew discrimination because of color and we knew discrimination because we were poor whites that just took the epithet of "Trashy Hillbillies." The Civil War was long over, but some had still kept family ties to old ways that said money and possessions somehow made you better. To this day I wish I could talk sense into many of the people of my county who got stuck in welfare and class systems that existed like poison oak and scream at them to get some grit and pride together. It isn't too late for an end to giving credence to the term, "White Trash," birthing babies for cash, taking the drugs that keep you from feeling anything, and sitting on your butts whining about your lot. I want to scream at the poor of my county to stop telling tall tales, better known as outright lying, watching trash TV, smoking killer cigarettes, and drinking cheap booze, for most of your fathers gone before you were better than that. I want to remind them in some loud voice that the top of the mountain is in sight if they just look back a little, remember how hard people worked, and believe, for God's sake, truly believe that you are the harbinger of your fate. You can change destiny for your children by showing courage.

Maybe poor folks need to march again, and march and hold hands with the brother up the road, rich or poor, black or white. Sit down to some jam and bread and a nice glass of iced sweet tea and know that together you are the sum of something great which can still come to the poor communities of the south that people have conveniently left behind. Yes, time has moved on, but some of my home folks are stuck, and I want them to make some changes, not for me but for all people who just lie down and decide to do nothing. The angel you might meet if you can just get up and walk is the spirit of the old folks of the poor south who walked those back roads and reached out, because beyond nothing there is something and somebody, and you are it. As Mama might say, "You are real people." I do not want you to forget this, so get your marching shoes on. There are a lot of us out here for you to become heroes to. We'll be waiting to lend a hand, not a hand-out.

Chapter Nine

Black beauty, black souls of slaves, black people—I knew so little about any of these things when I became involved in some very beautiful days in a cotton field. I remembered Mama's words about folks who seemed just like us. One day I was to pick cotton at Mr. Gordon's, the nicest man I might have ever known other than my Uncle Clifford Bain. Back then, I was very surprised that it was me, a few more white people, and a black family who had been available to help in Mr. Gordon's field that day. My life had become a series of daydreams about the fact that a person such as me could have been adopted or stolen from their real family, for it seemed that I had become the ultimate "hand." I was a cotton-picking hand, a child-care hand, a cleaning hand, and when Mama needed help, a hand for about anything else a farm kid could think of. But this day was different from all of the rest, for there in the white field was a woman that looked like the real Aunt Jemima, just like the new cornmeal and pancake mix. There were the first African-American kids that I'd ever worked with, and I treated them as Mama and Daddy had mentioned—like real folks—for that was how we all talked together as we went up and down the rows.

I remember there was talk that the mama went around the county with her kids picking cotton for money, and I wondered where the daddy was but I did not have the nerve to ask. We talked about schools, the black schools and the white schools that were going to be united soon and that maybe it would be a better thing. The mama looked at me once and said, "Girl, you're filling out," but that didn't mean much to me, because I did not know where, being a stick at the time with no bra and only clean panties to show on wash day. She had a boy whose name was Damian and how I have remembered that name through all these years, I do not know. He was a boy about my size but shorter, and I had so much fun with him chasing up and down the cotton rows when we got a minute to play tag and run like banshees, as my mother called kids having a good time. By the second or third day the mother was saying that maybe Damian and I were sweethearts, and I went home that night pondering the ramifications of what that meant. Dr. King had been preaching on TV about little black boys and little white girls walking hand and hand together, but then I saw George Wallace blocking the entrance to the University of Alabama with his body so a deserving student who was of color could not get in. I heard grown folks cheering as black people got the hell beat out of them in a place called Selma, and there was the story of three young men killed because they wanted to promote integration in the southern United States, and here was a mama that looked like Aunt Jemima telling me that I could be her son's sweetheart. Something didn't seem safe to me, so I sort of quieted down in that cotton patch.

Another thing that I noticed was that the mother and children sat on their cotton sacks and ate fine biscuits and drank water for lunch while the rest of us got invited in to the house for a nice hot meal. Somehow I wanted to sit with them, for that mother hugged her kids, and they all sat close like a real family should, and they talked up a storm. I wondered what it was like to be left in the field while everyone else went in for lunch, except that family did have it nicer than my brothers and sisters and I did when we worked at Granny's in her fields or at some of the uncles', especially Uncle Ralph. All the other kin help would go in for what I imagined to be ham and pie and all kinds of vegetables, while my brothers and sisters and I were thrown stuff from brown bags that Uncle had picked up at some store. He didn't even ask us what we wanted; he just brought the same thing all the time, something like Vienna sausages, beanie weenies, maybe a bunch of bananas, some colas, and if we got really lucky, some crackers and Moon Pies. Sometimes he considered it part of our pay. Often we got two dollars and fifty cents for a hundred pounds of cotton which took a little kid a whole day or more to pick. No love came in those brown bags.

Aunt Jemima's kids looked loved, though, and she would laugh, and we would laugh about anything under the sun. Maybe someone was chasing an old heifer cow down after it had jumped a fence, or perhaps a chicken decided to see if there was a willing rooster in the cotton patch. Whatever it was, it was funny. Once she got her dress caught in the crack of her bottom, and none of us told her. I think we all got down on the ground and rolled with laughter for we were all keeping the secret and she being a hefty woman caught us and she called us a bunch of little devils which made us laugh even more as she finally pulled her dress out. I wondered why we all couldn't be so happy.

I kept remembering a children's story that I had read in second grade about a little black boy who was afraid of tigers, and once he found himself in the middle of those tigers, and they started chasing each other so fast like a merry-go-round without a stop, and their tails all hooked together. They got so hot that they melted into jars of butter which the boy then took home to his mama. She was so proud that she made him pancakes and forgave him right away for having gone out in the jungle where she had warned him that danger was around every corner. I just knew those kids I was picking cotton with were having pancakes every day before we hit the field which they ate streaming with melted sweet butter and honey. Maybe that's how they got happy.

I would never see that family again, and I wondered what happened to Damian and his family. Would he find a path like me or would he get lost in some city jungle without his mama and brothers and sisters because the sticks and guns broke his spirit somewhere along the way? He'd never know that some little white girl took him to her dreams on those soft autumn nights or that she wished his mother could give some lessons on loving kids in a proper way and without shame, laughing at the smallest things to the point it was infectious, even if you were trying to pick a hundred pounds of cotton that even then wouldn't buy you a dress for school.

After I went to Washington, I would meet one of the handsomest men ever. He was African-American and he looked like a lawyer and was a little older than me. He wanted us to not just walk around DuPont Circle and the neighborhoods around D.C. together, he wanted us to be a couple. The late sixties had come, but my memory was too locked into all the threats that I heard from white boys with guns, and I looked at him and knew that he had a black parent and said, "Please understand that I like you very much, but I could never take you home. Someone would hurt you or me or both of us if I took you back home."

Strangely, he showed me some understanding, placed his arms around my shoulders and said, "I get it." Compared to some of the white guys that came into my life for a while, I had left a prince, but I told him the horrible truth. I would miss him just like I'd miss meeting Damian and his Aunt Jemima mama. Please understand that I would not have given her this name, but for some reason she never shared hers, and she addressed me as Little Missy or Ma'am.

Again I was daft, for I did not get that she still lived in a world where a color barrier had been so formalized that she did not realize how much a child could respect her. Maybe I hope that some of her family is still around Franklin County, Tennessee; maybe, just maybe they will remember a mother or a grandmother who could make the ground shake with laughter while we did a hard day's work for small pay. I'd even like to think that somehow I am making amends for sins of fathers and mothers who taught their children to hate based on color. Don't think for one moment that I haven't had some really bad black supervisors at times who maybe did not hear Dr. King's lessons on getting to the same goals together, but I've also had a life that involved a lot of white folks who never even bothered to really listen to such a lesson, much less the words of Jesus which were all-inclusive. My favorite scripture probably will always be, "Ye that labor and are heavy laden; come unto me and I shall give you rest." I do hope that Damian's mother found such rest, and I hope the man in Washington, D.C. found a true love that could take him home without the assumption that they would be jungle lions chasing each other to get away from predators called "Men without Conscience" for the world did change.

This is probably not written in a form of political correctness, but that it is written and the stories are told is a part of the healing that I must offer for anyone who ever thinks they are the lowest in the field called life. Oh Glory never faded away; it just became more gallant when a person was recognized as a human being no longer bound with chains. Think like a child sometimes, and you might find a bright spot in the darkest of places.

Chapter Ten

There were very few days when we were not expected to work from early morning until evening fell, but if there were a free day, then it was apt to happen on a Sunday afternoon after church. Were it springtime when the milk check was a little bigger, then we would be thrilled to have banana sandwiches, a whole plate-full that Mama would make for us. She would have to be feeling really well, and after we had full stomachs, then without words the older sisters, Violet and Rose, might decide that we would go exploring together. I would follow, and what I did not know that day was that they knew exactly where we were going.

Normally we'd walk past our old gray barn, climb the fence down to the lower pasture, and head for the pine thicket that we thought had been planted as a windbreak. Later we would learn that it had really been put there to hide the moonshine still on the other side, which my sisters had wandered upon one day much to Dad's horror. It was not his still, but he knew that young girls wandering around where white lightning was made was very unsafe, even then, and he told the girls to keep away from there, and he meant it. They described barrels and pipes and a few bottles lying around, and to them it was a great mystery. Dad could hardly stifle a smile as he scolded, but scold he did and with enough fear in his voice that the sisters never ventured that far again.

This Sunday, though, the girls had just started walking and they let me follow. No one said very much, but it was almost as if they were in a hurry to get where we were going. One thing about children and people who become close to one another which one notices is that words are not always necessary; you just know that a time has come to do something and each one follows as if the plan was set in motion long before the day began. It was bright and sunny, and the newness of day still lingered in the hollow as we traipsed down the hill together. I looked at the girls, and for that moment it was perfect family love, for they included me when usually I got left behind with Mama and the babies.

Dad, were he home, was apt to be plowing and embarrassing us to death, for only sinners plowed on Sundays, The Lord's Day as we would always know it. That is what we heard at church, but we did know that you could rescue a sheep by the roadside, for Jesus said so. What we did not know was that we were the sheep and to have food on the table Dad would have to shame us and work on Sundays, especially when he had to go back up north and be there for the next morning's work at the brickyard. We did not know then that if he got two hours' nap before Monday, he'd be lucky. All we could hear was about the sinners working and sheep being rescued, for children—and some adults—think so literally about what is read in Sunday school.

We walked and almost ran into the middle of the tall pine thicket, and there we became entranced, for before us was the most beautiful thing which I had ever seen: wildflowers which were hidden from the sun and waited for us to pick them. At any moment there could have been white rabbits popping out of unseen dens, princes with wands turning us into ladies in pastel and magical dresses that looked like Cinderella's, or a fairy with a wand that changed us from ordinary girls into women walking up to a palace in that hidden place. Instead, before us lay the last of the dogwood trees protected from the sun and a scent of perfume which I will remember with my last breath. There before us, sheltered by the pines and kept clean by a new washed floor of pine needles and as lovely as anything which would ever take my breath away, stood within reach, the pink honeysuckles. They were everywhere we looked, and we danced around them and placed our young faces within their bowls, for they were like no flower we had ever seen before.

We tasted them like birds sipping sweet honey and began to gather them in bunches, trying to find the very prettiest to take our vision home to Mama, trying to save the hour, the day, the magical forest that was ours alone where no danger seemed to lurk, only beautiful, beautiful pink honeysuckles, hidden from all the world except for us. We smiled and played;

we ran and we gathered, and we'd break stems of dogwood and reach down for some purple violets that were hiding with us in our secret place where magic was possible. We did not get angry at one another nor worry about Sunday labor or who might be watching little girls fill their arms to the brim with flowers that seemed more magical than any other flower or tree we'd ever seen. Everything became about us and the gathering and how we were going to remember this place and this time forever, but most of all, we were going to make Mama smile and feel happy.

We had found an abundance of a gift that was simple, free, and ours for the taking, and no matter how many we picked, it seemed as if there would be enough for all of the forest spirits to enjoy once we had gone. When our arms were filled, we raced back up the hill and found some stray lilacs along the way, and when we got home our faces must have shown like the sun, for Mama was happy to see our gifts, and she began to gather Mason jars, the only vases that we had, and all of the sudden the rooms became so beautiful that it was enough to make us all cry.

All of us would remember what mother said that day: "I used to do that for my mammy, when I was a girl." Her face smiled as if she too had been with us on the carpet of the pine forest floor and had been able to leave all of her sorrows there. We three girls who were there with her at that moment flushed with pride, and as she helped us scatter our bounty of flowers about, we knew that we'd do the same thing year after year until we were too grownup to enter the magic kingdom which bloomed only once per year.

We would go to the hidden garden of pink honeysuckles just to see our mother smile, even though forest flowers wilted by the very next morning. They did not take to being stuffed in jars away from the shadows of the pines. In the worst of times, that day would come back to us as it does even now. If I open my heart and listen above all other sounds, I can still hear the whisper of the pine trees on a late spring breeze with its "hush, hush," a tender sound almost like a soft rattle of a baby's breath. More than any other sound, though, I can see Mama acting all surprised and smiling as she so rarely had reason to, and her voice. "I did that when I was a girl." I wonder if Grandmother Hood had gathered her empty Mason jars, too, and made Mama feel as wonderful as did we when first I learned the enchantment of pink honeysuckle and the sweetness of remembering that mother was a girl, a little girl who had her own magical garden some secret place where we had never been.

Sweet sisters, all sisters, all sisters wherever you are, I give to you this part of me, the memory that I can go to when all else fails to soothe. I have known magic, and the magic cannot be just mine, so before I continue the story, I give to you a small petal from the pink honeysuckle that now grows very far away but lingers within the very essence of who I am who my own sisters are, and I give it to you as your very own. This hour I am one of the Magi and it is the most perfect gift which I have to offer, and it is with holy intent that I can offer such a small portion which pleased the soul of my mother.

Chapter Eleven

By this point in my story, I am opening a new chapter which I warned you early on was coming, and it occurs to me that I feel like a script writer challenged with setting up a crime scene for some kind of life's script that is beyond my comfort zone. This is a true story, a serious crime which went unreported, and the problem is that I know that I have to be the victim of something that happened so many years ago for which the perpetrator and others like him will never face justice. People tend to find stories more credible if they can see that river of justice catching up in a great wave with the evil character or persons who are involved and then see them crushed before a judge and jury with the suspense mounting each moment. This will not be the case here.

I feel as if I must take you where I found my aggressor lurking. You've heard a little about my maternal grandmother and must have some awareness that her home was enviable compared to the one my family was encouraged to move into. Hers was a white two-story home with pretty flowers which she cultivated, bucolic in setting and off the main road just enough to be private. It was always sparkling clean while she was alive. There were white Adirondack chairs outside for seating at the side of the house, a big welcoming porch always painted some shade of grey or blue with nice rails, a firm foundation, and Granny's prized doormat that you had better darned well wipe your feet on before walking on her polished floors. She had two living rooms, but both were also used as bedrooms, and there was a large dining room with plenty of table and chairs, a long bench, a pie safe, and well-dusted pedestals which were so thanks to her grandchildren's labor.

She had hot and cold running water and a real farm sink, and she had the most British-looking pantry attached to her kitchen that I ever saw anywhere outside of a theatrical production. There she could use her huge bread counter to make pastries of all kinds, and the pantry kept that faint scent of sour milk, dough, and sweetness all packaged and ready for the next baking day. Two porches came off these areas. From the dining room, one could walk out onto what we called the well house which was really a covered cement porch with a well and her newer wringer washer that was under cover, so in the worst of winter she could use a few clotheslines strung there rather than traipse in the bitter middle-Tennessee wind or the occasional ice storm or snow. The side porch off the kitchen had the original recycling bin that every home where hogs were slaughtered for curing had a bucket of leftovers that wasn't eaten by the dogs or humans—their own personal slop bucket which many a pig would grow fat from. Anything edible from nature could be thrown in there from apples that rotted on the ground to grapes that had dried on the vine plus any food that was deemed kept long enough. Next to this was a freezer which my grandparents kept stocked with edibles most farm families could not afford like store-bought ice cream, cheese, extra chickens, and maybe bags of sweets Granny was saving for special occasions.

I must admit that I almost laugh out loud at some of the recycling practices of today, which are costly containers. Farm families were recycling everything from the time of their birth until the time of their death, and a great big lard bucket was the ultimate composting bin or slop bucket as we called it. Canned goods from the orchard and garden were kept in a smoke-house which one could see from the kitchen, all beautifully displayed and in no particular order other than by the color of the fruits, vegetables, and soups which filled those wonderful canning jars. Going into the smoke-house was such a delight, for there was always the scent of cured hams and bacon, winter or summer, and the thick walls of it simply kept that place cooler or warmer depending on the opposite season on the farm.

Though they did not have a bathroom during grandmother's lifetime, they had a great outhouse. How can an outhouse be great you might ask. Well, in summer and autumn there was a small vineyard of concord grapes that kept the air sweet even around there, intertwined with old weed-variety honeysuckle which would try to choke them out without success. Being a two-holer and having the nicest catalogue collection one could ever want, not to mention wonderful magazines now and again, this was about as good as it got, especially if the cousins were willing to sit inside or outside with you and talk woman talk. I think most of my cousins had more knowledge of menstrual cycles, babies, boys, and female conditions at age ten than I would when I graduated from high school.

Their mothers were younger than mine, and maybe it was diet, but most of them matured physically a lot sooner than my sisters and I ever did. Maybe you never knew that there was joy and purpose beyond the obvious for an outhouse; but we found it to be a fine place to gather if you wanted a little privacy. It was such a natural path and privilege to visit a well-kept privy, especially since Dad had been remiss in rebuilding ours after it was blown away in a tornado. In my own devious humor, I often wondered on whom the remains of our outhouse fell, and did someone see it as a sign and wonder of whether or not shit from Heaven would turn to gold?

All of the other outbuildings were kept in good condition as well. Grandfather had all the tools most men of his day could want. I believe that I've come to realize that much of this wellbeing came about as a result of sons who had gone to service and had helped their mother and father out some as the uncles did. It was to me an amazing place, and the curious thing is that I had little understanding that this was my mother's parents place for all the reasons we've gone over before, but we were not there on as regular a basis as the other cousins for social and family events. It was to me as if these people were not mine at all, but belonged to some other privileged world which we were only allowed in for work or if no one else was going to be there.

Sunday summertime was most likely the only day that we could actually visit, unless it was to watch The Lawrence Welk Show on the Saturday nights when Daddy had come in from Chicago. Daddy knew that if he brought home a coveted bottle of schnapps for Grandfather Hood we would get to watch television in spite of Granny's natural aversion to all of us except for our eldest brother. He had been only a few years in age removed from my beloved Aunt Mildred and Uncle Woodrow, Granny's last babies, and she found great satisfaction in keeping him away from our mother and father as much as possible. That woman had serious issues about her eldest daughter which went with my mother to her grave, but some light may be shed on certain issues now that you have a picture of where Grandmother and Grandfather lived as compared to what they had allowed our Uncle Ralph to find as a place for us. Sometimes I think living in the smokehouse might have been preferable to living where there was no natural source of drinking water, much less living at the end of nowhere. To my sister's recall, Grandmother visited Mama one time in the years we lived back there, and their memory is better than mine. It could have been a visit from the Queen of England as far as poor Mom's preparation was concerned.

Maybe you have some picture of the Grandmother's world as compared to ours, and perhaps it will come as no surprise to you that in spite of all the grandchild cleaners, the aunts' attempts to help, and the uncles living nearby that Grandma ruled, and when she died, this house and grounds became the main meal for termites through the lack of new paint, poor roof repair, and general neglect. One might say that my Grandfather let it go to seed, for he was left with few cares, having no one to keep him from being drunk most of the time, as well as being the lender, the quick drink source, and fishing buddy for every other alcoholic in the county. Mama thought that it was a sin how he had let her mother's place rot and along with it he even left all of the clothing and linens that Granny had kept so carefully ruin while Mom, his daughter, was lucky to have a decent dress to wear.

I need to walk you through Granny's house, for it was where the crime that took my childhood and almost my life from me happened. And by doing so you get the picture of my grandfather, Mr. Hood as everyone knew him. He took his old jeep and lulled away the hours going from the house to the river's edge where, for him, the fish were always biting, but from whom no loaves of kindness ever came to deserving grandchildren, much less to Mother. On the little white graveled lane that led to his house servant children would come to know that evil people sometimes leave you with no alternative other than to hate them to the bone and wish they had died with the slaughtered pig seasons before and been ground as feed for the rest. I know, I'm procrastinating. I'm writing words, any words, for the next words I write must be truth, and I am still devastated and feel no remorse in my anger toward this horrible man.

Sometimes at night when I work I hear the mockingbirds, but I have told them that they cannot sing on this night, nor can they mock the sound of the voice which I make as I cry out for help as I tell you about my story of the years of Grandfather's abuse of me. As I remember it, I cannot believe that I was his only victim, and when my mother was more than eighty years old, all she could say to me was that she married at sixteen partially to get away from her father, and then she would say no more.

I do not know the year it began, but Mama would always tell us to go and give old Granddad some sugar, and we were obliged to go and sit on the lap of a drunken man with snuff all over his fingers and spittle from snuff dripping down his chin. Snuff was very popular among the people of our mountains and valleys well into the 1960s before any bad tobacco ads began to come out, and even some of my beloved mountain aunts were snuff users. Most homes were apt to have a place to spit even if they did not have a handy ashtray. Thus, if we went to watch TV at Grandma and Grandpa's house, this was the first order of business. If we were lucky and gave him a kiss on the cheek, he would sometimes give us a nickel or a quarter. Usually the more alcohol he had taken in added up to twenty-five cents, and that was enough to buy a Coca-cola with salted peanuts and a Moon Pie from Mr. Crouch's general store, or if you save up enough, you might even have enough to buy some fabric for a dress after we learned to sew.

I was too little to care about sewing much, especially when I got my nice pink nylon dress as a hand-me-down from one of my friends. It was a type of nylon that one cannot even seem to buy now. Soft and pink almost like my honeysuckles in the hidden forest, and I liked the way it touched my skin in church, for I was so proud to look dressed up, but this one afternoon we went visiting over at my grandparents' house, and my turn came to go and give Grandpa his usual affection, and suddenly it happened, something that I knew was very wrong but did not know how to scream or to run or to get help in anyway. His hand with the snuff-stained fingers slipped under my dress and started to probe and hurt parts which I knew only God was to know that I had. I wanted help so much, but his chair backed into a wall, and I tried pulling down my dress as far as I possibly could. I know that involuntary tears began to stream down the side of my face that my parents and Granny could see, so I thought someone would notice that something was very wrong.

No one responded except for Mama who said, "Oh, just give your granddaddy some sugar." He kept probing and poking me as I tightened my bottom and knees as much as I could, and it was hard for me to imagine that no one could see the sobbing. If I told the truth, then and there Daddy was going to kill Grandpa and go to jail, but Mama was going to agree with her daddy. He would say something like, "That cross-eyed lying little bitch." Then every grown person in the room was going to beat me up.

Finally, I gave in, and I kissed Grandfather on the cheek, took my quarter, and I pulled away as hard as I possibly could for a girl that weighed about eighty-five pounds then. I went outside and walked and wandered, for, you see, I thought maybe this was the way that someone placed a baby inside you. Understand that to this day where I grew up terms like intercourse, pregnant, sanitary napkin, and birth control are things kept quiet in front of children. My friend Joan Mason had told me that I should know that menstruation meant that I was going to have blood coming out of my butt, so I had been expecting a rectal bleed, but never in my wildest dreams did I see a Grandpa who could place a baby inside you with his nasty old hands. Over and over again this would happen, for I was only about nine years old then, and each time we went over to Grandfather's house, the same thing would happen to the point that I began not even to cry.

All adults were authority figures, and no one but me on the face of the entire world had ever had to go through such a despicable act again and again. No one was going to believe ever, so I might as well stop my tears and tighten by knees and buttocks, hold my clothes tightly against me, and take the inevitable. I began to make these plans. If I had a baby fall out of me, then I was going to keep it down at the little spring where we got water, and I would let it sleep in a cardboard box. My mother still had some baby clothes, then when I was ten years of age, along came my sister, Linda. I would take some bottles, for Mama had some from when the two previous babies were born, and I would keep it just like I had my rubber baby doll that had disintegrated because I bathed it too much. Sometimes I would get sick at Lexie Crossroads School, and old Mrs. Ruder would send me home because I was crying and shaking, and I'd tell her that my stomach hurt, and I needed to go to Mama. Mind you that I had to walk more than a mile, and Mama would put me in bed upstairs, and she would always want to know: "What's wrong with you, girl?" How could I tell Mama that her own daddy was putting a baby in me with his fingers?

One week things got so bad that I could no longer go to the bathroom, and in the morning before school my vaginal area became so inflamed that I burst in to tears. When Mama asked what was wrong, all I could do was to say and to point at my body to show her the wicked "Down Here." She decided to take a look and obviously knew that I was in misery, for she sat me in a pan of hot water with Clorox and Lysol in it. I sat there again crying like a baby, for my sisters were sort of making fun of me not knowing themselves what shape I was in, and I told Mother that I probably had cancer like Grandma Everett had died from. She only replied that I didn't have cancer, to sit in the wash pan and I'd get easy. Strangely enough, I did, and for the first time in about a forty-eight-hour period, I was able to use the bathroom. Her method of curing such vaginal irritation might sound crude to you, but Mama and all the country women had ways of dealing with such pain that they'd had to find out on their own, and though you might not appreciate Lysol and Clorox in hot water. That was a day when it saved my life. The pain eased up, and I got back to school. About a year had gone by, and the baby had not come either, so I began to think that maybe I was safe from that kind of harm.

Chapter Twelve

I became a master at finding ways not to go to my grandfather's house until Granny died and I would also begin to know that boys and girls had to do something more to get a baby. At this time in my life I also began to develop a tendency to go into a serious tremor at the moment of any stress. I was an artist at hiding distress deep within me that was going to boil over in years to come like a kettle exploding from being overfilled to the point of destroying its contents and everything that surrounded it. I believe Granny's death happened around my twelfth year of life and she would be followed in death by my Uncle Ralph who was said to have gone off the road hauling a load of cattle. I told you that Mother cried for her Mama and I would wonder why, and now she cried for a lost brother. Again I could not imagine why. I was losing the ability to know grief or pain, so when Uncle Ralph died I supposed that maybe there would be more time to be at home to take care of our own things, much less the fact that it was with him or another Uncle when Daddy would try to show that he could knock back whiskey just like they did, but would lose all grasp of reality, get sick, terrorize us if he was home, and then Mom would get him so tense that he would do something really stupid like take out a shotgun at which point we all figured our time was up. I could not understand how my Mother could ever find grief for the lost brother who placed us in an almost unbearable living situation. My only hope was that God would have mercy on our souls and get Grandpa out of the picture too.

Instead, Mom decided that her dad needed help more than ever, so she started the business of sending me over to be his weekend maid. He knew that I had grown up some, so he wasn't as willing to try something with my parents in the room. I cannot tell you how much of my life is like a dark moon that even I could not see at this point, but one night would be the last encounter. My friend Jean had gotten off the school bus one day, and then we never saw her back at school, for a baby did come out of her. Her parents denied it until the story got around that my uncle who delivered the baby had told her father, "You may not think this girl is going to have a baby tonight, and maybe you're right that it is a virgin birth, but the last time this happened on earth Jesus was born, so I am going to get along with delivering it." I never asked my uncle, Dr. Hood, if he had been so clever with the verbiage, but he did deliver most babies in the county at the time. What happened to Jean was not going to happen to me, though, and at first I thought maybe Grandpa had mended his ways.

Then one night as I got into Aunt Mildred's bed to get ready for Monday and school, the door to the room opened and to the horror of this early teenage girl, all of my misplaced trust was torn to shreds, like a quilt with the rags of ages spewing out of an open seam. This grandfather in his mid-seventies crawled into my bed, and I got away from him and as close to the wall as I could, before he was tearing at my clothes and asking me if I couldn't get my drawers off, meaning my underpants, as he tried to place his sorry hands against my body again. No one was there, so I began to gather enough sense to grab hold of anything which I could and God had mercy on my soul, for I had placed my purse in that bed, and I picked it up and hit him as hard as I possibly could. Ordinarily it would not have been hard enough, but I had used a couple of his old quarters for a big can of Aqua Net Hair Spray and I will say this vehemently that I would not have cared if it killed that son-of-a-bitch. It undoubtedly packed a mighty blow, for he went off in his usual drunken stupor, whining about whether or not that was any way to treat old "Grandaddy." Had I landed one hit on his head, the rest of my life would have been spent in jail. I'd stand up in court and hear that I got the electric chair, and my legacy would be "The Aqua Net Killer."

It was dark and late. I could not go home or call home, for they were going to see the truth this time. Daddy was finally home from Illinois, and he was going to see his girl shaking like a leaf, unable to utter a word, and again I pictured my father, a most respectful man to daughters, behind bars for killing this Grandpa that was as useless as a dried turnip in midsummer. I piled all the furniture that I could, even things on top of the dresser, to bar the door, for I could not sleep and sat on the bedside in horror waiting for daybreak. By then he'd gone out to tend cattle, so I tore down my barricade. I ate nothing, for I couldn't without vomiting it back up, and I dressed and I ran over those roads to wait for school. I cried and ran, and when the school bus came, my dearest friend Betty Ruth had a place for me to sit beside her. Betty could read my face and that morning she placed her arms around my shoulders, the youngest kids in our class we were, but she knew something was going on, and I do not know even to this day if I ever even told her what happened.

I would not even tell my parents until I was about thirty years of age, for Grandfather lived to be well into his eighties, and when I did my baby sister ten years younger told that he'd chased her around the table a few years earlier, but she called Dad, and Dad came right away, and she never would go over there again. I still got tremors, but I tried to finally tell them the whole truth, my parents, my sisters, and brothers, and per usual I would go into shakes really bad as I recalled all that was now behind me. Later in life I would find a therapist who managed to pick up the scraps of me working with me for years, and he did save my life, for even married and with children I would go back in to terrible remembrance as if it were all happening again. My husband helped in every way possible, but my parents had the oddest reactions. Dad said that "Grandpa wouldn't have known which hole to bark at" and held his head down, not out of amusement but for lack of anything more that he could comfortably say to a grownup daughter and more likely, because he had been part of my rationale for remaining silent through the suffering. Mom just kept saying her Daddy was a "No Account Man!"

Only near the end of her life, would she make the confession of his attempts to get to her and she worried about one of her sisters. She would not tell me what he did to her, but for her to walk up the mountain at sixteen years of age to meet and to marry along with her next words said all that needed to be said. She said that she was ashamed for letting her own daughter become victim of this evil person she called her father. I couldn't ever tell the aunts or the cousins, but now I know that some of them were also not spared, and I hope that my open heart will not offend them as much as to tell them that it is finally all right. Step up, for I cannot be the only one he chose to abuse out of the many. I can say for each of them almost to the person that they will not want the story to have ever been told.

That is still a problem where I am from. Bad things can happen in families of color, among foreigners, or to people far away, but in a community where people keep Sunday sacred, get together with the family for every holiday, and where a man usually still heads a household, one does not share such issues that might taint a family history. You keep shut up and you go to your grave with the secret; then maybe the next generation might get spared your lot. Unfortunately, girls I went to high school with would wind up being called insane. Some girls would, and still do, commit suicide for unknown reasons. Good and decent white folks are just supposed to get on with their lives and luck, no matter what fortune has in store. There is still the concept of predestination, of bringing things on oneself, and bad stuff doesn't happen to nice folks. Every one of us grew up with the old 1950s song "Whatever Will Be, Will Be" singing it and believing it. We were not people, especially women, who believed that we had control over our destiny. I see changes there now, some mental health services, a great niece who is a social worker extraordinaire, but there are so many women my age still in denial and without resources.

I wished the mockingbirds would quiet, for I needed time to write this part of my unhinged life, but now I want them to sing so loudly that eardrums almost burst to every mountain top and to every valley where women feel trapped in a gourd of guilt and anger hanging on a lonely vine, hoping that mercifully someone, someway will pull them away and carry them to some sweet grace and mercy where it is safe. I want the birds to sing and to whisper that they are free to open their voices, to hold each other's hands, and please not take to the grave the haunting edicts which so many of us had to face before we could carry on.

You are the flower, the welcome flower on mockingbird hill, and your song will be carried if you know that we are all listening out here. That too was a song we sang again and again, that we were welcome as a flower on mockingbird hill and sometimes in my hiding I would just sit on a hill and wait for something to ease the pain in my heart, just one beautiful bird to fly over and to speak for me, sing to me, and to carry my voice when I could not speak. For you, my sisters of long ago, I speak for you, for the dear girls who were not lucky enough to win a battle because you did not know when or how to fight back and for me it was a can of hair spray bought with blood money given to me by my perpetrator.

My body and soul ached for some kind of whispers from one of God's angels to help me get through the days of pain which my grandfather had left within my heart, much less what was inflicted on my body, but I took meager comfort in the fact that my abuser was apt to burn in hell's fire, for there was usually some guarantee at Sunday morning church services that people who committed evil would suffer such a fate. The preachers of my past were thoroughly bent toward warning sinners that such a fate laid ahead of them.

My total sin apparently was that I was becoming a woman - Oh yes, a lustful woman. "Women, cover yourselves, for men are the head of the household," said the preacher. And it was showing through my clothes, or in how I walked, or if I made eye contact with this elderly man. I personally had made this whole thing fall upon my shoulders, for I was female and a part of the original sin of Adam and Eve. Women really took verbal beatings back then, even in church, where you might hear about the seductive nature we were born in, the inappropriate feelings which we caused, and we all knew the neighbors whose wives stepped out on their men, went up town, and who sold their souls for money or for drink. Yes, it was born in us, and brothers, sisters, mothers, and fathers could not help us one bit. We didn't stand a chance for salvation unless we got ourselves baptized into the church and cut out all our evil ways, so when Mama told me that it was time to "go forward," I knew that she meant that I was to accept the call to walk up to the front of that church and to have my baptism day, because I needed a cleaning. I was going to get rid of the "Tail Waggin'," which I understood as "Tell Wagon" which seemed odd, but I saw no harm in it. Yes, I figured if you wanted to talk to a wagon, no harm was done.

Chapter Thirteen

I had put it off for as long as I could, for I pictured myself back at Bean's Creek in front of the Pickett's house, and I was going to be that girl it finally happened to. As they lowered me into the water, with all my family and friends present and glad the day had come for me to be "washed in the blood of the lamb," a school of water moccasins which Mama kept telling us had eaten a man uptown was going to strike me just as I hit the water, and I would die instead of being saved. My salvation time was at hand, but I wasn't going to emerge from the waters of baptism unscathed.

Fortunately, they took me down to The Huntland Church of Christ, and there they had a baptistery built right into the floor. Now folks who have not grown up as New Testament Christians may not know that most churches which require full-body immersion have these pools about big enough for a 400-pound sinner to be fully and thoroughly covered in water as was Jesus in the River Jordan. The baptisteries lie under the floorboards in the front of the church or are hidden behind curtains for such special days.

When I grew up and traveled to European cities, I would learn that the great cathedrals all over the continent had baptisteries which were usually a separate building used for the very same purpose. However, in the oldest of early churches the construction was as such that the one being baptized would be raised up from the west to the east, to symbolize the newness of the day and of their life's journey, thus born again. "Born Again"; Free from sin; I'm happy both night and day, could only fulfill saving the sinner.

After my baptism in my youth, though, I was passionate about learning and being the kind of Christian that was advocated by the families which made up our church. I thought that something magical would happen for me, not that I would get a pair of wings or something ridiculous, but that all measure of doubt and pain about myself would disappear and maybe it did for that day, because Mama said she was proud of me. I got to be the center of attention for about twenty-four hours, and I tried to believe that I had a new and non-violated body. That may not seem like much, but to me it was the first sign that I was healing in any manner. It gave me more armor, more cover, a thicket to hide in where wild roses with their thorns could protect me from anyone who dared touch me, this precious new creation. Now no one else had to be involved with my injury, which is how most people liked to keep things where I am from; tending to your own business was about as kin to godliness as making certain your house was clean all of the time. There had to be order and to keep things orderly one disturbed nothing, and the intensity of needing to keep family business at home only increased as one accepted more responsibility when becoming a young adult.

Other than having lewd dreams about Gene Autry and Dr. Kildare, Richard Chamberlain's Hollywood character, saying an occasional curse word when totally disturbed, or mumbling something mean to my brothers and sisters to cause somewhat of squabble, I must admit to probably having graduated among the purest of seniors who ever left Huntland High School. I was as dogmatic as any Appalachian Christian girl could ever manage to be. I even tried to stop reading song books to avoid being bored to death by the preacher and sometimes I listened to sermons. Then it was the new person born on baptism day. I was out to change the world and even considered what it would be like for a woman to preach scripture. The church was one place where I could go and feel as if I was a member, sitting in my best dress, which was probably the old dress of the person sitting next to me. Evenings would come, and shadows would fall, but simple faith would abide as I continued my life. Fortunately, I was always reassured that my trials were not over, but looking back I think that having heeded the call to baptism at least got me to thinking there was a chance for some redemption.

Mama, bless her heart, would sit on the porch during evening thunderstorms and become extremely fearful, as the lightning flashed from the peak of mountains in a total arch across our fields that the time of Judgment was at hand. She had a dreadful fear of lightning, and she would begin to speak of Gabriel's trumpet beginning to blow and Jesus' return to earth, to separate the wheat from the chaff. When you are a kid and hear this from the time you are five until you leave home, you are fairly convinced that at any moment the entire earth is going to be on fire. Call Mama crazy if you like, but the truth is that her fears were not too different from the apostle Paul's, for even he believed that Jesus' return was at hand in his generation. He had no guidebook of his own such as the scriptures, but instead had to rely on his own miraculous conversion and the revelations which he received from the Holy Spirit. I can see how Mama had arrived at such a fearful point, for every other week she would go and hear about the passing away of the earth and the atonement which she was about to face.

I wish that I had known a lot that I know now at this point in my life, but I resent with all my heart and with my soul all of those who discount the "hillbilly Christians." My ancestral fathers and mothers would become many parts of what I like to think of as one large body and as Christians before them, they had to bond together and become a community. Most faith groups, including my own, could take lessons from the Bible Belt of America on how to congregate, to share meals, to talk before and after church, hear the news of neighbors, family, and friends. Too often country people, especially in the southern United States, are set up as the butt of jokes, a reason not to examine organized religion further because of fundamentalism, when most people outside of these areas have no information other than trash TV ministry on which to make judgments. I have deep admiration for the love and support of the old-time religion which I was brought up in, and it was one of the few sources where the locals gathered together without class distinction.

This night, I can smell the wild roses in Mr. Leon's field, and I can see us as a family walking over that field to rest at a day's end among those almost blood-red rosebuds. The sun has not set, and we all have some look of peace. It is our chapel for a time, and if I look in the distance, there are some storm clouds coming out of the western sky, but on this night and at this hour I know that I can, carefully, break a few stems of these pretty flowers, take them home, and set them on a table which Daddy once built for Mama. When and if the storm does move on in we can sit on our porch and this time I can tell my mother the good news that she no longer has to fear. I've learned that she was ready for the Lord and had been all along.

Chapter Fourteen

Some methods of coping had so much to do with when those blessed angels disguised as people would somehow come into our lives. One who grows up without the benefit of toys or even books in the house has to rely on a vivid imagination, but what opened our eyes the most to other family experiences and what made us genuinely happy was the gift of a television! It started with a man we called Uncle John Mason.

He came to live with my neighbor's family, the Masons—Mrs. Marie and Mr. Leon—during the time when we were often home alone with our mother. Out of the blue, Uncle John gave us and Mr. Kirby Christian's family the most precious center of a house known to mankind then, a television set. We had not asked for anything, but this gracious and generous man reached beyond himself and somehow thought to do such a kind act. We could not thank him enough and there were no words to express our gratitude. I believe we tried to find the words and somehow it came to us that he gave the two families the gifts because he felt sorry for us, but whatever the motive, this television brought us into the heart of the twentieth century and made me aware that Hollywood can change lives for the better, and it now has the power to cause harm and pain. While right now programming has become so vacuous and has no skills to teach the average child, TV in the early years was all about families, values, and the pleasure of musical variety shows where we saw people happy, dancing, playing, solving TV game quizzes, and reinforcing American standards of kind and gentle family life.

My imagination could draw me away from most painful events as I saw the lives of Lassie and Timmy, who also lived on a farm, unfold before my very eyes. A wonderful dog could find ways of saving his master or any hurt individuals by coming and leading Timmy or his family to where trouble was brewing. Shows like *The Donna Reed Show, Leave It To Beaver, and Father*

Knows Best were our first insight that fathers had anything to do with family life and their children beyond dispensing an occasional whipping. Oh my God! Kids talked to their parents and parents gave reasonable answers to life's most pressing issues, whether it had something to do with a social or a simple school task. Grandmothers and grandfathers always provided good things like hugs and cookies, and mothers wore lipstick and earrings while they made meat roasts with potatoes and vegetable, not to mention there were fine desserts like ice cream to be had just for the family around an ordinary meal.

It never seemed strange that on *Ozzie and Harriett*, the father never went to work, for we decided that must be the way it is in the real families which we watched. On the old cowboy movies, no matter if it was for cattle rustling, drinking too much, or for pulling a gun on the Marshal, bad guys always lost. There was no greater gift that Uncle John could have given to us or to our mother, for it was the ultimate escape into a happy world like the one Beaver Cleaver lived in where his mother would tuck him into his own personal bed at night and give him some good advice. On all of the shows mothers and fathers washed away the tears and fixed everything up as if nothing bad had ever occurred in the first place. My sisters and I knew that all of these were real families and we were just unfortunate. Around the bend, we were going to be like the TV families, for we were good and suffering, and it was just a matter of time before we would be taken away by one of those men on TV that were the perfect dads, and there would be no evidence of a life where children had to fear. I honestly think that believing in these TV families and the possibilities was a divine intervention, for it was out of simple Christian charity that a man who did not know us changed our lives in such a profound way. We would be able to see that Uncle John received a blessing out of the whole thing also, for within a few years, he would meet the widowed Aunt Lottie and they would get together and be married. We were ecstatic to learn that some people had real lives after the grief of lost loved ones. Occasionally we would visit the house that they bought up on the main highway and I will tell you that never a visit went by when we did not mention the wonderful gift of our first television.

We know that there was no motive, beyond kindness, that caused Uncle John to buy us that precious Zenith television. He did not realize, nor would we, that TV reception then was something less than wonderful. It did not matter that most times the picture was snowy and hard to see. We could make out the images and through that snow we got it: out in the world beyond our fields and communities was a world of kindness and of cheer. Walt Disney was real and the Mouseketeers were real and we were going to get out of our mess and become as privileged as Annette Funicello and we were going to have Shirley Temple-looking little kids who could dance and sing and pull off untold pranks, much less go and find a real Grandpa in the Swiss Alps. Because we saw and heard all the wonderful news of the life on that planet called television, we were actually inspired. A child could leave behind all the cares and difficulty which they might experience within their lives because they believed in the reality of such good situations. It made it possible to pretend that our lives could imitate the stories of these good families and children. Imagination so removed from reality might seem dangerous and perhaps to some it was, for they could see disappointments which lay before them, but our reality was so stark that to imagine meant we were left with hope and for us, that gave us the ability to get through the interminable days and moments of our genuine existence, and if one has hope, there is reason to carry on.

It certainly splashed over into how we played with each other and pretended to be family. Rose, Violet, and I, had we a moment to spare, found the greatest joy in playing house. Our playhouses were made up of pieces of Dad's trash lumber, anything scavenged from a fence that we could make as dividers between our rooms, any old tin can or cola bottle that someone might have left behind, and that precious ingredient which made all baking easy—mud. No, we did not build real houses, but we would lay our boards and twigs around to mimic a perfect ranch home and each person had their own rooms. Rocks could be cars, and old rags could be drapes, and why ever we decided that cleaning was the best part of the game of house playing, I will never know, for cleaning was the everlasting farm chore which mother might wake us up for at four in the morning to get started. "You never know when you are going to have to call the preacher or a doctor in." Mama never let that one go. Thus we always had twigs of cedar for brooms. When I recall how very lost we would get in our playtimes, which usually came between getting the cows milked at day's end and darkness coming on, it is as if we could change our identity. Again, our pretend walls were as satisfying as genuine walls and God help the one who accidentally stepped over into the other's turf! That was cause for a good smacking straight to the face! Territory was essential in our games.

The building materials were usually divided by the eldest sister choosing the best boards, though Violet could hold her own. My house was apt to have a few more sticks, and if I had a role to the sisters' games, it was as the child or a student, though sometimes I was also something to be trained such as a circus clown made possible because we somehow came up with a hula hoop one summer's time. I had to learn to jump through it in case a circus performer was needed. My sisters, again depending on the age, could rank as teacher, mother, father, or undertaker if it was decided a death was to occur within our houses. I did what I was told to do, and, as a result, my sisters had pretty much taught me to read, to tell time, and do math homework before I entered the first grade at age five. Mama needed me out of the house, so the girls had me prepared knowing mother now had other babies to care for.

All of these things were a part of what we learned from television, though. Thanks to Uncle John, the girls would become more like those TV characters who were real moms and dads, so I did not get wacked as much when we played house. Ozzie and Harriett would not talk to their kids in that tone, and a good Mouseketeer wasn't about to leave their baby sister dumb and uneducated. Oh yes, imaginary friends and houses and nice words—the power of network television on our growing brains turned out to be almost like having a good mother sent to you through mail order, for play reflecting good influence was certifiably an exquisite building block for our years to come.

Now there were things we had not anticipated in our new world of escapism and that was called electronic failure, the weather's effects on the old antennas which picked up the signals, and the fact that we got to use our newfound wealth of entertainment depending on if mother decided she was going to pay the light bill, as it was called then. The house had no electricity when we first came, but Dad was finally able to have the power company run the line further out, but we were not wired for much beyond a couple of light bulbs. The TV would suddenly become unwatchable, and though we could act out our stories in the playhouses, we had to wait until our eldest brother, Ira Neil, who knew all about electronics thanks to the U. S. Navy would decide to drop in home from Mississippi or Virginia or whatever state he and his family had moved, and we would watch him amazingly get our television working. We then could continue to broaden our perspectives on life and for us to catch up with how we needed to be planning our futures again according to *Father Knows Best.* Oh we ached for brother to come home and help us out.

Praise Uncle John and his good spirit for what he did for us. I suppose the internet was supposed to have similar social ramifications. Unfortunately, media at the present time holds tools for so much destruction. Most network television is absolutely vacuous and without redemption. Exemplary living has been replaced by mainly trash talk television, the most unfortunate and wide-ranging horrible news in history, crooked politicians, and sex. All of this sells and were it not for some television programming such as public-supported TV stations, having access to such media is apt to harm instead of help. The his-and-hers advertisements for sexual arousal pleasure are an absolute new low for Hollywood and the advertising industry. Ejaculation problems, libido problems, sex and stupidity, urinary, bowel, and those nasty old menses products are the new Rice-A-Roni we longed for. Most poor people who are home all day never turn the television off, so I hurt from the messages all kids are indoctrinated in to from an early age of growth and development all centered around beauty, sex, materialism, and how cool it is to be the dumb, non-conventional family. PBS offers some hope and options, but it is most apt to be parents with education and chances for a better world who will monitor their children's choice for such quality television. Oh, you suggest it was so sappy back then and so without spice and color, but you are wrong.

That weird, precious piece of furniture was the gift of a saint to us. It made our black and white world stream with both imagination and color. My children and grandchildren will hear the story of Uncle John and the magic box which changed our lives. How could we be destitute in those years and in that place, when one person provided the most pleasurable gift a child could long for? It was the equivalent of giving poor children desktop computers which their friends probably received long before them. We would dream and believe that somewhere voices still come from the ghosts of a better California.

"Children, come in it is time for supper."

"Alright Father/Mother, how was your day?"

"Well, not a lot happened, but it means the world that you would ask."

"How's that homework coming?"

"Well, I'm really having a problem with fractions."

"And Mom, Dad, I saw a little boy who didn't have any lunch today, do you think that I could take something

extra for him tomorrow?" "Certainly son, and the next day and the next."

With this corny recitation, I leave you to your own thoughts about your family and I enclose it with some love, for it is going to take a whole lot of love to hear the preciousness of such trivial, but refined thoughts ever again. For the child you are interested in is too bombarded with trash talk to hear anything which resembles such kind words as may have been spoken a long time ago in that Hollywood which once meant something to the fate of the youngest and the poorest of its generations.

Chapter Fifteen

Angels and blessings. I keep counting them as if I were standing on a star-studded field. Along with remembering the times my sisters and I would play, I am now recalling what was always the most blessed week in my life every year for about a dozen or so years. My Aunt Ruth lived in the little town of Winchester, Tennessee, which before the roads were improved seemed to be a real trip for us. We only went to this town, the county seat for Franklin County, Tennessee, if Dad had business at the courthouse or at the bank. On the rarest of occasions we would go there if we could buy shoes or maybe we might be just taking a family outing when Dad had some time free from the factory in Illinois. Once per summer, though, and on a rare Christmas season, Mama would decide that I could pack a bag, and for one blissful week, I was able to spend time at Aunt Ruth and Uncle Buster's house on the corner of North Cedar Street.

It was a tiny house which had probably been built in the 1950s, but it was home to my mother's next youngest sister. My cousins, Peggy, Philip, and Floyd, and a baby, Mechele, grew up there, and to me it could have been a mansion. I loved the hardwood floors, the kitchen with crisp little curtains, the pretty bathroom where my aunt had her wonderful creams and powders, and the corner lot where it felt so very safe at night. Always as the late evening came on, one could hear trucks going to some place far away taking some shortcut to Route 64 passing my aunt and uncle's house on the way to somewhere, and as their engines would pick up a little speed to round the curve, I would imagine places Dad spoke of—Indiana, Illinois, and Ohio among them, places with people and factories, the Great Lakes coming in somewhere there, and the lives of people from all of those Chicago suburbs like Peoria, Gary, and all the places we would hear about when a Chicago radio station was powerful enough to infuse itself into our world on a clear weekend night. I felt so safe and free from all the things which terrified me in my rural existence. It was as if those trucks and their sound gave me some hope that someday I could move on to a place where families such as the television families really lived, and dreams took me to the ideal family land. I felt sleep would come on soundly and refreshingly as it rarely came with all of the worries we had at my house.

School would usually be out for the summer, and if I could, I'd like to take you to this town, for it was beautiful then. Before all of the Wal-Mart and super stores killed them, each little town like this one had a town square where one could purchase most anything in the Sears catalogue, plus home furnishings, appliances, and those clothes for special occasions. These owner-operated stores even changed the window decorations along with the seasons. There was a restaurant, a Rexall Drugstore, and the most wonderful dime store ever made. In both of these places one could order fountain drinks, milk shakes, ice cream cones, and sit at a counter to be served. The main building on the square, which remains in operation to this day, was The Oldham Theater, and once a summer I got to see a movie at The Oldham. Milk and egg money was good enough then that I could see a movie, get a treat, and still save ten cents to buy my mother a present. I wanted to make Mom happy in the worst way, and she did keep the little figurines which I bought for her all of her life. I would go straight for the bin which had little glass figures for five or ten cents and once I picked out her favorites: two little porcelain dogs which she kept on the coffee table. Little did I realize that these would all become collector's items. Back then to have things which said Made in Japan was like buying something which might have said Made in Hell by the devil himself, but I did not understand why until years later as I became aware of all of the American GIs who had fought and died in the Pacific arena. Only the luckiest kids on earth could live near a five and dime!

All of the streets of Winchester seemed to be so safe and so very relaxed and pretty in an Old South way. Most were built as frame houses, painted all white and crisp. There were several streets of houses built for the soldiers as affordable houses, all so predictable with two tiny bedrooms, a living room and dining room, and a kitchen so small that three people were a crowd. There were always little patches of garden, both flowers and a few tomato plants, but it was the purple petunias, the red, white, and pink roses, the four o'clock bushes, and the fragrant iris of Tennessee which gave the places such charm in the summer hours when children played, marking chalk trails as clues for a game of hide-and-seek. Almost every house had a porch swing, which seemed to be in use in late afternoon for neighbors to drop by and to share news of the day. How I loved those swings which, as they creaked back and forth, seemed to call one to walk up a few steps to a neighborly greeting, as if the swings themselves were saying; "Come to me, come to me."

There was virtually nothing which one would consider to be today's ghettos, for people loved their little houses, and everyone took pride in ownership or even just renting. There were few house trailers, and here and there sat a rather stately antebellum sort of place, which was a reminder that the north and south United States really did have a separate and severe unpleasantness once upon a time. These were lovingly preserved until people simply could no longer afford maintenance on such dwellings. There was Dinah Shore's childhood home and there was a home we were taught to stay away from, for a real, "witch," lived there. That was rather tragic, for I never knew who lived in that nice house, but sometimes kids would throw rocks and break out the windows, and our chalk trails would certainly have to include a trip to that neck of the woods. How such a rumor got started, I'll never knew, but whoever lived in that house must have experienced much grief through the years, especially around Halloween, when there were more tricks than treats.

Winchester was about as sweet as a little southern town could be, and it breaks my heart to go through there now and to see all the places where I played on the best weeks of my childhood as torn down, unpainted, broken sidewalk areas, with all of the town having packed up and left for what are now new housing developments on the outskirts of the old town. Anywhere else in the world such houses would have been treasured for a century or more, but people never thought a lot about adding to homes or saving more for the next generation. New was the way to go and were it not for some old roses, a few remaining four o'clock bushes, and a couple of streets which have been rehabbed, I do believe that you would not be able to imagine that these ever were the homes of wonderful families and a respite for a farm child to place her hopes and dreams, much less trust that peaceful and gentle neighborhoods ever existed beyond the city's square.

My cousins would come to the farm and think our world was the very best, for we had a large garden from which to gather our food, animals to tend, woods to play and hide in, and the freedom. But they were not there when it was time to do the chores. I will tell you more of those days when we played, but right now my heart lingers in all of the sweet towns all over this country which were given up for big box stores, fast food, and for the atmosphere of suburbia. What a sadness that we gave up so soon on these national treasures and that the interstate highway system made it possible for people to leave so much that was beautiful behind. We keep leaving, keep mowing down trees and destroying the distinctive small farms once dreamed about by young people as that which would make their lives worth living.

The system of country cousins and town cousins sharing each other's worlds made each know the possibility of a different kind of life, and the city existence was a whole other realm which we would experience later on. Small-town America had the best of so many lives after World War II, the American dream shown in Norman Rockwell's paintings and captured in song and verse for many years thereafter. It is beyond me to even understand why such lifestyles became yesterday's memories so soon, only for many of us to search our entire lives for that consoling feeling of the porch swing's swaying on a summer's night, the buzzing bees of sidewalks going from flower to flower in a constant hum, the smell of cornbread and bacon going from house to house as supper-time came on, and children trying to eat as if they were not in a hurry to get out for another hour of playtime before the sun would set. We captured hours and counted them, for there were no days when we were bored or without during the weeks of reprieve from our homes and families, and when they were winding down, we'd try to make up reasons why going back home was a better alternative for us.

I knew, though, when I was in the house on North Cedar Street that I was living a few days in a dream and when the dream was over, I would be looking back at them as among the best times I ever had, and I wonder if the spirits of playing children ever freed the witch's house from its legend and if the scent of flowers seeps past the houses now falling in from time and lack of care. Will those dear old streets awaken from a three-decade summer and nourish the souls of other families in time or fade away like falling seeds on four o'clock bushes as evening falls and the trucks heading north simply pass the old town with the sound of a long good-bye.

My dreams would follow me to school and would get me into trouble. Sometimes I feel as if I am writing to the wind just as I felt as a child when I would pray to the passing breezes and hope they landed on God's ears, for as I build my world and my story of who and what is me both now and then everything seems strangely silent—as if I do not want to hear or see the path behind much less the path ahead of me. Now, as then, I pick up pieces of my own puzzling existence as a woman from Appalachian culture, and I carry on even if my heart is breaking. I need to explain that to one emotionally and physically scarred from a hidden world as was ours in the rural south—I never knew the word "interlude"—but the brief interludes and joy which came with play or a visit with my aunts and their children were among the tiny morsels of safety and pleasure that gave us the strength to hide out for the rest of the time within our shadows.

One teacher tried to place me in a slow reader's group, because of my tendency to sit with a fixed gaze as if I did not know where I was. First off, I would have already read the book through three or four times just to pass the school day, but most of all I was preparing for the magic moment when Elvis was going to come through Lexie Crossroads, stop at the general store, and notice that I was there in my best pink nylon dress. And there I would go on the back of one of his fine Cadillac cars heading west toward Memphis. There were days and even years when I planned my escape, and it was going to be the same each time. Elvis was going to see me in my church dress and he would order his bodyguards to pick up that little girl and I would be heading up the road. It seemed totally logical to me throughout what would now be called the 'tween years and even my years as an early teenager. I had seen covers of movie magazines where he did unusually kind things for people, and I saw it as a natural course of events that he could come and claim me as his own and no one would say a word because no one would argue with Elvis.

My manners would be impeccable and there would be no one in Lexie Crossroads who would ever forget the sight of me taking off on that day and God knows that my parents wouldn't be upset, for there would be an empty space at the table. I do not remember when it came to me that all of this might be simply imagination or my way of escaping my own reality, because I did not want to be awakened from my daydreams. Within them I could create any world I chose until the school bell rang and it was time to go home. I have to confess that I had the most incredible sadness at the end of many days knowing that each had not been the day when Elvis Presley had chosen to pass through our neck of the woods. My dreams could even continue into sleep if I willed them so, and often I had to, for things would be so dour and painful that to live in a dream state was better than to consider the option of ending my life.

I warned you that Grandpa would not be the last deviant I would have to deal with, so maybe I need to tell you a little more of the reality which was going on about this time. Mother had chosen me as the girl to go with her brother, my Uncle Robert, to The Primitive Baptist Church which he attended once a month, and she said that I needed to go because Uncle Robert liked to hear me sing "Sweet Hour of Prayer" and that seemed good enough to me. I wasn't that great of a singer, but if he wanted that song, I could carry some kind of tune.

For many Sundays for a couple of years, I went to my uncle's church, but, unfortunately, my version of "Sweet Hour Of Prayer" didn't sound a thing like what they were singing. It was here that I would learn the term "quarter note" singing, which is very similar to music called "sacred harp." These were methods of singing which either included a four-note or a seven-note pattern, making it possible for all of the congregation to read their music in four distinctive parts. Later I married a professional musician of symphonic level, and he still doesn't have it figured out, so please do not ask me to endeavor to explain to you how it works. Strangely enough, I believe quarter note has the seven basic notes and that sacred harp has the four basic shaped notes for this melodic mastery of music in a few basic lessons. I do not know what the Primitive Baptist sang, except they sort of summed it up as "shape note" singing, and Mama knew what I was talking about when I told her that the music didn't make any sense.

To this day, the main mastery of this music is to be found in the southeast states usually near the mountains and valleys along the Appalachians, though much to my surprise and to yours probably, there are groups that gather from coast to coast. I am talking about groups from Los Angeles to New York City who gather and enjoy this spiritual music for both worship and non-worship purposes. To the untrained ear, untrained in shape note, it sounds mournful, maybe as if someone is yelling a song instead of speaking it or, as we called it as children, something akin to a long suffering dying cow music. I have heard it done well by one group and that was The Mennonite Conservative congregation which moved near my folks during the last decades of their lives. Mom and Dad loved it so much that we asked the Mennonite community to sing at their funerals, and it was beautiful. Our beloved friends of that community would eventually visit me in San Francisco and in the gayest of gay communities. There they performed for us one evening. My husband's family home happened to be in the Castro and Noe Valley area of San Francisco. That night on our hill on the west coast occurred the most diverse of diverse events in the most harmonious and pleasant of places. Our neighbors, mainly gay and lesbian couples, commented on it the next day, and they did so in a pleasant manner, as if maybe God had paid a visit the night our Tennessee friends came to stay. The best that I can tell you is after all has been explained to me and to the man I married, the word, "harmonious" is most associated with this passionate singing of the old hymns.

A few years went by when I had to sing at Uncle Robert's church with his congregation, and I would just sort of close my ears and sing with compliments from all as we parted. One weekend I was to go on to Uncle Robert's house. He usually came in without Aunt Martha and her most impressive collection of fancy flowery straw, flowered, ribboned, colored, and netted selection of hats. Apparently Aunt Martha was often "down with her bowels." Sure enough, Aunt Martha was there to greet us, and when she took me to her mother's place, they discussed her bowel habits from the time she was young until that day when I visited for the first time. It seems she had developed constipation and her mother knew something must be wrong for as Aunt Martha explained, "Mother, you know my bowels have been loose for most of my life!" I will spare you the rest of the details of the conversation.

I was to stay with them until the next meeting day at the old church back home on Highway 64, but it was to come earlier than usual, for there was a revival to start that coming Wednesday. I did get to see some of Chattanooga, and Aunt Martha, being a fourth-grade teacher was rather nice to me, even playing her new Baldwin Organ just for me. I loved the scent of the fresh sheets on my bed, and for the days I was there, everything seemed like maybe I had found a refuge. I even wondered if they might like having me as their girl around, even if I had to eat their curried scrambled eggs. I knew little beyond salt, pepper, and cinnamon, but curry sounded like a fancy kind of term, so I decided I would relish my breakfast every day and help Aunt Martha however I could. I was a little sad when leaving day came, and the reverend from The Primitive Baptist Church came over to preach at a Chattanooga church, and he and my uncle were to take me back over the mountain toward home. Before the day ended, though, I would know that there was no place for me on Signal Mountain Road in Chattanooga, and I had gone to sing for my uncle for the last time, unless it was at gunpoint. No beating would get me back there—ever.

The Sunday finally came when it was time for me to put my things in my brown paper bag and to leave my aunt and uncle's house. I must say that I was a little disappointed to realize that Aunt Martha would not be going with us to the church where my uncle was to meet up with the Reverend Song, a name which I will give him to protect other good pastors who may have carried his name. Uncle had brought him to his Chattanooga

Primitive Baptist Church to preach, and the Reverend Song was dressed in his best suit and had his head of white hair combed as if he were going to a dance at a Shriner's Elvis look-alike contest. He was feeling mighty proud to be preaching in the city instead of the little country church at Bean's Creek. I do not know why my aunt had chosen not to come unless she was down in her bowels again and I thought for certain she would be with us wearing her white pill box hat with a brim of lilacs, which looked almost real if you were dumb and didn't realize that lilacs have a very sweet smell and are a little more purple in the southern sun. But she did not get out the hat box, and she did not come. I could not bring myself to ask her if maybe she needed me to stay and be her girl, since she did not have any, for it seemed pointless as she bade me goodbye and didn't say a word about my coming to visit any time soon again. I certainly hated giving up my clean sheets and her organ recitals, but I guess she figured that I was better left with my big family to have some good vegetables picked for her next visit. I cried, for I cried every time I left a place where I felt safe. Aunt Martha patted my shoulder and off I went to hear more of the revelations of when the world was going to end and to sing "Sweet Hour of Prayer" for I knew that was my job even if I sounded like I didn't know which part to sing.

Reverend Song was known as a "singing preacher," and I am reluctant to tell anyone who loves rap that this white man had a way of preaching that only a rap artist could do. This was long before boom boxes and sexy lyrics, but everything else was about the same. He would begin, "I want to tell you and you are not going to believe this, brothers and sisters, but I met the devil. Did you hear? I said I met the devil. Mama had sent me to the chicken house to get some eggs, I tell you some eggs! Then, Glory! Glory! I picked up a big fat hen, and she had no eggs, but a big chicken snake was sittin' in the nest and the snake began a talkin' and my heart started apoundin' then Hallelujah Brother! I wanted to run, but old Miss Hen, she got a voice too and she said, 'Song, you are meetin' with the devil! Aren't you ascared?' And I was so scared, so scared that I was shakin' in my britches!"

By now the congregation was fanning themselves from heat and the reverend was singing, "Oh glory, did you hear me say it, glory," and the congregation would go into tears and the preacher would be in full rap mode by now and the congregation would answer, "Glory," caught up in the moment, scared for the boy in the hen house. "Mrs. Hen got up and a light came in through the rooftop of this roosting place and I heard a voice calling, 'Son, I want you, and I want you now, you can listen to a snake and an old hen on the nest, but if you got the spirit, I am your Lord God and I'm willing to save your sorry skin if you pick up your cross and come follow me.'" Reverend Song said the Lord sounded strong and wise and the snake began to tremble and the hen fell dead and the room filled with, "Praise, did you hear me? I said praise."

"Praise be," the audience would join in as they sweat and cried and knew that there was salvation going on here. Reverend Song said he started preaching to the hens and roosters and he said, "Get behind me, Satan, for the Lord has called. The Lord called me, said he and I saw that snake start to squirm and hiss and I knew that he could not touch me, for then and there I accepted the call to teach and preach and this old Primitive Baptist has been preaching ever since. Sisters and brothers, that chicken snake got rattles on its tail then and it stood up as if to strike, but the light in the window struck it like a fire, and God told me, The Reverend Song, 'Don't you worry, boy, for this Satan's going to be gone. Reach out your hand! Say, Get behind me Devil, for I am going to follow Jesus. I'm going to save souls and you worthless serpent ain't nothing but a pile of chicken feed,' so I stomped it, I stomped it and on that chicken house floor lay one tired old snakeskin worn out by the sun. That was my Calling Day, and I said, 'Yes, Oh Lord!' and 'Goodbye' to my sinful ways. Amen my brothers, Amen, my sisters."

Then he would invite us to sing something like "Come To Jesus" and he would invite those without faith and those who weren't Old Baptists to mend their ways and to come to the Lord and he would cry and the congregation would cry and if everybody got lucky, some sinner would answer the altar call and come forward for baptism. Oh, it was inspiring, especially when I was used to a old farm boy who pushed the plow during the week and came in to our church Sundays to speak for a few hours about the sin which surrounded us, especially on Sewanee Mountain, where those Episcopals were preaching almost like the no-good Catholics. Our neighbors were going to hell too, because they were not the true "Church of Christ." I liked the singing preacher, and his version of The Call was fascinating even though I did not believe him, because I was told that my way was the only way to being saved by the Lord. It was a confusing time, but I never pleased my uncle by getting saved his way.

The Reverend Song, Uncle, and I went afterward to some church member's house for Sunday dinner, but with my ribs sticking to my backbone from hunger, I did not get to go to the table. The men ate, and the women cooked. The fried chicken smelled so good that I could have eaten my blue sweater, but Mama had taught us not to put people out to any trouble, so I said, "No thank you, I'm not hungry," when it came time for the women and the girls to pick the bones the men had left. I thought those curried eggs would keep me until nightfall and maybe Mama would let me have a banana sandwich for being so good all week long and pleasing her eldest brother.

After dinner, we began our trip back over the mountain from Chattanooga back to my home in Lexie Crossroads, or so I thought. I was sitting in the back seat quiet as a mouse, for my uncle and the preacher were having lots of talk about the folks they knew and how some of those sons of bitches couldn't even cough up a dime for the collection plate. We were nearing the mountain's top when my heart began to pound and pound. I was sweating, and all of the sudden I was an old hen in the chicken house, only I wasn't hiding a snake, a snake was biting me. The men's words were audible as my uncle looked back at me and was whispering to Reverend Song.

"You don't have to worry, she won't say anything." And then they were talking about my innocence and that no one would believe me in the first place. I had heard such words before and my uncle kept staring at me and then they were talking about where they should take me and would anyone notice. Uncle Robert did not know about Grandpa's advances toward me and he did not know that by now I knew what they meant. I began to tremble uncontrollably and to ask God to help me. I believed there was no help, for we were on the mountain's top and I did not know if they were planning just to have their way with me or to kill me. I had heard about people disappearing on Sewanee Mountain, so the tears began to fall down my cheeks uncontrollably and Uncle would look at me and then look away. He made no effort to comfort me, but there was a miracle to come.

Old Reverend Song said, "Robert, we've got to stop at the gas station. I'm sitting on empty. Within about a mile was a gas station near Mount Eagle, and when we stopped I got out and I was going to run or beg the people to help me, at which time my dearest uncle would have told them I was a half-wit and they were taking me home, but on that mountain top, in the middle of nowhere, Mr. Paul Carr, our 4-H county extension agent and his wife were also stopped for gas, a good couple of hours from their home. I remember Mr. Carr saying, "Honey, can we help you somehow?" And I was so ashamed, for I said, "No sir, I don't want to put you all out."

Mrs. Carr then said, "Don't you want us to take you home, for we are going that way anyway?" Look, no one is ever going to nowhere for no reason, but these folks saw a young girl tormented and troubled. They said, "You just get in the car, for we are out for a Sunday drive and everything is going to be all right." I almost fell into their arms and I told my uncle and his co-conspirator that these folks were going to visit Mama and Daddy, and I appreciated everything, but I couldn't turn down the fact they were going straight to my house.

The two primitives said little and they had been spotted by someone who knew me, two angels in the most unlikely place you could ever imagine, a place so remote to my valley then that no one ever went up there from Winchester without purpose. I will remember Mr. and Mrs. Carr until the end of my life, and I wonder what they thought when they placed this child in their back seat who was so wet from tears and sweat that I probably should have been hospitalized from sheer shock. Again angels had appeared within my life, and when I got home they told Mama how they had just run in to me coming over the mountain and they wanted to save folks from a drive out of their way. I hugged them and thanked them again, breaking down as if I had lost my family to a lightning bolt, but they knew a troubled child and they knew they were my saviors that day. They bore my cross and never hinted to Mama or to Daddy what they had seen. They were my answer to a prayer and my belief in happenstance would be forever gone from that day on.

My light through a henhouse ceiling was a sweet married couple with two little children. I see them in a divine remembrance, and if Christ appears now and again, then they became living Christs to me that day. I would never spend another night at my uncle and aunt's home, and I see them often as I make an inward journey to where chicken excrement falls and snakes crawl. The Carrs are the beautiful light; they are the gracious light which appears among the darkest of clouds, kills the standing snake, and rescues the helpless servant from the false Christians who hide out in chapels of hell. Oh me, I wish my soul could put this all to rest, but about the best that I can do is to thank God again for the miracle and the angels which appeared on the mountain that day. "Amen, Amen, won't you sing with me the great Amen?" For I was spared one Sunday afternoon on the wings of a bird and I shall call my bird, "Grace." My angels always showed up in unusual places and they saw through me as if I were paper transparent and torn. I wonder about them sometimes and wish that I could ask them if they remember the days they saved my soul and body. So I wish I could ask Mr. and Mrs. Carr, do you remember picking this broken twig up around Sewanee Mountain? Do you remember me, beloveds, for I have never forgotten you. They would never know the girl who was trying to find her face in the mirror. I practiced personas in the bedroom mirror when I could get away with closing the door. I thought that if I could make just the right face that I could be a real girl and I'll tell you that around the time of my rescue on the mountain, looking at myself was getting harder. I saw an ugly face looking back and how that mirror kept from shattering beats me! I had to believe that I was almost faceless, for Mama and Daddy seemed to be able to look past me not seeing that I was in so much pain, so filled with grief and angst. They looked at me every day and yet did not see that I was being torn like a shroud on a shrunken head.

Chapter Sixteen

In the mirror, I could practice being a class clown, so if someone made fun of my crossed eyes that helped hide a lot of my story I could cross them worse, make a joke about my ugliness, and have the class in stitches. As I entered my teenage years, I practiced the face of the intellect, for my body felt cursed, but my brain was always working. I looked for something angelic about myself. I could still have some secret and divine nature only known to me and to God. I had a secret shield between me and all hurt, which I could bring out sometimes, for I was aware that it was going to take a supernatural component to my being to not be discovered for who I was becoming.

The trembling was getting worse and nights were sleepless for fear that the only thing between me and death was to get through the darkness which was consuming me. Here I go making you feel sorry for me! I do not want you to, for my coping skills were invaluable. A teenager whose mom was going through menopause and craziness ever since they took her thyroid gland out, develops the ability to forge nails with bare hands. I practiced being a school comic from TV cartoon characters and even I had found fondness for acting out Pepe Le Pew. Being a skunk was alright with me if it would get a laugh. Some among you might ask, "Why did you choose to portray a television skunk?" I do not know, except it went along with some of my other favorite characters like The Beverly Hillbillies, Tweety Bird, and a Smothers Brothers-style of entertaining which my friend Betty Larkin had made into a female dance and song routine which brought the house down at Huntland High School at a school talent contest. We even got ten bucks for first place which was enough money to last me for a couple of months, and all I had to do was to interrupt our song and dance routine with, "Hey Betty, I thought this was a beauty contest," looking as dumb as the mirror allowed. I am telling you we had an auditorium full of people laughing.

My early love for opera singers led me to practice operatic sounds with the new rock songs of the day, so this was something I might bring out in the cotton patch to get a laugh. Now and then if I heard a funny joke at school I would absolutely have no control over the fact that laughter was like crying to me. Once I started laughing it seemed to become infectious and everyone around me would burst out laughing too. It was uncontrollable laughter and being very small then, I would have to hold my ribs with both arms as it poured out like a cackling hen. One day on the bus, my friend Joan asked me if I knew the joke about what happened to the cowboy after he ate a pot of beans the night before and when I heard the answer, "He woke up the next morning and shot his parrot," I almost got kicked off the school bus. Country kids lived with bean jokes all of their lives, so if you don't get it, then you are not missing much.

Later I would hear Judy Collins sing "Send in the Clowns," and I almost felt that the song was written for me. "Where are the clowns?" Over and over I would hear that song and I knew that no one had earnestly ever found the one I became for a year or two. Where better to hide a clown, than behind a clown's face, but my clown was not from the circus. No, it was the desperate child, hiding in the mirror awaiting my moment of being discovered and hiding sorrows like broken balloons that could drift until the wind sailed them to another time and place. Being a funny girl seemed to work for some time and at high school's end, Dennis Walker and I would win the category of "Wittiest" in our class.

I never did tell anyone that Elvis had been going to come through Lexie Crossroads and whisk me away to Graceland, for he married about that time and my dreams and hopes were permanently placed behind, a relic of where I might be found. No one ever knew about Uncle and Reverend Song, Grandpa, or my other realities, for I had become such a great actress to save my family more shame that even now, on Oscar Night, I think maybe the knock is still going to come to my door and there it will be, the Oscar, Hollywood at my door, and it will be the prize I deserved for being the girl who could fool anyone into believing that her life was real. And yet I worry there may never be a prize for a maniacal child controlling her world in a clown's rage.

Chapter Seventeen

I know that there is a time where I will put my childhood thoughts away, but there are a few places and some people who you've not spent enough time with. So today in May when the pink honeysuckles are finishing their sweet bloom in what is left of our pine forest and the remnants of our footsteps within springtime mud hardened with the ages, I want to share some sweetness of not being poor alone. I've talked about the Christian family, one of the four families that were about a mile away and up the road from us, but I haven't told you much about them. If our heads were bowed low, then sometimes theirs were bowed lower, for Mr. Kirby and Mrs. Nellie, their mother and father, both had drinking problems.

I lived among them in that Appalachian valley for about fifteen years, and I've known them for this lifetime, and yet I know almost nothing about them. Where did they come to our woods from? Why did Mrs. Nellie always wear a do rag when we picked cotton together and who took care of her Allan, Agatha, Bennie, and Billy Ray? After all of these years, I know for certain that no Christian love was leveled out to this family, for all people could see was the unkempt house, the children's rarely washed clothes, and the store-bought food which Mrs. Nellie called cooking. They didn't have the adapted skills to live in a place as remote as Lexie Crossroads, and they kept to themselves much of the time. Poorer than dirt was an elongated adjective used to describe them, but to us they were almost extended family. Thus my shame is deeper.

The Christian kids could "kick ass," and if you picked on one of us Everetts, then your sorry ass might just get kicked by the family that watched over our family and my baby brother, William, especially. The boys, all the way down to little Billie Ray, were ready in a minute to defend an Everett, for we all were sinking on different boats, and we worked the fields together, played together now and then, and never were any of us victimized by any of the boys in an inappropriate way. Their manners were very good. In fact, I do not think that we were as generous to them as they were to us in many ways. It looked bad in the community if you associated with non-churched folks, and the Christian family didn't go to church. Mr. Kirby had seen too much in the WWII arena and Mrs. Nellie and he probably couldn't drag themselves out of bed on a Sunday morning.

"When we all get to heaven," words from one of my thoroughly read hymns, sticks in my mind, for I know that the choirs of angels are going to be asking folks from our community to step aside and explain where the help was when Mr. and Mrs. Christian lost their twins. There were rumors of twins and one more baby that Mrs. Nellie might have had being buried in their backyard. Every time I passed that house there would be a dead wreath hung at the side of the house, and I knew that it was for the babies. If one dug up the old backyard, would there still be any sign of tiny bones that didn't even deserve a shoe box much less a headstone? We heard all the rumors, but the family would not tell their needs. Pretending seemed to be a sorry gift where I was from, to pretend a mother had suffered, labored, given birth as a cause for gossip, not for neighbors to gather, bring the family the comfort of a meager meal, or to hold that family in their arms. None of this kind of godliness happened. Mrs. Christian hid her pregnancies, or so she thought, and I don't know how folks knew about the backyard burials. In Heaven, I am going to get answers, for these were good people who had to cloak themselves in endurance while tongues wagged and people shoved down their early evening suppers.

"Being like us," meaning your every-day Appalachians scrounging for a living, took precedence over most realistic thoughts of kindness, and if you weren't like us, then you were outcasts, like the Christian family. I once wrote a Christmas story about this episode in the Christian family's life, and some of it came out as almost humorous. Considering that I thought I might be going to have to raise a little baby placed in me by Grandpa Hood's stinking and snuffy fingers made none of this hold any humor, and I do not even know where my own folks stood on this matter. Mama did go see Mrs. Nellie Christian and took her a couple of jars of tomatoes. Daddy would have hung out on the porch and smoked with Mr. Kirby, but no one ever mentioned what had gone on in that house. No one took the usual cakes and pies or prayed. Everyone pretended that all was well, but Mrs. Nellie was a little skinnier. I should have known something was wrong, for when we were pulling the cotton bolls the year before, we had a lovely conversation about the nice size of the breasts of various women in the community and that was one reason I loved her so. Mrs. Christian would talk to us in the fields about such things as breasts, how beautiful her hair was under that rag, and how Mr. Kirby hugged and kissed her and called her Baby Doll. Most men called their wives, The Old Lady. I thought to myself that it must be a real love affair, just like Dr. Kildare and his nurse on TV and I was surely convinced that words like Baby Doll and Honey were a whole lot nicer than being called Old Lady or Old Heifer. That was the nearest men around our parts came to calling their wives pet names. If the women got called by their first name, you knew they were either being ordered to the barn or the field. Perhaps they were being summoned to the kitchen for a third meal of the day or someone in their near and dear family had died.

Maybe Mrs. Nellie was among the only women I ever knew to be truly loved and among my souvenirs somewhere I have a picture of the house with the dead wreath. I wanted to replace it when I was back to visit my folks once, but something told me not to go near there, for there would be snakes around the house sitting at the edge of marshy land, so I couldn't possibly force myself to do so. Even now, I would like to see the community get together to pray over the dead babies, to help put away the shame of indifference, stitch a garment of white and place it in a shadow box and give it to Agatha to remember that we all felt the family's loss. I want stones where the babies lie, and I would love to plant flowers in their memory, for until we do, we remain monsters pretending that we were human when we let the most innocent disappear under southern stars and we left them out of sight.

Allan, Agatha, Bennie, and Little Billy Ray, God does know and I know and we have made a long journey together. Their little angels live, for when I go near that place my arms chill and tremble like a winter's wind on a baby's breath. At last the sin of indifference to this family may be apologized for. Our family would like to thank them for making our days bearable just living over the road and being ready to pounce on evildoers who might harm us. Thank you, my friends. Oh, I do thank you, and I'll be seeing you down the road, and we'll all have some grape sodas cold as ice. You will remain brothers and sisters for all of us. The robins sing the love song your babies never heard before. It is day's end, but they sing and the rushes through the old lover's lane swish with angel's wings which belong to the children who would have been pulled on their Mama's cotton sack just like us. Lullaby, hush now. This is a sacred lullaby all starlit on this valley night.

Chapter Eighteen

I dreamed like any other girl about boyfriends, the feasibility that another world might be out there for me, and I wanted to be loved, so incredibly loved. I knew the movies showed women and men, even older teenagers, enfolding each other in their arms, and I saw high school kids get married and drive around the old town as if they were in middle age and some even looked as if they might be happy! Happy folks. It was a word which almost did not exist in our dialect of Appalachian laws of faith. We were put on this earth to suffer, for Christ suffered for us. Our mothers and fathers suffered; if we were not suffering, then we were certainly not living the life which would lead us to heaven where streets are paved with gold and all sorrows end. There were times when I felt that if I cracked a smile, then someone was going to smack me in the face for being a sinner.

As the years moved along, I began to hear about parties at other kids' houses. I saw flirting in the hallways, and all of a sudden, I did get a clue that I might be missing something, but what? The cheerleaders danced and jumped for joy, and the boys who were on the ball teams seemed to hook up with most of these same girls, who, on Monday morning began to talk about who was seen with whom at The Campus Grill, what movie was playing uptown, and conversation about back seats, whatever that meant. I know that I was a buried turnip, for I was about as important in my head and had about the social skills of a vegetable hidden underground unless you were talking television manners where everyone was perfect, but I did not know anything about natural attraction.

I thought maybe it was because I was being called for ministry, and I fully know that had I been Catholic then, I'd be a Mother Superior now, because while others talked about their weekend exploits, I might be writing something poetic and scriptural or I might be telling one of my classmates the truth of The Holy Spirit as I knew it.

"You are going straight to hell unless you are baptized into the Church of Christ." I never doubted that on the day when fire ravaged the whole earth in one mass nuclear explosion, I would only see the folks from Lexie Church of Christ being called to the right hand of God. Saving the world from this inferno had become my passion when I wasn't running from a switching, because I'd called Mama an "Old Cow" or when I wasn't being asked to get in a truck with some old fool offering to give me a ride to the store.

One night my cousin Princess Anne was showing me night garments my uncle in Illinois had supposedly bought her. The one I remember most was black baby doll pajamas that had straps which would cross to expose her rather large breasts for a girl younger than me, and there were some extravagant bra and panty sets which my mother would have set on fire with her eyes had she seen them, but knowing nothing I looked at my dingy old slip dress and thought that my cousin was just way ahead of me in the women's apparel department. Some years later when she had a child that none of us were supposed to know about—except we did including birth weight, date, and the hour when it happened—then the picture of another victim was unfolding before my eyes, even though I did not know to put my arms around her and whisper, "Don't hide, my cousin. Don't hide. You are beautiful and somebody might be willing to believe you." She became an imposter like me, because of my silence.

A high school mate was knitting all the boys penis warmers behind Ms. Laws' back during free sewing time, and Perky, a very wild funny gal who was never prepared for school, but who kept all the boys happy, wore her Frederick's of Hollywood dress which her grandma had ordered for her as a birthday gift. These small hints began to somehow consolidate with what actions I saw on a regular basis in the barnyard, pasture, and when Tom, our cat, had visitors. Worst of all, I began to want to order my Mark Eden bust developer and the padded and pointed bras shown in the back of movie magazines. I did feel that I was failing in my quest to bring the masses up to speed in their life's direction toward hell, but someone appeared to be having a good time and it certainly was not me. I blamed it all on my crossed eyes, which even the older kids made fun of, but later on I would learn that most boys didn't give me a second look because I was too pure. No one was going to be flirtatious with the purest girl in school, especially when her father had a reputation of being one of the best shots around when squirrel and rabbit season hit the valley.

Oh, I did begin to love boys and through my friend Betty Larkin I found a phone boyfriend. There was a boy by the name of Mark, Betty's phone friend, and her brother told me about a guy by the name of Scot who would not mind my calling him. As Betty and I kept on the college reading list her brother brought home, we found something to talk to the guys about almost every night and, God Bless both of them, they were at The University of the South, and most guys who went there were training to be Episcopal priests. We had to have been their community outreach projects, for had either one of them come to visit either one of us, I think they would have high-tailed it back up to Sewanee Mountain and changed their names to something like Pete and Ezra, anything to keep these goofy high school girls from calling every evening.

For all we know, the boys could have been sadists or toads, but we talked about our boyfriends and I think we may have even felt a little superior by then, for we could hold attention with conversations of alienation and sexual issues of the day. I didn't have to have sex, for all I had to do was read a little William Goldman, Albert Camus, pitch in a little Byron, Shakespeare, and I could simply imagine the fire of physical love burning within. I could hide myself and feel the burning desire which I kept as mine in the pages of a book.

Wherever these young men wound up, I do not know. We saw them for the last time when we got them to play at the first high school prom Huntland High School ever had in 1966, organized by Betty and me. If somehow they run across this draft of my Pink Honeysuckle life and story, I just want them to know that regardless of their motivation, they helped two awkward and innocent girls have a reason to dream and to pretend that we were loved by some very special fellows. I hope they became priests and teachers, good fathers, and wonderful lovers. They deserved the best for giving one damn about two valley girls who were lambs. I love to presume even now that they had social service reviews where they went over our progress from week to week and a dowdy professor gave them a 4.0 for having learned about the life beyond the Southeast's Oxford look-alike campus. "Gentlemen," he may have said, "You chose a project which up to this point, I presumed to be non-achievable, talking with heretics from down there!"

Maybe it is sad we'd never meet again along life's way, for Betty and I became college girls and we were pursued by guys just because we did grow in to womanhood even without the bust developers and back-seat romps. For a while I even became an Episcopalian, along with a stint as a non-believer, a Buddhist yoga mama, and then a Catholic. I wish that some other college guys would realize that the brains do not stop at Sewanee Mountain's edge nor does faith come without study and redemption. Isn't it shocking that one may never meet some people they would have loved most, because class distinction is so pervasive in this society? I thank you, boys. Oh I thank you and I will never see you grow old, nor will you two ever see what became of Betty and me, but I mean it when I say that you changed our lives, and I'll love you always for being there. I wish I looked like Bette Midler and had the voice to sing out over Winchester, God I thank you for Scott and Mark somebody or the other, for you made Betty and me feel like eagles soaring above the melancholy of high school courtships.

The beads and peace signs, the silly kids who cannot sing worth spit, and old hippie attire can still be bought in Haight-Ashbury close to my California home, but rarely will the truth of the 1960s be told, if it is not told with the fact that poor girls and poor boys were not the ones enjoying the dance. Do not endeavor to take our time in history sweethearts; even we Appalachian sisters knew then that we had to make our own circle of love. Betty did not have to hide with the telephone as I had to, and could you say that we were early provocateurs when it came to phone sex? We knew of no such thing then; But it added a lot to sweet dreams. Since dreams kept me going, I needed little more to be satisfied.

Chapter Nineteen

I try so hard to find sweetness in the life of a Bible Belt Christian, and here and there I can gather stems from the vine of Sundays and of appreciable kindnesses that could happen when people were allowed to express their sorrows. Sometimes I almost wished that our house would burn down, because when people had fires or a storm struck, then the community came with whatever they had to give. We had zero to give, but I can guarantee you that when we knew of other's sorrows or illnesses, then we would give the very last thing we owned if that is what it took to show a generous heart. All Appalachian communities, hill and valley, still share much of this measure or thought. One might have to get out and search for a bucket of ripe persimmons in the autumn, or crawl around in dark, dank places where we usually didn't go to find the fresh eggs of springtime, but whoever was known to be in need brought out community in a way that is rarely seen in other places.

Mother was always talking about, "Why if this house burns down," and then she would tell us to go to sleep with that fear in our hearts. I thought it might be a good way to get a few new covers and underwear to get us through the weeks of winter when the cast iron wash pot would freeze over at times, and somehow Mom had not gotten the idea of hanging lines on the leaky old back porch. The first washing machine came along when I was about seven years old, and I loved that old monster with its wringer and the big aluminium washtub that came with it. I didn't think too much about clothes as long as I could get warm. One could have counted the kids in school who were going without if they looked around the classroom on the first frosty morning and saw all of us who had britches, as we called long pants, under our dresses. I really felt sorry for a poor boy by the name of Paul who loved to grease up his hair like a lot of boys did then, but he lived in our neck of the woods even further down, and kids made a lot of fun of Paul when he'd get to school with icicles hanging down from his well-greased and obviously freshly washed hair.

Here and there, families even seemed to get together just because they were family. Only as I grew up would I learn that most of our relatives would cringe if we dropped by, partially because of our retarded brother, James. We may as well say retarded, because James could not help himself, for he knew that he would get one whipping after the other for things he would decide to do. It was not unusual to knock out a preacher or two, but now and then he'd be running wildly with a shovel ready to bash in someone's car windshield or ready to put a cat in the nearest pond, but where was the sweetness? No one offered to help or to try to give him any form of diversion. They wanted to see bruising and blood, then they would probably have been satisfied if we'd tied him to a tree like a dog. In our county there were so many challenged children that it was very questionable that all of these children were conceived under normal circumstances as was my brother. I probably didn't know about incest until I got to college and saw it in a psychology textbook, then things started to make more sense. In hidden places off the main roads, and I would later learn in cities and towns as well, incest was seen by some fathers and brothers as a God-given right. Girls and women were property.

Some families just handled things better than others, for they had been taught better while growing up. So here and there, I was so amazed to see people take pleasure in counting cars go by, gathering at a fence post at day's end just to rest together, and there were people like my friend Joan and her mama, Mrs. Marie, who milked their old milk cows while listening to a radio and singing together. Here and there, mothers would laugh with their daughters about something funny at school, and if I was really a good kid for a day or two—whatever that meant in Mom's mind, then I might get to spend the night with my friend Marlene. That was really special, for her parents had the best job in the world to my way of thinking; they cleaned the school, and I got to help them! They liked it, and I liked being with them. I especially loved to polish our small chemistry lab, and between Marlene and her parents, Mr. and Mrs. Davis, we cleaned that place up in a hurry, and it was cleaner than most folks' houses.

When I first started helping clean the school buildings at Huntland, I would pretend what it would be like if it were my big house, and I had all these secret places to play. Sometimes, if there was an evening school activity, then Marlene and I would get to drop in just because her parents were so nice as to let us be young girls for those few hours. I know that I am sounding pretty hard up by telling you that I found joy in being a janitor, but it beat going home and dealing with Mama and worrying about whether Daddy was going to be depressed or not. The Davises had a life that I'd have given my right arm for, for they did love each other. I never saw Marlene yelled at or punished, and when we got home Marlene's favorite meal was a Bumble Bee tuna sandwich. They had no idea that they might as well have been serving me fillet mignon, for tuna fish sandwiches simply seemed the end to a delightful evening.

No one affected my life like my friend Betty Larkin's family. I just about moved in with them the last two weeks before I finished high school. Things had gotten unbearable at home; everyone knew that I was leaving, and the Larkin family had picked me up and salvaged a girl who was almost beyond being pieced back together. When I went there, we worked on 4-H projects and baked pies and biscuits. They loved Tennessee Walking Horses, so there I learned to ride a horse, to a degree for I was scared to death of feeling that high up on an animal. There were bicycles enough for Betty and me to ride, and we would go visit Mrs. Campbell and swing on her front porch. Mrs. Ruth Larkin would come home, and sometimes Betty and I could work out some kind of play or song to do at school. The Larkin family did not bury themselves with the usual concerns of housekeeping and church every Sunday. Mrs. Ruth worked all the way at NASA in Huntsville, and Mr. Gus worked in Winchester's Dobbs Hat Factory, but when they got home it was all about kids. Homework was encouraged and made fun. To be creative was expected, and I can tell you there were many nights when Betty and I would have to dive under a pile of clothes to find a bed to sleep on, but this was the happiest place I ever found in all of my childhood.

Mr. Gus began to notice that I had terrible strabismus, and he spent about a year seeing that I got seen at Vanderbilt Hospital where I had the first surgery. It was through his Huntland Lions Club, so throughout the years I have tried to send back home memorials to that club. Unfortunately it would be at Vanderbilt also where it would be noticed that something else was wrong with this girl, whoever I was, for I would have tremors so badly that the physicians could hardly examine me. I remember the resident that was in charge of my case, Dr. Daniel Lev, and I will always feel that he did the best he knew how to do at the time with my surgery, but the result would take too more tries. He was kind and would hold my hand and talk to me to help me calm down, but what he did not know is that his observation that I had severe anxiety would eventually cause me to completely fall apart with no one but me to run and get away before I would up in some mental ward for the rest of my life.

Here I am trying to tell you about this blessing, and it is turning in to a curse. I entered the hospital with such hope and love for Dr. Lev and for all of the nurses who were especially nice to me, and I began to think that night that I was going to beg them to just keep me, for being at home was no longer safe. I hid again inside of me, I read a little girl who was to have another surgery some scripture, and even when they were getting ready to release me to my mother and aunt who had come for me, I again thought, "This is your chance," and every quivering inch of my body wanted to beg them to keep me away from home, for I could no longer bear the beatings. No, I've not told you much about the whippings, for everyone as a child in Appalachian Bible Belt country knew that you were born with Spare the Rod and Spoil the Child written on your back, but it was out of hand at my house.

I had to relearn in my own life with my own children processes of diversion, and I was not always successful, but no one attacked their children the way mother began to attack me. She would purposefully beat me across the face so I would have to go to school scared. Rock throwing became a new tactic when we learned we should try to get away from her and she would laugh maniacally if she could get a hold of me and have a younger sibling kick me in the privates. Coat hangers, real old wire coat hangers, belt buckles—you name it, if it left a mark, then it was used. I lied to people about my bruises, but the shakes just came if I felt that anyone was getting into my world. I did not want Mama or Dad to be victims of humiliation, for I was certain that the next mark would be on my grave if I did.

Chapter Twenty

Do you mind? I started out trying to find blessings, and maybe I could find it amusing even myself that I loved to do janitor work, but I need to go to the woods again, for the last time with Rose, Violet, and me, just us to walk to our magic garden carpeted with the pine needles. I gather them and look at Rose, for in my life I pretty much knew that after she graduated high school and took a job in Washington, D.C. then we wouldn't walk on the pine carpet of needles again among the pink honeysuckles and white dogwoods, so we gathered them with a zeal that appeared as if we were gathering gold from an endless mine, and if we left all of the sparkle would be gone. We did as we always did, took them to Mama, and they made her so happy that I thought maybe I could let my eldest sister go away in peace to seek a new life. The government used to recruit secretaries from our area because we did not complain, and Mrs. Marjorie Kennedy prepared us to be those great office assistants. It was that or get married to some boy, and Rose did have a boyfriend, but Washington opened her eyes to another handsome boy from Pennsylvania. I was right, for all my fear was that she would not return home to marry Walter like Mama wanted her to, but that one last day we played in our garden like the little girls we were when we first stumbled upon it, and Mama's Sunday was complete that day.

Every family I've mentioned here in some way touched my life with angel intervention, and Rose did find another life and married at age nineteen. Only my angels who let me play, who let me clean, who let me create, and who tried to fix me are the ones I want you to remember from this part of the story. The scars are gone, the ones which you could see, and the angels dance around me with moonlight and memories on their wings. I am all right—maybe just all right—but I feel like my folks hit a point in life after we left home when they tried to make everything up to us. They did to us what was done to them as children, and I forgive them and I love them. With everything within me that was the message I wanted them to take into their heaven, and oh my friend, surely they did. I pray that they did, for all of our experiences were simply the sum of what they had learned in lives and times worse than ours. Tonight I feel overwhelming love for them, though even as an older child Mother in particular would endeavor to create a kind of chaos as did her own mother. I pictured Mom and Dad this past springtime in our pinewood garden taking the nectar from the pink flowers, and they got to be hummingbirds and take the longest drink a beautiful wisp of a bird could ever swallow. Birds, pretty birds and nature's call to them to sing and hum, and to tell stories with their songs; So I see the ghosts of my parents so very real – pretty birds; Sweet birds. I know your disguise, we will meet again.

Do not worry about me; you will soon see the mad girl beginning to blossom and the past is left behind only for the days I care to bring it up when I'm thinking of other suffering souls. Laugh at me, if you must; You can weep for me, but only because I am letting you know here and now that many kids felt loss and many failed miserably at making a life for themselves. But we did get a gift that carries us across the years: we are able to find tender mercy in the remarkably unremarkable path of simply existing.

Chapter Twenty One

For Mother

I cannot imagine how my mother felt on that October day when she left her mother's angry soul to climb to the top of Sand Mountain where she had arranged to meet my father, her brother, Ralph Hood, and a pastor whose name still remains in the small family Bible that her mother gave to her as a wedding present. Though it was supposedly a surprise to everyone, somehow Grandmother had managed to sew Mama a new dress to go to the rock on top of Sand Mountain, which became her wedding altar. All that she took with her was the clothes on her back, maybe a couple of nickels and a change of underwear. To be truthful, I would expect that Mother had little else to offer as she made her climb to meet my father, Amos Orsbon Everett. She'd met him when he came to her valley, below his place at that southern-most tip of the Appalachians where he had grown up.

Her mother and brother were doing the daily milking as they watched her go away. With her fragile courage, Mama began her climb without smiling—she was never self-assured—lost in her thoughts of what it was going to be like to be a grown-up, wed to my dad and away from the valley life which, though difficult, she would miss, with little brothers and sisters left behind. The last words she would hear were from her youngest brother remarking to her mother, "I hope the old heifer never comes back here." Then their mother simply focused one last time on the eldest daughter as she disappeared among the boulders, the mountain oaks, maples, walnut trees, and to the hum that is the song of life in the woods. The birds were Mother's wedding song and Mama kept thinking about the boy whose loves letters had been kept from her by her mother, a valley boy who Granny thought was less suitable than one of the Everett boys. Mother would have been as fragile as a magnolia blossom about to break from spring frost on this autumn day. Her cheeks were porcelain to pale, a fading flower, and as fearful as a little girl headed to an executioner. For God's sake, she still wanted a Shirley Temple doll like all the other little girls next Christmas, but on she went.

I asked her why she had married so young and she told me how her daddy had begun to point at the area where her dress did not meet her ankles as she took his lunch per Granny's orders. She would hand the old sot his lunch as he was working with the fishing boat that he would rent and tell the other half-drunk slime there to fish, "Just look at that girl tempting us. Just right for mashing, because that dress doesn't cover everything." Mom said she would hang her head in shame, but never told Granny for the razor strap would be ready to whack her a few times for lying about what she just said. This is a theme that seems repetitious as I go over my own life, and I don't like telling you about Mama, for she was so private about such matters, but somehow I have to show you how a beautiful mountain lass became a woman crazed, abusive to her own children, unable to care for us half the time, and without joy to give except for a few simple and secret times with Daddy.

Her wedding night that mid-October would be spent at the home of Dad's brother, Weaver Everett, someone else known to be about as kind to women as a mule driver. She could not tell me what it was like to lose her virginity, to not know how to take care of herself, but one thing was for certain, wedding night or not, she was to be up the next day fixing biscuits and gravy and ready to send Dad out 'till the noon hour, when she would have made another meal. I have a natural affinity for cooking, but all I can see is poor Mom troubled over how to get a whole meal out in one iron skillet. Who ever heard of a honeymoon? Even I did not know that people who got married were to expect wedding presents until I got married, for every woman that I ever knew from our world just woke up one day and she'd gotten hitched. Mom got some of Granny Everett's old things. Dad built a couple of pieces of furniture and over the years, if they got a little ahead, then they would buy something like a pan or a paring knife. A butcher's hell would be to have to use the paring knife which my mother used throughout the days of my memory, for it was no sharper than dull finger nails, but somehow she used it until she cooked her last meal some sixty-five years later.

Mom could never do anything to please her mother, but she was desperate from the day she left to be with her Mammy, as she sometimes called her, for that was the way of her Scot-Irish world. She said that she felt so grown up, and she loved Dad's sisters. Years later I would learn that their favorite pastime was bickering with or about my mother and I've come to have this savage wish that some of those critical on each side of the family will have the misery of having to put on pantyhose over their slimy bodies when they enter the gates of hell. Dad did not know how to be a husband other than to have a wife servant and to curse, hit, expect three square meals a day, and to have his lady, come time for bed. Mama said they had some good times, though. It turns out that when things were good, they might go to a movie with some old friends or with anyone who had a car. Money being scarce, they'd make candy from peanuts, sugar, and powdered cocoa, and they liked to visit; Oh they loved to visit and to have company, so much so, that having company would later become a focus of their lives.

Mother was supposed to prevent all of the pregnancies which kept occurring, but lets get this out now while I am atoning for my own sins toward her: the woman wasn't able to stop pregnancies. Daddy did love his sweet baby who, to his pride, grew fat through the years. Yes, he could be vile, but if Mama was troubled or in pain, then that trouble and pain caused Daddy to walk the floor and to sometimes simply melt into tears.

Now at that time, to my memory, there were three known methods of birth control: abstinence, condoms, and diaphragms. If loving is all you've got, then abstinence doesn't seem like such a great option. Women did not know how to graph their fertile times back then. Condoms cost money and if a woman went in a store to buy one, she would have probably gotten labeled as a whore over the next three counties combined, for gossip was the mode of all news outside of the U.S. mail. Then the diaphragm; do you really think anyone ever sat poor Mother down and said, "Well, Mrs. Everett, we are going to show you how to use this device to aid in family planning and we've got this stuff called lubricant that you can use to stick it in"? And if there were spermicides widely available then, would they have told her? No one can quite picture pulling your baby on the cotton sack, nursing between rows, getting food on the table, then having time to plan that on such a warm southern night you may need to stick your little rubber hat over your cervix, planning ahead as wise women should do. I absolutely feel no sympathy for anyone who would criticize my mother for having so many children.

I often felt that it was as if my mother had some knowledge that other country women didn't have. Remember the rock on the mountain. Mom at her young age had committed all of herself, her thoughts, her hopes, her energy, all that she had and promised to give without refusal because men of the Appalachians heard the great "obey" of the apostle Paul's missive to love and to honor much more readily than they heard the end scripture which specifically ordered husbands to "love" their wives as God loved His bride, the Church. To most Christians, there is no church without the Christ, so I have long been at odds with those who get stuck on the obey part. I would go so far as to say that this particular scripture is the most misread, purposefully misunderstood, and troublesome of scriptures in the New Testament. But Mama tried to comply with the only word she heard, too. She was the obedient wife who opened her arms no matter how tired she felt and with no regard that child after child was wearing on her body.

I want to make a small summary of problems my mother was saddled with as my memory began: four older children, me, James—our little broken boy, and a grandchild or two having been born in the meantime. Her husband had left because he had to go all the way to Chicago to keep a job for six years, so we could eat well enough for Mama not to eat red clay dirt as a vitamin. Her mother visited her a total of once before she died in 1964. Grandpa helped Mom by calling her and letting her pick up the rotten fruit left in the orchard to can. Some had talked about our mom as if she were a whore wallowing in a vat of mud, waiting for another pregnancy.

They even dared not encourage Mother's own son to treat her with enough respect to visit her after driving five hundred miles supposedly to do so. She couldn't even breathe for a while, for a goiter was severely blocking her airways until it was removed. Then, there being little medical genius, she went without thyroxin hormone replacement for most of the rest of her life. She did not drive and wasn't welcome most places because of brother James, even if she could. Her brothers and sisters saw her now and then, but I can seriously say that Mother gave her all to receive those visits, working herself to death in the garden to have something to give. I will never know the truth of why Granny Hood was out to break my mother, but you may imagine with me whether or not Mama had any control over any such acts of evil.

She was heavy, and she'd developed arthritis and suffered from depression from the day I knew what a face was and before then as far as I have been told. She had the confidence of a rabbit with its hind legs already being fried in a skillet. Her father let her mother's clothes rot in the closet, while my mother wore rags because there were no hand-me-downs for her. She was terrified of the coming conflagration of the end of the world, for she felt nothing could be worse than living. Then things got a little better, and she began to look for a job after Dad had a car again and was home. It almost appeared that we might have our Mother after the children were all born, then, as if mercy could not exist, she became menopausal. By the time Mom was in her early fifties, she was probably a certifiable closet maniac, and the worst part was that my brother Van and I became the whipping posts.

So why would I ever love this woman? It took me a long time and it took a lot of years for me to see that she was disabled from her own youth, from the work of a marriage where they had to understand that they were the best either of them could have ever had, and I had to learn that my physical pain gets taken care of whereas she suffered. I will tell you that when she was beautiful, she was a magnificent woman. She loved where others despised and made light of her infirmities. She made a home that any grandchild who walked into would remember for the great effort my parents gave to give them boundless love. Yes, I owe her big time, and the time has come and gone when I can look at my mother and to say face to face, "Mama, I understand. I wish that I could have helped you more," but I know that when I meet her again in the bye and bye, we will eat her coconut cake, her banana pudding, and her rabbit cooked to taste like chicken, and we will laugh.

We will laugh about the only time I ever saw her run, when she knocked down a hornet's nest. We will laugh when I asked her why that nasty old bull was sticking something wet and slimy in our cow Daisy, and we will roll over laughing about when the tornado took our outhouse and how we hoped the contents landed on a select few. Oh Mother, I know how sick you were now and I feel shame, but I also know you. You quietly forgave those who tormented you and you and I forgave each other. I heard the last words you ever said. Yes, I arrived and we all saw the joy on your face when you struggled to say, "Barbara."

I became your night vigil in the end, and I thought of your coconut cakes and banana puddings, when you made ice cream to try to cheer us up the Sundays of Dad's years away. I told you that I loved you, words which did not come easily, but that I needed to say and words which you needed to understand.

Yes, Mama, we will laugh in the bye and bye and we will gather the mountain laurel which lingered into October, for in our heaven, we will know one another for the first time and I will listen more and I will understand, as I never did before, that you were a super woman placed on a common earth to achieve amazing things, even if it was through the fog and distraction of years of madness. This is a memorial to you, my angel mother, so touch me softly in the night and whisper as angels must, that you have found another mountain top and from there you can see the world, but most of all you can see us and you are watching, watching like you always tried to do even when you were in so much pain that you could not breathe. Oh, my mother, we will laugh again and maybe we'll stir up our own storm and let the bits fall where once we were not welcome.

A little baby is born who would be another great-grandchild, and his name is Gabriel and you would love him. We'll have to wait to hear what is his favorite cake for you to bake, as you did for all of the children. He is wonderful, Mama, and he has an angel's name, the angel of the Annunciation, so he is really special. You would want to know, "Was the labor hard?" I would answer yes and the phone lines would be on fire as you notified everyone. That was your way to hear from others, our presence, so now we depend on our fragile prayers for you to awaken and call the saints to announce a blessed birth. I will talk to you later at sunset, but between then and now, Mama, do not go looking for a hornet's nest, for you need no such trophies for us to know that you were among the bravest women we would ever know. We must admit that your eyes and the way you ran though would have competed with any freight train endeavouring to pass you from behind

Chapter Twenty Two

I have heard about the codes of silence when it comes to criminals, and I am sadly amused, for what is common behavior in the areas of Appalachian Mountains and the valleys, which lie below, is a type of silence which is almost deafening in the hum of its ancientness. I do admit that the crimes do seem to have become more brutal, but my mother and father taught me from a very young age to love God, to help my fellow man, to look before I stepped into the unknown, but perhaps, more fervently, "Keep your mouth shut when it comes to the neighbor's business!"

I can honestly say that is probably the only crime my parents ever participated in; silence. We knew all the moonshiners and later we'd hear about drug dealers. We knew that God-fearing people did not talk about their neighbors' peculiar habits. It was perfectly normal for a prostitute or two to hitch a ride on our school bus halfway up to Winchester, and we just said, "Yes, ma'am," if they wanted our spare seat, for after all they were someone's Mama even though they were not pillars of the church. The codes of silence probably began immediately after the Civil War when the new south was in its infancy because people had to hide everything they had not to get it stolen or have it claimed by the new government. When we heard the word "feds" it was not spoken with any particular respect. I hate to think of us as the purveyors of gangs which would eventually take hold in most American cities by the early twentieth century, but many of our rules were applicable to what went on.

Good people did not tell on their neighbors for breaking laws that supported the demands of the community. Even when white lightning was still being made after the package stores freely bought and sold legal liquor there were still guys making liquor in the old-fashioned way, and we lived right in the midst of it. We heard all kinds of stories, of bodies being found under bridges, of people we didn't know disappearing, and my mother would have made them banana pudding before she would get involved with gossip of such. We did not see things; we did not hear things. And the poor people who died mysteriously were always said to be "skirting the wrong side of the fence."

In later years houses would get bombed or burn mysteriously, and there was even rumor that drugs were being run from Florida in movable toilets, but it was all gossip to us, and you let it happen around you as if blindness came and went like the setting sun. Our biggest curiosity was whether they cleaned the johns first, if there was such a racket going on. Call it crazy, but also call it survival, for people who chose to talk did seem to have dates with unusual events that threatened their welfare as well as the welfare of families. Ordinary families such as ours and most of our neighbors were solid rock, down-home Christian types, and they determined that the devil's work got done, too, but if you stuck your nose in it then you would get your nose cut off. For as good as God is, evil is and was powerful and it involved itself in all kinds of corruption, much of which we did not hear about.

My mother was a clever historian until the day she died. Driving with her out to Sand Mountain and hearing the names of all the people she could tell you about from house to house, remembering dates, hours, and places of goodness or unrest, she could reel off stories that would make your hair stand on end. "Now they found this boy back there under that bridge we just passed, and his throat was slit from one end to the other. He must a told on somebody," Mother would say, and we would have to stop her, for some of the stories involved atrocious crimes against humanity. Instead of enjoying the scenery, we were anxious to get to the safety of home. I was thus in a world of low-class Al Capones who were just as dangerous, and our folks let us know that from a very young age.

When there were few phones I think everyone eavesdropped. Then everybody was on a party line, sort of like your phone Facebook without the hassle or cost. How could you totally stay out of people's business unless you knew what was going on in the backwoods drug fields, old whiskey stills, or people sucking white stuff up their noses, but it wasn't enough to call the law in about.

There was the great movie *Walking Tall* about a place like those communities that still thrive all over the land of our fathers. But best you be warned that what you see there usually should stay there, because things are back to the old ways of taking care of snitches. Add to all of this that a good person at that time felt that God would be there soon to sweep away the debris of evil, so why would men try to do God's work of doling out punishment. Daddy and the humble men who abided by the law knew who in the community controlled things, for all was controlled where there was a little money, and your children and family losing their lives or homes was not something anyone was going to risk, especially since you could not tell the law makers from the law breakers when most of the time, they were enjoying their fine dinners together. Poor people needed no more trouble than they woke up with day in and day out. Mistrust was at times a little too much, for we needed all we could get from the county considering options for health care were minimal.

I have a feeling that the county health nurse and Mama had equal respect for one another, because that was messing in Mama's child rearing. Mama did appreciate that Mrs. Marie Mason would be taking us in to a clinic for shots and, bless her heart, most times Mrs. Marie would let us get a treat at a tiny restaurant in Huntland. That got rid of the health nurse for a year or so, and I would be out of high school before I ever heard of a case where The Feds came in, and that would lead to a sad story about a murder over on one of the mountain roads.

Folks worried that somebody's boy had said too much, and no one talked about it in the churches except Mama got to tell what an amazing thing it was to have cargo trucks of marijuana hauled out in such large quantities. And added that she just didn't know what this world was coming to, and Daddy said he reckoned it was nothing she could fix or anybody else for that matter.

Next came the meth labs, and Mom thought she had a lot of protection from the law when a deputy sheriff of a nearby town moved a half-mile from her and she boasted how safe she felt. Somehow or the other though, the next thing she knew, that very neighbor was being hauled out by law enforcement himself for running a meth lab. "Yes, I can't believe it, a law man making drugs for people in his nice big trailer!" My mother was afraid at night and all of the sudden she became more fearful because her deputy sheriff had been hauled off, so we had to comfort her. "Mind your own business" is as pertinent as listening to the word at Sunday meetings in that world, and I came to understand it more as the years went by. As long as you lived and let live, for the most part, people got along. It may seem curious to you now, but when I was a sixth grader, we still had teachers who wanted to talk about the injustices of the Civil War, for they had elderly fathers or certainly grandfathers who had participated in that period of "late unpleasantness." After seventy-five years, people still had a mistrust for anything federal and you have now seen the southern states growing into one of the largest voting blocks in the country for the hope to see more states' rights and less government intervention.

When the fox comes home to lie, people will try to protect their own, one way or the other. To live in silence was a first lesson, a mixed blessing when you think of all the other atrocities that would come into our path, but even recently I met a beautiful man who grew up in a coal mine patch or village of coal miners as far away as the Pennsylvania Appalachians and the theme held true there also. The community was fixed and satisfied as one could be with their faith and duty toward neighbors. A man with an official-looking suit meant one thing and that thing was trouble. We weren't oblivious to our surroundings, but we owed something to those around us unless they took something of ours. We are watching a lot of Southern poor kids, just like other kids, falling under the mystique of drugs, especially those that kill and are cheap like methamphetamine. Like most Americans, we look in horror and we wonder why the government doesn't come in and protect the communities from these horrid chemicals which destroy the young people who are falling as victims, and we ask, "What can be done?" and the answers are not there. The foxes do come to our homes and attack, but their dens are still more dangerous than what happens to people who accidentally fall into their turf, so the old rules of silence prevail. Our kin and children find out how best they can live, and to avoid becoming a "snitch." I am not proud to say that my people had discovered the awful word and consequences long ago. The risk of losing friends and family, this folklore of Appalachia, is now the unspoken law of the gangs who now torment inner city neighborhoods.

I do not accept that we were criminals or protectors of evil men and women. We just did what we had to, to live and to get along. Part of the time it made little difference, but now generations of children are being lost. Maybe someone has an answer to such societal debacles and if you do, then please let everyone know, for you are going to win a Nobel Peace Prize. We depended on a greater God, a greater punishment that could not be imagined in an earthly realm. We sang "What a Friend We Have in Jesus" then we got on with the work ahead of us and prayed for forgiveness for our weak spirits, with aside prayers for the health nurse not to check on us for a good long time to come! All the while, we knew that there would always be corruption, robbery, prostitution, alcohol and drug addiction, but the speck we were in the universe made no difference and in some kind of amazing grace, now and then people got caught and justice was served, but silence will live among children of the hidden southern communities long after the lamplight is out on the new day. It is embedded within us, deep within.

Snakes. Just think of them, all swirled and ready to bite if their cover is blown. They are all over our woods, and some are so blended with autumn leaves that you could reach out and touch them. Their color is as pure as nature's earth dying to another winter. They have shelter and are deadly. They have dens and places to procreate just beneath your feet. They hide behind trees if you get close and hiss before they strike, but once you've reached out, you have gone too far. Stay away little children, stay away, you've heard a mother say. Father cannot reach you in time, so do not enter what you can't get out of and if the Lord should return, He will understand why you had to keep the secret. It is just another line to write on your heart like the ones you wrote of Mama when she was bruising your skin, but bear it all, and wait for Judgment Day. My greatest desire on that day, outside of seeing all you old friends and loved ones then, is that there will be streets of gold and the old peddler's truck will be there with a frosty RC Cola and a Nutty Buddy in his freezer case, for we'll have some time to spare while God is rounding up the evil-doers, and I did always long for that old truck to come when I felt my worst. Innocence kept our minds away from a side of darkness, and we knew the circumstances over which we had no power.

Chapter Twenty Three

When my sister Violet graduated from high school and went off for a career with the United States government, I became the eldest daughter left at home with the three children younger than me to help with. Mom's insanity increased because her latest daughter had left and there were a few years ahead before my father would find his Lord and Savior and join the Christian community. A lot of things would begin to change, but utmost among them would be our move to the new house which Dad and Mom had been able to have built through the utmost generosity of the FHA, the Farm and Home Administration, which I came to see as a pathetic friend to farmers. I am certain that giving loans to people such as my folks who had no money was considered to be a risk for the United States Treasury, but the people around where we lived would turn out to be the best buyers the federal government could ever have, because it represented people who were honest to a fault, who thought that if Uncle Sam gave them a loan, then it must be sacred, so the foreclosures so common in the early twenty-first century did not happen. Those ten-thousand-dollar loans probably were among some of the best spent money LBJ put out there, for it would take poor folks like Mom and Dad the next thirty years to pay it back. Every small county had its small-time builders who had their unskilled housing inspectors who would pass anything for well done if Mr. Builder kept bread on his table, and Mr. Builder knew every Mr. Banker who would be glad to take the government's money and shell it out in under-the-table deals. I cannot tell you this is what happened to my parents. Just let me describe moving day.

The house was located on the very end of my dad's property then, closest to the main road, so now and then we would get to see a car pass by on the way to the wooden fence which led back to an old road where the drunks liked to come and hang out on weekend nights. As strange as it may seem to you, I never went in to that house to see it until moving day when I was sent to carry the typewriter our brother Robert Van had given us as a present so many years before. It was treated with the respect of a Limoges vase. I felt a little guilty as I looked back at our old salt box settler's home that we were leaving. Through the misery of heat and storm it had somehow sheltered us and I had come there as a three-year-old and was leaving it at age fifteen, and I had the strangest feeling as if inanimate objects had emotions, especially houses, that some of your soul would always be left there. I tried to act happy, for even though this was not the day I would be getting my own room, we'd have a bathroom that would actually have a flush toilet, and Lord of Hosts, we would retire the Sears catalogue for good.

That evening and night would bring on the first truths of our new life. A house with three rooms meant that Mom and Dad were going to share a bed without a little child. I got my little sister as a roommate, and the only two people getting their own beds were William and James. James made a point of wetting his bed until he was in his twenties, and our observant big sister Violet decided she was going to give him a taste of his own medicine by making him stand and scrub his sheets until his hands were red. This was the first great blessing of the new house. James never wet the bed again. That was all it took, some adversarial behavioral psychology from a woman who turned out to be a major success as a government employee. They must have known they were getting a cracker jack employee when they got her, one with a ring in the box, for a ring that fit a child's finger was the luckiest of all cracker jack toys. She had a gift for negotiations and contracts. It was probably a blessing that she'd left home in the summer, for we did not gain one thing in square footage in the new house.

When you walked in it smelled of cedar and hardwood. Everything looked too clean to touch and I would learn immediately that Mother had put me and my baby sister just off the kitchen so she could have an even firmer control over my study habits. She was sick! She did not want me to study, and she found that it was much easier to start beating me at four in the morning if I was not already up and awake to give the house a good cleaning before I left for school and I had to see that the other three children got off and fed also. Most times she and Dad were going at a yelling match by five a.m. anyway, and one day she told me that she thought maybe she was going to poison his coffee—all of this and the joy of a new house, too. She always kept rat poison along with the poisonous pesticides for the various plants and vegetables she grew. I often thought that it was up to me to save Dad knowing that Mother had this on her mind, but by the next afternoon, they would be out discussing something funny that happened at one of their county jobs, so I decided that maybe some of the arguing was simply sport, and I was not going to die for a ball which I was not guilty of throwing into their unpredictable wrestling ring.

There were a few quirks about the house that I would learn through the years. The kitchen had kitchen cabinetry that was so cheap it was called knotty pine. One was not supposed to notice that here and there a knot a hole had been plugged up. The cabinets were built into the wall and they were so poorly attached to the studs that the rats found it to be a very comfortable winter destination, there among Mom's old pots and pans. I was convinced that they filed their nails with that dull plastic-pearl-covered paring knife which Mama was so proud of. We had no dishwasher and no window at the back of the house where the dining room and kitchen were placed, a mere oversight in an un-air conditioned house. Kindness was shown to the reptilian world also, for the crawl space of the house was hardly big enough to allow a plumber to work, but it proved to be an awesome place for poisonous snakes to breed. Every time a rattler showed up in the yard, my folks blamed it on the timber-cutters. I thought the snakes had come out for sunning after a rest at the Everett under-the-house reptilian spa. The dogs usually killed the unwelcome demons.

Our bathroom fixtures were so cheap that after one year of Comet cleanser—which Mother loved—the glaze was already coming off our bathtub. Every heater cover was so chintzy that rust developed each season as the silver-colored paint wore off in each room even though we could only turn them on if we had company or if Mama said so. The upstairs storage attic which was built to maximize our cooling and heating situation and to give Mom extra storage was so small that little people could not have used it for anything bigger than a puppet theater, though somehow Mom got her plastic Christmas tree and boxes of old cards up there. It also made a great home for the wasps which would often nest there. Other anomalies were the faux pink linoleum crud on the bathroom walls which was asbestos-laden and the toilet that would rarely flush because the drain field was put in upside down in the first place. Even the least interested home inspector might have noticed that sewage by its nature begins a flow down hill; of course it had been overlooked that such an assertion was reasonable and the septic tank had been put where our backyard had a slightly upward grade. We may as well have gone over and salvaged Granny Hood's old two-holer for cleanliness sake.

To Mom and Dad, it was beautiful, though. Through the years, Dad would add on to it, building several outbuildings for his tools and even building himself a two-car garage with a side room where Mama could put her canned goods to boil in the summer time and to freeze when winter came on, for again there was a tin roof. Mother loved to get people in to that side room. In her heart, I felt that it was her own Motel 8, only you had to hide out back or come inside, just hoping the toilet was working. Then their voices come to me from near their life's end: "We had everything we wanted or dreamt of, and what we didn't you kids gave to us." Their closets were too small for me to hide in to assuage the shame of what little it took to make them happy in this life, for their closets were built as an afterthought and were made for women's undersized clothing. Mama's dresses had to be pushed in sideways to close the doors.

I loved the new house smell, and I was proud to show my friends that I had something which resembled a room. They probably realized, as did I, that the old one had better "bones" as Dad called it, but we were now one of the community with our new house. Dad said he worked for the state board of education and mama was a nutritionist. In other words, even though Dad's crew built schools, he was a maintenance man, and Mama cooked at the local high school, so they were in "Public Works," as Daddy eventually called it. Compared to how so many families were losing all pride as Mom and Dad aged, Mom and Dad had built their mansion here on earth as far as they were concerned.

Yes, acting happy on moving day was all that I could do for them then and for several years thereafter. I will tell you, though, that what we gave to them was zero, the bunch of us, compared to what they accomplished from where they came. Any grandparent can only hope to achieve minimally the status of greatness which they did with grandchildren who rarely got to see them. The elder and wiser grandchildren learned that love was a modest house on their grandparents' lane in a valley that looked back toward the mountains from which it all began. In my darkest hours, I long to go there, for I had to miss so many years of the best part of these good people who were my parents. I can only share with my sons and the others who knew them well, as my Mary came to know my mother, that as plain as they were what they shared was a wellspring from their hearts. Carry them with you, my dear ones, and you will remember what the eyes of Grace come to look like even when they are too blind and too old to see your faces well. Carry them, and you will never be alone.

Chapter Twenty Four

I would change my condition or my needs to get through years. There are days, perhaps years, which seemed to pass as if they were so stark that we became trees standing numbed with the winter wind. I can see myself standing next to many trees where I, like them, am grey and gnarled, and I am so very cold inside and out. I twist and turn, and my limbs groan for the want of some kind of warmth in my life, but I see the other trees and I am just one alone. We shiver, quake, and we crack like the icicles which drip from us—drip, drip, drip—then we are moving more easily and somehow we know that the birds will come again. They will tell us in laughter that the folks up north think it is warm where we are, for we live in the southland, good old Dixie! We try to speak, but we are one with the trees, so we scratch notes on old leaves and twigs to fill the beaks of birds for making their new nests. The notes say something about how we have heard of warm places called Florida and California, but where we are, the snow sometimes falls in drifts up to the porch rails, and snow ploughs hardly exists, and here we are one with the earth.

I scraped on the old leaves, dancing in a final swirl before Mother Spring came with this message: that any person who had never experienced the wind on a cold Sand Mountain, Alabama, day knew little of the nature of winds and mountains. If ordinary people would just come, I would take them there where your skin could be exfoliated by the blasts of winter which blew so hard that no one wanted to leave the hearth but to bury their dead or to help a neighbor in need. It seemed almost wonderful to be a tree, to shiver as I wanted and then to be reconciled that soon some redbuds would be coughed out from the others around me and any big white magnolia friends which bloomed with great exuberance as their flowers would almost burst forth like a hairball from a cat. I would be a pine, though, and when I let the pink honeysuckle bloom beneath my magic carpet, then all the earth would rejoice. From that day forward we would be safe until we had to don our coats again.

We who grow up close to the earth take on kindred spirits as if we are the earth itself. We are better pretenders than most people, for we are alone enough to think. As a fragrant pine, I didn't have to change what coat I would wear or worry about what season I must be in. Being an evergreen helped me to avoid feeling anything. for me and for others in our small world. It was not madness, but one of the ways we simply searched for ways to yield to our ordinary days—"ordinary" to us at least. We had to get through them somehow. How many times have you been a forest or coughed up a flower or even ran as fast as the wind to become the wind? My guess is that many of you instead went home and said the words so engrained within your being, words we could only dream of saying something so humble as, "Hi, Mother. I'm home. Do we have any food in this house?" The television gods again gave us an idea that there was some usual greeting and pleasure in coming home, other than to take that first step from school waiting for the first command about what must be done before dark and the angry consequences of failure to do so. Pretending and protection became words almost synonymous with our ability to survive.

Certain events marked time for me much more than seasons. I believe that I was able to purposefully stop my menstrual cycle from coming until I was almost fifteen years old, for most girls were yakking about it in phys ed long before I knew what the heck they were talking about. We had to wear gym clothes for the first time and my friend Beulah said to me as we dressed for President Kennedy's new fitness program something like, "I don't want to see those nipples again without a bra over them." That was part of my coming of age, so I went out and bought a bra that next Saturday with my cotton money, for I didn't have my maid assignments made out clearly then. The only problem was I learned that they came in sizes. The 36Bs seemed plentiful, and I could get two for the price of one, and though I thought A's in school were better grades, I earnestly felt that I could do with the lesser B bra. When it fell down to my hips, I did somehow work out a deal where they'd go to someone else in the family, and a bra that accommodated bones and nipples proved suitable for me and it was extra quality, for it was an AA.

The awful day of the menstrual flow meant to me that I would cry for about the next year, for I did not know how to take care of myself. Was seven days normal or long? The worst was when I tried tampons—the sexy girls used those. My problem was partially caused by the Tampax Corporation's inability to show pictures on the outside of the box. I honest to God thought you used one piece of cardboard to shove the other piece of cardboard inside yourself. I spent about a quarter of a year until I opened the box and read something called "instructions." I truly suffered as one might expect secret cardboard-carrying females would, so when it came time to push my babies out, it was a cinch compared to having what felt like a corncob in my vagina before I learned the proper technique. I just wanted to do what the other girls did, and I could only get occasional instruction from my friend Lyzette, aka Joan Mason. Joan was more interested in trying to help me fix my unruly hair that went straight as a horse's rear no matter how many bobby pins we stuck in it.

It is not unusual, as a child of the mid-south, to be asked long before all of this, in fact, by the time you are toilet-trained, "Who's your boyfriend?" The adults in your life start trying to focus your mind as a young boy or as a young girl toward boyfriend and marriage after your toddler phase of development. Any guy who would say hello to me after the age of five immediately could take that role if I had to designate an answer. I made up boyfriends to shut people up, though at six years I did have a crush on one of the graduating seniors from high school who was one of my brother Van's friends. I have said that I felt invisible to boys even by the time I was wearing my AAs, because no one appeared ready to marry me immediately.

Adults always asked girls and boys back then, "When are you getting married?" It was just a joke, but children take things literally. It was not unusual for a younger teenager to get their mamas to take them to Ringold, Georgia, for you could get married there with a parent's signature much earlier. The more I heard about folks running off to Ringold, the more I heard about the babies I've talked about that were supposedly preemies at seven or eight pounds. It would take me a few more years to know that people got married as kids too often for the purpose of legitimizing sexual relationships, and as I examined so many of the families including my own, I was having a hard time understanding why any fool would ever want to marry other than to get away from home like Mother had. Only I would be running from Mother and Father's terrible threats to each other and Mother's abuse—if I'd even known a boy who wanted to marry a good girl. After all, I wasn't certain that I wanted to have sex until I was around twenty-one years of age, and I was still trying to reach Richard Chamberlain in Hollywood.

Mrs. Hannah's family and kids seemed to have the best marriages with husbands in town in several cases, nice little homes, and sweet children. Now and then Mama would let me visit one of them to help clean dishes and they would let me play a little. I wanted a life like that with kids, Saturday morning cartoons, and Sundays at the Methodist Church in Tullahoma where they had a nice Sunday school and not much preaching. But best of all, Mrs. Hannah's daughters and daughters-in-law got to go to Mrs. Hannah's house and play by the spring, eat great Sunday dinner, and leave happily to do it all another time. Their husbands even had jobs! They were my sisters and my first peek into an Appalachian family who grew even closer through the years, angels who would show us that marriages actually worked out fine sometimes even over rough patches. I longed to learn from them and to get out of my pretend world. The symbolism of the tree was that I was growing in to early womanhood, and what I was seeing of many in a similar state was another form of terror. I was entering another door, and the girl, me, was afraid to stay behind but more afraid to leave.

The blushing bride was pregnant at the time of marriage and she was apt to have a child or two by the time she was hardly twenty years old. Her health would begin to decay from lack of prenatal care, and the face of the girl she once was would already be disappearing from poor diet and her little knowledge of how to make much food outside of biscuits, gravy, cornbread, and coffee. She would pick up cooking skills, for that would be the one thing which usually pleased the boy, now calling himself "man" and calling her "my little old lady." She might begin to become plump, but he was apt to hit obesity way before her, because the tractor had allowed him to spend hours in the fields sitting on his rear, while the little wife tried to care for the little ones, please her mama by doing part of her chores, somehow scrounge up clothes for her babies whose diapers needed to be changed most times, and I will swear, a lot of those women spent so much time with husbands whose shoes always smelled of cow excrement that it didn't even bother them that their poor little babies smelled as if they hadn't been changed all day.

I remember when I was a teenager, my Aunt Mildred gave her beloved little boy Randall a really nice shower with all of her baby products, and she was drying him, hugging and kissing him, and then she said, "You smell like such a sweet baby!" Considering what most babies smelled like, that frightened me until I learned that she powdered, oiled, buffed, and petted her wee one until he smelled sweet like the Johnson and Johnson commercials said your baby was supposed to. Randy was one of the lucky kids who lived in a home where love flowed throughout his parents' being for a lifetime.

Most women did not enter the work force as other women had in and after WWII, for the few factories around were closing. Albert Gore Senior was a senator then from Tennessee, but he took care of business in Nashville, Knoxville, Memphis, and maybe Chattanooga. He spoke at my sister Violet's high school graduation because somewhere along the way he had befriended Mr. Homer Laws, our high school principal. I remember little of the speech, some foreign policy garble, as if any of us thought he gave a load of horse manure about anything going on around us. In the 1950s and 1960s, our area had feelings of serious hopelessness, and we admired that Mr. Gore was taking care to put out some projects to help the poor little black children in the United States, but we all thought he carried a bunch of hot air insofar as poor southern white people. I will add that this was absolutely a critical time in what would become the destiny for our communities, for if jobs had come to our area at that point, every farmer would have willingly let their fields go fallow for an honest day's work and for minimum wage. We needed help so desperately, but the real changes would not begin until around the 1980s when the south was recognized as a place to locate industry—because of cheap labor.

Thus the women stayed home and this might have been a typical September day for her. The kids were back in school, so she had gotten up to make coffee, start a fire in the heater hoping she had laid the wood in the stove the night before. She would then make breakfast, milk the cows, see to the babies as best she knew how, and then got the older ones off to school. Next it was time to go to the garden, for it was harvest time, so she would gather food to fix noon dinner for the men or workmen who were at her house, and if she had time before noon, she would be expected to go to the field for a while, especially when it was time to pick cotton. She washed dishes from dawn to dusk until the daughters, if she had any, knew they must take over that task. Canning was nonstop from April with early fruits through sometime near the end of September each year. She spent all summer preparing for the winter when the lady of the house was expected to make certain everyone was warm by quilting, never letting the heater burn out, the never-ending washing with a wringer washer unless all was to be hand washed, and then there was ironing everything. When people got to where they could afford the new polyester, it was as if even the saints in heaven finally knew that these women were going to crack at some point.

If you had a TV set, afternoon was the time to catch up on ironing, and if you were really lucky and didn't have a blown-out television tube or a storm between you and Nashville, then that was the woman's pleasure for the day. Women adored the soap operas and took their dreams of lives portrayed on *Days of our Lives* and *As the World Turns* to bed with them praying that they'd have such a loving scene the next day. I can still hear Mrs. Hannah saying, "Well, it's time for my programs," and once I was lucky enough to get Mama hooked on something called *General Hospital*. After Mama saw one that she called "Old Love Story" she was as addicted as a baby to its mother's breast. That was one of the few shows when I could sit with Mama and she could just shut up about the ten other things I could have done to make her life easier.

Afternoon meant more gathering in of whatever was in the garden, and, folks, you need to know that garden was started from seed in late January or early February. In our climate, when you planted the tobacco beds which protected those delicate slips, you also planted spring greens and onions and the seeds for the real garden for transplanting. A tobacco bed was a poor person's greenhouse, a logged-off rectangular bed and some kind of cloth and straw would protect the new plants as they began to grow for spring. The work was endless.

Afternoon was soon followed by the rush of kids home from school, cow milking time again, and then cleaning everything up for a last effort in preparations to make the next morning easier. There was no loving after you got off that school bus, and for many of us, books were the last thing you were going to get to think about. My sisters could use a crosscut saw by the time they were eight years old, for when Daddy wasn't cutting timber for us to burn come winter, then the rest of us were either sawing, carrying, or stacking wood. The only respite was if Mama got a visitor which was scarcer than hen's teeth. We were not supposed to work on Sundays, but Mama would decide that to break a washtub of beans was relaxing and the Lord wouldn't mind. As we grew up and older, she longed for us all to come home, for she could get some company and some rest. We didn't mind helping her, but Mother had this annoying habit of still getting us all up by daybreak, and if she wanted to go to bed at seven, "We might actually get to share news and talk for a while.' Men did men's stuff like killing hogs and planting fields, but the women cleaned, butchered, and preserved the meat brought in. I always wondered what Dad's secret was for looking more rested than everyone else in the house, and it turns out he did two things Mama didn't get to do. Sometimes he took naps under the shade trees, and he went to a dentist.

Can you get the picture that becoming a bride by going before a JP was about as wonderful-sounding to many of us with a brain in our head as having an arm sawed off without anesthesia? Some few of us resisted carnal temptation by reading the Bible a lot and praying for the life of the few lucky people who had jobs in the local towns and who visited and were generous to those who needed food. The luckiest people of all got to go as far as Tullahoma to the Piggly Wiggly store. I was holding out for that life, college, anything, but I did not want to marry a home boy. I had heard the women when I had overnight stays with their cries, "I am just too tired." And I'd heard the man's voice coaxing, and then the bedsprings. I didn't understand what was going on until much later or when debauchery would become almost a hobby for me, but those poor mothers and their mothers and all the women before, I want them to know that I know now why they were too tired and how they simply had to accommodate their husbands. I believe that most of these poor souls came to feel that sex was about as pleasurable as tooth decay.

Why did mothers not tell their daughters the truth of their lives? The best time they could ever look forward to was when those daughters got old enough to understand that they must summon some energy from within their hearts to help lighten their Mama's workload. We broke Mother's heart, for we abandoned her. When she was older and cried and wished she hadn't hit us so much, we almost had to thank her, for had she not, the circle would probably have remained unbroken—early marriage for a passion you might understand. Lack of formal education, and being a doormat for the men often seemed to be your only option. Yes, Mother and mothers of the mountains before you, we are sorry that we had to leave you, and we are sorry that we could only come home now and again, but you chose not to tell us your story, and we were afraid to ask.

Can we say, "Thank you for half beating us to death, but we love you at the same time?" Had you been kind, it would have been too hard to say goodbye. I know that it sounds somewhat shabby for a once-disadvantaged southern white Christian girl to say that. I think maybe none of us would have had the chutzpa to hit the road and work for a better way of living if those beatings hadn't drilled it into our minds that all we wanted to do was get out of there.

I learned to love you all, my Appalachian mothers and friends. Oh I love you now more, for I see the bigger picture, and I know that you suffered your own whippings from the men most of you would bury in your old age, but you would have learned to love them, too. Time so swiftly whispers to us that we missed your fate by a thread, and if we could have had anything, we would have asked you to hold us in your arms even when you hurt. We would like to have known being washed and loved and stroked on our heads for doing such a good job and you would have gotten the same amount of work out of us only more, for we would not have been so hurt. Just to have felt loved, to have felt your arms around us, and to have you call us your babies, that is the difference most of us would ask for. We understand better, though, each passing year, and we still miss our time with you.

Your arms hold us in our sleep and your guiding spirit leads us to seek love in unexpected places just like your TV hour. The ones we left behind, Mother, some of them are having a really hard time, and we cannot help them, for we must summon courage from ourselves to be without you. Your beautiful eyes still pierce our own, and the faded luster is too late understood.

We loved the grandmother you became, and we are glad that some fathers that are our home boys are giving their wives the lives neither you nor us could have had in the old days. We long for our fathers who became the examples to young men after their wild and mean years and we have loved and know love to this day. It had to be learned—like staying away from wasps' nests when we were children—but we learned. When the afternoon comes, I would almost like to watch the stupid stories, but your stories are so much more interesting, and we have a different kind of labor to attend to, for we are the new daughters and grandmothers. Our worlds lack perfection and will never be filled with sappy TV love, but help us, whisper to us that you kept some good secrets too. Let the rainfall wash us and caress us, and help us find grace similar to that which you finally left behind as your way of loving in the end.

The forget-me-nots have bloomed on the mountain, and it is a Sunday afternoon, so I will not work as you once said we should not. We no longer have to worry about broken telephone lines, just the distress calls that come sometimes, but we are strong, and we can usually fix our broken selves. When we cannot then we pretend that you are holding the little girls we were, and the sunbonnets you made are the shade under which we can take a nap and rest when strength does not prevail. "I Am Weary, and I Must Rest" is among the best of the spirituals which call us homeward.

Chapter Twenty Five

"You ain't getting any younger, so you better be gettin' yourself a boyfriend." Yes, those words would not stop as I hit that ripe old age of fifteen, and this would continue until the day I would marry, a story for later. I had the college guys on the mountain on the phone every chance I got, and I would have sneaked in some time to hide in the woods or to catch Mama gone for a few hours to read like a maniac, to memorize Ms. Nell Baker's latest Shakespearian offering or the classics like Blake and the one I adored most, Walt Whitman. I was able to make my telephone college boy, Scot, whom I had never met other than through our phone conversation, interested in this valley girl, curious about how I knew so darned much. I certainly was not going to tell him about the small school library where I took comfort resting and reading or that I did not even know until I was in ninth grade that we had a little school library from which one could borrow books. I somehow remember that Betty Ruth and I had aggravated her brother, Ronnie, to find us a couple of college boys, and maybe he just asked two guys from this all male school to make his only sister and her friend happy with a few calls, but as I see pivotal events, this would be one of them, because the high school boys just were not that interesting from then on and the one or two that might have had clout with Betty and with me showed no interest at the time anyway.

The closest real county library in Winchester was an unknown to me until cousin Peggy took me there once, and of course I could not check out books because I had no way of getting them back. This was not a service made available for the kids from Lexie or Huntland, but no one happened to mention that we were part of the public who was entitled to use this "Public Library." Any moment I could find after I got homework done between classes or when it was official Study Hall time, that is when I set out on my evil quest of reading and memorizing—for me and for this boy on Sewanee Mountain, whom we must agree was a darned saint to take calls almost daily from a desperate girl hiding from her mother in the hallway. Mother liked to gather garden gifts and to wander at the pasture's edge now and again, so to the phone I would go, and there I had the greatest boyfriend imaginable. I could see him in my heart as we talked about our latest classes and the reading—our common bond over those many months of chatting and even sometimes laughing together.

If he asked me what I was up to I would bring up something about my family that lived far away, and how I really had more of a connection with Chicago, Illinois, because my daddy used to work there for so many years before returning to the farm. I was even fairly adept at putting on the Chicago accent after having listened to my sister-in-law who was a pretentious loon. On those clear nights when the Chicago radio stations made their way all the way to our corner of the world with their great power then I would learn about the goings-on in Peoria, or Gary, Indiana, what the teenagers were dancing to, and who was winning in sports around that section of the Midwest, so I could even bring that into my repertoire now and again. Scot must have been somewhat confused, but he accepted that I might be a little different from the other girls in the valley below. I had no idea that if he ever came to our place, then I would be outted for the Appalachian country girl I was. It was definitely a *carpe diem* life I was living, and it gave me some reason to want to carry on. I guess that I was really a fraud, but when you are desperate to find a love, even if it is just a voice on a black rotary phone, fraud seemed a small crime to commit. I was fairly lucky to be able to pull the whole thing off. Once Mama came in with her turnip greens or having watered our faithful dogs. Then I just said, "Time to study, Scot," He'd agree, and we would go away until I phoned him again.

Now and then he might mention that we had to get together, but I just left it there and enjoyed the words. "We have to get together, indeed." I would hold myself really tightly to bring into me this secret love as if it was really going to happen. As I look back over everything that would transpire over the years to come maybe he let a girl get away who might have been worthy had he been able to see past our place at no where's end and my impoverishment. That just did not happen to girls from Lexie Crossroads, and I knew it certainly was not my time just then.

I wouldn't have known him from the Holy Spirit had he tapped me on the shoulder. I did not know until a few years later that the phone line was my comfort zone, for no matter how horrid my existence, I became the antithesis of myself on that telephone, and best of all, I could hide the tremors which I had developed. Why were they getting worse? Was it the rocks which caught my head sometimes as Mama flung them without regard to where they were going to land, or was it the whacks with stow wood (stove wood), which all the neighbors and my family always were either gathering or stacking or using as weapons What do you think? It occurs to me that terror and tremors are too very similar words and to have twenty miles as a safe zone between this and my true love made a safe place to hide both.

I think that Mama may have sometimes listened in on the phone calls, for there was logic to her curiosity. Though she had decided to make me her recipient of all the madness which came with her thyroid disease and the menopause which was kicking in, as a point of logic she pretty much knew that if I got married young, then she would have a daughter to act crazed with just like her own mother. She would have me for the rest of my life no matter who the boy was. Gracious Lord. Possibly the cruelest thing a mother could wish on her child was the early marriage. Marital bliss was a fraud but most Appalachian girls fell for it because it was the only way to soothe that unholy ache which came to all, for nature planted the seeds of procreation.

Some are luckier now and find exemplary spouses while others still see their only role as to follow the past. A lot of girls sleep around just like all other teenagers across these United States and are able to keep it hidden from the mamas because birth control is available at the corner stores. What is so ghastly upsetting to me is that these girls have become like inner-city girls in that they think a baby is supposed to fix all things, so now they are not only stuck with the need to marry early as seen appropriate by their elders, they are having babies at a rate which exceeds or at least which matches national trends only with fewer support systems. "A woman's place is the home," says the country pastor, and that is accepted as truth while the Bible is smacked to emphasize this point.

The female abuse has become even more dangerous in quality and quantity, and my hope for them is that more mental health care is available if the women will reach out and ask for such. Silence remains the prevailing code, and there they suffer in silence, and the boys on the mountain aren't as generous with the small talk. Shades of hope have become obscured by the trash which lines roadsides, the rusted old trailers on the back roads, and even the decline in church attendance as younger couples unless they are bonded with parents decide it just isn't worth their time. The WWII daddies have died off, and crops are few and far between, and I have not seen a field of crimson clover in a very long time.

The theme of Dolly Parton lyrics like "We might not of had much in our house, but there was always love," was more or less the basis of old country music which still plays even as the women go about their days dragging one more smoke if they can afford it, one more sip of cheap wine available in every store, and wishing like hell that they were anyplace other than where they are stuck. White southern poverty is even worse now, because they do see people around them who have made better communities in their own places easily overlooking the back roads where evil deeds all stay out of sight. I am so tired of witnessing women and children being impoverished because it is so easy to hide the needy behind the fence of indifference. Again there is a code of silence when it comes to spousal abuse.

Oh, young mothers, if only you could pick up one foot one day, and the other the next. The journey forward will begin with all of you, so let me keep writing this story and hoping that someone comes and takes a look at where America's most hidden sin is found. Poverty is black and white, but if you are a southern white or an impoverished Appalachian lost in the big cities of the north, you are still the easiest people to hide on the face of the earth by virtue of your color. You are assumed to have all it takes to move forward, but I know who you are. I know of your burdens and of your pain, and I'd like for a few more young men and young women to come down from Sewanee Mountain sharing that in this great big country, there are places where love has washed away fear of being a wife and mother. I want you to hear the words that you are beautiful, and Franklin County, Tennessee is a glorious place. A little help and kindness builds bridges even up to mountain tops.

Chapter Twenty Six

Teaching and nursing were thought of as fit jobs for women even when the 1960s brought women out to seek other professions, and though I would finish my education at another time in the realm of things, I am going to risk losing the Laughton/McCovey Silver Bowl for advanced authors, by bringing these two professions into my musings. I would like to think that these thoughts thrown in as I faced career decisions might awaken the hearts of a nation of women who endeavoured to do the best jobs they could, from the time such became noble aspirations for a mother's daughter. It seems early to talk about my career choice, since my personal story is a long way from completion, but I owe something to both nursing and teaching, so maybe it is appropriate to share my abiding respect which lingers for both.

Only when I reached high school, would I come to know men as instructors, for teaching was a shelter for women through the years, while men went out and became the auto and steel industry workers with high pay and good unions. Or they would become the academics, the lawyers, the doctors, and the professors. Women's rights pressed heavily from the mid 1960s through the 1980s and 90s, and even after the millennial change, women would still be struggling for equal pay for equal hours worked. Professional women are returning to some of the old home places, and they are coming home burned out and tired in far too many cases.

I saw as a nurse who went the academic route through a university, that no matter where I went, men as nurses would progress faster, usually be promoted first, and the minute they walked into the room, they had to convince the patients that they were not a physician. Perhaps a more highly trained and skilled nurse could walk in the same room with ten very important things which she needed to do for a patient. The male nurse was apt to get a smile and a female of higher training would hear, "Mother said that her lunch today was not hot enough. And I wish that you would just look at that light fixture! Do you ever dust around this place, and while you are at it, we think Mom would really feel better if you finished with her medications and massaged her right arm."

It isn't that as women we did not care about the right arm, not to mention the dust balls hanging from the light fixture, but it was not unusual to have five other patients waiting for their medications at the same time and no one presumed that we had gotten beyond technical school status, which I say with deepest respect, for the greatest tips I ever received usually came from a sage and kind LPNs. Nursing was coming in to my mind just in case I needed a backup plan for Elvis's discovery of me as he drove through Lexie Crossroads, and in case I could not write a nice letter and get a scholarship from George Washington or Vanderbilt, because I did not know much of another way of getting in to a great college and university program. I shall leave it as a mystery of what I would become, but I will give you this glance in to what I thought might be another place to save the world as I planned my career, thinking I was going to be a spinster at the age of 15 and 16.

I have long lamented that long fuzzy disposable handled fluffy extension dusters were not something we knew much about before I left my life as a nurse, for I could have made stethoscope, dust busters, and handy wipe-away gift goody bags for nurse graduation presents, and even throw in some butt paste for that itch that a person could no longer scratch until a nurse got in the room. Never mind that hospitals do have housekeeping departments. Among the stupidest things hospitals ever did was to get rid of most orderlies, to have on-call with housekeeping services 24 hours a day not to mention around the clock technical nurses who could do tasks like bathing, massaging, and all of the things which can be easily done by a non-university or technical school graduates fully capable of doing tech chores which in no manner required an RN. I place RNs higher on clinical skills than most new college graduate nurses, but a four year nurse from a university program was going to have usually had more pharmacology, anatomy and physiology, psychiatric nurse training, and you would not know the difference unless you asked them, and in most situations, they were not willing to tell you there was any difference. Some of us would immediately begin masters programs from college, people like me, and I found the intense course of physical assessment to equal most starting MDs level of skill, because a nurse had more hands on patient contact.

I came into nursing just as they were taking away jobs such as IV therapist, respiratory therapist, and extra dietary services. Nurses got to be the pick-up for most such jobs which the lower paid technicians could accomplish in a third of the time. They were great! I would suggest that any time you see a student nurse coming at you to start an IV, it is probably a pretty good point of advice to ask for at least a trained nurse. Most of us are not as good as the IV therapists were at getting them in, but if you do not like needles, grab your arm and protest. Med tech jobs saved time and were respected.

What should a good nurse RN be capable of doing? I would answer you that she should probably know what your medications are and see that you get them in the way they are prescribed. She or he should be able to keep up with all the doctor's orders as soon as possible and make the necessary calls to physicians who are too stupid to leave standing orders for medications which every other patient needs, antiemetic, anti-anxiety agents, sleep medications, laxatives, or whatever it takes to keep a patient comfortable during a hospital stay. A nurse needs to examine a patient, for there are many things which happen when the physicians are not in the house. There is always a need for grief counseling, hand-holding, constant explanations for changes in a client's care, not to mention keeping up with the as-needed medications such as pain meds, using good judgment about insulin, nitroglycerine, and certain pertinent bedside meds which have been prescribed for particular patients. I could go on ad nauseum about fields that have all but disappeared, but I believe that I have touched upon such fields here, and I would applaud a public who would ask for nurses to be allowed to be the professionals they are. Never has there been a genuine shortage of nurses, but it is more like women and some men realize that we have been unable to educate the public to the idea that we have a high level of training which is misused by hospital administrators who do not have the courage to protect a female dominated profession. When there is a nursing shortage you see coverage by nurses from other countries who can speak some English, and our pay sounds high within their homeland, and then folks get the ads about how much nurses are respected all ready to burn out a new crop of females and some males who gave it their best until it became too overwhelming to take up the slack of other disciplines, not to mention wiping off the cobwebs after you finished housekeeping and bath chores

To younger nurses who have grown up with computers, computer charting was seen as a no-brainer, but as I have watched these same nurses in hospital settings, I still see hand-charting having to be accomplished and for everyone who wants a fully electronic medical system of charting for the medical system, my recommendation to you is to keep your own chart, or have a family member keep a written chart for everything that happens to you within a hospital setting. If hackers can get into National Security Systems, then God help our souls when computers go down or when med dispensary equipment fails.

Nurses in smaller communities have an even harder ladder to climb. I can just see young boys in hysterics as they sit in the quiet of their own computer-savvy worlds giving Grandma with end-stage coronary artery disease a few whopping doses of Mr. Jones's Viagra. Please, for so ever long as there are electronics, and high technical equipment, there is also going to be some brainiac out there who can figure out how to break the codes. How many times do you hear of such hacking going on and have we not seen our country almost brought to its breaking point financially by greed more than once in our history by man's ability to reset how things look on paper to make things look so very real? Rural communities are desperate for more doctors and nurses who understand their ways. How about more medical school scholarships based on giving no less than five years of service in a rural community in return for one medical school education?

Now that I have gotten it off my chest how important highly trained nurses and their former support job holders are and were, then let me go on to the people who changed my life, who kept me up when all else failed me, and who are directly responsible and cherished by me as the arbiters of where any great society shall go. Teachers seem more apt to understand that they are heroes in a country and off the expressway school.

My earliest teacher probably had to have a hand-crafted double coffin, for I never saw her weigh less than 400 pounds. She was so wicked that I would virtually believe that the devil himself wouldn't want her in hell. We called her our favorite name for such old bats, the Old Battle Axe. She classed children, felt free to make fun of our clothes, our hair, sat us in the classroom according to whether or not she wanted your parents' influence, and purposefully made fun of children in front of the entire class if they had a lisp, or eyes that were crossed, or were crying for their mothers.

She would use the paddle most days, a real wooden paddle, on little children, then that child went around the rest of the day with wet pants, for their immediate reaction to this witch of blubber was that they were so afraid of her and that paddle that she used with such vengeance that little kids simply wet their pants once she made them bend over. And the parents let her get away with it. Most folks didn't have a way to school unless they walked about a mile to catch a bus which we did, or someone gave them a ride, and, if you can imagine this, some families in our area only had a mule or two if they were lucky to pull a wagon and plough—not to mention, parents just did not interfere at school. Most of the parents had been kept home in the fields as children, and it was only our generation in which going to school became mandatory, though even then some parents would just send their kids now and again. I have to get past telling you about this horrible old bat to get on to tell you that teachers with a soul put themselves out for ridicule and for strife by trying to help children who were so impoverished. They were the first people to look at me with eyes that said, "Something doesn't fit with this child," and we can't fix it, but somehow and some way we are going to help her.

An anomaly to me, too, is that so many of the ones who did their best to help were childless themselves or had very small families. A form of birth control which has not been experienced by most adults is to put them in a classroom full of students for a week. I would be the first to vote that every parent who sends a child to school should be required to spend one week in a classroom to observe what teachers are doing in reality—managing to keep a classroom of twenty-five children quiet and teaching them the manners their parents just couldn't abide forcing their little sweethearts into obeying, like sharing and having a meal together. People come and scream at teachers because they do not recognize the special qualities of their little brilliant kids, always the brightest child in the classroom or the most special of the other twenty-five brightest and special children, and they expect that that teacher has some magic brew of how to isolate that one child and give them all the special attention which they get at home. It is apparent to me that most people who agree to be teachers probably have some sadistic nature toward themselves or they would never decide to accept such a profession where the parents are expecting miracles for Jane and Junior which no mortal could possibly pull out of a basket of tricks.

The role models my teachers would become would follow me for a lifetime, and many of them I kept in touch with until they were elderly, so elderly that they could not hear the words of thanks and appreciation which filled my heart and on through several other generations of children whose lives would become their mission. It all began at home with one idea—that teachers are special people and if you upset them then you offend us and count on knowing that if you cannot listen you will pay at home! Meet my other angels, the school teachers of Huntland School who deserved all of my respect and admiration. Angels, not mortals, sign report cards.

I have just described to you what teaching would be about when my children came along. Public education lost the cord to home life, and now it is a "Once upon a time" story. The parents in the country and in the city disappeared, and only the elderly realized that schools were for education, not babysitting.

Many parents just gave up on parenting, because they were entrusted no more with disciplining at home. No, children did not need to be beaten, but to respect an adult and to learn does need to begin at home. If parents need lessons on how, then get out a few more specially trained health nurses. They saved our lives. Thank God Mama is not here to listen to me say as much.

Chapter Twenty Seven

My last four years as a girl beneath the shadows of the southern Appalachians, which could be seen from some of what used to be our land that Dad deforested for cotton fields and for pasture land for his small herd of cattle, would best be described someday as intolerable and not compatible for human existence. I was dealing with growing up, trying to keep up with school and being sent off as a maid on the weekends from Friday evening through Sunday afternoon. For the grand total of ten dollars I was sent off to be someone's slave. It was usually for my Auntie Carol. She wanted me as often as possible, for I cooked, I cleaned, and I took care of her four children who probably did not ever realize that my mother was their father's eldest sister.

Auntie Carol relished her role as the town doctor's wife and had she lived in the Martha Stewart era, she would have considered herself a chef par excellence, and I was the maid. One of her favorites, as far as cooking, was to plaster every counter with whatever pastry making and baking she was doing and coming out with something which resembled bread, cake, or pie, then calling me in to clean up after her. I can clean a counter which has been despicably trashed because I lived with Auntie Carol. My dear uncle was stupid enough to marry the class blond before he got out of medical school. Neither of them was stupid, but they were careless enough to have two children prior to medical college's end much to Grandmother Hood's delight. The other two would be born after he was established in practice, and their mother immediately stuffed their brains with some sense of self-importance. I was the nasty poison ivy growing along their wonderful and learned oak tree bodies.

At one point Auntie had promised me that she would teach me how to cook as she did, and Lord help me! That caused an immediate ache within my heart after she said it, for we did not have enough dogs back at our house to lick up the messes she made for me. I do believe that the one thing that woman taught me of value was to use a paper towel to grease a pan instead of a pastry brush. I did not know what a pastry brush was then, and we couldn't afford paper towels, but to this day, I will even spread olive or truffle oil on a pan with a paper towel, for I do not like to feel oil on my fingers unless it is for intimate purposes.

I worked hard there, and when I got home on Sunday evening, I still had Mama's dishes left to do, and then I began to think about the four a.m. beating that was the optimal choice to begin a new week of being awakened to clean our house and to chase my brother James down from running near the pond where he was apt to pick up a rattlesnake. I will add here that my brother could have been a snake charmer, for he just thought they were any old toy, and if he picked one up, the snake would just kind of look at him stupidly as if to say, "I do not know what this fool is doing, but let me slither out of here before I find out!" Oh yes, my weeks began as they ended, in servitude at home with Mama coming at me with something to beat the hell out of me for things which she got stuck in her mind that made absolutely no sense.

"I know you've been thinking about them old love songs again," and I did not know exactly how to fix such blatant accusations, but I would take the beating at the time. One of the ones she despised was "Love Me Tender." She thought that Elvis's voice brought on convulsions of sexual pleasure within me. Again, I would take to singing "Sweet Hour of Prayer" at the top of my lungs just to drown her voice out. Mother never just screamed, she shrieked, and somewhere I was going to have to take a stand, for the bruises were mounting.

One day Aunt Carol's middle son was sitting and watching Saturday morning cartoons and decided to give his baby brother a candy bar. I was running around doing my usual chores for Auntie and my uncle were having a wild game party that night. They were going to have pheasants to eat and the greats in town were invited to dinner including the lousy surgeon who would eventually sew my mother up with surgical sponges left in her leading to years of suffering. There was to be bear, deer, wild turkey, and I saw the baked Alaska, and I knew I'd be cleaning this one up the next weekend. I was sent to the nursery after I had done all of my work to prepare for her dinner and I was hungry, the babies were unhappy, and I could hear all the frolic outside. At times I found my face wet with tears. It became late in the evening, and the little baby boy woke up nauseous and covered in his own excrement which kept coming no matter how much I cleaned and carried, walked and cried, prayed and shuddered, for I did not know what to do then.

On one occasion, I could have used Mama there to smack them around with a stick or to shriek like a hyena. I had to tell them, "The baby is sick. I need help." The baby was the only person to whom I felt responsible at that moment. I decided this was time for his father. Auntie was highly disturbed that I would come in to their room after they had fallen asleep. They were resting so soundly, that I finally had to pull the covers back and shake them, and for the first time in my life, I would see a man in full erection. My mind was so focused on the baby, though, that I just wished that my brother James was there to grab that snake and get it out of the room. I finally got my uncle awake, but the baby began to quiet then.

I did not know that I had already done all that they could do outside of start an intravenous infusion to do fluid replacement. I fear that was not part of my medical knowledge at the time. My uncle was very kind. He reassured me that it was good that I had awakened him, and I went back to the nursery where I had a bed to sleep near the smallest children. It made no difference that I never ate, for all appetite had subsided, and in anyone's house, no matter how many times I had been there, I was afraid to do anything for myself, even to eat from the plates left on the table for me to clean come early morning. I feared from Auntie's scowl that I had committed a horrible sin, but it was not my choice to see naked people. I just wanted help for a sick baby.

I slept fretfully, for somehow I knew that I was going to get scolded, even though I had taken care of the situation as best one could. And sure enough, there was Auntie Carol on her broomstick the next morning, blond hair teased, so mad at me that she was calling the optometrist to see if my folks had paid for my latest glasses, so she could have something to shame me with.

There was an admission in early morning that her son Little Davy had given the baby his candy bar from the day before, and beside his chair where Davy watched cartoons, Auntie picked up a wrapper and said, "Do you see this? Weren't you watching the child?"

I said, "Yes, ma'am," but I was in the next room doing the dishes—shoveling up the crud was more to the point—and I figured it was alright for the babies at eighteen months and about three years of age to watch cartoons with their ten- and twelve-year-old brothers. The eldest was only about two years younger than I was!

She then threw the foil toward me and screeched, "You tried to kill my baby, and here is the evidence."

I took one look and I knew that her vacant-looking son Davy had given his little brother an entire package of foil-wrapped Ex-Lax, and I simply trembled. I asked her, "How could I have possibly done your work and been responsible for an older child being so stuck on Porky Pig that I could have stopped him from giving the child Ex-Lax?" She raged at me. "Your parents haven't paid the eye doctor for those glasses yet and you said they had and now you've tried to kill my baby. You are nothing but a lying little witch, so you just get back to the kitchen and get yourself working, and nothing like this better happen again!"

Rage. I felt it myself, and this time I did call home and I told Mother that even if I had to walk twenty miles, I was coming home, but could she send someone after me instead and Mama did. Everyone in the community knew Auntie as a nut case who had actually gotten into the College Conservatory of Music in Cincinnati by being a privileged Huntland, Tennessee, girl but rather than finish past a first year, she and my uncle got married just in time for him to finish college, go to medical school at UT-Memphis, and have four kids in the process. Auntie's lunatic parents cared for her as if she were a crown jewel, and back in those parts, a physician's wife really did not have to do anything. They were our community's rock stars.

Granny Hood and my sorry Grandpa Jim kept them supplied with meat and vegetables and took care of all holidays. Woodrow's elder brothers saw that he and his family had housing covered, furniture, clothes for the kids, and everything else they needed. No, they could not help their eldest sister, Mama, in any way, and we could starve, but by God their brother was going to be the town doctor, and Auntie Carol was going to be Mrs. Franklin County. Her one year at the conservatory made her an expert in piano and voice which she was always practicing or trying to teach one of her kids. Sometimes I amuse myself still with the realization that she taught none of them anything except for piano and show tunes popular from the 1940s which was the only music she knew. Was I ever relieved when "Moon River" became popular, for at least she was not bellowing out the World War II marching songs or old Doris Day revues. When she wasn't singing, she was carrying on about her menses or down on her back from something really strenuous like the year she decided to decorate her Christmas tree with great big red bows and all big red glass balls, and I returned home quite amazed that she did not have fruit jar lids with little Christmas card pictures stuck to them like the ones we would make for decorations. Decoration for us was one string of lights we put on even after they burned out.

I left there hurt, though, because if someone told me I was a failure and then brought my parents into it, I could do nothing but believe them. I even left without my ten bucks, and it was almost evening Saturday when I got back home, but Auntie C. had made a mistake, for she had pissed off Mama. Mother knew her well enough to know that she had trashed our family, so I would never go there again. Instead, Mom started sending me just about anywhere in the county to pick up my weekend maid service.

I was amazed to see that there were other people with good hearts, people who would wonder about the girl who worked so hard, yet trembled much of the time until she was comfortable with them. I would even wind up going to houses where people would be ashamed by the end of the weekend that they had accepted help from such a child. The best couple were Brother Jimmy and his wife Martha Jean Walker. I had known

Brother Jimmy as a pastor and his wife Martha kept up with me until early adulthood. Brother Jimmy taught history at our high school, too, so I got to see him in the classroom, and he was always very chatty, very kind, and the only man I ever knew who could have doubled as Clark Gable on a *Gone With The Wind* movie stage.

Mrs. Walker did not let me work hard, and she let me sleep until six in the morning at least, and I just had to care for the kids a little bit. They were recovering from a family tragedy where a little boy of theirs found Drano under the sink and had done his esophagus in, and I wanted to help them so much. Though they had a house full of boys, I found out they wanted to adopt a little girl. My heart broke, for I wanted to ask, "Would you adopt me, would you just let me live with you and adopt me? I don't need ten dollars for a weekend's work and I can go without school lunch, but if you will just take me and love me, then I will be your girl until the end of time." But the words would not come. They were stuck in the back of my heart, for no one could ever want a girl like me, not then, not ever.

It was people like this, though, who lifted me up—rare angels who would smile at me and thank me for being there. Now that I look back at them, I do believe that I might could have found a home there and I could have been a big sister, lived near Mama and Daddy, and they might have let me, because I would have been a preacher's girl and that counted for something then. I did not know though what my little brothers and sister would do, and I knew that my lot was to finish out life at Huntland High School or to simply die trying. I can tell you that by then I would walk past a mirror and instead of seeing a girl who had fair skin, a trim body that had begun to blossom, and who was certainly competing with the smartest kids in class, all I saw was some kind of faceless ghoul. The mirror was witness to everything I thought about myself, that I was so ugly no one could ever love me. That the bruises on my body were deserved because I was some kind of sin-filled monster who had on occasion begun to dream about other boys, not just the boy without a face on the phone, and to think such thoughts left me bound for hell.

Mama needed to beat more sense into me until my flesh would tear, and she accommodated that wish everyday as she did without her thyroxin or any kind hormonal replacement therapy since for women of her era such therapy was simply not there, especially back in the country. I could not look in that mirror by the end of it all, for it would burn with the intensity of the dissatisfaction of the soul looking back at me. Everything and everyone possessed beauty except for me. And it was going to be that way for the rest of my life. Just about all of Auntie's family, including herself, would wind up in drug or alcohol rehab at one time or the other. The last time I saw her she looked like Elizabeth Taylor's maddest version of *Who's Afraid of Virginia Woolf?* Try as I may, the only sorrow which I could ever feel for her or for any of her family was that they actually started out with possibilities and here they were with their mother, the madwoman looking as evil as her heart had allowed her to be. The children did well enough for themselves, all but the youngest and most charming who gave over his life to his family's curse of addictions. That little baby that I rocked and held for at least a couple of years never made it beyond young adulthood before he was hooked, and I wonder about the morning his brother fed him the chocolate laxatives and whether he had brain damage that night from lack of fluids. How could I have made a difference in their lives? The faceless girl was always trying to fix everyone, and someday she would begin on herself and maybe she would find out that she was as lovable as the bear-skins that were taken as tokens from the big hunter's wild game party nights. "Lovable." I did not know the word, but I knew the feeling, for now and then an angel or two would pass by. You will probably not recognize your angels either until after glow burns them into the yesterday of memory, for angels do not ask for reward for themselves and they serve like soft mittens on cold hands just to soothe, to comfort, and then to rescue.

Chapter Twenty Eight

A best friend is something every child should be able to experience, just like my friendship with Betty Ruth Larkin whose family my mother despised because it was a distraction from my chores at home and took me away from friends that she thought were more suitable, such as the girls more apt to stick it out around Lexie Crossroads. Besides that, they only went to The Church of Christ now and then. Mama disliked them for that reason alone. Mr. Augustus Larkin and Mrs. Ruth tried to protect me any way they possibly could, and if I had an important school or 4-H project or if I had an appointment at Vanderbilt for my eye, they took care of seeing that it happened. With their help and friendship, I would look almost like a normal girl when I graduated except for the stupid glasses which I chose to wear at the time. When it comes down to truths, these were the people who were the ultimate angels, and they flew close to the ground and were willing to pick the child that was me up out of the dirt and they helped me accomplish as much as I possibly could as if I were their own daughter. Whatever I won or did was not resented by them or by Betty. It complimented their endeavors, for I was their protégé and they applauded me every step of the way.

Through the years I will never in this life be able to show them just how much it meant to me. By the end of my senior year, these are a few of the merits which I had achieved with their loving help. I edited both my high school yearbook and the school newspaper where I could write anything I wanted much to my delight, as long as it was decent. Having found a newspaper on the floor which Mama used to protect her linoleum, I saw something called "Letters To The Editor" in the *Nashville Banner*, so over the high school year more than once I had little letters or poems published in what I did not know at the time was a paper that went to the White House as a state paper for all of Tennessee. I thought that anybody who wrote something got it printed and had no idea the scope of their readership.

Every year that I could remember, as did my sisters, I had poems published in The National High School Anthology, and that was an honor back then. It made Miss Nell Baker so proud of me and she would say, "You are going to be somebody when you grow up." Betty Ruth and I both would be given the highest awards one can receive in state 4-H. The camp was in East Tennessee and had once served as a German Prisoner of War camp. I cried as I marched in that processional, for I knew that everything I had done in 4-H had required a pint of blood given as an extra workload at home, for Mama would occasionally let me go with the Larkins to the meetings but only if I worked myself to the bone for about three weeks in order to get the privilege to stay over at Betty's folks place. It helped, too, that every time I won something it would appear in our little *Winchester Chronicle*, and Mama and Daddy sort of liked seeing our names in the paper for it would always read "Barbara Ellen Everett, daughter of Mr. and Mrs. A.O. Everett of Lexie Crossroads."

They would allow me to go to 4-H camp when I won the right to do so through public speaking, what would now be called motivational speaking, contests. It was beautiful up in McMinville, Tennessee, and at the camp was something which I pray that no one has torn down. There was a recreation hall or gym for the prisoners, and the prisoners of war had painted each wall from floor to ceiling with pictures of their Rhineland. You could almost walk into the pictures, as if they were some kind of magical gateway into a homeland left behind. I do not even think any of us knew what a piece of history this represented in the very place we were learning square dances and doing cane-jumping in. That I could learn either seems quite improbable at this point in my life, but youth was a time when I pushed myself to the limit and hoped to come out minimally sane on the other side.

When Betty and I organized the first junior-senior prom that we'd ever had at Huntland High School during our lifetime, we finally got to meet our Sewanee Mountain college boys. They played rock music, and we were able to come up with the donations in dollars and pennies to pay their fee for the evening. My Scot and Betty's Mark must have thought they had landed in total skidsville when they came in and saw the bunch of us. I did not even know what a prom dress was and I guess you can say that I accidentally dressed up in my best business attire, for I remember a vest, a skirt, and a decent pair of shoes. I did not see anyone other than our young men who we would see that once and never see again, even though I think we called them until we all graduated.

I wanted to look official, somehow, and had no idea that across this nation impoverished girls were helped to dress for one night to feel beautiful, for their senior prom, if nothing else. In that regard, I think that Betty was about equally as naive. There must not have been many good prom scenes from our old TV shows or we would have known better. Worse, I did not know that it was a mutually accepted thing that you were apt to have a date and maybe even make out a little in this rite of passage! But we accomplished seeing "Prom Night" as a yearly ritual partially to see the faces of the boys we phoned, and they were more handsome than the voices ever could have shown. And I wish that I could tell you if the prom continues to flourish, but I haven't asked, even when I was invited back to Huntland High to be keynote speaker at their alumni banquet and dance. The event is recorded for posterity in our graduation yearbook.

I also tied with Johnny Williams, a nice scholarly boy, for a senior academic merit award, but Johnny got the one medal shipped in and I had to wait for one to come in the mail. The DAR would give me what was then probably the most special title a senior girl could get, and that was their Citizenship Award. The day I heard that news, I almost fainted. Me, crazy, shaky, Barbara Everett, had been voted to receive the award for the senior class girl of 1966. I wrote a peace essay on a whim, entered it in a contest, and got a check for fifty dollars, a ribbon, and another medal and all of this was happening at the end of my school life, because one family cared for me. I had no idea that anyone outside of Miss Nell knew that I had a brain in my head, and all the 4-H awards were an amalgamation of all of the work that I had put in to hiding it from Mama with Mr. and Mrs. Larkin helping me on the side. No one told us how to apply for college, but I was just going to write letters.

My number-one goal had been to enter Vanderbilt in pre-med but no one had advised me that you do not get into Vandy without lots of credentials or without going to some high school where your chemistry teacher is not accredited to teach agriculture nor that there was also a legacy policy. A man came through one day, though, and I was called to the principal's office to be interviewed about college, and the worst of the worst shakes set in. My voice could only tremble, but he told me who he was, a worker from the Tennessee Department of Vocational Rehabilitation. He said the principal was worried and he was worried because I seemed to have a nervous problem. In this case with all of my awards and good grades, he said it wasn't a bad thing, but he wanted me to see a special doctor in Chattanooga, and Mama and Daddy let me go, probably with Mr. and Mrs. Larkin.

I did not know then what the special doctor was, but he determined that I did indeed have a nerve problem, and I should get some help for college. I had to repress the urge to say, "You son of a bitch. I would like for you to live my life and you would know that maybe I don't have quite the 'nerve' problem you are speaking of. I want you to go and live in my shoes for a few weeks and see if your sorry ass is still standing." Through all of this, I was continuing my maid service and running after all the kids for Mama, and the beatings were only stopped when I threatened her with a butcher's knife a year or so before I left home. I did not know what psychiatry really involved, but if it would help me go to college, heck, I would give it a go.

Next thing I knew, Middle Tennessee State University was giving me grant money because I guess I looked pretty darned good on paper. Betty Ruth would be going there, too, but her mama had told her to broaden her scope of friends. She was my best friend! There was one thing left to do before I left for Murfreesboro and that was graduation which began with commencement Sunday.

On this day the word of God was preached especially for graduating seniors right there in a public school building, and Mr. Homer Laws, our principal, usually was able to come up with a fairly good speaker. I would sing with the glee club both at commencement and at graduation, another activity which I fit in my busy school schedule. Mr. Jimmy Walker, our director, was so fond of "The Bells of Saint Mary's" that it was sung every year and it was so sweet that everyone would tear up just a little bit for we were disappearing into another part of life out into the seas of being where we had never swum before.

We would sing hymns like "Amazing Grace" and the alma mater of our school, and no program was complete without the patriotic songs like "America the Beautiful." For a school choir, we weren't bad. Then we would march in as Miss Nell played "Pomp and Circumstance" and every heart was full, so very full, and I do not think we really understood why. The ladies of the community would have hauled out the old school vases which were filled with snowballs, Tennessee purple iris, and roses, and the smell was so sweet and fragrant from year to year it was hard to differentiate between graduation and a funeral. We wore the caps and gowns of ages past, the blue and the gold, and we would give the tassels to our mothers and fathers. I think I received my first carnations at these events, and as we marched out, some of my school angels came up and gave Betty and me special little gifts.

Miss Marjorie Kennedy, our business education teacher, Miss Nell Baker, and Mr. Kenneth LaFever's who had chosen me to teach an afternoon class of kids who needed a little extra help all came and gave their good wishes. The kids I had taught gave me almost six dollars in dimes and quarters they had collected and tied into a handkerchief, so by then I was simply weeping. When we processed outside, I looked around at my classmates, and I probably looked very vacant, for all that I could think of was that in my own way I loved them all.

I'd never dated any of the boys, for I was the good girl, the extra-good girl. I thought that all of the girls and boys would be married in a year or two, and I knew that there were a couple of girls rumored to be pregnant at the time, but these were the home kids, even the kids whom I considered to be privileged. I realized that we were never in our lives ever going to repeat these special days together, that I would remember their faces, though not their names, as the years passed by. That we had all been young, maybe stupid, and perhaps a little too harsh to one another at times. For a while, I just felt the deepest sadness that anyone could have felt.

Out of the blue, Mama threw a dress at me and said, "It's new and it cost me twelve dollars at Hammers." Honest to God, the woman threw it at me, and I somehow caught a white dress with little green roses as she went on to say that she had even taken it off the rack, not out of the bins, which was big-doings back in our area. I thanked her, but Mama knew that I was leaving her for good, for I had told her that I wasn't coming back.

Graduation day passed, and with the forty dollars I had received total, I bought what they said I needed for college and arrived in Murfreesboro with my white dress with the little green roses which I knew was a color Mother loved, and if I do say so myself, I looked pretty good. Dad never said much, but as the awards kept coming during the weeks before graduation and the pictures of me were plastered in the paper, the yearbook, and announced on some radio programs I would see him smile just a little. The day I arrived at MTSU, I declined Dad's offer to give me a little money. With five dollars left in my pocket, I expected to be all right for two weeks—at least until I went to the grocery store for I knew I couldn't afford the cafeteria after one look in there. My daddy was trembling, though, with his hand out, and he gave me the one-armed hug which was all the emotion he could bear, and I knew that I had made him happy. I vowed that I would do so again.

I had turned seventeen near the end of January, and then gone to Murfreesboro in June. I was at college to begin summer school and a journey that would leave me wiser, shaken, worried, and unable to stand straight at times, but for that moment it seemed as if all things were going to go well. I had left my mark at Huntland High School. Let us say we all left a mark, for we were among the last classes just before drugs hit Franklin County. I did not realize my classmates who were boys would be enlisting to fight a war, and I did not realize that Dad would get himself saved at sixty years of age, changing the context of how our house was run, but here I was standing in a parking lot looking at the rest of my life before me.

In spite of everything I'd accomplished on the wings of my angels, I would leave high school feeling like I was the ugliest girl in school, for I had never won one beauty contest, had never been homecoming queen or one of the court, and beauty seemed to begin as a mark of the culture with baby beauty contests on, so this girl had failed to achieve the pinnacle of high school endeavors. Someday I would know that academics and a golden heart were far greater than the beauty of the homecoming queens, and that I might even be more attractive than I realized, but for now, I was just a kid who was given divine graces, and they would go with me. I would have no idea how, but somehow I would not disappoint those who dared to believe that I was worthy of their time.

> Rose, Violet and I all left and for the first time since the war years, Mama and Daddy were going to be left home with younger kids. Now who was going to chase James down when he hurled song books, trying to shut up Preacher while Mama cried? Who was going to get Bill and Linda off to school and leave our house clean, much less take care of dinner with Mama still in public works? I could only ask, weep a little longer and conclude that we all had to make it on our own somehow.

DAD AND UNCLE HOMER WITH HUNTING DOGS – ALABAMA

Dad and Mule – Alabama

Dad with Both Mules and a Thrasher – Alabama

Dad (kneeling) and Uncle Homer – Alabama

Paternal Grandmother Barbara Ellen Durham

Grandmothers Myrtle Hood and Barbara Ellen Durham visiting in Tennessee

Mother and Uncle Robert – War Years

Robert Hood, Thelma Hood (my mother) and Ralph Hood – Raccoon Valley, TN

Mother in her new kitchen – Tennessee

Thelma, Arbutus, Annie Ruth, and Doyle Hood

THE FIRST HOUSE IN TENNESSEE

END OF MASON EVERETT ROAD TN

Chapter Twenty Nine

I think that I was paralyzed for a few minutes after Mom and Dad, the brothers, and my sister drove away. We had gotten my few worldly possessions up to my dorm room which was a three- to four-stair walk-up I would be sharing with a girl from Winchester who was from one of the better-off families who'd sent their children to college if for no other reason than to find themselves a proper mate.

In fact, the mother repeated this two or three times, "Now remember, honey, we are sending you here to find yourself a nice husband." Then the woman kept repeating it as if her daughter was a deaf mute.

Finally the girl responded, "Yes, Mama. I know."

I sat on my bed with watchful eyes as this pretty girl and her mom unpacked, and the mother would look at me for validation of the need to have worked your ass off in high school to come this far to find yourself a husband, and she asked me, "That's what you are here for, isn't it?"

And as a good southern girl must at a few months past my seventeenth birthday, I said, lying through my teeth, "Why, yes, ma'am." I wasn't about to tell her that I had really wanted to go to Vanderbilt Medical School now that I was made aware that no decent girl desired a college education when she could find some man that would take care of her and her mama.

The room got stuffy, and my roommate was so cute and perky—nice to a fault, in other words—probably in shock after seeing this hayseed of a girl roommate with her mother's Bible as the one thing I brought from home without permission. After all, I was here to save the Methodists, Baptists, and Presbyterians from the fires of hell, so when they opened up their hearts to the New Testament Christians of The Church of Christ, I had to have Bible in hand to validate my every need to educate these heathens, or "heatherns," as we knew them. I walked down the steps having already realized that Daddy had at least weakened my lungs with his cigarettes, for as strong as I was in the field, climbing stairs left me breathless day in and day out.

Going outside in Murfreesboro on this early evening in June, I saw a fellow who appeared older than me, and he had a buddy as a cohort, and he began to talk to me. I wish that I had known then the smart answer "You talkin' to me, fool?" But he was suave and began to say what a great day it was when the freshman girls got in to town.

He said things like "You are always so fresh and pretty, and I just like to check you all out first," and "Lucky me, the first one I meet is a pretty girl like you." I looked around to see if there was the shadow of another female behind me, because the girl in the mirror still had no face, but maybe it was my green-flowered dress that fit just right, the one Mama had given me on Commencement Sunday. There was no shadow, and he was talking to me!

I could feel my voice tremble a little bit, and I was searching for words like "Listen, buddy, I have never talked to a man before, and most of the ones I've met are sorry and no count, and why in the world would you lie so despicably and tell me that a faceless girl is pretty?" Instead, with some stammering, I was able to tell him my name, that I had just arrived, and to ask him a little about himself.

His name was David, and he was finishing a master's degree in political science and, to my amazement, he was twenty-seven years old. He was stationed at AEDC, an Air Force base nearby, and had some rank as an officer because he was a college guy. His buddy was along for the ride on this mission of checking out the incoming freshmen for the dumbest, most naive, and least likely to deny you the privilege of fondling her later in the week.

All of a sudden my head went into a spin, for I was finding that I liked this guy from Natchez, Mississippi, immediately. He seemed smart, and we chatted for a while, and he sort of made it clear that he would be back the next evening. I tried to think of what other piece of clothing I could possibly fit in to. It did not occur to me that those straight-line dresses that I'd made in home economics were going to be nothing but a pack of trouble.

I decided that I would go down the next evening, and, sure as heck, there he was. He had a sweet disposition, took my hand, and we began to walk.

I had never even seen a fancy little sports car before, but he had one, so we began to take drives, and that summer was off to some kind of wonderful start. Holy cow! My roommate was searching for a husband, and as far as I could surmise one was waiting for me the minute I arrived at Middle Tennessee State University. He was suave and slow. Any southern man worth your time is apt to be a little slow in how they approach you, for being unblemished produce, they could see us coming a mile away. They were not going to touch the skin until the young girl was beginning to have feelings she had never had before. Oh yeah, I know that he wasn't Gene Autry or Dr. Kildare. In fact he was just good-looking enough, but I would dream about him in some of the same way I would about the TV boyfriends, and I kept holding his hand a little tighter, and we would walk the summer away in the shady old town near Nashville.

Next, we began to walk with our arms around each other, laughing and talking. He would always tease me about needing to marry his landlady's schizophrenic, somewhat pedophiliac forty-year-old son who was probably still a virgin unless some farm goats had drifted into town a time or two. Once he introduced me to some gal by the name of Rose who said, "And when am I going to see you again, sweet fellow?" And I looked down and realized that she was pretty, and she wore the same silver sort of ballet slippers that the woman who'd died from heart failure back in my old community wore, who was known as the one who serviced the football players' first masculine needs—not that I knew what those needs were—and I got a knot in my stomach, because I knew there were circumstances beyond love which they had shared.

One evening he picked me up in his beautiful car, always a gentleman, and we just drove around that night. I thought that I was out with my man, so things began to escalate into something I was not prepared for. I had on some short skirt, shorter after I got Mom out of sight, and I had bought a blouse that might have been described as sweet, 1960s gauzy and a little open at the neck with some pretty elastic and ribbon at the top, and

I felt good. I did not know that what I felt was absolutely sexy! We got in just in time to avoid my curfew, and David hugged me very tightly, and the street lamps seemed to glow on the top of my shoulders and my skin felt so very warm, a lot warmer than that summer's night. He reached over from the driver's seat, and he began to kiss me, and then to passionately kiss me, and I might have felt a little worried, but David seemed to be a relatively steady boyfriend, so my brain and body left my quaint and untouched self as he began to remove my blouse and Marilyn Monroe style bra away from my breast.

Kisses went down my neck, then I felt him begin to kiss my breast, and my face felt brilliantly flushed with perfect skin next to his hands and to his skin. That was the first time that anyone had ever made me feel beautiful. I was simply a peach fallen from an orchard tree being tasted for the first time.

Yes, his hands went to my thighs, but almost as quickly as it all started, it ended. I am well aware as the years passed that going all the way was not always the goal. It didn't have to be. For some guys like David, they just needed the newness of a fresh body, to conquer it, and that was enough for a while. Guys then, young women, sometimes actually had the decency to understand that you were a virgin. And at age twenty-seven, smart, a grad student and Air Force officer, David was also aware that he could get enough sexually without making babies an issue. He was beginning to bring up the subject of prophylactics, and for the life of me that sounded useless with what I knew would be an impending marriage! As you've wisely concluded, marriage was the last thing on his mind.

The nearest we ever came to actually making love was when he took me to his house with company there, and he led me to something of a den with a couch. He had me lie down, and he again had my brain and body, and this time I wanted him. Per usual, he was able to get along fine just with me as a pretend recipient of all of him, and I began to feel the frustration of a lover. I wanted him big time, and I was going to have my man from Natchez who saw something in this silly little girl from the Appalachian Valley. And then the process of teasing me about his landlady's Chester, the visits to her house where women were not welcome in his quarters increased, and the late summer leaves and early autumn would find me lonely and grieving even if he came around, for I had made a passage into the realization that the lady with the silver slippers got all of him. She knew how, and I didn't, and I would hear from him words that would ring within my ears over the next couple of years, "Barbara, you are such a good girl." This Bible-toting girl longing for genuine sexual and physical contact was too good to be broken, so the essence of my virginity remained intact. Still, I had made the giant leap to lover—only a twenty-seven-year-old guy wasn't buying it.

He now didn't want to see me, and he began staying away, and my heart ached as if I had been beaten worse than I ever had in my entire life. I tried to see him, and I would walk the places we had walked, autumn leaves crunching under my feet, and I was ready to tell him how very much I loved him and how happy we were going to be as the years went forward. I do not hate him to this day, for I know that what he sensed was exactly what was happening. This year's ripe fruit was a serious girl with an attitude, a complex attitude. I would still remain a girl who believed that men like David took the time to love, because they loved you, not for some prurient delight of just getting a girl and changing her to young woman status. I believed boys only were with you if it was alright to look at marriage, to think of babies, to fulfill all that I had been taught about sacred intentions. I had learned nothing from the girls back home, absolutely nothing, and had it not been for some interest in writing and another older guy that was a student teacher, I think I would have been a suicidal nut.

Instead, I began to endeavor to let David go. He would know that I still existed, though, for the next thing I became was a student. I was interested in journalism, and I interviewed people for our school newspaper, and the next thing I knew I had my own column called "The Roving Raider." All of a sudden I was bursting with energy to talk about the differences made between men and women—everything from curfew times which gave guys extra time to get in to the idea that women could accomplish whatever they believed they could with integrity by getting out and demanding it.

I was probably the first woman in the history of Middle Tennessee State University to begin writing about women's rights, my favorite subject for my column, and I have saved the articles to prove what I was doing in 1966 and 1967 before I had ever even heard of the old bra-burners.

My journalism instructor had written for the *Nashville Banner* as a Second World War correspondent and was well known in his circle. Somewhere among the souvenirs of my life is a letter from him telling me what potential I had as a writer, and I treasured it like the Ten Commandments. My GPA shot up for a couple of semesters, and I met Tom, a great-looking guy from Pittsburgh who I would keep in touch with through many years. Tom was acid rain, and I was water vapor in so far as brains, and he was good looking, very handsome, very funny, and he could make me laugh so easily. I would later learn that he stayed just about drunk enough and stoned enough most of the time that he actually didn't remember much of anything about how we met, what we did for one another, or that he even was the catalyst for my knowing when it was time to leave Tennessee, my mountains, my heritage, and—for a while—the God I had grown up with. He was a total atheist, and he slept with any woman who was willing to walk up his apartment steps.

We lived about a block apart, and my precious friend Betty Ruth Larkin had taken his class and told me how much everyone just adored him, his energy, his funny jokes, his abysmal behavior among a very churched group of town folk, and so I went with her and her newfound friends, most of whom had boyfriends from the local funeral home, strangely enough, and I fell in love immediately. The only problem was Tom had zero in the suave southern category. I knew him ten minutes before he asked me to go to bed with him, and he told me about how many dozen others had been in ecstasy between his sheets after he had arrived in Murfreesboro. He introduced me to Bob Dylan records, to books of all kinds, and the existentialists such as Albert Camus.

I hung on to his every word, my hero, and he said, "When one understands Camus fully, then one understands life." I read these depressing books back and forward, tore the seams, and began to become as much like Tom as I could.

He had traveled all over Europe, had been in the service, and had been to New York City to what everyone knew as "The Village" where the 60s art scene was so vibrant. He had great tales of party-crashing and important people he got in to see. He was so full of himself that it simply boiled over and filled me with wanting to be his lover. On the other hand, in the make-out department, he had me figured out already.

"You are a nice girl, but I have a kid in Pittsburgh and I don't want this to happen to you." If we had made love, it would have been because I initiated it, because Tom was a free spirit, and the free spirit wasn't about to get caught up with this "nice girl," so we just visited and talked, and he had the nerve to tell me to just stay away from "that David," for he wasn't anything but a pack of trouble. I think he liked his role as my mentor, and I figured he just wasn't interested in my body. The old "just your mind" scene from plays which could not possibly turn out happy then, had to focus on alienation, and alienated enough meant "sleeping around." It would be another year or so before he would invite me to his bed again.

He kept telling me though, "Go. Just go somewhere, because you are not going to find what you are looking for here." Through the years I would learn that he was essentially a narcissistic SOB who thought that he was on a plane quite a bit higher than the people of our region, and it would take me almost a lifetime to know that I did not need him to justify my spirituality, to make my own way, and to enter the world myself, but if I give him kudos. He was the first person to suggest that maybe there was something about me that needed to be nourished by something outside of a place where a mother would tell a daughter when she entered college, "You know, you are here to find a husband."

My downfall was almost as rapid as my ascent to college life. I still missed David, and I thought that I loved him. I did! It is just that it is true that one abused, broken-hearted girl from Sand Mountain and from Huntland, Tennessee, couldn't tell love from passion. In a way, I never forgave David for he did not even have the decency to give me a proper good-bye when I left after three semesters as my sophomore year was coming to a tragic end. Sometime later I would hear that he went home to marry the girl from Natchez, and I had about begun to believe that if there wasn't someone in their back-home past that they would not go back to, then men were apt to be the stupid young guys whom I had come to detest with their frat-brother mentality, their church group falseness, and their untrained tongues not speaking but slithering back in your throat on the first time out. So I wanted grown-up men, the Davids, the Toms, and men who knew how to gently remove a blouse and love a shoulder, to be gentle, and consider that a young woman might even be more innocent than they could have ever imagined.

I became aware, too, that the boys were disappearing and something was happening called Vietnam. I tell you with sincerity that I earnestly believe that before 1966 and 1967, this war was unknown to a lot of people, and when it was made known the people were not ready. Hadn't life been better without war since the 1950s, and who were these Vietcong? No one wanted this war, but in the end most of us would feel deep shame that we had not supported the young men who fought it. The only woman from my church in Murfreesboro who gave me a sense of being personable, intelligent, and a woman before her time of strong character, for she was a state government employee while most other women stayed home, lost her only son in this war, and I was somewhat of a healing balm to her. She introduced me to a few of his service chums, but most of them were there for a drink, a chat with her, then they were off to the young girls they'd come home to see.

Perhaps one of the better articles I did for our college paper involved the death of her son and the memorial she set up in his memory. I lost her when I went to Washington and decided that I would try Catholicism over my newfound atheistic Albert Camus-types. She was elderly, and she didn't get it. As smart as she was, she was tied to the faith of my fathers and mothers which I could no longer accept as my ultimate truth, and the last letter I would ever receive from her would address this very issue. How could I possibly leave The Church of Christ, she wanted to know. And I couldn't tell her that both David and Tom came from Catholic backgrounds, and another love in my life left the seminary six weeks from ordination because using that explanation was a flimsy excuse. Besides that, when you are debating going to heaven or tumbling into hell, you've put some thought behind it, and she thought Catholicism was a great big cult especially since it wasn't very prevalent in the Bible Belt.

I was a traitor to her faith, and I was not the girl she had met, the innocent girl with the New Testament to quote word for word. She did not understand the need to search, when to her it was so logical. My theory is that we go to our graves searching for some kind of spiritual truth unless you're a most hardcore San Franciscan where all truth seems to be evident as something new age with old religious ways as the archaic entity of the uneducated. For me, though, it is more complex than that, and any mortal who can walk the ancient trails of religious history might find ample evidence of other prophets, but the influence of Christianity on our art, as part of human history, and people's own changes of heart as they suffered persecution, died in the name of faith, and even today's communion with saints leaves me to feel that no one should be quite so certain that the Divine does not exist.

Narrow-mindedness has never been a one-way street, and it just seemed so consoling to me to know that with all of our imperfections we are forgiven just for the asking, and I will take the heat of agnosticism and even the absolute conclusion of atheism as one's choice; just do not endeavor to polish other souls with the same cloth, for we may find it to be lacking. The struggle for the open heart against a closed door is not something that always concludes with an opening when one knocks, but in spirituality we have to give it our best shot, screw up often, accept our own imperfections, and if we can do these things then we might have achieved the ability to know what it is to love. As it's been said, "we are only human," and that means we all have inner journeys to take, and some are beautiful just for a moment.

Middle Tennessee State University: Time to Run
The Angel Speaks Again

The summertime would fly by and though obscured by the passage of years and the changing seasons, I look back upon that summer of 1966 as if I found myself in a state of raw emotion, which had no refinement, but would grasp at the woman who I was to become. I would see church as I had never witnessed it before and I would know that the troubled life which I had left behind in Lexie Crossroads was not just a scar, but a millstone around my neck, so when the dorms closed for a week or so, and even the library where I worked, I seemed to have little choice but to go home.

Some of my friends with wonderful names like Janie Deavor, Rose Cernacola, and a new boy trying to get in my life whose name was, I kid you not, Hub, as in hubcap, helped me feel some sense of connection, and I diligently went every Wednesday to the Church Of Christ Student Body Meeting and there I met the face of a church that was not soothing like the old home church in these Sunday faces of the bigger church in Murfreesboro. As I looked around me, I saw couples, a few loners like me, and about the most unfriendly, pompous, and non-accepting group of human beings that I had ever met. I tried reaching out to people sitting near me, but all faces were usually focused toward the front where someone led us in the old songs and a sermon was preached. The next exciting Wednesday was announced to have a content most similar. Meanwhile you were given scripture verses, and the ever-standing altar call was all made with the thought, "If you should die tonight, are you saved?" It would have been a good thing to have pretended to be non-baptized, for everyone would have gotten so excited to get to trek across the street to where the biggest congregation had the font of water and salvation right under the stage floor.

I decided that the Holy Ghost would not be too pleased, but the mere acceptance as a new being in Christ would have at least brought me a few companions, and if I'd gotten lucky, the ladies of the church would have taken out the food never in short supply in the Protestant refrigerators. I knew that I had been baptized and once was enough. Then my friend, Janie encouraged me to join her at the Baptist Student union, for it seemed that the Southern Baptist group, though smaller, did a few fun things together. So hesitantly I went with Janie to one of their meetings.

On my soul! We went to a park, had singing, a cookout, no preaching, and then you were free to socialize. I do not recall ever having been in any city park before, but who needed park land down near my home when the whole world seemed like a field of grain or a cow pasture? They told me it was a park and sure enough I would have the miracle of my life happen there, for this boy, whose name was Hub, decided to invite me on one of the many trails where we could walk. It was mesmerizing to me, a perfectly groomed little path with some plantings and some wildflowers, and a nice-enough-looking boy escorting me, talking as if we had known each other for a long time. I was ready to be a convert, but we kept walking, and then it was dark within the woods and we seemed to be where no one else was.

Next thing I knew, I was in the grasp of what became octopus hands that clumsily grasped at my body and soon I felt his tongue deep within my throat, but this time nothing magic happened. Where was David? I wanted this to be David or Tom, and I wanted his tongue removed from my esophagus before I threw up. Maybe he was shy like me and maybe he saw me as love at first sight, but all I wanted to do was to get out of there and all that I could feel was Grandpa grabbing at me again, and that was enough to give me the strength to finally get this moron off of me. I figured that I was about to be fully raped, but I was blessed, for it would not be too long before the BSA bus would be coming to get us all back to campus. Girls in by 10:30 sharp, and boys could hang out until 11:30, but that bus was the only salvation I found that night.

I didn't want to see him again, but he would show up now and then to take me for rides on his motorcycle, and I loved the backstreets with the wind in my hair, and he probably loved that I always wore a skirt. Good girls wore skirts which just came to their knees, and this good girl did what she was told. I would look at him and try to figure out why he was not a boy that I could like, and I came to the conclusion that once you had been loved by the older guys, then a boy seemed rather trivial, so I would reclaim my tongue, run up the flights of stairs with my wild long hair, and say evening prayers which usually included that I hoped David or Tom would show up and Lord, I know that you are trying to give me the husband my roommate's mother ordered her to find, but could you please just have Hub give me a rest? I am not interested. He is clumsy and I can live without being a motorcycle diva.

David would come back for most of the next year and a half that I would spend there, only his teasing about his house mom's son began to really bother me. He would make a point of taking me when this royal nut case, whose name was Chester, had time to hold court and sometimes he would leave me there with Chester and his Mom, where I felt that I was in an old movie set with ladies upstairs in the bathroom preserved in formaldehyde awaiting a Halloween resurrection. I thought about what David had said, that I should marry Chester and become one of the wealthiest girls in town, and that I would only have to deal with him until he kicked off and Lord knows he was in his forties where death could be imminent. However his mother was kissing ninety, so I wasn't sure that would be the case. Again, marriage sat in front of me, and I was avoiding even the chance at making my family's life in Lexie a little better by becoming a seventeen-year-old bride to a monster. What seemed worse, though, was that David actually seemed to believe the whole thing was feasible.

He would still come around, and each time when I was with him, I would hear my heart skipping beats and hope that was the time when I might become a woman, but, most of all, David's woman. Instead, with some perception, I was becoming aware that there was never going to be a David and me that Natchez, Mississippi, was a long way away, that his father owned a mill there, and there was always the girl back home. I went home that summer feeling emptier than before and thought about checking out David's church group, something called The Newman Society, the Catholic faith's college campus ministry and the smallest student organization on campus outside of The Skunk-Neutering Club. I thought that since David and Tom had Catholic backgrounds and they were the smartest men I knew, they must know something I didn't. I would walk by the Newman

Society and think of going in, get almost to the door, feel like a stalker, and remember the Catholics were all bound for the fires of hell, especially if they had taken one of my Church of Christ pamphlets and read through it learning the absolute way of salvation as the New Testament Christians and thus I never gave one to David or to Tom, because I wanted them to stay ignorant. Then God might forgive them and let them in to heaven.

We were told that if you are ignorant about Christ then God might understand your wrong turn in the road, and that seemed as logical as it would get to me. Right now there are more Catholics in the entire state of Georgia than any other religious denomination, and the larger cities of the south are always breaking ground for the new Catholics coming in with their job changes, and for the first time maybe there is more brotherhood growing there among the Catholic and Protestant churches, but the truth is that Appalachia is still an enclave for religious zealots. Those who came preaching and teaching out of the Appalachian Mountains and into the valleys below left an indelible mark that has been there since that mass migration toward the western sun, for many hiding in the mountains were originally hiding from the established Puritans and Church of England holdovers, the Episcopalians. Those country Protestant churches still have great clout in the Bible Belt, and people still gather in their own little clans of worship.

In those church communities good works are done, and help comes in fire, storm, and strife in a way that so many other organized religions cannot bring in. If you are bringing in what is still considered to be "false doctrine" then you had better look where you are building your house along that road going over Crow Mountain to Alabama, for you are not appreciated. Judaism and Catholicism still tends to cling to the large cities and to the coastal south, but slowly but surely the pendulum is swinging to the ancient faiths brought over from Europe after the Puritans. I grew up hearing so much about how we fought for our religious freedom only to find that we could be less divisive by looking back over the waters from which we came. I would be quite old before I realized that the first religious colony to establish, "Freedom of Religion" as part of its colonial law was the Catholic colony of Maryland. History seems to have a way of getting skewed over time and place. As with the Word; it can say whatever a good orator wants it to say.

Somehow I stayed a few days at home waiting autumn quarter. I had almost gotten through the stay without having my mother threaten me with murder, but she got revenge in an amazing plot of fate. I was bathing myself on Saturday evening preparing for the last church service before I would return to school, the library, David, Tom, and whatever came my way. I had the usual Prell shampoo, Mother's favorite Ivory soap, and I found myself happy for I had created bubble bath by using enough shampoo to drown several cats, and the night had fallen. I almost felt like a real college girl getting ready to go back when I heard Mom's yell.

"Barbara, you get out here. This boy has come all the way from Murfreesboro to see you." And she was excited. Then she said, "He said his name is Hub. You get out here!" Mother's voice had almost that sound of hysterical laughter when she would get so carried away while beating me that she would go into some state of mania which included laughter.

I told her in no uncertain terms to send him away, and the water began to get cold, and the bubbles popped, and I had trembling problems again. "You send them away," I said for it turned out Hub had brought along a male friend of his and so it was two against one. That was more than I could deal with. I could not call my mother into a bathroom and tell her that I had anything to do with boys or that this boy had almost removed my clothes when I went out with his Baptist group; instead I cried and I shrank and lay in that bathtub as if I could wait there until I died. Mama kept entertaining the boys just knowing that I would appear. In her mind, simple as it could be at times, she saw a college boy with his own damned truck, and she thought he was nice-looking, so she had sat them down to wait me out. No one was going to get that a truck and a body were not enough for me. Had Hub known how many men had shotguns out there on a Saturday night who didn't like strange license plates, they would have hightailed out of there in a minute, but they stayed, and I continued to cry and to shrink. Maybe an hour passed, but finally someone got the message that I wasn't going to move an inch, and the franticness of my state at this point had taken on Herculean resistance, for I was not going to feel my Grandpa's kind of loving which this boy had come for.

I heard a motor start, and I began to breathe rapidly, and soon Mama crashed in the bathroom door. I did not like her to see me unclothed, and she was frantic.

"Now you've done it. That nice boy just got up and left." I believe Mama knew exactly what she was doing by not sending them away earlier. A new school year was about to begin, and if I got this boy—or better, if he got a hold of me—there might be a chance that I would be sticking around. While Mama was hearing wedding bells, all I felt were the sobs coming from deep within.

I think that it was about that time when I said, "Mama, you should have listened to me and not shamed me so," but she never really heard. The bubble bath ended and so did my patience with seventeen years of letting my mother get away with such hurtful behavior. I would leave again on Sunday afternoon, and I told her that I would not be coming back. "Ever," I said, and the second semester of my freshman year arrived with that conviction.

All of the humiliation in the world had gone down the drain that night with my beautiful bubble bath which ended in the grief of a girl who had learned self-protection was what I could depend on. That, and I would still pray, but I was going to pray looking for a glimpse of a forgiving God. I did not know about mercy, love, or that grace cannot be earned, only given, but over the next few years I would start the search. I had washed and washed and cleansed myself with tears, and I was not just going back to college, I was going back to find a life. I wanted David, but I was beginning to expect that he had another life. I began sharing poetry with Tom whose brother was a playwright in San Francisco and had poetry published in reputable magazines, and I began writing just to rid myself of hurt. On paper a story seemed to be unfolding, and Tom thought that I wrote very well except he did not like the God that I included and gave such credence to. He wanted to see me write about me, and I could not bear to tell him that not only was I a girl with an invisible face most of the time, but my soul had gone down a bathtub drain on a river of water which partially came from my heart.

He taught writing, so he should know if I was actually showing some talent, but the drain kept sucking me in, all of me, so with Tom I began the new school year in a new apartment and with the hope that some few bubbles had not burst, and that my spirit was floating around me somewhere with my voice. He was now a non-believer, Tom, but he seemed to know beauty, and I thought that maybe one of the magical bubbles had seeped through his pores, and that maybe, just maybe, it would find me, and I would meet beauty, too.

What about me did this Pittsburgh industrialist's grandson know? What could he possibly know that kept him coming back with the smiles, the words of encouragement, and the invitation to the bed I never accepted—but that he would continue to offer until he left and found a wife. Angels and demons are sometimes one in the same, only some have better ideas than others, and I loved that someone could open this school year with the gesture of giving me time, just time, which I needed to try one more school year. Once again I would dream the dreams of being loved so fervently that my mind and the classroom would fail to mesh. Living on day dreams was the spring water for the thirsty bones of the rabid fox. Even a fresh drink though might not offer the solace of the fox's den. Still waters were calling me.

Dr. Capers, The Mystery Quotient, was about to appear. I no longer remember if it happened in the summertime or if it began in my autumn semester, but it turns out that there were strings attached to receiving grant money from Middle Tennessee State University. The vocational rehabilitation person who had come to our high school and had gotten me all the papers which I needed to sign had stated, "I notice that you are a little shaky," and I did not think much about it, but it was arranged that at some point before college I would be evaluated by a doctor and the doctor just wanted to talk to me. Mr. Gus Larkin and Mrs. Ruth must have wondered about the head doctor at my evaluation in Chattanooga, but they just got me there – their other girl. This evaluation was very surprising and was rather curious, for it consisted of several, what I suppose were, IQ tests. Then the doctor talked to me for a very long time, asking me a bunch of questions that Mama would not have wanted me to answer, so it made me more tremulous, and I would tell him small things about myself, but I tread extremely cautiously.

Somehow, though, I got the feeling that this doctor had seen the likes of me before, the cotton-picking children who were having a problem with nervousness, fear of adults, and who would only talk with their heads down if it were a serious matter. So before I left he agreed that college was the best thing for me and reassured me that in Murfreesboro there would be a physician, not unlike himself, who would just talk to me. That seemed like a pretty darned good deal, no examinations, no shots, no looking at my throat, just talking to me, and I thought maybe they had some secret words or something which were going to make my life different.

Oh he seemed ever so nice to ask me about my brothers and sisters, my mother and my father, and just what I did every day, and he began to ask me about things and people which frightened me. He seemed most interested in my recurring dream of an old man who came at night and who was planning on killing me if I could not come up with a word only known to the two of us. I think about the most that I told him about Mom and Dad was that Mama made nice banana pudding and Dad liked to hunt rabbits when we didn't have much to eat, but he seemed satisfied, jotted some stuff down on paper, and he let me know that I was college bound. I was in tears with this great news, and he just sort of wished me well and I never heard from him again.

I would not even remember him until I received some note that when I got to school I was to see a Dr. Capers on a particular date, so I found my way around downtown Murfreesboro and was so relieved that I had come to the right place. His receptionist had a nice smile, and over the weeks she would greet me smiling as if she had just won that washer and dryer which I wanted for Mama from the "Queen for a Day" show, the one which made it seem so logical that anyone could get out to California and become a winner. The doctor, dressed in a suit, was an older man, and he had hair like the Reverend Billy Graham. Just being around him made me more nervous than I could possibly hide. Time is integral only in this context, because his "interventions" would again change the course of my life. Supposedly Dr. Capers was somewhat famous in some circles, and I did notice and began to understand that he was a medical doctor who specialized in psychiatry, though what psychiatry meant to me seemed to have little relevance. It seemed that I had lucked out in his ability to take me on immediately as was the desire of the doctor in Chattanooga. I knew that my dreams and my hopes were not reality, but when life is too messed up, a dream world can soothe some of the pain. I did not know that seeing a therapist meant that I automatically became a lunatic as I shared such with friends.

My idea of crazy was someone who went out and finally shot everyone in their household and then turned the gun on themselves, and I was a very non-confrontational person, especially having been raised to believe that physicians were extra-special, like my uncle who had become the popular local physician. Dr. Capers, week after week, kept asking me about my home life, sometimes about school or church, and sometimes I would give him a few clues that there had been some trouble in my life. But I just didn't like him, especially with him looking like a Baptist preacher. I'd had enough of a fright from the one Baptist preacher, not to mention the boy with hands which went places where he wasn't invited and who would not give it a rest trying to go out with me, so this psychiatrist was someone who was not going to get any news to publish in his journal about me. I did notice that he kept a clipboard and wrote the whole time that we were talking.

My school grades began to pick up that quarter, no thanks to him, but I had decided to make college my stepping stone to my next goal of finally getting to Vanderbilt which was about as likely as one desiring to take a trip to Mars on a jet plane. The Dean of Women called me in, and she wanted to know how I was doing so well, and if I think about it, she was probably insinuating that I was somehow cheating on my exams. I just told her that life seemed to be better, and I planned to be somebody.

That is who Dad wanted us to be. "Somebody," he'd say. I also was able to successfully appeal to her sense of earned credit by letting her know that I was going to church regularly, and I thought the Lord might have a hand in my success, so she was satisfied. Then she sent me on my way. I felt ten feet tall, for the Dean of Women wanted to know why I, Barbara Ellen Everett, was doing so well. Had she known me in high school, she would have known that what was impossible was usually my finest goal. That would be my great semester. I was gaining such personal notoriety with my Women's Issues editorials and my own column "The Roving Raider," that even David and Tom seemed to be impressed.

Christmas came, though, and I decided not to go home for I knew there wasn't much reason. With my library money I sent my sister a doll, and I got something for the brothers, Old Spice for Dad, and probably some nice powder for Mama. I even got on a bus and went in to Nashville to do my shopping, but the department store was so overwhelming with all of the choices that I just got a bus back to my little world of Murfreesboro which I could handle. Something else happened at Christmas, for all the sad Christmases had left marks deep within, and I went in to see Dr. Capers, and I could not stop shaking and crying. The "Billy Graham Look-Alike Doctor" got all excited because he enjoyed being in control of broken-hearted people, and even I thought maybe "the nervous breakdown" was my relief.

I cried the tears of ages, the tears for a lost youth, the tears of loneliness for a comfortable home, and the tears of being at school during the break eating beanie-wienies and snowballs for Christmas dinner. Yes, I cried, and I could not stop. Dr. Capers kept asking me to tell him what all was wrong, talking about some kind of breakthrough, but meantime I wanted to tell him to go to hell and leave me alone and that I didn't want to see his ugly and scary face anymore.

Instead, he went to his back room, and he brought out pills. He gave me the pills without an explanation of what they were, what they did, or how to really take them. Just stuff like, "Take a red one if you feel nervous and a blue one if you are feeling too sad." Surely he, a medical doctor, knew what he was talking about, so I began to take the pills, and I began to notice that I wanted to sleep all the time, and if I did not want to sleep then I had the shakes and I would go to class and remember little of anything which was said there, so I started trying to take more of the pills to feel better. It was just like a bad seed had suddenly been planted in my world where life had been getting better and my resistance began to weaken in how I talked to Dr. Capers, for I began that winter and into that spring to tell him about Mama, Grandpa, Daddy, and the shotguns Dad would scare us with.

He was ever so much friendlier and I began to think that maybe I had misjudged him and I would tell him about my school problems. Then he would mess around with other pills from the back room, and I thought it was the nicest thing that he was going to all this trouble for nothing just giving me all of these medications for free, though I would later learn that he was reimbursed by the state's Department of Vocational Rehabilitation, but I kept taking the medicine with his promise that he was curing me of the ills which were keeping me from being able to get through a normal school day.

David began to come around less and I so missed his affection, our walks and our talks, and the little bridge which we would go over that had a street light which made everything so atmospheric and romantic and where we would usually stop for a time just to hold one another. My friend Tom, though, kept telling me, and I do not know how he understood this, except he was usually high on something, that I needed to get out of there. He was older, and he was seeing things which were beyond me, and he understood about people like Dr. Capers. Even though Tom would prove over the years to be as narcissistic as I had sort of known him to be, he would become my angel through the horrid invasion of my privacy which was going on.

I was particularly upset one day as to why David disappeared, so I began to cry in Dr. Capers' office, and he began to yell at me. "Did you let that boy touch you? Did you let that boy touch you?" I could not lie, for it was something I knew was a reason to go straight to hell, and I did not know that he meant it as in touching me in the area below the waistline, so I told him the truth as I understood it. "Yes."

He shamed me and told me not to let it happen again, and the next thing I knew he was in his back room fidgeting for medications. I took them, then all that I could do was to sleep, and if I had an assignment, I would take caffeine tablets trying to get through it so my grades on my best subjects began to hit bottom. Worse, I got a call from Mama as the semester was ending, and she said, "That Doctor thinks you've been telling him a pack of lies and he thinks you might belong in that state hospital."

For the nonbeliever, you cannot imagine this, but exams were about to be over, and it was like a chorus of angels telling me, "It is time to go. Go to Washington, D.C. Do anything, but get out of here." Within a week's time I had gathered what I could take of my things and called Mom and Dad and told them that I was going to the sisters' already working in the D.C. government and that I wasn't coming home again for a very long time. I pitched the rest of Dr. Capers' medications, having learned that he had conversed with my mother. Mom had convinced him that I wasn't telling any truth about what had happened to me at home.

"Why, we never whipped her." Mom had made it sound like I was a flake in a pepper pod of fine upbringing outside of being poor, and the bastard doctor believed her. He was going to have me placed in The Tennessee Psychiatric Hospital from which I would probably never have emerged, for people did disappear in the places as late as the 1960s. Please remember that good psychiatric medications really were not available until probably the 1980s, and Mama would have out of spite, for my telling the truth, signed those papers.

She had one small problem. Two of my little nephews not much younger than me needed to go home to Silver Springs, Maryland, just at the time she and Dr. Capers were talking about getting together, so I had bought my one-way ticket with what I had left from library and grant money, and I found myself getting on the bus with my nephews headed into the great unknown. I had no money, and I knew nothing of public transportation. All I had were the mystics which tell you sometimes from some place of divinity that you must go, you must go, and so I did, leaving at the end of spring semester not knowing anything about tomorrow or what had happened to me, or worse, what was about to happen to me if I did not leave, so I held those boys in my arms through that night.

I bought them breakfast in Bristol, Tennessee, then we went through Virginia, and I must have fallen asleep, for as if I were in some kind of amazing time machine, the monuments of Washington began to appear. I had seen them in books, and I recognized them as we passed and something said that I, the slave girl to my own family, the crazy girl who had to see the psychiatrist to go to school, saw something else. It was as if I had followed the North Star and had made it to Ohio with dogs chasing me, this white girl who was freed, because two little boys needed an escort, and Mama saw it as her chance when I said I was going to get them on that bus. The boys will only learn in reading this that they were my guides, not the reverse, and my life would soon be forever changed.

I felt so sad, for David had come to the dormitory just before I left, but he would hardly say goodbye. I do not doubt that Dr. Capers had gotten to him as a man, too, for nothing a child under twenty-one said was private then, and David just said goodbye. The romance was gone, and he shook his head as if something unimaginable had happened. I would contact him a few times, but I would never see him again. I would later learn that it was true that his family had a factory in Natchez and I was told that he was getting married, though I did not believe it at the time. I think that his father had told him to lose that nutty girl! Dr. Capers was probably about the worst human being I could have ever been assigned to, an old man with old Freudian values, and obviously absolutely no knowledge of the psychiatric medications which were coming on the market as fast as they could be developed.

The medications, when used properly, were freeing schizophrenics, and maybe some bipolar sorts got a reprieve or those who came back from wars shell-shocked and numb, but those medications were not for the kids from the hidden areas of the white south who needed support, love, and gentle counseling to get them over the evils committed in the wisdom of a nineteenth-century world which lingered in the hills. We were not crazy, hopeless, or throw-aways, but my story is one of the better ones. Especially girls would find themselves being sent away for "a nervous breakdown," another way of saying they were probably being raped by their fathers and their mothers having suffered the same lot felt that their daughters could do the same, but times were changing and it would not help our area of the country much because there is still a blindness to the needs of impoverished southern-bred Americans. Many remain the invisible people. They are simply gorked out on worse drugs now. The welfare system has replaced the work ethic, and the churches still often keep people feeling that the only heaven they will ever know is not here in this place. No one cares when it comes to white trash in the country or in the city, so why should politicians? Feed them a hot dog to get a vote and go on your way as some big deal to Washington.

I have never left my people in so many ways, nor will I. They are a village away, and I want them to know that if I have achieved anything, then they can achieve more. I knew the years in Washington were going to be hard, but it was divine intervention that told me to go and save myself. I will begin taking you through those fields of living and walk through the cherry blossoms just as I had walked through the pink honeysuckle vines, and we will drink love, grow up a little more, and we'll find our way. It will be several years before I take you back to the foothills. I am waiting, so come with me, my friend, for the Appalachian girl has a life to rebuild. I would end this vignette with this advice: if you ever meet such a physician who would be proud of a name like Capers just run for your life. If they scare you from the beginning, then listen to your heart and never reveal more of yourself than you are comfortable with, for when it is the right person, then you will not be afraid to share the innermost darkness hidden within your hearts, and today patient confidentiality has meaning in the courts of law. Mental health services in this country have been mercilessly cut by allowing insurance coverage almost "emergency" medicine out of the sheer need for basic listening and behavioral modification. Hospitalization is unavailable to many who suffer.

A lot of what should be basic psychiatric intervention is instead being left up to over booked neighborhood health clinics, social workers, and to nurses, and, worst of all, to the criminal justice systems. Incarceration of the mentally ill and the drug addicted means we have lost about thirty years of chances to change lives, talented younger people who have contributed to society, and we have placed mental health care in the column of shame once more.

Those who contributed to such loss would do well to bow their own heads in shame and beg forgiveness from the souls who shall haunt them in the courts of justice.

Chapter Thirty

Washington, D.C.

Sometime during the early morning hours after having fed my little travel buddies, I must have fallen asleep, for when I awoke, I suddenly found myself looking at all the picture postcards I had ever received from Washington, and the Greyhound bus driver had begun to describe the monuments and marvels of the capital city we were entering. At this point in the trip I can see the Washington Monument which my friend Tom Bissell used to describe as the world's greatest phallic symbol. That description somehow did not fit into my brain cells as to exactly what he meant, still believing as I did in the puritanical things and people who had seemed to govern my previous life. There should be some noble statement here, but I think that I felt more like General Lee's horse at Gettysburg when its bereft general saw that the South and its effort for secession from the Union was a dream about to be lost. I was an exhausted beast of burden embarking upon a new life, and I must tell you that there is a black hole within my life.

To this day, I have no memory of who picked up the kids and me, how I got from one place to the other, or what the next few days had in store for me. Everything is erased until I get little flashbacks of my sister Violet and her roommates getting ready to go out on the weekend or I find myself about to board a bus to downtown D.C. to try to find myself a job. I just went along with my sister, some report cards in my hand, some records of awards, and I had no itinerary or knowledge of which great big building to go into. They all sort of began to look alike, the government buildings, and I felt the terror of a wounded lamb at nightfall when all of the foxes are about to feed. I knew nothing of résumés, government service, or what you did to get a job outside of asking, so that is what I did. I went around giving out résumés and tried to look intelligent in my country clothing.

One day, I struck up a conversation with a girl by the name of Jean Hewlitt and she told me that her father was a string writer for *The Washington Post* and that she was bummed to be back in Washington, but she had to get some money together. She said that I should check out the insurance office where she worked at George Washington University. With only her as a reference, I went there and was told that I could begin the next work week, and I probably hugged the man who interviewed me, thanking him for his generosity. It was going to be over six dollars and fifty cents an hour, and I even told him that he didn't have to pay me so much, but he said, "The college education you have counts for something." I was so relieved to tell my sister because two days of walking Washington streets and trying to meet back up with her at the State Department had taken a toll on my relationship with her.

I would not know until years later that she had just broken up with a boyfriend that she loved so dearly that she was ashamed to bring him back to our neck of the woods to meet all of us. It would be a mistake of her life, and our sister Rose had married a Pennsylvania man who was wonderful, wise, and loving and expected nothing of us other than that we were his new little brothers and sisters. I did not understand what anyone had to be ashamed of just because my little brother James ran around beating up things between rocks or pulling the heads off of chickens. Sister also apparently feared having to explain one of our parents' rip-roaring battles, and the whole thing was just too much for her. We each took a different tack as to how we handled our lives in the early years of adulthood, and what I know now is that we had no idea how to help each other.

The three weeks at Violet's place left me lonelier than I could have ever imagined, since she needed mainly for me to move on. She had built a world with roommates mostly from northern Ohio where her beloved boyfriend was also from, and they would spend their weekends going to bars and hooking up with all of the military guys that were hanging around Washington at that time. Daddy would have called it bees out for honey, but D.C. was the place to be a single girl then. Those girls had developed what would be a lifelong friendship, and my dear sister was unable to let her guard down one moment for me. She was doing what we had been trained to do. To survive no matter how unfamiliar the setting might be, but I was a distraction sharing space which was non-existent with her and the roomies.

I think three of us had to share a bed at times, but this wasn't unusual for me because the only place I had ever not shared a bed was at my friend Marlene's place back home. Only the luckiest girls in the world had twin beds. We knew that as early as the *I Love Lucy* show. Lucy and Ricky Ricardo had matching bedspreads and twin beds, and that was what I was going for!

I had a nice surprise when I got a call from my old friend Tom; he was passing through Washington where he said he came on a fairly regular basis, and I had given him my telephone number there. Way too bad for me, but he was on his way to South America or somewhere to pick grapes. It would not surprise me when years later he became a wine connoisseur of sorts, and he gave me some reassurance that he would see me again back in Washington. My friend Jean called me, too, and she told me some VISTA volunteers lived below her and were looking for a roommate, and would I be interested. I almost exploded with excitement, and when my sisters saw the area they both almost died, for it was in the heart of Washington's ghetto district. Poor blacks covered the streets with glazed eyes and brown skin—then here we were a bunch of white folks barging in on their turf.

As I have said, I never learned to be prejudiced as a child, for I loved picking cotton with the black children and that my parents could visit "Negro Joe" and his wife. All I saw was the city, R and 17th approximately, and the apartments were over the Flamingo Restaurant and dance club which led to rather interesting sounds in the evening.

I moved in, and I became the working stiff of the group. The VISTA kids got a stipend for food and for housing, and they were supposed to be working and rebuilding community as part of their assignment. It worked this way, or so it seemed. I worked at George Washington's hospital matching insurance accounts to payments, then Jean and I would go back to R street. The wonderful group I worked with had some assignments to go to meetings and to interface with the neighborhood kids. It was supposed to be breaking down barriers. In the evenings we would have parties, discuss love, peace, and politics, and for the first time since I left high school I would become aware that there was a real war going on over in Southeast Asia called Vietnam.

I began to see myself in a role of some kind of peace activist and humanitarian just like the VISTA and the Peace Corps volunteers who would come back through Washington sometimes before returning to their homes. My friends were Kathy, a girl from Ohio who had left a convent; Natalie, a girl from Nashua, New Hampshire; and Carol who became a best friend, a well-off young lady from West Covina, California. Believe me, you were not going to find any cotton-pickers among the volunteers who gave service to America. These were all middle-class, and in this case, beautiful young women, and I loved them and wanted to emulate their every motion. I considered myself the girl with the lazy eye still, the country woman ready to take care of them all, and the outsider, but they all seemed to love me, and I loved them back with food on the table and whatever I could do just to feel a part of something. These were my new friends, and there seemed to be a common thread among each of us. Each had boyfriends, and there seemed to be a need to have other boyfriends along the way, especially a black guy, because that meant that you were not prejudiced. Black men caught on to that one fast, so the girls usually did not have to wait long.

My friend Kathy had me fixated on a story of a beautiful evening when everyone had just gotten stoned, naked, and jumped in to a pile, and she said that it was among the most beautiful moments of her life filled with love and all barriers were erased. It was just everyone being loving and kind, then they sort of paired off and made love. I guess there wasn't much action in the convent. I was rapidly losing my southern accent as the weeks passed on living with girls from all over the country, and I was picking up a little ghetto which came in handy now and then. I had decided to join the Catholic Church, for it seemed that all of my friends had a Catholic background, and I was looking for something in the way of continual divine intervention and introspection. As I wrote people back home about my decision, the letters came that I was a good girl, but did I realize that I had just damned my soul to hell and other such small items. I loved my friend George Takos from upstate Ohio, and he was only a few weeks from ordination, and he acted as my sponsor.

George loved Kathy so much, and they would have made a great pair, but she had her eyes on a guy from the Berkeley set who was a peace activist, a Peace Corp volunteer returnee. If I wasn't taking Natalie's cast-off boyfriends, then I seemed to be taking everyone else's, for I wasn't going to do anything which upset my friends. George was an obvious match for me with Kathy just always keeping him on edge and teasing me. Six weeks before ordination he would come to me, the world's premier virgin and ask me if I would help him to make love for the first time, and for a while I thought that George and I might just be meant to be together, and I tried my best, but Catholic guilt was still worrying George, so we put the whole thing off for a time.

I so wanted him to be my first love, but I was trying to keep it to one boyfriend at a time for the pure sake of decency. In so many ways we were a perfect pair, though he was almost ten years older than me. He was handsome, romantic, and loving, and he would understand about James's love for chicken decapitation, for George had that kind of heart. Years later I would learn that he married a German girl and settled in the Washington area, and he will never know how happy that made this girl from Lexie, but I have carried his signature on my baptismal certificate, and each time I see it I can feel George's wonderful hugs and his telling me about *The Velveteen Rabbit* for he thought that I was one who needed to be loved before I could give love, and I can think of no better place to be than in a child's story all worn and frayed, picked up, kissed, and carried off to one's sleep as something lovely. George deserves more than a line in my story, for I think that he began to give me a true sense of literary beauty, and I was becoming a real girl as long as I would know him.

It happened that Catholics were taking a licking before Vatican II when the good Pope John decided to bring the church into the new age.

Upstairs from us lived a couple, another Barbara who worked for the district government and her ex-priest boyfriend, known in the neighborhood as Moose. Moose and Barbara spent most of the time the lying in bed, and once he asked me, "How does this make you feel seeing us lying here and unmarried?"

I heard the truth coming with my words. "Maybe a little uncomfortable." Then I told him what my faith had taught, and he did not demean me in the least bit nor did Barbara. They just listened, and they held each other closely. I would visit most evenings just to be a part of everything going on in the house, but one night I went up, and the bed was empty. I could hear conversation and saw a flickering light in the front room, so I gently knocked and went in to find Barbara, Moose, Jean, some other people I did not know, and they all just looked up at me. My eyes became fixated on a tiny burner they had in the middle of the floor, and in it was liquid melting in a small vessel, and there were empty medicine syringes, and there were more being filled. I kept coming into the room, for I was curious having never seen such a thing before, and I wanted to be with Barbara and Moose just then.

Suddenly, I heard Moose say in an angry voice, "Barb, you have got to leave. You are too good to get messed up with this."

I heard myself protest just a little, for I still did not understand, for everyone looked so rested, and he said the same thing again and I knew that he meant it. I left not knowing that I had been to my first and only heroin party.

In the days to come I stayed away from Moose and Barbara's, especially after I heard that Moose was out to beat up some guy for selling him bad stuff, and I now knew what that meant. I feared for his life, but I would remember him as another saint that saved mine, and I wish I knew the end of the story. In my heart I want to think that he got it together and became something like a prison chaplain, or that he pulled it together enough to get off heroin and to help the others who were trying. My worst fear is that he died in some back alley in Washington after having had the hell beat out of him. Moose had become his nickname because he was as large as a Washington state timber, and the little guys wanted a piece of him. I wondered why of all the people in that house he had protected me, but my explanation would remain the same through the years. God shows up in many forms, even in that heroin addict who once was a priest and chose to dance with the devil, and that I was good meant that Moose saw me like a part of some communion that was stuck in his mind. I think that he had enough love left in him to recognize love in action and maybe a face that said, "I am afraid." My gratitude exceeds the boundaries of time and place, and I love that couple, that priestly addicted man as if I still knew him to this day, for he saved me from something way bigger than I was.

The year with the VISTA and the Peace Corp returnees will be treasured throughout my days as I remember their fresh and young faces. I remember standing under a blossoming fruit tree that early summer, the sun was out, and the weather had warmed, so all of the fragrant petals were swirling around me, and my skirt was twisting northward, and the long and dark hair which was natural to me blew in the same wonderful direction caressing my face, and all that I could feel was wonderful. Everything seemed vividly alive and real and I, the sad rabbit of George's favorite story, felt as if she owned the day, and the tree danced and I smiled at everything that moved awaiting the 16th Street bus to go downtown. The Greyhound arrival was no longer important to me, and I was redeemed and washed in the love of sweet blossoms which seem to surround me when I need a place to reclaim myself. Love was with me, in me, a part of me, and nothing could separate me from it at that moment as I danced the joy of pretty blossoms on a Washington, D.C. day of ecstasy. I would sing "Where Have All the Flowers Gone?" but for one shining hour of the day then I owned them—the flowers, the trees, and all—for we were acquainted from a woodland of long ago.

I was so impressed and happy with the VISTA crowd that the obvious came to my mind. Why not become a volunteer myself, for I had more qualifications than anyone I had run into. The Peace Corps group was a little different, for most of them had finished college, had some life experience, and they were out to save the world, but a lot of the VISTA group had way less experience than I did. I had proven myself in high school to be a great organizer of anything I set my mind to, and I had some basic college behind me. Some of the VISTA people wanted to go down to the Appalachian hills and valleys all across this country to help, and those were my people. I knew the language, the mannerisms, and I knew when there was a prayer for intervention and when one would be wasting their breath. I agree that I did not know the ways of the inner-city black communities, but neither did any of these kids from Ohio, California, or other mid-western bastions of civilized living. I could cook, sew, preserve food, plant a garden, and I knew generally how the mothers tended their babies and, perhaps more importantly, I knew the spiritual fears and hopes of the poor. So it seemed to me that I was a perfect candidate.

I think my friend Carol Skelton from West Covina, California, had prepared me as best she could to be disappointed, though. She told me a lot about the interview process and the importance of the essay. Little did she know that The Roving Raider was in her non-medicated state a darned genius when it came to essays, or so I thought. Besides that, their monthly stipend more than met my monthly requirements for money, and doors would open for college with VISTA on my record to make up for the fact Dr. Capers had me so zoned out during third semester that I was almost unable to function. I saw my path clearly, the walk hand in hand, going off with my own training group, and I had been a reading teacher in high school helping kids younger than me.

Everything just fit, and when the day for the interview came up, I was a little tremulous, but I was less so than usual. A very serious middle-aged white man interviewed me, and he hardly looked at all of my rewards and treasures. He said that he wasn't certain that I was VISTA material, to which I looked at him as if he had just said, "I am afraid to tell you this, but you are actually the color chartreuse and you do not fit anywhere, for we do not like odd colors around here."

He said, "I see where you have written here on your essay, 'I just want to do my own thing.'"

He was right, for the VISTA and Peace Corp kids used that term all of the time. It was about the equivalent of using the word "like" as a prelude to every word that comes out of the mouth of anyone born after sometime when ignorance became bliss in language around the 1980s or the terms, "I go, and then she goes," another of my most hated forms of dialogue that came along around the same time, and now even grown people use these same terms. I thought it sounded pretty cool to write down that I wanted to do the things I knew how to do. Daddy had always said that we should be proud that we could walk fast and that we would probably be the most likely to survive a nuclear attack, because we had already learned to live on nothing.

Mr. Middle-Class interviewer did not get my point, though, and he looked at this girl from the absolute tip of the Appalachian chain and said to me, "I do not think that you are suited to our program," and all that I could see before me were the uncalloused hands of my roommates who had never pulled a cotton boll, milked a cow, split one piece of firewood, or prepared one tub of beans for canning. Apparently to be a Volunteer in Service to America, you had to look as if you had never done a lick of service for America in your entire life. I could not collect my thoughts, for I think that I had gone into the zombie mode which could come over me when I was absolutely devastated and with shame. I went back and told my friends of my failure in not gaining a spot on America's team to help the impoverished, supposedly because I had written, "I want to do my own thing." They gave me appropriate, but not surprised sympathy, for it was true. I was not one of them. My impoverished life had prepared me to remain impoverished in spirit, because of some really stupid white guy in Washington who should have been out selling vacuums door to door instead of interviewing kids for volunteer service.

I carried that hurt around for many years, and even today when I look back, I long to open my heart to that man and to tell him that he had just denied the rights of my people to be helped by their own kind. He didn't know about the ancient signs of when to plant the garden or when the weather was just cool enough to slaughter the meat. He didn't know about how to avoid the old men and how to leap like a leopard through tall grasses where rattlesnakes could be having a convention, but most of all, he did not know about the poor and how their hearts needed mending before you could bear the good news that their children might need to finish high school.

He was the arrogant and ignorant of many components of our federal government at that time, which would establish a welfare class of people within our country who cannot get out this day for the life of them. Things could have been different if they had gathered us from the farms and the hills to teach survival skills and to instill pride instead of to embrace the poverty that became the yoke to bear and to cast the ever-growing class structure which we have now where the poor keep getting poorer and the rich simply choose to wall them off on the back roads and towns where merely visitors go. Why wouldn't they look for those of us with the message that we can all get somewhere, but that we've got to go together? The knowledge we could share would make a genuine difference, because we would work, just harder, and with more zeal as a class of people who woke up and noticed that we had been achievers all along.

There would be other joyful hours with the VISTA and Peace Corps kids throughout my years in Washington and for many years afterward. I especially liked when the boys from one of the houses came over, all great-looking guys back from overseas, and at least they knew about well-digging and other languages. Usually I was so busy protecting my chastity for the hour of my marriage bliss that most of them really paid attention to the other girls in our house. One evening at a party, I met a Peace Corps boy by the name of Mark Schneider, and Mark asked me to dance, for that night there was alcohol, music, sex, and me the chaste girl from Tennessee. Sometime later Mark would tell me that he had picked me out because I looked so lonely. That would have been wonderful if he had also picked me out because I was a girl that he wanted to spend some real time with.

He was an upscale military-raised kid whose father had obviously screwed with his mind for Mark wanted to be everything except what his father had disciplined him to be, the next military man in the family. We were in a room just off the kitchen and evening light came from small fixtures on the side walls. Couples were pairing off to drift in to slow dances, and I saw this boy coming toward me who looked remarkably like the description of the boy whose name was Christian, portrayed in the novel *Moby Dick*. I believe that his eyes were blue and his hair was cut neatly unlike most of the boys there, somewhat sandy to blond in color, and he was tall and beautiful. When he asked me if I wanted to dance with him, I looked over my shoulder, ever certain that he was really asking someone other than me, but there we were, he and I, and he placed his hands around my waist.

We danced for a while, and he began to hold me a little more closely, and I could feel my breath coming faster out of fear and still not certain that I was whom he wanted to be with. Next, both of our arms were around one another, and he placed his face on mine, and I felt warm and so very happy and in total disbelief that the sweet and beautiful boy was holding me closer and closer. Soon we were looking into one another's eyes, and he looked very serious and then he began to kiss me. But unlike with Hub, the creep from the Baptist picnic, something important happened. I did not pull away and I let him kiss me and I kissed him back and he was the first boy that I opened my mouth for just like my heart, and we kissed each other long and hard and very sweetly, both of us not wanting to go anywhere. We stayed that way for a long time, holding each other to quiet music, and if our arms were not holding each other closely, then we were face to face again, like grown-ups, and I knew for the first time what it felt like to have the French kisses the girls used to brag about, the tongues exploring the entire mouth as if there were erotic sweets to find or secret places of mint and frosting and I fell in love then and there. I wanted this boy and I wanted him a lot.

After the party, people were sleeping everywhere, but since I paid for the space, I had the front couch, so I took his hand and we walked there, and fully dressed we held and kissed each other again, and he smiled at me, massaging my arm that was around him, laying his head into my chest, but still not undressing me as if to say, "I have time for you." We fell asleep that way, he and I, and there was no sex, but insofar as sex goes, maybe it was one of the sexiest experiences I've ever had. I left his arms the next morning to go to work, kissing him one last moment and hoping that he would not move for the rest of the day.

Weeks passed like that, and during this interval I had given my usual speech about waiting for marriage, and he would often just sleep with me and kiss me and I knew that he was "the boy." How many boys keep coming back just to be loved that much and then fall asleep in your arms? He had to be the boy and I never dreamt that either of us would be anyone else's lover ever.

One night, way too late and with a driver that had more to drink than was safe, someone got the idea that we would all go to Rehoboth Beach in Delaware. So about eight of us got in a car and on this weeknight we took off for the ocean. I had never seen the ocean before. This was so perfect, for I wound up having to sit in Mark's lap which seems impossible now, but I only weighed about one hundred pounds on my five-seven frame, so I made myself as light as I could, and the perfectly normal thing to do was to cuddle and to caress him all of the way there. It might seem impossible to be kissed for two hours, but when you are eighteen and in love, the time passed remarkably fast. I think poor Mark's legs were without feeling by the time we got there, but he held me and he loved me and before we knew it, we were there.

The moon was full, so we walked hand and hand to the water's edge, and I was overwhelmed that anything could ever be so massive, beautiful, and so full of color in the dark sky of the night with stars sprinkled like golden specks so high above us but so near in sight that it felt as if we could touch them. I could see the darkest blue waves and the white foam lapping at our feet and Mark put his hands over my shoulders and pulled me to him and I am certain that I told him just how very much I loved him. I saw my guy then look out over the water, distant, and I wondered what he saw, but I had no idea that what he saw did not include me. We stayed for as long as we could and continued a love fest all the way back to Washington as the sun began to come up and for a little while, we were able to lie on our couch, Mark sleeping and me kissing his sleeping face at intervals, for it never occurred to me to just miss work this day, and my life changed in that few hours.

After that, the boys would come over, but Mark would rarely come with them. We moved even further into the ghetto, the VISTAs and I, for they felt we were not living enough of the ghetto experience, and soon it became apparent that Mark was never coming over. One night he phoned and his friend Larry Holcomb answered the phone and my face must have lit up like the stars on the beach, for I could hear Larry telling Mark, "Yeah, you are still the number one," and I finally got it. Larry was giving my love that message, because as long as that was perceived as truth, then when I was around, Mark was not going to show up anymore. I was not an ignorant girl, and I got it, and I went and hid and simply cried for I could see Mark's eyes looking out at the ocean again, and I realized that his hands on my shoulders and the mysterious look on his eyes had to do with what to do about me. Was there a girl back at his old college? Did he decide that he did not love me or that loving me was too dangerous? I would not have been the girl his parents would have chosen for an officer's wife. Thoughts raced through me like pricks of knife in a steak, and none of them helped. Every insecurity that I ever knew raced back in and I could feel those stars at Rehoboth Beach falling around me and breaking like glass as Mark looked away, and I would wonder, as all young lovers wonder, "How do I go on after this? What did I do wrong? Can it be fixed?" Everything inside of me knew the answers and they were all "Nothing, nothing, nothing," and I just cried more.

I can say to every young woman or young man that you will carry your first real love to your grave, and you will remember everything about those hours when the world seemed too perfect to believe, and most of you, like me, will live an entirely different life from the one which you claimed as a first love. You will never be the same, for they will open and close the door behind themselves and no one and nothing can ever replace that place and hour when you claimed them for your own. You will see them like seasons, bloom, turn colors, change temperatures, and see their rising and settling within your soul, but you will never within your entire life experience that day when everything was so clear and so very new. You are apt to love over and over again and you may have a short walk or your path may be much longer, but you are apt to fall in love again. I have no consoling words for you. First loves are sort of like the first time you see an ocean or that you cross a dateline into the unknown. They are irreplaceable, but love again, bear hurt again, and place the one that was first somewhere sweet and kind and hold it like an old comforter now and then before locking it away. Hold on to it, to them, and someday even the pain will feel good. It sounds like the essence of rhetoric and misplaced energy, but you will deny yourself something as valuable as the day you were born if you do not look back to remember the splendor of your first romance.

It is the essence of what is there and what is possible, the child's heart summoned all of the love you could bear and you do not wear it like a token, but you keep it like a key to open your heart when a true love comes along, only this time you are wiser and you will know what the eyes are saying and you will soothe the wounded child with each passing year and the tenderness of a new love when it swells like the sea's mouth kissing you once more with sweet and white foam. Love is like that. It is only real if you hold it dearly close to you, and when it is lost, if you can take it out now and again, breathe deeply, and cherish its every moment, for if one tries to kill the source and the beginning of first loves, then, subconsciously, you are denying something as important as the day you were born or the day you said, "Yes," to the grace of falling in love again.

And, yes, we remain children to some degree, for we all long, at least sometimes, to be new and to take that walk back to our youth again, but we are also grown up, or most of us are, and we know that the best that we can do and the nearest we can get to that place is to gather our memories and to love them, to hope for our tomorrows and package the treasures from them and to open our hearts for those who have given us the best and most lasting love they have to offer. I feel lucky to know both places and do not take for granted that love at its best is difficult, but we are so very unfortunate if we never experience this ultimate gift. That "God is love" is no accident, for whatever else could possibly matter?

I would be failing my southern sisters if I did not at this time tell you something of the difficulty that was becoming apparent in the early months of my independence. There is an old adage, "You can take the girl out of the country, but you can't take the country out of the girl." This would become far more significant than I could see at the time in the last half of the 1960s, and as I peer back, I can see the subtle little nuances, the patronizing smiles, and the constant misunderstanding of what a kid from "Back There," as they tended to call Bible Belt America, might be encountering. At first there are the references to language.

"Oh would you say that again—it was so cute," in reference to the southern accent which I was purposefully setting aside. I had particular problems with words that ended with the sound of ill, as in Bill, pill, hill, and people would find such humor that I absolutely at first could not say any of these words without double-syllabling them. The sounds always came out as, "Bi-ill," as in my brothers name and I remember even Mark going over and over again with me these words in an effort to show me that I was saying them differently. I could not hear it, but I worked and worked and I got it down to pronounce one syllable words without the high/low emphasis which seemed to separate me from people with the so called "normal" use of language.

My friends often had most enjoyable moments if I came out with something which was just normal in my former world. One which set them off in to laughter was, "I could just stomp you." In my world that was a good-natured way of saying that I could hug you, I could kiss you, or I am so excited about what you just did for me. I emphasize the concept of normal, for I have generally learned from traveling across this country that each region has a less than pure dialect. The Midwest is somewhat more nasal with, "goin'" and "comin'," as immediate thoughts of differences in sound. The ing sound must be well emphasized in school or it will just not get pronounced.

The easiest example of eastern seaboard states' differences is the inability to pronounce the letter R as in "car" and "far" and the very proper use of the word "bath" with the *a* as an "aw" sound. Going west one gets more of a combination, for the language seems a little slower and words more purposeful as if well thought out before, but it is just the easy west where life is not so hurried. Once we really get out west into the Pacific coast states, there is a greater purity of the English language with no immediate exceptions, though most people are going to understand a lot more Hispanic words, a lot more of what I call stupid slang, or just making up a word that gets added to the English language like "hella" as an adjective or "That's just radical!" In other words, I disagree that Californians are without language anomalies.

In the 1960s, "groovy" and "radical" and "Well, like, man, do you really believe it!" These are all clichés that have hung around from the days of Haight Ashbury and the urge to get out to "Frisco." But Southerners get the litmus test on language even to this day, for it is very regional.

Words came out of the mountains from the mixing of Old English with Scottish, Irish, the tribal Indians, and even showed up from the Spanish explorers as the Melungeons came about from marriage of blacks to Indians and to some whites with sixteenth- to seventeenth-century wanderers up into the Shenandoah Valley. Not only is there the concept of the southern drawl, but from southern state to southern state the dialect and pronunciations are different. I can easily tell a Charlestonian apart from someone from Nashville. Tennessee is mid-south and probably more mountain-influenced, especially in Middle Tennessee where I was from, and as with all southern states in this area because people are heading toward the sunbelt still, it has less of the deep south sound. I had been nowhere, though, but again, thank you, Miss Nell Baker. She had taught us enunciation and the 4-H public speaking had given me lessons about elocution, so I had a head's up on some of us who went toward Washington, D.C.

"Did you just here how she said 'cat?'" At first I thought it was complimentary and then it became embarrassing to me. I picked up the language of the girls around me within the first year, and I have ever since been accused of having a pure German dialect secretly hidden in my soul, so go figure that one. In dress, I did not have a clue, except I would go shopping with the girls and that was the period of time when you could have put a flour sack over my head, and it would have looked good. My sister Violet picked me up at George Washington University one day after work and immediately said, "That is embarrassing. Is that the best coat that you have?"

I looked at my coat, which was the only one I'd had since the sixth grade, a hand-me-down by a factor of about ten users, and I suddenly became ashamed, for it was all that I had to keep warm and the autumn leaves were falling in Washington. Night would fall early, around four-thirty in the afternoon on the shortest of winter days. I hadn't noticed my frayed three-quarter-length sleeves, the torn linings, and the fact that the coat belonged in a garbage bin. It was my damned coat for better or worse. I also knew absolutely nothing about hats, gloves, scarves, or leggings and boots. I am not kidding you, and to this day if I see a child without gloves on a cold winter's day, then that child may wind up with what I have on. Mama did not knit whatsoever, so we had no outer comfort apparel, and most kids in school were lucky to even own a jacket. We sort of just kept layering clothes on top of each other, therefore we never smelled except for outer layers, and they just smelled like moth balls.

Mama would yell at us on cold winter days and tell us to make ourselves a "head rag" as she called a head scarf. Therefore, I was probably one of the few native-born Americans who went around Washington looking like a peasant grandmother from the Russian countryside. Violet insisted, absolutely insisted, that I buy a coat, so we went to J. C. Penney and I bought the first new coat that I had ever had. I looked at myself in the mirror, and I was almost looking at another person who looked like a college or business girl. It took probably half of my sister's salary to see that I was vaguely warm that winter, for I would have to learn about other warm accessories as I ran through the snow and ice storms which pelted Washington from before Christmas until the end of the early springtime. I still had only one pair of shoes, and even into years of plenty, I still tend to wear one pair of sensible shoes. Boots were about the most amazing things which I ever wore, for I had never known that legs could be warm, and the last thing which I ever dreamt was that boots were very sexy, for they zipped tightly against the lean body of my youth, and between that and deciding that I liked outrageous tights, I began to look like a city girl. At the time, though it hurt me to learn that I looked like something out of the sad old book, *Trailing Arbutus* about a girl that was just made to look homespun, I will never forget the day my sister had the mercy and generosity to get me in to street clothes.

It was presumed immediately that being a girl from the woods that I should stop at every place where telephone and electrical guys were working, for if I was with my VISTA gang, we got a whole lot of attention. The girls always wanted me to respond to the whistles and cat calls from these guys, and probably many of them were nice fellows whom I might have had a good time with. I would smile at the girls and not say much, but I knew that I did not want to marry a laborer, for there was this promise stuck in my brain, this defiance of my species of Southern Womanhood, which had declared that I was not going to settle for the life people expected of me, for I was going to make Mom and Dad proud and one way or the other I would pull it off. I would go to college.

I did not know that I was about to fold a time or two under the pressure of having older men love me, and I am talking PhDs, physicians, lawyers, and university geeks. I did not know just how afraid I was every day of my life to just get up, get to a job, and to endeavor to meet the demands of becoming a larger player in a big city than I was ever prepared to be. Mainly, I did not know that sometimes I would just like to be back on Tennessee turf, sleeping next to my sisters under the quilts that had begun to disintegrate with the passing of time, but taking one thing at a time was what seemed to get me from day to day.

Another thing happened that I need to apologize to Damian for the little black boy whose family picked cotton with me and who played up and down the fields with me. I began to be terrified of black people. I never went to Washington as a prejudiced person, and I naively lived in a ghetto or near ghetto areas during much of my stay there, but within a year after having moved there I had my purse snatched twice, each time by a black guy. One had a gun, and when he asked me where I lived as I stood in front of my basement apartment after taking my purse, my brain said, "I live up the street" and that's what I told him. People were coming home from work, and I guess he decided that maybe I was from too far away and so he made me promise to hide in the basement well until he was out of sight. That was the only thing that saved me from getting raped that day.

A few weeks later, a group of little black boys feeling their oats attacked me on 16th Street three blocks from the White House, and they were endeavoring to shove sticks up my dress. The oldest was less than ten years old. Suddenly and without warning, I would fear black people for the first time in my life, whereas in Tennessee, we had just been poor together. Little did I know that all of this was like some symphonic production where the prelude to the theme of rage was only beginning. America was about to burst open like an inferno, and the ghetto blacks of Washington were so full of hate and rage for white people that they could not contain themselves when it came to what appeared to be a very white girl who just passed by them with some kind of big smile.

I would learn that once more the Civil War had left blacks and whites as divided as before and those who came to Washington and settled after Mr. Lincoln freed them, were still slaves to a million masters, to the white upper-class, to the criminal justice system, to drugs and alcohol, and to lack of schooling. And all of the promises of equality had never manifested as truth as was the plan even after almost a hundred years of being free. I didn't like black jokes and I wanted to know the families. I thought that there was good in everyone and face to face, I would learn that hatred is such a bitter pill to swallow that even blacks outside of the south had given up. You are my brother. You are my sister. I wanted to say these things, but people of color had become as petrifying to me as the German shepherd dog our neighbors kept that had torn my dress off my back so long ago, and I would tremble in the presence of black men.

I had become prejudiced for the first time in my life and doesn't it seem odd to you that the prejudice did not begin in my little clearing in the road in the boundaries of the South, but in the nation's capital? I was like a disappointed child and only later, through some understanding roots of poverty and lack of opportunity would I ever get beyond beginning to feel my own taste of hate. To this day I wish that I had gone and sat on some porches with black families and told them about our cotton fields and how we were all just poor together, but we did not have the voices we have now which say it so beautifully as President Barack Obama, "Let us begin the conversation," and there would be few conversations before this country was on fire with a rage. There was supposed to have been some happy ending in 1865 when the Civil War ended, but instead, poverty bred poverty, and the black people of America had to be informed by Dr. Martin Luther King that it wasn't just about them. It was poor people everywhere. Keeping us in our place guaranteed the greater society wealth beyond measure and left us blacks and whites to dislike each other because we all needed food from the same table.

I would later know that I was capable of standing up and walking for all poor people and for singing and saying, "Too many people have died." My voice was just a little squeak in a bullhorn of all the poor living and dead, but I would learn what happens when a society finally cracks like an earthquake. The late 1960s will remain historically as the struggle without arms, but with locked arms walking, talking, going one way together, for that was the only way any of us had any power. History will recall that decade long after we children of the cotton fields are laid to our rest. Bless you, Dr. King, President John Kennedy, and Senator Robert Kennedy, for you must dwell among the saints who cry for mercy.

Moving On

With the hope of Mark out of my life, I began to feel an old and familiar sadness, almost like when someone dropped a box of used clothing at our house during my childhood and my sisters would so happily find things that fit. Since I was an amazingly late bloomer, oftentimes the box would be emptied and nothing in it would have been something I could use. Mama would do her best and find a couple of things of my sisters' that they could pass along to me and she would simply tell them that they had gotten new stuff, so Barbara was going to be receiving something cast off from them. We wore anything and everything that was sent to us, and we fit in with most of the country girls, for if we found a pair of spike heels with the toes pointed enough to remove a tonsil, then we had found church clothes. We also painted our lips with lipstick thick enough that one could plow through it, and chewing gum was not only acceptable, but it was expected to be that one thing which kept your teeth white and kept your breath juicy and fruity just in case that moment of being discovered should happen when fame would knock at the door before Sunday school.

I only add this in here for it reminds me of my endeavors to once again become a good Church of Christ girl when I found one on 16th street in Washington. There was a very large congregation as I had never seen other than once in Memphis, when I was on childcare duty with Uncle's family. And Lord knows, though Catholicism recognized the bread and wine as the absolute essence of Christ's body and blood and offered communion at all masses, the Church of Christ also offered communion each Sunday. When the invitation was given to come forward for baptism or repentance, however, once again, the only significance of the bread and wine was symbolic and in spite of the Last Supper of Jesus, when he declared before the apostles that when they took the bread and the fruit of the vine, they were partaking of Him, these same people called Catholics cannibals for eating something which seemed mighty darned important. I was searching, pretty certain that I had found my way as a happily blessed Catholic sinner, but when one feels down, church is something like going home, or so I thought.

I dressed up just like I would back at Lexie, lipstick intact and high heels on, only this time I think that I added fishnet hosiery for the new 1960s and 1970s fashion required some fairly kinky wear, and one went to God's house with their Sunday fashion magazine clothes, which I was beginning to buy now and then when I had some extra money. I hooked up with a youth group who had broken up in to smaller groups. We would have a Sunday activity together before evening church.

At this time I had a roommate from Odessa, Texas, a very pretty girl who taught nursery school, enjoyed eating, smoking, alcohol, and other vices which I would soon share. We would become roommates for a while after I had to give up on my life with the VISTA group once they settled in the deeper ghetto. On two week nights, my precious high school ring had been stolen that I'd worked all that summer before graduation to pay for and my entire take-home money which I had hid in my sewing box, and another rape attempt—all of this had convinced me that since I had a work life and the VISTAS did everything together, that I was no longer safe in the midst of Washington where the crime was so bad that a task force had been set up to try to just manage the killing and robberies. The neighborhoods were falling to drug thugs and pimps. Thus the moving from place to place had begun for me.

You might have presumed that I needed a place of comfort, and the youth group seemed to have some promise as I still debated religious life. It soon became apparent that the meetings after church were gatherings where couples paired off again, and there was one fellow in the entire group that I was interested in, the twenty-seven-year-old group leader, but so was every other woman his age, under his age, and above him in years, for he was one of the only good-looking guys in the entire group. Most of them were in Washington for a short while, working as pages or studying to go home and pastor churches of their own, and again this seemed to have some promise for me. The fellow they paired me up with was as nice as he could be, but if you've ever been licked by a dog that is very slobbery, then you'll know what I mean when I say that as his mouth came near mine, I felt as if I was being forced to kiss one of Dad's old mouth-dribbling pups before the shotgun was brought out to put him out of his misery. He definitely did not have kissing down, and he was over twenty making me wonder how many other newbies they had tried to stick him with just to find him a life partner when he went back and took up ministry. He always had *The New*

Testament in one hand and held my hand with the other and gave me those God-forsaken kisses of spit and drool. If I could go back, maybe I would say, "Sweetheart, you are awfully nice. You're a good Christian, but the slobbers have got to go." He tried to take me out several times, and I went back to the church for maybe three months, but I found that the social life was very lacking and in a bigger setting, I was finding that a back-home girl was just as comfortable at Catholic mass and in many ways much more so, for I could be unto myself.

My Protestant life finally came to a permanent end when I saw this guy one last night, and I do not even know what all I said, but I used whatever ghetto talk that I could manage such as, "Forget the spit. I prefer the skin." And I know that it wasn't very nice of me, but I was using it to alienate him and the whole group of people. I wanted them to say that I was hopeless and if they prayed for my soul at the next Sunday's group meeting, that was all fine, but I wanted back with the people that I had come to love. After a few more moves, a few more roommate tries, and feeling the great loss of the VISTA and Peace Corp kids, I looked them all back up again, and we picked up where we left off. They had gotten a little beat up themselves, and most were beginning to think about returning to the hometowns of their youth, but while I could be with them, I was going to, and I was there to learn how to live in a foreign land which happened to be our nation's capital city.

I may as well have moved back in with Kathy and Carol now, but I was on a mission to find a place before they would leave the city also. A trail of my roomies included a girl that I had gone to high school with and who I have not seen since she left Washington D. C., for I think that there is nothing I could say to her that would not admit that I feel like I damaged her emotionally to the core by having her come to Washington. She had come from a very good home and family and she was just looking for a job. Instead, I paved the way for her to find boyfriends like the rest of us. In other words, to become the almost hippies that we were and to give up her Appalachian valley ways, but she needed no such change, for she was comfortable in the wisdom she'd learned from her father and mother and her brothers. She would wind up despising me as a person who had misled her into a life which held no promise for her, the entire experience of the move, and this land beyond her comfort zone. Once she got really angry with me and told me that she thought that I had become a heartless bitch, an amoral shadow of my former self, and certainly not her friend.

I had taken advantage of her hospitable soul, and I had stripped her naked for the world to see—a girl from my world who was satisfied with a country morning, who missed her family, and who had left a world of comfort for what she saw as my place of becoming a spoiled love child. And then somehow a miracle happened. A boy from back home came through from his Vietnam experience, and they fell in love. I would feel that there was reason for her place with me after all, but as well as the ending of her Washington days seemed to have come, the worst was yet to come.

She married this boy, and he died in an airplane crash, and though I wanted to console her, all that I felt she had left in her for me was disdain, and I somehow accepted that I was the beginning and the end of everything she had treasured. At age eighteen, that was me lying down and setting myself aflame upon the altar beyond redemption.

Before moving from the 16th Street apartment building, I would meet a thirty-five-year-old psychologist who was a Hungarian Jewish man who kept a pistol hidden in case he ever needed it. I think that he had been married previously, but that was long over. He had parents in New York City who, along with him, had escaped the Holocaust. As hard as it may be for anyone to accept, I knew nothing about the Holocaust or Judaism, and he would begin my lessons. In retrospect, he was probably a bit of a pedophile, for as he began a relationship with me he began to teach me more about grown-up kind of love-making. He once remarked with me in his arms, "God, do I ever love little girls." And here I thought I was getting on up there, getting past eighteen and being so experienced. In spite of whatever he was, he began a new wave of consciousness for me that involved World War II, what happened to the Jews, the Gypsies, and to many Catholics who could not hide out as Aryans, another new term for me. He gave me a book called *I Never Saw Another Butterfly* filled with the last pictures, poems, letters, and drawings which were copied from the walls of places like Auschwitz and Buchenwald, other places that I knew nothing about.

I began to read the poems and look at the pictures which were in this holy book, and I wept. I was crying so hard that every part of me trembled. Robert could not comfort me, so he held me in his arms long and hard, and stroked my head as I cried for the children, the living and the dead, and I have cried for them ever since and hear their voices. And the butterfly flies by and I see their spirits, and I knew then that evil beyond all words had occurred. Two decades had passed, and no one spoke of it to me even in God's house. In Catholicism I would always appreciate the butterfly as the symbol of the Holy Spirit and the freedom which it exerts, and I treasure their entire cycle of life from cocoon to colored wings, the moments from emerging from the cocoon just like the few children who would be saved. People of the United States and the Allies when they dared tread on the devil's grounds and to take it from the demons of darkness who put the children to death and destroyed families like cord wood.

I needed to know Robert, and I needed to know about the *schoene Schmetterling*—beautiful butterflies—for I was in darkness until he opened my eyes to a world so much worse than my own had ever been. For it was the beauty of the creatures of earth, the flowers, the winged birds, and the butterflies which kept me breathing. The children's pain became my pain, and I began to read American history again, realizing that I knew more about the Civil War than I did about the war which had touched every other family in the Appalachians. Send the country boys to the front lines. Appalachian boys could shoot, and they were uneducated and dispensable, and I would later learn that we had heroes all around us back home, well before I was born.

Even now I can see the shining suns and the happy children from my special book, and I do not feel used by a man who loved me, even if he thought I felt like a little girl. Compared to the lost children I was ancient and for a while, I would be Robert's girlfriend to the extent we would work together, for he found out that I needed a new job, so the next thing

I knew he had me working at a society devoted to writing textbooks, plan guides, and new curriculums for the nation's public and private schools. He watched over me like a good father and that he was a lover was no particular secret at our work. For the first time I was with the Yale and Harvard graduates, people like Dr. Sheldon Steinberg, renowned for his academic textbooks at the time, and though I mainly took their phone calls and subbed for the girl who was the research corporation's executive secretary, I found a dimension of myself that was hiding, the scholar, the prideful young woman, and I again found a body of people who loved me.

Washington was a haven for Jewish people for some reason then, probably because a lot of brilliant Jews found their way in the hub of national policy and academia, so I learned everything I could while I was there. My friends were the Levys, the Steinbergs, the Fishmans, and every Jewish name you could think of, and like Robert, they treated me like a daughter. It was a glorious place to work, University Research Corporation, and I met there the woman, a *schikza* like myself, who would be the bridesmaid at my small wedding in a year or so to come, so the depressions of youth were beginning to subside somewhat.

My last memory of Robert had to do with having become angry with him when he brought a woman down from New York City, all poised and decked out in diamonds and fur, which was not considered too excessive at the time. She was an on-and-off real girlfriend for him about his own age. I was defensive enough to have come out on the roof and to unexpectedly find them embracing, something natural for people like them who were more appropriately suited for their age group, but I was insulted, too, and I said something regrettable about her delicate age to which I could see Robert's eyes filled with spears and daggers. It was springtime and lovely and I felt somewhat bad about interrupting what was obviously a better and long-term relationship for them.

Around Fathers' Day, now loving him and feeling sad that he had no children, I slipped a note under his door and tied a rosebud to the door knob. Suddenly I heard knocking at my door, and Robert appeared serious and he held his chest. "If you are pregnant," he said, "then you are going to St. Theresa's Girls' Home to give birth," and then I caught on. Fathers' Day, a good wish, a note and I had scared Robert half to death. He thought that I was carrying his child, and soon we were both laughing at this confluence of innocent events. After that, I realized that the woman with the diamonds and the fur coat was probably more suited to this New York City Hungarian Jewish guy. The most we had in common was work now, and he had done a study of the snake handlers and the evangelicals of the Appalachians, but we remained in contact for as long as he was in Washington, D.C. and for as long as we had the blessing of being the best of friends, though I never quite forgave him for threatening me with one of those birthing places. It is just that he could not fathom a world in which to bring a child that might never see another butterfly, and I knew that and loved him no less for it.

Chapter Thirty One

I can never believe this of me, but now and again I would long to go back home, to see my brothers and little sister, to be the one somebody was baking a cake for and to see if there was a life for me surrounded by the Cumberland Gap of Middle Tennessee and beneath the shadows of Keith Springs and Crow Mountain. These were all areas which we had to cross over to visit the family that I never really knew very well, my father's line, who lived on Sand Mountain, place of my birth, and Lookout Mountain, where the bones of my Confederate Great-Grandfather Samuel Clay Everett and his wife Annie, and most of their children were already at rest.

I never knew, nor shall I ever know, why my dad would not discuss his family, but I would learn in later years that my sister Rose had asked him, "Daddy, what is your first memory from being a boy?" And Daddy looked with his eyes cast down and as if he were someplace else and he replied in his, the-conversation-ends-here voice, "You really do not want to hear about it." And my sister knew that it was more than he could ever possibly share.

Dad's family had come from near where Gainesville, Georgia, now stands where Dad's great-grandfather owned about 800 acres at one time before the Civil War. It was Dad's grandfather and his great-grandfather there along with Dad's Uncle John Everett, another Confederate Soldier known to have fought all the way to Gettysburg during the saddest days of American history. My great-grandfather, also a Samuel, joined up as a boy and wound up being captured twice. He cooled his heels in the prisons of the cold northern states. In Maryland, Point Lookout Prison, and then to a well-known prison in Columbus, Ohio, called Camp Chase. Great-Grandfather's last imprisonment came on Sherman's march through Georgia, and we know that he did not get out of that prison until the end of the war, if not afterward. His federal pension papers show that he was released in April of 1865. Family history is something which no one ever discussed when I was a child, so all of this I have had to find out about and to search for on my own.

We know that there is an Everett family cemetery in South Carolina where we believe Great-Great-Grandfather Everett and his family are buried, but I only bring up the family history at this point to tell you that somehow my father became the son of William Everett, my grandfather who wound up in a land dispute with his father, the second Samuel and who then relocated his family to Sand Mountain, though Great Uncle John and Great-Grandfather would remain on beautiful Lookout Mountain, which looked over at a yet even higher mountain from their home which still exists near Collinsville, Alabama. It was a beautiful home with wonderful farmland, and once there was a school within a mile of their house, where William would be taught, along with his brothers and sisters. They learned math and Greek and had a better life than my family could have ever imagined. In following my genealogical record, though, you will note that I would become the granddaughter of those who not only left Georgia, but who also separated themselves from the main body of the family in Alabama, forfeiting our legacy. My grandfather, William, left a broken family with many broken souls, and my father would be sixteen years old before he would visit his family in Collinsville, and that was when Great-Grandfather Samuel died. So generations before me, we had left the main body of the Everett clan who probably came through the port of Charleston, though some evidence now points to an arrival in New York in 1809, heading west. Then Georgia was part of the more western places.

Just to make the picture a little clearer, the 1820 Georgia census shows that my great-great grandfather Samuel Everett was residing in what is now Cherokee County, Georgia. Great-Grandfather Samuel Clay and his brother John would then move to Lookout Mountain near the town of Collinsville, the first to part the original family, and they would reside in that area until their deaths. Grandfather, William, after marrying an Indian woman which was frowned upon in those days, would lose that wife, and we presume also the child she bore after he left Collinsville. William L. Everett, my grandfather, would next marry Barbara Ellen Durham of

Chavis, Alabama. He would move her to Jackson County, Alabama, and their family, insofar as I know, would all then be born on Sand Mountain above Scottsboro, near a little place called Rosalie. The next large move for the Everetts would be when my father, Amos Orsbon Everett, who married my mother Thelma Hood, a Tennessee valley girl whom Dad met walking down the mountainside to go fishing and to use her father's boat along with his brothers, took the family to Lexie Crossroads, Tennessee. My mother was born in Meigs County Tennessee, part of the Irish Clan, the Varners.

Mother longed to go home, especially after her folks moved from Coon Valley. She would see all of her brothers and Dad's brothers go off to World War II and with her folks moving a time of work in a Chattanooga thread factory where she would spend weeks away from the farm and from Daddy. After having two sons, my brothers, Ira Neil and Robert Van, Mama would begin to long for her mother and father once more. She was only sixteen years of age when she married Dad and before her thirty-sixth year of life, she would have three daughters as well—Rose, Violet, and then me. I would be the last child that would be born on the mountain before Daddy would give Mother her wish to move to the Tennessee valley near her folks. The other children—James, William, and Linda—would be the born in Tennessee. Dad, even after he was an older man, would long for that mountain-top, and along with his sister Aunt Helen would be the only children to locate themselves more than a day's drive from home. Aunt Helen would find a good job in Oakridge, Tennessee, in the early days of nuclear research there, and Daddy had moved us to a life of hell ordained by my mother's brother Ralph.

The farm hands had arrived! Daddy let Uncle Ralph find us a home. And as I've mentioned before, it was basically a two-story unfinished house with no plumbing and no electricity and with little land for cultivation, so that left Amos and Thelma's kids as Ralph's field hands and as cotton choppers, pickers, housemaids, and caretakers for Granny Hood and any other family members. Sand Mountain was at least home, and Granny Everett seemed to love us, and Dad and his brothers showed some mercy for one another, but we had come to a place without help or kindness. Somebody sold asbestos-laden tar paper, which was supposed to look like red brick on the outside. It looked like tar scored with a red brick stamp on the house.

This almost needs to be diagrammed like a sentence, but if you have followed the line with me from the Georgia mountains then you will have noticed that my brothers and sisters and I were always a part of the family who broke away. Things were not perfect in Alabama, but we were Everetts, and we probably seemed somewhat like a clan. But once we were in Tennessee and with Mother's own family who had broken away from their East Tennessee roots, then we became the loneliest and at times the most without souls under God's heaven. The Hoods and Varners had large families in areas like Soddy Daisy, Tennessee, Meigs County, Tennessee, and mainly in the areas where the white folks and East Tennessee Cherokee Indians had married up with one another, but we became the nobodies who moved in The Old Solomon Place, as it was called, and we were not among any even known to be kin to Mother's family, the Hoods, because we came in late to the life of Lexie Crossroads and Huntland School. Grandmother and Grandfather Hood began to treat my father as if he were the least of men who could not provide for his family, and they gave Mother only grief letting her know that they did not like her or her big family and insofar as she was concerned, "You made your bed girl, so lie in it." Mother never got the loving support of parents or grandparents, only more hurt than she could bear. Most of Mom and Dad's children are very white, but the Varners and Hoods, especially Grandpa Hood, looked like the mostly Indian he was.

I looked back upon it all, though, and when I would think of going back to Mama and Daddy, the brothers and sister, I had to challenge my heart to go on and to stay in Washington until I could get back in to school or until I married, which did not seem likely at the old age of seventeen and eighteen with not a clue as to how to find a life's love, not certain that I even knew if love existed for anyone and with no one waiting back home except for a few high school boys who may have taken a second look, for I had blossomed in many ways, late though certainly apparent, so I would put the thought of returning to my valley, to my mountains, to all of the pain and sorrow that had called me away. Yes, I would put it to rest. I could not help anyone at home until I could make something of myself and I would hate be called "a work in progress," but I felt that way. I would not drag myself back to become another beaten wife or girlfriend left if a baby came into the picture, not on your life. When I would return, then I would have something to show for having left in the first place.

It is a strange thing, too, for when I pictured myself going home at all, I would see this little girl with bare feet, and she would be walking around the graveled road from the old tarpaper house. The new grasses of spring would have those little blue flowers and Daddy's peanut stack would have by now composted down to almost nothing, so there would be no more for roasting. Winter would be passing, and in a distance were the blue mountains, the backdrop to the emerald green of spring. The little girl might sing or stop and make a few mud pies where the ruts of the road had been carved in winter and where the melted ice gave water to help mold the mud into all kinds of forms. She would be walking to the corner where Mr. Hannah's barn could be seen from the road, heeding the warning not to go further. She would stop and admire cattle grazing, push on a tooth that was about to fall out, and she would be so happy not to be cold, to be by herself, and looking no further forward than to the moment it took to think that life went no farther than the garden's gates, the fences that separated the farms, the Masons, the Hannahs, and the Everetts, and it was a hopeful child that stood there, too young to know all that would lie ahead. For those moments, she was the girl that was hope-filled. As long as I could only see the little girl that was me and the world that stopped there, then I could not go home again.

A gentle elderly man by the name of Alvin Reeves would tell me about my Lookout Mountain family when I was much older, and I would see the house near Collinsville and see the old soldier's grave who was my Great-Grandfather Samuel laid to rest there with Great-Grandmother Annie and all of their children except for William who was buried on Sand Mountain and Great Uncle John who is buried at The Pleasant Valley Cemetery with his wife and family. As I looked upon those old Confederate graves, I realized that they had left their children with a message which they did not intend. It was that they were on a losing side of something, a Civil War, an embarrassment to a nation, and the thing is they never were anything but a bunch of good old farmers who knew their homeland was being invaded. They had no mansions, no slaves. They were a part of the Indian land grab which will live as a great sin of the forefathers gone before them and into their generation, but in their lifetime they would have known a broken South for most of their kind, and they would again become families apart, minding their own business, doing their own work, and prospering to place food on the table and to provide for their families. They would take consolation in the faith of their fathers, but they would also remember a country in peril and how good it felt to come home when it was all over. Loss meant picking up their labor where they left off, staying tightly woven to the land and to the community around them.

Loss of the Old South, to them, was simply recalling the sons who did not get to come home. It was in my nature to wish for no more or no less in moments of despair, for I was born to ages of people who cared for nothing more than the safety of place and time. They would not believe that their granddaughter of the South would watch Washington, D.C. burn from the top of her apartment building on 16th Street in the riots that plagued the country after Dr. Martin Luther King died in 1968, and that in every city when we were not mourning for Dr. King, then we were mourning for John then Robert Kennedy. It would be beyond them to know that not only could I see the nation's capital on fire, but federal troops were in tanks just below us to protect the way to the White House and to stop the madness. And I thought of these things as I decorated all of their graves with flowers, their feelings of loss, our feelings of loss in our time, and how most of us did not have the most basic thing which all of these people did have surrounding them at their hours of greatest need—that when it was over and done, the word would go out that one of their own was coming back for homecoming and as soon as they could all get together, they would all celebrate under the old trees which shaded the yard and provided rest for a family that went unbroken. I have felt their spirits within me like a patchwork quilt keeping myself together even as the fabric of my life sometimes seemed too tattered to bear. Something of color and something of beauty held me in one piece and I hold dear that I found them, even though it was their resting place.

Chapter Thirty Two

That first year in Washington, D.C. would bring my friend Tom Bissell back to D. C., and as usual he was without work, though he had picked grapes somewhere in South America for a time, and he had sent me a post-card to let me know that he had not forgotten me. He was about twenty-eight years old by then, and he was remembering a girl in England who he thought maybe he should go back and marry. With great trepidation and the risk of the fires of hell, though, I had concluded that he was not getting away without being the first love for me. If it was worth his coming through to be with me, then he would not go away disappointed. How incomprehensible it was to think he wanted to see me again. Me? I had even begun to like the way that he usually smelled of some sweet wine, and that he always wore the same British-schoolteacher sport coat which smelled of mist and warm tweed as if he was an expatriate frat boy, but he always looked great.

Other than to simply reminisce about Murfreesboro, Tom felt good for saving me from being locked up in "Backwater," where no one returned even halfway sane. Coming from a Pittsburgh, Pennsylvania, guy that was somewhat judgmental, for the mills still spewed their grit and grime into the air along that Allegheny valley, but he always had that one-upsmanship for he was an expert freeloader, and women and girls just loved him, like me. So he could make me feel as if he had come from a very urban center.

He was it, my chosen first love and his coming back to Washington was in my simple reality about me and not about him. Within a couple of nights he could get the following: food, money from someone with whom he chatted as if great secrets were compelled to exist, a proper bath and grooming, and the absolute right of any way he passed. To be wined, dined, and then laid—then he was good to go. It could have been a scene out of some glorious movie as he and I walked over 16th Street headed up to

Lafayette Park, and I think that he was almost as surprised as I to realize that I could stop on the avenue headed toward the White House and to share kisses that I had never shared before. I do not doubt that there was vivid steam coming from both of our bodies as we walked along that night, and he began to offer me the hotel of my choice for my chosen seduction, but I did not know about hotels and who needed such when a work friend had offered me the keys to her place, since I was apartment-sharing again.

I, for the first time in my life, felt as if I was wanted in a desperate way, and by now I was eighteen at least, and my newness, Tom's experience and inebriation—it all kept us tightly in each other's arms until we got near George Washington University where I still worked and where I had planned on our being together at the apartment that my so-called friend had offered.

All saving myself for marriage had taken a dive into the abyss of all yesterdays, for Tom and I were together! He had come back as he said he would, and I decided that there had to be something divine involved, for in my heart I'd thought that I would never see him again.

He told me how wonderful I felt in his arms, how pretty he thought I was, and asked himself why he had waited so long to get this involved with me, almost a year since I had become seventeen, and how we made it through the door much less into the bed I am not certain. I took my time for I was so afraid that I would disappoint him in some way, and I never wanted this feeling to end, that someone was actually almost trembling to have their arms around me, and Tom, being the natural instructor even as an undergraduate teacher at college, told me everything to do. Then I remembered Aunt Mildred's books which said that everything just sort of comes naturally, so I began to give and to receive a kind of loving which I had never known before. Everything about me was an ember longing to burn, and I did not understand any of it, just that I might go to hell for letting it happen. I loved Tom so much in those moments that an apocalyptic event would have to occur to make it all end, and it did.

Cynthia, whose apartment it was, walked in just to check the refrigerator's contents and to tell us all about the care package her mother had sent to her, and I, among the shyest girls in the world, just covered Tom and me up, and he rested on my arm while she blessed the soap, the toilet paper, the Bumble Bee Tuna, and the Campbell's Soup, and her great new box of Sugar Pops. Tom kept settling in more and more next to my skin, and he fell asleep in my arms, and soon, before I could even protest his resting she left, and he was asleep, gently asleep, and I held him with my eyes open until daybreak. We would lie that way until about eleven the next day when he would awaken me and realize where we had left off. We did all of those things young lovers do, brushed our teeth, freshened up a bit for each other, and all of the feelings were there again. He began to instruct me in where the most sensitive areas of his male organ were, and I would show him that I had read the books well, and I knew how to excite him, too. We were taking great time and care again, and he began to worry about "protection" and I could not understand why, for he was with me, the girl he had led away from back home, and if I got a baby that would be great. He could marry me.

He was finding, though, that I definitely knew how to keep him excited without any form of penetration, and he told me that he had a daughter and was terrified of getting someone else pregnant. I insisted, though, and he began to relent, and his body came over mine and we were ready, and it was awkward, for all of the faces of the perfect church people I knew began to make me anxious, and when we finally just about had it right—crash, clang—in walks Cynthia again with an "Oh I am sorry, you guys." At this point I went into tears, Tom realized he could not risk fatherhood, and after Cynthia went back to work we got up and went to breakfast, paid for by me, of course, for Tom always had a way of not having enough money yet being able to catch the next airplane to London or Paris, or to meet someone in Barbados, things I would later understand that young rich men got away with, because they are born to upper-class parents.

He loved me and held me for a while after breakfast, and he said he would be leaving for Europe on that day and it made me cry, so cry, for I was in love emotionally and physically now. We had known each other for two years now, and that seemed like most of my life, but he said, "I want you to go with me." I told him that I could not, for I still felt that I needed to pay my sister back for her winter coat, and I needed to make money for my family back home, and I walked away from him after we said goodbye.

I took a taxi back to my place on 16th, and to this day I hear Louis Armstrong singing on that radio, "I see trees of green, red roses too. I see them all for me and for you, and I say to myself, what a wonderful world." I heard Tom say again that he would come back, and I wanted to get out of that car and run to catch him, but I had no imagination of what could happen between us if we did what half the old hippies were doing then leaving for Europe, or hitch-hiking out to California, for I only knew that danger usually lay in wait without a guide, and I wasn't certain that my love was a guide.

He would come back through a few weeks after that, but this time he just called me, and he had gone to Cynthia's for a place to sleep. Cynthia had one bed, and he had one need for one night, and I knew it. I fell apart in one million pieces, threw down the phone and wept, and cried like a baby, as they would say back home. I did not understand even by then that men whom I loved were often interested in the carnal, not the soul, or the girl that was me. Just pure and carnal recreational sex. I did not know such a thing existed, for most girls that I knew who had babies and got husbands with the deal, so I thought they married each other out of love, and some few did, but this was not what was happening for me.

Later, I would understand that Tom had Washington as one of his stops on his jet-setting days, and maybe he cared a little something for me, for he and I at least were acquainted with the land beneath the Appalachians, and he had seen when a young woman needed advice, and he gave it to me. He would enter my life now and again after those years, even after we were married, but in a sober state. He claimed innocence in knowing all that had transpired, but to this day I can still picture the yellow taxi cab, Louis Armstrong's throaty wish for me to have shared the trees of green and the red roses too with the man of long ago who smelled of sweet wine, a warm evening, and the love story which had to end just like the mystery books where one must draw their own conclusions. Maybe no one is guilty of the harm done, but I was a broken girl for several months after that, more broken than I had been since Dr. Capers called in Mama.

Most seasons of our lives we can put into some kind of proper perspective and move on, yes, move on and feel better that we passed that way. I can see the comedy of Cynthia's morbid curiosity about the handsome man in her bed, but I am left to this day to wonder if I was really part of the love life of a young man, or just a gateway on his journey. Either way, the story somehow needed to be told. I will promise to laugh with you at how very naive I was if you will understand that this girl with the best of intentions to love wholly and with all of her heart never was less fragile than any one of you. So many country songs bring up the thorn in the rosebud, and I think that is what we have to become sometimes to make our path, the thorns which prick us until blood is drawn, and then we are chosen to find the flower petals which will mark our path.

Chapter Thirty Three

I Listened, at times, for the pine forest to call me home, to shelter me from the Washington jungle I was in, and even now I think that I can hear the rush of wind through the pines when the snow is about to fall and when all of the pink honeysuckles are hiding until the new mystic of spring touches their tops with some magic wand and the forest bed will open up pink again. I wanted to find home, so I moved around from place to place and somehow wound up sharing a place on 16th Street where I stayed longer than at most places except for the year with my VISTA and Peace Corps friends. My roommate was an Odessa, Texas, girl, who I've mentioned before and older than me by several years, she was already a teacher and I meandered, if you'll remember, somewhat back into The Church of Christ with her. Half of that church had come from the mid to lower southern states.

She was beautiful, absolutely Texas beautiful in some ways, and she and I would spend days walking around the capitol area when people could still wander freely among our government buildings and even eat in the dining areas where senators might be having lunches. She took me to an Army Band concert there once and I was absolutely amazed. You could just sit on the steps around the Capitol Building and listen to great-looking young men play band music, not a favorite of mine, because I was already hooked on Bob Dylan and lived for Judy Collins' *Wildflowers* album, of which I would learn every song and sing over the next twenty years or so. I remember that as we walked out one of the band members started chatting a little with me, and I felt as if I had met royalty. I would not know until a year had passed when I would meet one of the President's own United States Marine Band guys, how gifted these musicians were. But I give this roommate, whose name may have been "Cherry"--no kidding, credit for giving me my first look at what would be great symphony musicians in years to come. They came to Washington to audition for the service bands because it was a no-brainer to do so with the Vietnam War fully on and the draft still legal.

We will call her Cherry for the sake of it and I do not have a lot to say about her except those Texas girls needed to be dipped in a pot of testosterone to get over their need to be Christians on Sundays then to be endeavoring to make love to every guy that pulled back a sheet every other day of the week. This girl got all dressed up once to have lunch with the good congressman from her district.

Holy cow! What a visit she'd had with him, this stalwart gentleman from where I will not say—ever—take it for what it is worth. Apparently he had told her what an absolute unloving wife he had been married to for darned near forty-five years, so awful, in fact, that right there on his congressional couch, my roommate had eased his pain and future days would come when she would need to console him more right there in the congressional office building. I would not have known that guys older than him could even still be courting the back-home girls, but he surely did and my roommate would go in with a bustier and girdle to endeavor to hide some of her curves and come back tell me about the love bond which was being established.

He slowed her up at some point, though, something about their families knowing each other with my thinking, "You do not know just how well these Texans do know one another." I decided that without reason within my lifetime, I could find no rationale to pay a visit to my congressman or senator if this was what went on with social calls. I am not here to suggest that there was one other male elected to the United States government at that time who got so close to his constituents, but I do understand that Washington never was a bastion of men above the fray of calls from nature and the girls back home, not to mention certain movie stars, congressional aides, and others who would rule the air waves in years to come. The sacred code again came down to the old line that Daddy said of the moonshiners and those doing God knows what else—that we should keep our mouths shut. I swear on a stack of Bibles that I do not remember my roommate's last name, and that congressman died a long time ago after a life of service to his fellow man, so I will let him rest in peace.

Having unfortunately been taken in after my breakup with Tom and after my beloved Mark was out of the picture, I was once more given boyfriends the VISTA girls left behind. One was a prominent D.C. attorney, and after having lost Tom without ever consummating the relationship, I wasn't about to let anyone else that I believed loved me get away because I would not be their lover. The attorney's place was very nearby, and he too had a wonderfully sad story of why he was divorced, alone, and free of guilt. Thus he gained my trust, my love, my body. I should have known my friend Natalie had kicked him off her list for some reason, but I was giving up on the good girl ways and this thirty-five-year-old, good-looking, and successful man easily claimed my heart. He smoked so much that he is probably dead now, too, but we were together for several weeks just before Woodstock, and I was very hurt to learn that I was not alone in his treasure trove of women to call upon.

I cried again. Another lost love, and Cherry listened and decided that this creep of a lawyer needed a good talking to, and I was ignorant enough to think, alright, she is older than me, and I have listened to her lost love stories enough. When dawn came the next day Cherry came in looking as if she had been in a cat fight with "love bites" all over herself. I absolutely went ballistic. "You spent the night with my boyfriend!" Being the gracious member of my church as she was, she could not tell a lie. "Well, we didn't mean for it to happen, but once we started talking, we just knew something was there, and we couldn't help ourselves."

I threw things, swore at her, called him up, and I am unable to confide in you what I said to him, for I do not know, but I can tell you that as I entered this point in my eighteenth year of life, I knew that I was just not able to rationalize anything about this thing called "love-making." It was more like the new words that were taking over the nation at that time: "getting screwed and the heck with love." I decided that I needed some mental healthcare.

My brief treatment led me to staying in an in-house setting for a while, because I had insurance and maybe Dr. Capers had been right. Maybe I had some wicked and horrid mental disease, so I went to an ER and got myself checked in, for I obviously had the common sense of a duck trying to swim through a vast of quicksand and God couldn't care about me except that he did allow George, my old beloved to escape the priesthood and to continue to love me. I loved him through it all and without question. So I did it. I shamed myself, the family, the universe, and I checked myself in as a mental case and they would give me medicine that turned me into a mute. I kid you not. My mouth could not project words and somehow I got my sister Violet on the phone and she came, saw what they had done to me, and she sprang me from that little visit to 1960's mental healthcare.

While there, I learned that most of my "inmates" as I called them were spoiled drugged-out hippies who were exchanging crabs from room to room, and we are talking critters, not the sweet Chesapeake Bay variety. Fortunately, I met a woman who was reading *The Good St. Anne* who I would later find out was the Biblical mother of Mary, Blessed Mary, to whom I would later see as a guardian angel in my own life. This sweet-spirited quiet woman saw me on my way and kept me away from the, free-sex-if-you-don't-mind-a-dose-of-crabs, and Violet would be mad at me for a while for going there in the first place. But her face would show also that this time she somewhat understood. She had been through lost loves herself by then.

I pondered the goodness of St. Anne. I can see the girl who read it as her salvation and thought about how my life kept bringing me back to St. Matthew's Cathedral. I would go there to pray and to breath in the incense which hovered over me, that special scent that washed my body and cleared my head. I would have my baptismal certificate from there, and I would endeavor to understand that love was not a frivolous state of being, even though in Washington, D.C. and all across the country, a sexual revolution had taken place and there was no going back to the early years of absolute innocence.

Chapter Thirty Four

There cannot be anything that just passed simply then into yesterday and washed away, for I had a follow-up appointment with a resident at D.C. Psychiatric Institute, and I would run into a guy whose name was among my favorites—Mark—and we sort of laughed the whole thing off as best one can laugh off having been given a medication that turns you into a mute person, and we began to talk. Then the next thing I knew we were going out. He was handsome, in a different way than I was accustomed to, for he was more olive and had wonderful dark hair neatly trimmed, and it turned out that he was just doing a psych rotation, which he was glad to be leaving, He told me that he was a New York City boy by birth, but he, like a lot of bright Jewish kids, went to George Washington University for medical training and had an apartment out in Hyattsville, Maryland. I would say he could have been a very dark haired Warren Beatty stand-in.

Here enters my old friend Cynthia again. She was sleeping with some sleaze-ball that she'd met at Dupont Circle, and they both told me that I was going to be nothing but a *schikza* to this guy. I didn't know what that meant, but they made it sound pretty terrible.

"You just wait," Cynthia and her boyfriend said. "He'll come driving up in his great big Cadillac and you're going to be his whore." So now we had the words schikza and whore together and I still did not know what they meant. They waited in the lobby with me trying to get me to turn around. And I will be damned, but this left me ready to run: a white Cadillac sure enough appeared in the driveway and there was the newest, "Mark" in my life driving it. He did not get out, he just invited me in and was very sweet, a little affectionate, and well-dressed, something most of my friends were not those days by most mothers' standards, and we drove away together with Cynthia and her drugged-out boyfriend still screaming out my fate.

After we got to Mark's place, he made a drink for the two of us and said something like, "Are you alright with this?" as we sat on his small patio.

He said, "I sent my roommate out for the evening."

I replied, "That wasn't necessary," forgetting too soon what had gone on with Tom. He must have thought me even more open to adventure than I was, but I did begin to realize that he had a one-bedroom place nicer than most medical residents then, but we had another drink or so which he made, and I felt comfortable, and I was daring to let myself feel easily a case for debauchery, so when we went back in and he turned back covers and held me sweetly, I thought we might be a fairly good pair together.

Next thing I knew, I was locked in his arms, clothes disappearing, light softly dimmed, and he was sweet to be near. I felt I was receiving some kind of blessing by this guy that I had met in an ER. After all, my naive world kept telling me to find a way back to my medical school journey which was my original intent when I left home, so maybe Mark was the sign, the wonderful love charm who would lead me that way.

Unfortunately one thing they had obviously not taught well in medical school was love-making, for it was like a drill. " Clothes off, a bigeer kiss than usual, hold tight, and then tighter, and coordinate parts and like a spark made when one plugs an old toaster in; his body burned within, and we were a single being. One, two, three, collapse, and we were done." It was as if I breathed in, breathed out ,and it was over, and after it was all over, he seemed to think that I might tell him how great he was, so he could write the girl waiting back in the big city of his exploits.

By then I was beginning to get the picture, one that was a little familiar, for I knew about "The Jewish Mother's Club," who like any good mothers wanted their sons to marry in their own faith.

I could just hear his conversation with his girlfriend back in New York City.

"Inez, I met this innocent little country girl from the South and I mean she is so sweet!!"

"Mark, don't you tease me like that, you schlemiel. You know that our parents have discussed the wedding with Rabbi Rosenbaum, and we are both supposed to keep ourselves pure for our wedding night, don't you darling?"

"Inny, I am pure as a crystal clear goblet, and you've known since kindergarten that you are my first and only love, alright? She's just a distraction, so don't worry your itty bitty heart any more."

I began to put things together. I had just been had, the sacrificial Caucasian from Tennessee and I turned as bright as a menorah, but strangely, he kept up with me even for a few years after he returned home and even wrote me an invitation to visit him long after I had left Washington, married my husband, and expected yet another child.

For some reason, I had seen all of the stereotypes of Jewish guys, but it turned out that he was a fairly genuine soul, though his mother would have had him back on a moped instead of in his shiny white Cadillac had he ever really brought me into his life. In one weekend I had been baptized physically into the stereotypical role of *schikza*, the Jewish doctor's mistress, and yet I know something more had happened.

Had I been willing to risk it, I could have gone in to his world, and he could have been welcomed into my own, for neither of us really had gone into any of it thinking we were anything but a couple of younger people that had some more to learn about love. To this day, though, I wish that he had shown up in a beat-up old Ford so that Cynthia and her boyfriend would have had to spare me the Cadillac joke, for it went with me. I could tell him now with such love that many of my best friends are Jewish, and I know now that you are part of a special tribe whose daughter Mary was asked to bear the human Christ. Keep your faith, and let me be the white Christian girl that you tried to love one night. You were not very good at it, but you tried.

I think that I was supposed to get different mental health counseling than I wound up with and wouldn't old Dr. Capers, pillar of Protestantism, have gotten a swollen head had it happened, but instead I grew up a little more, and I have had all kinds of Jewish mothers in my lifetime who have been friends, guardians, and guides. We have laughed together, for I learned that most of them couldn't own up to being virgin brides, and

I share a great fondness for celebrating the Jewish holidays and dressing a little tribalesque. Maybe I wish the experience was more memorable.

Back in Appalachia, there are the sketches from early people, probably Spanish explorers, when they would have to hide in caves to keep out wind and mountain snow, and some of these are similar to the petroglyphs of earlier times done by the Native Americans. But some folks swear that they look like Hebrew words left by the Spanish Jews who hid out in the Appalachian mountains, married up with the Indians and blacks, and some of the mountain folk called them the Melungeons, while others liked to say that they were part of the lost tribes of Israel. I have heard such things at family reunions and Daddy said the cousin making this claim was just a blowhard, but I like to think that mystery is still unresolved and there were tribes called, "The Bad Indians," who were found in the Shenendoahs, for instance who would speak a dialect of Spanish, African, Portuguese, and had created a language combined of a blend of these cultures as early as the 17th century. Thus such speculation is recorded as truth for all of posterity and today many Melungeons and are endeavoring to trace families back to that period, and names such as Collins, Mullins, and even Presley fall frequently in to the background of such a people.

As daughters of Mary, we Christians feel privileged that our lineage is traceable through the line of Mary's and Joseph's kin where we saw that monogamy was the goal; and false gods made by man were soon to be looked upon as pagan.

Somehow we got away from the idea that Creation is still a mystery. But whether it was God's "big bang" of a universal ball, all people share the common thread of the first man and the first woman who stood up one day and said to their Creator of life, "This is good, even our humanness."

Chapter Thirty Five

The old friends, my family, of whom I thought of through another hot summer beginning to pass would not have been very proud of me. I was not the girl who'd left, and there would be many times when I would debate whether it was worth staying in the city away from all that had become familiar to me. I would look around and think that the Greyhound station wasn't so very far away, and then I would wonder how I became the girl who would brave the city streets to hear the cat calls of morning. I would get out to work after my brief period of deciding that it was a good thing just to give up and let the madness and the heartbreak consume me. Old roses were waiting along the same paths which I had walked all of my life, and maybe I could go back and break tubs of green beans with Mama, hear the Sunday sermons, and keep the house clean in case someone died in the night. I knew if I went back that's how things would have to be. All it would take was holding on to a few weeks of pay, packing two suitcases—which was still about all I owned—and going back home. I was afraid to stay and afraid to leave. My tour of the ER and coming to know the young doctor from New York City would lead to a complication I did not know about then.

It wasn't a good thing to have a job where employers could look back and see that you had checked yourself in to an emergency room because you were depressed. From then on you would have to hide any such information as best you could. One may as well have had a party line with all of the old gossips who liked to listen in, only this was on paper, and I would have to go through a job or two to learn that people would not let you keep working if it was recorded in your insurance information that you had gone to an emergency room in the mid-1960s to simply say that you were so depressed that you could die, even if the admitting physician turned out to be your first real encounter with intimacy. So I would go through a couple of jobs and a couple more places to live before I found the job with the District Government of Washington, D.C., and mercy found me again before I started street-sweeping just to keep from heading home.

John Richardson was a gentleman in his sixties who had been hired by the Washington, D.C. government to endeavor to make the D.C. Crime Commission Report something workable beyond a bunch of papers scattered about in his office. Through my job searches I came to meet him. That he had been city manager for the city of Portland, Oregon, meant little to me, for I had no earthly idea how important it was to be a city manager anywhere, and then for him to get called to Washington, D.C. to straighten out our crime-riddled city at the time just did not ring a bell to me. I thought that it was sort of nice that he worked with the mayor, not for the mayor and that he actually would get called up to Capitol Hill now and then. If you worked in his office, you got to be driven around in a car provided by the mayor's office. I was in no way acquainted with such a man before, but somehow I walked around and got a call back from the city planner's department because Mr. Richardson thought that I deserved a chance, and he looked at everything else which I had managed to do.

I interviewed with Mr. Richardson one early morning having walked all the way from one of the VISTA places around R Street to downtown, and I did not know much about interviewing. I was not the world's best typist and I had my shorthand system that I'd made up for myself, the one where I could scratch notes as fast as someone could talk, remember the letter long enough to type it, and make it look pretty darned good. But Mr. Richardson wanted to hear all about me. So I answered most anything that he asked. We even went so far back as to talk about my days of reading the stacks back in the library at Middle Tennessee State University and to my college writing, and I held back a little when he asked me if I had a boyfriend. It merely seemed somewhat sweet that he would ask. I had on one of my summery dresses, and a lot of people had started to call me a hippie for my hair was about as long as everyone's outside of the Holiness Churches. I was prepared to leave, for I figured that we were enjoying a conversation and soon he would show me the door.

Instead, he showed me a little Degas print which he had brought from his place in Portland and talked to me about how he really had wanted to retire, but figured he might as well see if he could do something with Washington in a year or two of time before he firmly left the working world. He showed me offices, introduced me to people, and then he took me to his other office. It was enough that I looked up at him with great surprise and a look of concern, for it looked something like a hoarder's closet and I think that I almost gasped. There were papers in boxes, papers on bookcases on the walls, and lots of official-looking books. Where there were not books in the cases, there were papers. Out of his mouth came words that were going over my head, around me, and through me. And it was sort of like when I first started getting some awards back home in school and 4-H public speaking contests. Someone was asking me if they thought that I could help them out with this mess.

He said, "I guess you can see that I haven't got around to filing much since I've been here. But you seem just like the kind of girl who can put this place in shape for me." I told him that I believed I could, and I found myself weeping on this man's shoulder and thanking him for having given me such a nice job.

There were other people besides me that were a part of the office, but I answered to two people mainly: Mr. Richardson and his administrative assistant who I would think of as cold at first. He labeled me something like his administrative secretary. When he told me what my salary was going to be and asked me if that sounded reasonable, my inner being thought he must be teasing. No one had ever asked me that before. I was thinking I would do well to get about three or four dollars an hour. He gave me another term I was not familiar with—something like a GS-6, which in today's terms would be like telling an eighteen-year-old that you are going to give them a great mid-range salary with benefits and when could they start?

I told him, "Let me start today, and I am going to clean this mess up for you, which I will do in a record amount of time." Over those months I would not forget that going back and standing where the wild roses bloomed was an option, and I hoped that Mama and the kids were getting enough green beans canned for the winter, but visions of going to the Greyhound station would leave me. As I had done so many times before, I picked up the pieces of myself.

The first time Mr. Richardson sent me to city hall, I called for a car. I expected just that, some car. Instead it was a chauffeur-driven limo that said District Government on it, and when the driver turned around and tipped his hat to me I apologized.

I said, "You should not have gone to all of this trouble. I could have walked." He began to smile knowing that he obviously had a newbie to take care of, and I took the papers Mr. Richardson had asked me to find for the mayor. When the driver said he would wait for me, I was even further speechless, and I never talked much about my job for I figured no one would believe it in the first place. From that time forward I never had a problem getting a job again.

Mr. Richardson might have hesitated had he known that I was going to have put him on an entire filing system within a month or so, for we did not live in the early years of computer organization. Everything was done the old way. Even with figuring out the topics which were crucial and developing files for them to go into.. I had so much done that I was actually getting bored sometimes. Mr. Richardson treated me like a daughter, and when I showed him this amazing paper I discovered over lunch at the drug store counter next door, a paper which told of three-headed babies and reported the lies and lives associated with every movie star I had ever heard of, he helped me to understand what a paper labeled as a "rag" was, and I am glad to say that I gave up my life of passing time reading such non-newsworthy material, but I was bored, for I had the main part of my job done and had organized my boss too soon. So some days I just typed letters home or I went around seeing if anyone else had anything to do, for I feared that my boss was going to decide he didn't need me. Instead, he kept sending me on the errands to the various governmental departments and gave me a letter to type now and then. Sometimes he would just tell me something which he thought might need to be put on paper, and I would go ahead, make up the letter, go in and let him approve and sign it, and then we had finished another project. We were a team, he and I.

His personal assistant had been with the government for a long time, and she and I would go out, becoming very good friends. I worried about her being in her mid-thirties and having no children, but she was one of the newer "career women," and she wanted to hear my stories from the place that had been my home and what the schools were like. She didn't know much about our country churches, so I worried about her soul now and again. We only had a little over a year together before Mr. Richardson was ready to get back to his mountains around Portland, Oregon and a world that I dreamt might be somewhat like my own.

Curiously through the years, I would learn that we were talking about a land west of the Rockies and beauty which I could not comprehend. Most folks would have just bailed and would have run when they saw the mess of files, but once I had learned to dive in the middle of all the messes I straightened out in my life, I saw that John Richrdson's chaotic files were nothing compared to my old task of finding Auntie Carol's Baked Alaska caded counters with wild game hunting drips left everywhere. One man's clutter was my treasure. Being a child slave along with my library work at Middle Tennessee State University and even Mama's obsession with cleaning constantly in case someone died—all of it had prepared me to work that year with a very important man, not to mention the mayor himself at times, for I could go through and organize in a way most young women would have run from. Mayor Walter Washington was a gentleman and Julian Bond and Reverend Jesse Jackson were handsome and were sometimes around.

I cherished all of the people that I met that year from the driver on, and I would keep instructing him not to call me "ma'am" or bothering to get out and open the door of the limo for me, which just made him laugh a little harder or to see that I was always comfortable, whether it was an umbrella for the rain or a wrap from the cold. I had known so many difficult lessons through that previous two-year period. This was the year of recovery from many things, and the little Degas print Mr. Richardson handed me from his wall I carried with me over many years. Each time I touched my little print, I would remember a beloved man who knew that going to an ER once and trying to get help was not the end of the world, because you had darned good reason to know depression was no excuse not to give a person a chance. As all southerners know, we are to manners born, meaning we learned to behave well toward our elders and to present our best behavior, especially regardless of what might be troubling us, so I think sometimes that was the first reason I even got the job interview.

I ached when we all had to say goodbye. Were the Washington D.C. Crime Report Recommendations to substantially decrease its inner-city crime rate ever fulfilled? I would never really know. Mr. Berry and some of the people you've heard of in your lifetime were already there then and it would not remain my city for many more years beyond the first two, but being a part of that downtown was among the most special things that ever happened to me in my life. I was offered another job by the man who would become in charge of me after my beloved boss went back to Oregon, and it seemed logical to stay. But as I'd had a year of rose blooms, an old thorn would invade my life.

My protection and love of our office was dismantled when the new director called me in one day. He was speaking to me in a manner that I did not quite understand until my hair, my clothes, and what I might could do to make life pleasant for him came into the conversation, especially if I wanted to keep my job. This time I knew the signs, but Mr. Richardson was gone and there was the mayor and my new boss who was one of his appointees, and who was going to believe me that sexual harassment now came with the job? Your superior was entitled to ask, but when I said, "No," his brow furrowed.

In those days, no matter where you were from, you usually still had a man as a boss and this was the case again. It was not wonderful and flirtatious. It was a direct threat that I would be fired if I did not service this gentleman, so I did what girls and women had learned to do. I planned an exit strategy, and when the day came for me to sign the contract to stay in the office, I was able to tell him I had a new job offer and that the District

Government had been so wonderful to me. Then I left him with a smile and backed away as he asked if I didn't want to change my mind.

My new job was at the American Society of International Law as a lawyer's office assistant and I would be placed in the front as receptionist to greet both heads of state and senators who came into our offices on Massachusetts Avenue. I was able to smooth over my leaving by stating that I could not resist the opportunity, and even my aggressor had to agree that it was quite an opportunity for a girl who had been one of their office hires. This was my way and I got away again. The day was coming when I would know that it was my right to choose someone to love and that I did not have to always feel that I had to show the good manners of my heritage, for times were changing and women were finding a voice, becoming educated, and asking the drummer, "How much further can we go?" We believed that we would live to see women in higher public office, and some women began to use sexuality as a means for promotions while others got out there and said, "Gentlemen, step aside and share the dais." It would not happen all at once, but the march was on to see women enter the professions.

I somewhat resented the idea that we had to take on pant suits and seek to have the aggressiveness that had become common among males as administrators. I resented burnt bras and makeup tossings, for I felt very strongly that we should not have to put away the pleasantries of womanhood if we enjoyed them, not to mention the comfort of a cool dress on a summer's day. I never was the ultra-feminist who led cheers to push the men aside. I just wanted to be able to work with men without being threatened as often as I had been, and I wanted to see the women from the southern mountains and valleys share motherhood with fathers. I wanted the threats of women being wives who could be whipped if they got out of line to be put aside and for all women to feel more loved, especially the women endeavoring to change from the farms and fields to jobs which would help feed their families. Mainly I wanted to see an end to young women like me having to, again and again, be subjected to insinuations or actual sexual abuse by a more powerful employer. I was getting glimpses that we had some hope for these things to happen, and it would prove true that the next time I had a workplace encounter with a male; it would be by mutual consent.

Oh, mothers, my mother and yours. I want you to know, as spirits I see you watching over us now. We would see a day unimaginable from the Appalachian Mountains' tip in Southern Appalachia to the Northern most coast of Maine, we have seen a better world. And for those women still living with abuse and fear, you do have a place to go now. Just look around and call, speak loudly, and there is protection somewhere, for you are the daughters of the brave women who first questioned whether or not women could expect a better world, and even I am the benefactor of that world.

I heard a country song once by the daughter of a Harvard-educated man with a PhD in musicology. His family met up with the Cincinnati Symphony Orchestra in the essence of Appalachian homeland—Berea, Kentucky. His family, The McLain Family Band, brought country music to a symphony audience, and one song remained in my heart throughout the years. One of the daughters sang "Meet Me at the Trailways Station Honey" and her voice pierced that mountain air with "I know that you'll be there." And hers was a love song, but every time she sang it I was back at the Greyhound station in my head, leaving Mama and Daddy and my brothers and sisters in Winchester or I was arriving at the station in Washington, D.C. If Mama and Dad had waited for us as we left, we knew why they hoped we'd be coming down that road to home to remain there with them. And it broke my heart at times. Other times I would imagine the wild roses and stand with the women in the shade, watching white cotton rows turning dark as we picked the fields.

The year with Mr. Richardson was the time when I knew I wanted to stay in Washington, D.C., but never in my entire life would I forget that the Greyhound station was a choice I debated one day. I ended up meeting another holy man who led me in a different direction. For those who went by Trailways or Greyhound or sat six to a car heading away from the places of our mountain and valley homes, I know that some of you did go back and some are still waiting for that "Honey at a Trailways Station" and be that your choice. It was a fine one, and we will remember the roses from the other side have never been more beautiful than they were standing there with you, and even now it feels lonely just thinking of warm and damp hard-working arms holding us as their daughters. There was no perfect solution and we did the best we could with what we had.

It sounds, sometimes, as if I headed off to the big city and left behind a life that I did not consider worth living. It is true that I told my mother that if I ever left, I was not coming back, but what I was not coming back to from Winchester and Huntland, Tennessee, to Pisgah and Rosalie, Alabama, straight to my parents' doorsteps was to the degradation which was placed on poor women and children. I was never returning to a world where my father worked until his hands were raw and his flesh was burnt from sun; where he could not even enjoy himself for fear of losing everything, because a bank decided to foreclose after the thieves of the poor decided they had taken about as much as they could get from the backs of farmers who did not know that they were fighting a losing battle with a world of automation that had become bigger and greedier to the point where the common man no longer even had a face. With what I know now, I feel certain that my parents could have found happiness had they known to seek an Amish or Mennonite community, for they both loved that way of life.

I was leaving whippings of women and children sanctioned by churches under the guise of it being instruction, handed down by St. Paul and his ministry. We were washed with the sins of Eve, while it was somehow forgotten that Adam was cast out of Eden with the same shame and burdens, cast out together, not as separates but as equals naked and having shared forbidden fruit and all of their generations would be created together. No, I would not go back in to that world which justified all of wrath and sin at the feet of women and their babies, for I had begun to see the biblical responsibilities of both men and of women. Most of all I had encountered the blessings children brought, so much so that God had told Abraham that he did not have to sacrifice his son for God himself and with the coming of the New Testament we were brought further to the day when children were seen as the ultimate blessing by God himself. Too many men chose not to read St. Paul's command to love their wives as God loved His church.

Oh, sweet mothers, I wish you could have thought about Mary's visitation with Elizabeth and have thought of them as what you should have been. All women should have celebrated together that you were going to have children, admiring each other's girth, rejoicing as you spent your days together with the news, the good news, "I am with child." What incredible sweetness, what rejoicing! From naked and unclothed to the incubators of all human life, where the mother and father walked the journey together.

I could not go back to a place of fear, and I could not go back to what I had left behind, but the world there was changing, too. The one part of the puzzle that I had left out, that my village, my people were growing up, just like me, but in a different place. Schools were being rebuilt and the population of the United States was moving south along with factories. Institutions of higher learning were becoming national hallmarks, no longer simply open to the southern well-to-do and even my father would begin to bend in a most non-traditional way, to look to the future as if it was bright and open to not just his children but to his grandchildren. The sad old South had back roads becoming main roads. Our roads were even looking up until all of the old towns got shut down by Wal-Mart's greed and to get cheaper prices. The cheaper labor overseas' markets were awakened.

During all of these years, I would write to my mother and father regularly and call them when I could, for long distance calls used to come at a premium. Once I got my mama on the phone, she did not want to let me go. Or was it me? I had longed for her throughout my childhood years and not standing in front of her, I could hear in her voice the sadness that one by one, her children had left home, and even though there were eight of us, I now know that she did feel anguish, both of my parents. I was the last of the children to leave who had been born on the mountain, so I held some kind of glue between both worlds. Somehow Mama just did not believe that I, too, would go away, for boys did not look at me—or so

I thought—and I stayed unto myself so very much that I am not certain Mama did not think that I could ever make it in the larger world. Because there were six years between me and the youngest brother who was not disabled, I was almost her last hope for a protector.

At least before I left home, I had been there to raise my voice even louder, and though I trembled, I would put myself in the middle of my parents and Daddy might threaten me a time or two. I had a way of telling them both to shut up, and they were right in presuming that things were about to start flying off that table unless they did. I would be telling them of the shame they caused us, what they had done that shattered my soul, and I would even go so far as to ask them, "Are you going to be doing this to the rest of the kids when I am gone?" I would give them a sermon or two they hadn't heard during any of their church-going years of what a mother and father were expected to do and to be. Daddy would back off, call me a damn and leave the house.

Each phone call was a guilt and remembrance of my years with them. My mind would wander back as to sometimes when my father would put on his hat, leave his breakfast, and go outside "to wait for the, old lady." Next thing I knew, they would have gone off in the truck together for their jobs, for Mama was now cooking at the local high school, and there was no way in hell that Daddy was going to not get her to her job. I can honestly say that I do not remember ever having it get so bad that he would have her miss work. I do not doubt that they went over the road carrying on about "that crazy bitch" that they left with the smaller kids, but I got them out of our hair and out to work. The strangest part was they would usually come back acting as if nothing had gone on before they left. Maybe even with a little laugh about how Mama's friend Betty Rowe had mixed herself some of her famous cleaning solution, Ammonia and Purex, and it blew up the back of her car on the way to work.

In our phone conversations Mama and I would talk, though, and I would catch up on the news. Most of the time it was about things like Aunt Ruth having to let someone's wedding dress out around the abdomen, because she couldn't believe what she saw when their clothes came off for the fitting. Once, though, it was about Daddy, a story which remains with me and all of us to this day. We all have our theories, but being born in Southern Appalachia, I know that strange things do happen in those places where people find themselves alone and surrounded by nothing. Superstition is what you all may call it. The sixth sense is another way of defining it, and then there is everything from the supernatural to divine intervention, but something had happened to Daddy and the only other person with whom he may have shared the story, my beloved Uncle Clifford, died with it close to the vest.

Daddy loved his John Deere tractor, probably way more than his wife or his kids, and I know that man plowed his fields ten times even if he never sowed a seed in them. It consoles me to know that he used to go home from the Tuthill Brickyard in Illinois with a man from Indiana who had farmland so Daddy could get out in the country and plow with someone else's John Deere. I can tell you that our father probably thanked him for the privilege and took nothing but food for wages, and then he probably turned around and shoveled out their barn to endeavor to repay him for letting him have such a treat as to plow their corn fields, for once Loag and Sam, our mules, died the age of tractor plowing was the only replacement to consider. Mules had become as scarce as zoo animals then, so Daddy got away from everything after work, and he hit the hills he and the boys had basically hand-cleared for planting land. And once on that tractor, all worries were left behind.

Mama told me on the phone that day that a week or so before, Daddy had come home white as a sheet, trembling, and without saying a word to anybody. She thought maybe he was sick or something, but Daddy—who never told Mama much—did tell her that he'd seen something on the hill and to dress up for Sunday church, for he was going to be "saved," meaning that he was going to be baptized. Mama tried to get him to tell her what had happened, but he would not say a word about it, finally telling her something to the extent of, "Some things are best not to talk about and that's that." This was his way of not saying his usual "Shut your mouth!" She would speculate things like, "That tractor must have almost turned over on Amos," and that became the family story, but I never believed it, and I never shall. Coming out of a near-miss with his best friend, his John Deere would never have been enough to put the fear of the Lord in him. I brought it up once, and in later years he liked to talk to me about sacred and even supernatural kinds of things. This was answered only with silence.

We all had our theories, and one of mine was that he had stepped into a group of venomous copperheads resurfacing from an underground cavern from a winter's sleep. Mama, who like many Appalachian Mountain women was a great oral historian, told us the various stories she had heard from her youth, some of which I heard other places and from other people. I heard the stories that people had been in situations where rattlers or copperheads instead of dying from a blow with a hoe or whatever was available, actually stood up and came toward their offender as if they could walk, and when you hear it more than once and the sources are unrelated then you begin to have chills, especially if you are a growing-up child. Mama brought that up once, but sort of put it behind her, for she thought of it as a demonic event. Another story around our part of the country had to do with people meeting strangers who would appear out of nowhere and they would be dressed in black, have certain animal features, and would announce themselves to be Satan. Needless to say, confronted with such an introduction, most folks who spoke of such happenings would tell you not only that they had met the devil, but they were so afraid that they ran for their lives from him.

They would associate fetid scents, tongues of fire, and all of the things one could imagine with a Satanic figure, and again the stories would be extremely similar. Even in the last conversation I ever had with Mama about Daddy's conversion, some thirty-five years later, she would admit that he never told her, that she still thought he almost overturned on his John Deere. Maybe he had told Mr. Gordon Davis, Dad's best friend who survived the Bataan Death March, but he'd succumbed early from heart disease. Mr. Gordon probably knew, but a country man stood by his word, that if asked to not tell, secrets went into a vault, sometimes and came out near death, but in Mr. Gordon's case, he had a peaceful death in his easy chair from my memory, but no one ever shared Daddy's secret.

Legend has it that the area around Franklin County was considered by the Indians to be a "No Man's Land" and I could tell you that each of us had events in our lives that would make us think that this was plausible. The story was that there was a great tribal upheaval among the various Indian nations that came from near and far and that the very soil was so saturated with the blood of dead warriors that the Indian people would never return. We would look for arrowheads and Indian mounds, but I would have to say that it was almost virgin territory from all such things. It was as if any generation of peoples before us had left there so long ago that the earth had covered all over and over again, so that the secrets of ages would be guarded by the soil itself. Whereas farmers in the areas of East and West Tennessee were far more apt to plough up fields with arrowheads and things that farm children search for. In our land, though, even history seemed to disappear.

We will now never know Daddy's story. Did he encounter the Devil, this fearless man? Or did he walk into an old spirit left from when the earth seeped with the blood of warriors and where the unexpected seemed to be locked up and weary with some souls lost in the in-between. Yes, Mama and I had lots to talk about, for I was a child when I left and I wanted to know the stories, the old stories, the new stories.

"You mean it was a white wedding dress, Mama?" I had a natural curiosity about all whom I had left behind, and I had an inborn love for even those who hurt me the most. I appreciated that I was from a wellspring of natural philosophers and people who knew more about life than they were ever going to share with any of us, and I missed them all and still do in so many ways. I never once took my months, then years, away as making me some kind of messenger or person who had found the way. Quite to the contrary, I was like them: searchers. And we all searched together. When I would talk with Mama on the phone, I was the child in church again singing the old songs, and one that remains close to me had these simple words: "Tell me the old, old story. Write on my heart every word."

As I write this day I am thinking of that, and I can see me holding that phone in my hand, not wanting to let go. "Just tell me another story, Mama, and I will write it for you every living word. I've got to hang up now, Mama, for I know that you know this conversation is costing me, and Bell Telephone is going to expect me to pay them. Yes, Mama, I will come home when I can."

Chapter Thirty Six

Becoming a Woman

What day or hour do we become the woman on which we will begin to mold into the adult versions of ourselves? I came to Washington D.C. with more expected of myself than many people experienced by the time they hit middle-age, so what else other than relationships was it that would begin to define me as a woman? The women I knew from my childhood seemed to have hit a state of womanhood that was beyond my comprehension within a lifetime. Had we been women of biblical times, perhaps they would have shared such knowledge as we gathered water into our vessels in early morning, hot and sticky clothing sticking to our earth-covered skin before we bathed, and while we climbed the hills like pack animals helping each other manage our burden and as we placed the yoke on our shoulders to share and began our chores before the mid-day sun cast rays over the tents.

However ancient women shared the news with their daughters that womanhood was upon them seemed as if it would have had some relevance to all generations. Mothers and daughters had passed secret signs from the tribal desert life straight to the mountains and valleys where the women would give a knowing nod and add the changed girl as one of them to sit under their shade and to share the news, for once the blood sign came we bore the first burden of Eve, for soon our bodies could support the longing for birth.

I had experienced now what mistakenly was considered the error of the first woman by giving over my childlike body and heart to men who might have admired me in some way but who did not love me. I had endeavored in the foolish manner of bearing my body and my heart believing that such behavior led to womanhood, and I was left without fulfillment, for I looked to them for the sign which belonged to mothers and daughters. Knowing that these men knew nothing of this bond among women I was searching a missed secret sign as if I were the woman with the yoke and I felt betrayed by the women at the spindle making yarn to gird the loins. The Celtic wives checked the signs of the moon and stars to plant, so that seed was only sewn in the purest and the most beautiful hours. I needed you, and I needed Mrs. Hannah with her apron bulging with fresh spring greens as if she were carrying a last child in old age to tell me which day it happened. My womanhood—was I there yet? Was this how the day came? Without fanfare and celebration and without a Rite of Holy women to tell us we had left the girl within us behind? Was anyone ever as uninformed as I was?

Old friends from home kept telling me that the time was passing and saying right often, "You know who else just got married?" So I wondered if that was the flaw in my plan to be grown up, that I had not married. Women of the Bible who had husbands seemed to be wise, and the gracious women from my mountains and valleys—they were either married or they had settled on taking care of mothers and fathers. Here I stood clueless and waiting for the pronouncement that I was where I was supposed to be in time and place. An old family photograph showed Mother and two aunts from the mountain in Sunday dresses with nylons on and hair done for church, and I remember my Mama commented, "We were such women then back during the war, and God only knows how many runs we had in those nylons, but we were women, such grand women." I remembered that during the Second World War my mother was in her mid-twenties, so maybe I had a ways to go. I would go through other boyfriends, and by now some feared the "M-word," for they had a plan to remain free of children and to "chase chicks." That was an explanation that seemed of great concern to me that anyone would just use me or any other young women as if we were good for sport; have your way with us and chuck us out. I had up until this time never even believed it possible that being with a woman could be that trivialized by a man on fire saying, "I love you," without any thought.. So someone fix me, I thought, celebrate me or at least show me what test I must pass to be a part of the next expected role of my life. That of a woman, simply a woman. It did seem as if within my dreams the desert sister's life was easier. The woman had a place in her father's house, and her worth had to be offered to remove her from the protection of such a home, so the lover came to her. Only when all qualms of debt and bartering over her worth were settled—then and only then would she become a wife, a woman, and learn the forbidden love she had not known. Everything thus far had come into my life from the opposite direction of what I was taught made one grown up.

So I was beginning to become more insightful. I looked at my body and soul as if they were more valuable and to be cherished a little more, but in my dreams the wheel would hum and spin and spin and the golden threads I made would become tangled until I had to stop and gather them for thread, for more mending needed to be done. I looked for the mending, but instead I was still looking in the mirror collecting pretty buttons to use on a new dress for a girl like me. My celebration had not come yet. The mothers might cry out in my sleep when the time had finally come—or at least I hoped. And thus I waited. I would keep looking for the answer to the question of when I had left my girlhood behind.

I look back, and I do not want to say that the years of the most dramatic changes one could ever experience in such a brief time were for naught. I did learn lessons, and I would move on from them in a different way, more thoughtful than before. I hoped that I could, like Mother, find the picture that made me smile a little when I looked back so that I, too, could say, "I was such a woman then." And when it happens I want to hear "Ode To Joy" and "Jesu Joy of Man's Desiring." And if someone releases a throng of butterflies then I will know that my womanhood was celebrated, and the ancient sisters with dance and cymbals had called my name.

I remained afraid of so many things, even though time was passing since I'd left my graduation from Huntland High School and the semesters I spent at Middle Tennessee State University. Time was beginning to help me understand that the boy from Natchez, Mississippi, and my chosen life's love David had not been a boy at all, but he had been a grown-up man who found some fun while he could in innocent girls from the fields and farms, the small towns and villages which were still the back roads and away from the growing interstates. He loved us. They all loved us, for we were the last lilies in the field, so to speak. I would find that as life went on that finding the fresh and pure girls was like some kind of trophy to be bragged about, and I am not quite so certain that the Davids and the Toms were not the hay seed, for wasn't it wrong to injure beauty and the innocent? I guess there is no way around the fact that we were sometimes used. Whether it was the literature teacher who followed us around in college or the young Jewish physicians from New York City, we were the girls who would mistake affection for love.

Maybe it is only when one has arrived at this point of making strides toward womanhood that a woman can even see this all-important difference. I can only address the issues that girls from the middle southern states had to deal with both where we came from and leaving the comfort of what we knew. It would be years before I realized that the farm girls from the Dakotas and Montana or the girls who came in from places like Lancaster, Pennsylvania—we were all on this search for womanhood together. I believe that to a degree the moral standard of earlier centuries which kept our mothers silent to us was more prominent in the mid-South, for many of the co-workers that I would meet from such places as Pittsburgh and Cincinnati, Erie and upstate New York would be light years ahead of us in what kinds of conversations that they had had with mothers and older sisters.

The shame of a world where conversation among women was so limited about personal thoughts, feelings, and the physical part of us did not allow us to blend in as well and as quickly as many girls from other places when we arrived in the cities. I somehow want to own those words "Shame of Conversation" and to claim them for my own. When girls were instructed in becoming women, they might take the path of trying out things earlier which were forbidden, but they would not feel like the wasted fruit from old orchard apple and pear trees, another scent-memory that would immediately take me some place like gathering pears with Mrs. Hannah or being sent to Granny Hood's orchard to pick up the last fruits of the season. I was taught to be the first up for domestic help, and the last person to think about should be me. I was instructed only in how to work in an office, to be a housewife or to be a seamstress, with no thought of what my own physical and mental self was about.

Even though Washington D.C. would become a gathering place for those seeking human rights in the 1960s and early 70s it was a man's town—from the armed services to the young men who went to Capitol Hill and even to those who went to the predominant medical schools like Georgetown and George Washington. Women were the absolute minority but the United States Government wanted to recruit the young women from our area. Why wouldn't they? We were the hardest working, most obedient, and apt to do our share and the work of three others at any job where our high school and early college skills were marketed.

Two years after leaving home, I was more full of questions than anything. And if you question then that leaves a mind open to process the information I needed to grow up some more and to know my girlhood was leaving me. It is very sad in some ways to give it over, for the woman in me would have to spend a lot of time fixing the embroidery of me, surrounded by the wonderful color which I could pull from my past when I was at my lowest points and there would be many low points to come.

Hopelessly romantic, I would still accept a cast-off boyfriend every now and then. There would be the Italian guy from Long Island with whom I thought there was a prayer for a relationship. He was good-looking and among the only white guys who went to Howard University Law School, but he also, as was the case so often, had the girl back home. I would know her as Rose, and he would not sound very serious about her until I had to be very serious with him. It would be like Batman in his Batmobile how rapidly this guy would remember his old love when the thought of the possibility of pregnancy had come up. Mercifully it would disappear of natural means and days, and I would realize that I really did not love that guy any more than he loved me. Sainthood had not been given to me at this point, even though I endeavored to spend time with men who I genuinely thought cared for me. Later, once I had a working relationship, I would realize that I had screwed-up hormones after years of not even knowing what hormones were. Lord, I hope that he found his Rose, that after he finished law school that they had ten kids and I do hope that as educated as he was, that he finally learned that an amusing statement was not "a pisser." Perhaps a young woman is evolving also when you can finally just thank God you have given your boyfriend over with a sense of good riddance.

My ever-faithful friend Stan, another Jewish guy but from Los Angeles and part of the VISTA crowd, would always be there when I was in free-fall, and I loved him for it, but Stan and I just did not have a romance due to my discouragement. He was the only child of a Jewish couple in LA who had been through the hardest of immigrations to this country. Stan would tell me how his parents could spend an hour discussing whether a dishcloth was used enough to throw away, and he would finally become so perplexed that he would just grab the damned thing and say, "Would you shut the fuck up?" and finally take it to the garbage himself. He was kind to everyone to a fault, but especially to me. I think partially because he had been the Italian guy's roommate. He had developed a sense of kindness toward me knowing that I was going to be an easily-ditched girl. Everyone needs a Stan in their lives, someone who just loves them, who is screwed-up in their own minds about their own relationships, but somehow just hangs in as a friend even though you have told them that it just isn't going to get romantic. Those are words guys in their early 20s do not hear very well.

Whenever I needed a conversation, though, I had Stan. We kept in touch for some years after our Washington, D.C., days. I even think he may have visited my family later on. The last time I saw him was on the cover of *The Washington Post* on a kite-flying day on the Washington Mall with the cherry blossoms in bloom. He looked happy, and his kite was high and so, probably, was Stan, but he was enjoying himself. I sort of let him go after the last time I talked with him when he said he could never make love again without marijuana, for I feared that if I heard from him again, my buddy would be in the slammer. But again, I had become someone else. He was a man that I could have a relationship with without the complexities of thinking about marriage. We would take a lot of walks together on the streets of Washington, him telling me about his avoiding insanity in his parents old-world home and me telling him about the latest job or my tendency to obsess on my health, since I seemed to be enduring a lot of pain back then inside and out. I can admit that until my first child came along a few years later, I had never been to a gynecologist or even knew what the heck they did.

There would be the beautiful Greek God, Mahele who was just that, absolutely the most handsome guy on the face of the earth and his family had opened a Greek restaurant in Georgetown. He himself was an architect educated in Greece, so he was still going to have work to do in America for certification. I learned from Mehele that I would not just marry someone just because they were great-looking. There was no chemistry for me, another sign of womanhood. The mere words "Will you marry me," the words I believe a lot of girls prayed for back then, were the words he asked me more than once. Perhaps I felt that it would be useless, that there was no way of blending our cultures, for he had come from an Athenian merchant family. There was no problem when I met his family that had come to America, but I did not feel that visceral kind of love, and this time I was wise enough not to give the physical me, for I had made progress in putting away the girl.

I was finally reaching a point of knowing that there was something else that had to exist between men and women that made me worthy of deciding whom I would and would not love. I dishonored my family by having premarital relationships—or so I felt—as if I were the only one, but I now knew that I had a voice and I could make decisions and make decisions not based on writing home to say, Mama, I found a man! Mehele would seek me out for most of the rest of my time in Washington, but this time I was not the desperate female thinking my life depended on a proposal. I wanted to reach higher.

I never told Mama that I turned down a marriage proposal, for I was nineteen, and my mother and her sisters would definitely think that I had just blown off my last chance to make anything of myself. The girls I graduated with kept marrying and the cousins kept marrying, some over the fear or reality of pregnancy, but I was holding out now. I was moving in a forward direction, but I think some of the old values that my body and my soul had something to do with a greater God and a higher purpose than to marry the first guy who invited me to the altar also helped. Looking backward to find forward would not be that unusual for an Appalachian girl trying to find her place if she was to become a wise woman.

We had done this all of our lives in deep woods when we felt lost and we had worked through mazes in our lives which seemed psychologically impossible to get out of without a compass. Fortunately most of us had some compass of sorts which was moral and blessed by the Great Spirits from whom our land had been taken and given to our forefathers. We had natural instincts for protecting ourselves, for valuing simple gifts, and for not becoming the lost. Our legacy to the bones of those whose earth's blood we relied upon granted us this special status. Call it fate, but I call it reality that we "The Hidden People" of our rarely traveled youth carried a duty to those who proceeded us to find a path and share it, and that in it we would find respect along the way.

Here I was, born in Pisgah, Alabama, kissing the end of the Appalachian trail, and I did not even know that we had already been sought out as a people to walk among to find America. A man by the name of Benton McKay had gotten the idea of a footpath to bring you among our people and our places in 1921, and I would know nothing about him, but this little footpath or trail would become our country's longest walking trail when it was completed in 1937. It was designated as this country's Most Scenic Trail in 1968 as well as the longest at 2,181 miles and exceeding the length of the John Muir trail in California. It runs from that tip of Sand Mountain, place of my birth, straight through to Maine and even on into the beginning of the mountain chain that extends into Quebec. I could not tell people that this was the land of my people, for I did not understand the relevance of the ground that I walked upon as a child.

This was also because of "The Shame of Conversation" for our homes were taken from the great Indian Nations of the South, and when we would take our old roads back through Paint Rock Valley to see the family in Alabama, Dad would say, "We are on the Navajo Trail again." He became happy to have us all heading back up to the mountain and what Daddy probably did not know was that we were so near one of the greatest achievements of the United States in so far as the national parks and trails. We were at the Appalachian Trail, and our part had probably been owned by the Creek and the Cherokee nations, but we had a great heritage which we were not taught to be proud of. We were looked upon as some oddities of spirit because we had developed our own songs, our food, our culture, and our religions, but we did not know why we had a pride that could not be explained to others, for it was deeper than that to us and its explanation was withheld from our identity to the extent that we were not able to recognize or feel the pride of our belonging.

My heritage was beginning to knock at the door of my heart. "Who am I?" and "Where am I from?" Those were unanswered questions for me then. It would take many years before I knew that our woodland heritage, little towns, and farms, were the things of legend. I would go home, see things beginning to open up, see homes built from great timbers and solid like the earth, and I would eventually get that much of where I turned the corner from the girl who had come to Washington D.C. I was in each world. The two worlds would mesh in to one life, for that is the only story that I can be writing here, but that bigger questions helped me to regain some of the sense I had of building on and salvaging the life I was to become. That we get to a place in different ways simply makes me want to fall before the sisters and brothers, the fathers, and the homelands before me and lie there humbled in their presence to praise their toils and labors of becoming in an unknown land.

I think of all of the other cities that absorbed Appalachian citizens, and I immediately see places that seemed to offer so much hope until around the 1970s. Washington, D.C., would not be at the top of the list, for cities like Detroit, Cleveland, Cincinnati, and Chicago had so much more manufacturing. Areas such as Northern Kentucky just across the river from Cincinnati and down the road from Dayton, Ohio, still had manufacturing of everything from cars to home appliances. There were meat-packaging plants, breweries—everything one could find within a home from soap to cereal and even chewing gum was part of the great United States base of manufacturing. West Virginia was the absolute center for coal miners along with parts of Ohio and Pennsylvania, and Pittsburgh, the steel town. These cities were humming along until desperate people organized themselves to become unions, the proud child of the Federation of Laborers. People who had moved up from the South could still hardly feed their growing families on the salaries they came home to after the war and after the destruction of family farms.

There are areas which you can visit, to this day, in these cities where those southern whites and black people had come up in hopes of jobs. From post WW II they found each other in these cities and established themselves keeping their language and culture even down to basic food preparation. Modern ghettos were deep with Appalachian accents, religion, and culture over great swaths of communities, because once one got to the cities and the children married and children begat children, then Appalachia had just come down out of those mountains, out of those hollows, a form of new segregation based on poverty and background was born. People can only be knocked down and get back up for a few generations before there is a sense of hopelessness established. We were taught from a young age the concept of destiny, that "Whatever Will Be Will Be." And you begin to see that you are marked by your own culture. One of the old jokes that was supposed to make you laugh your sides off was, "A virgin in Kentucky is one whose Daddy hasn't had her yet." No one sees this as racist, because it involves a bunch of white folks.

Unions provided a living wage for people only until it became apparent that the large business owners had two easier choices. The first was the move to the sunbelt South where factory workers with a little farm income could make it, so we began to see Atlanta, Nashville, Knoxville, and all of North Georgia and areas of Tennessee where line work could be bought cheaply, and hands were willing to do the labor. Thus within the 1970s, the agrarian world where there were limited controls on land usage made the Old South grow again like one big balloon after the other, sailing right over the union cities. But by the 1980s, these folks who moved there wanted to make a living, too, and as my Daddy would have said, "Folks were getting to the point where they could not make ends meet," meaning that they could not pay their bills, live, and have bread on the table unless higher salaries came to the southern United States.

For this cradle Democrat, I had to applaud that during the Nixon and Reagan years there were more calls to "Buy American!" There were those of us flitting around in non-American-made cars who felt that we might should help our brothers and sisters out a little more, but once again manufacturing would take a hit. What once said Made In Japan became collectibles by the early 1960s, for there were the peoples of Asia, especially of India and China, who could honestly do everything for a fraction of what it cost to pay factory workers here.

It was being pointed out that we were citizens of the world, not just of the United States of America. The problem was that no one had quite figured out how the poor people of America were going to live when manufacturing was easily moved to third world countries. Unions became a dirty word and were associated with the old communist idealism so unions lost much power and we watch poor people are getting poorer, and the rich people getting richer like a runaway train. Once again it is on the backs of poor blacks and poor whites and Hispanic laborers. Before any election, you hear that old saw which sort of sounds like, "Bring us in and you are going to get a pot full of chicken." Folks who have grown older, like my Aunt Mildred, are apt to say that it doesn't matter who you elect—what you are going to get is a pot of "chicken shit."

I can safely say that I watched things begin to change in Washington, D. C., but it was long overdue help for poor blacks for the most part then, and though Dr. King invited white folks to bring their burdens in as brothers and sisters, once again, my Appalachian family and friends could not bring themselves to complain about the good life which God had given to them. The ultimate refuge is and always has been that there is a greater reward. It did not give the rich license to watch poverty grow around like weeds in a field. Jesus asked that our riches be shared here and now.

Chapter Thirty Seven

In moments of deep thought, when I find reason not to seek help from the God of my childhood, how does a life of faith still enter my awareness. The God of now comes in more quiet encounters, like whispers to me. Nature's colors are so incredibly perfect. I see the few green splashes in a Mediterranean climate, the blues of the bay against the blue of the sky. Both blue, but more like a sketch, and the flowers. Everywhere the flowers bloom in every color in the rainbow, but there are more colors than a rainbow, as if we are a painting made beyond all perfection.

I see little children sleeping, and animals scampering about. There are the sounds the symphonies of musicians endeavor to replicate, but the enchanting sounds of birds and breezes, the rushes of the sounds of water, not to forget the always-contemplative sound of silence. Again it all seems to have come about as something too perfect for simple evolution, so I lean toward The Great Creation, The Greatest Painter, Philosopher, Poet, and Choral Majesty. And again I see something larger than us, more poignant than the most passionate of scientists, The Ultimate Conductor, and I cannot come to any conclusion other than a perfect divinity. I shall lean toward it, call out to it, and conclude that I must call this master of all things "God." And I come from a people who took that to a level beyond my abstract thinking to the absolute conclusion that there is simply no explanation to any of this other than God.

I sometimes quarrel with the faith of my fathers, for there is so much wrong with the earth that people attribute to this God. From killing fields and battles that are as ancient as scripture and before there was the ability to translate "The Word" to the written for all men to see and to hear—I see the world in chaos and the hungry not being fed. Shelters destroyed by natural disaster and man, crazy at times, unpredictable man, with the power to destroy it all now if there is not constant surveillance and watch over which buttons it would take to push and to end all beauty, love, and perfection of this painting of mortals and earth. But I know that even with this, some will remain and shall the dead find the promised Heaven. I begin to think it preposterous to imagine that if we ingest the beauty of simple earth, sun, and the sky, that we are so tiny and insignificant as to not conclude that maybe, just maybe there is something even more remarkable that a sublime creator has in store for us.

As to the carnage, I would never have painted Picasso's "Guernica" even in the worst of times, for I also fear and believe that there is a confrontational and ugly core that aims to do away with all that is wonderful. My Appalachian world did see this in the darkness of time. The counter-force called evil has been trying to battle with all that is good since the great creation. It is powerful and has shown strength throughout the ages of mankind. Like the universal artist, it paints and it works, but it makes things intolerable for sustaining life. It is willing to starve children, to make war without provocation, and it is supernatural. My ancestors of the faith saw its name in the book of knowledge, "Satan," the evil one, the master of Gahanna and the netherworld which throughout mankind's history has been seen as "beneath." The shadowed hand chipping, chipping away at the beautiful garden, and we are to believe scripturally that there will be the day, whatever a day is within the context of ethereal time, when the last battle will begin to end it all. But that which is good, that who is God, will prevail, and then shall be created the new heaven and the new earth.

Appalachian heritage holds strongly to this premise that all good shall prevail with the greatest acceptance of the statement, "That man and woman born in God must die to see the glory of the Lord and from the expectation that bliss is yet to come." It was always very hard to concentrate on the reality of wonderful days and hours which were our lives. I grew into womanhood with this sense of fatalism, and I still believe that my people carry a heavy burden that has affected many souls into being taken advantage of those who preach goodness but who have evil intent. Growing up I did find it very difficult to hear, "Give us this day," and not to think that it was a far piece down a road which I had not taken. I still struggle with this thing called "happiness." What is it all about?

To look around and see the painting of life, to hear the avian chorus and the hum, the constant hum that is life around us, took a very long time for me to enjoy such pleasures. I think that when one grows up with the philosophy that fate is rarely on your side, as so many of my background came to accept, then it takes some work to carve out a little place to call your own. I have my dear old English and literature teacher to thank and to remember that she had us memorize the words of poet Countee Cullin, among the earliest published black poets in this country, who wrote, "A tent pitched in a meadow, A little meadow to call one's own." After all of these years I am certain that I am paraphrasing this, but we were taught by the whitest of teachers to respect this man who would speak of the ideal. Something to call your own. Most people would not question that "all your little own," as he phrased it, but the fact that she chose this verse for us was not surprising, for only a fraction of us would ever feel the concept of entitlement or having anything all our own.

I recently saw a movie called "Evening" with Clair Danes, Vanessa Redgrave, Toni Collete, and Natasha Richardson. It ended with an appearance by Meryl Streep made up to be an older woman and she brought to the daughters, with a mother who was dying, and who was an old friend, these messages. She told them women of mid-century did what they had to. Didn't we? We did. "Have you been happy?" And the answer was, "For the most part." Again, the kind of statement my people would understand, but the third message seemed to me the most powerful. "We are strange creatures, aren't we? And in the end does much of it matter anyway?" She also said of life, "There are no mistakes." I could not go so far as to believe that we are infallible, for I believe from my heart that we make errors often, but we are called to deal with our errors if we value the virtue and love of others. I seriously think that our humanness calls us to accept that everything is not all about us. We are called to share the tent, and we cannot call a selected meadow "all our little own" as the poet surmised.

Mistakes, though, are something we from the Bible Belt associate so dearly with sin that it is not good enough that we beat ourselves with the belt, for the buckle is harder, and the more it hurts, the more our flesh is torn. This is far too often the case. The scars remind us of our mistakes until we bleed and feel shame over things that are inevitable.

But to my hosts and hostesses of guilt and failure and to my peers, I could hope that we can find more forgiveness for ourselves and for others, for the kind of human beings we were taught to be are saints, and I wonder how many saints have walked among us in our everyday. The church door closes behind us, and we go on into another day, and if we make thoughtful choices, then maybe we have done the best that we can. Mistakes? There are mistakes like one sees in art museums when one goes to see the great masters of painting. The years have passed and in art museums like The Prado, a good art historian will point out the places where the oil has faded just enough to show you that another painting had been started where the marvelous work had taken shape over the painter's original intent. So is it less perfect?

Again I find myself longing to tell people of my birthright that we did well. We can be better and we need not keep giving up just because we are not certain which fork in the road to take. It is the strength within you that will prevail, not all of the outside clutter, so take one look across the mountain or down in the valley where the fields are being prepared for springtime, and take it all in, for you have a new canvas every day. The conflict is in how one receives the gifts and those who want to destroy it. I will never forget those youthful years when I was caught up in a story I did not know how to write other than as it was happening. There were many errors, offenses against myself, fear of the future, and the impending sense of doom that I had grown up in. But what matters is that I had the experiences, nurtured the ability to feel, and the chapters yet to be told are apt to say that all I worried about really did not matter after all. It is said and done, and yes, we humans are strange creatures, with one short time to get things done well. I am compelled to believe the luxury of another life, lies just beyond, for the elders will seem to speak somehow.

Chapter Thirty Eight

I would not go home again for at least another year or two, for I was still bandaging my wounds and calling on Sundays. Though there were many times when I felt like a girl alone, I knew that there was a purpose for me to stay in Washington. One job would bring me to meet a woman whose name was Diane Pierce, and Diane would not only become my work friend, she would become a new mentor to me. She had grown up in West Virginia, and she already knew a lot about what I had been through. She and a friend Elsa had come along to Washington about eight years before me, and when I met her, the times were about to change for me as if a good servant had plowed a garden path and said, "Follow. Just follow." And I said, "I will," as I turned and buried my feet into my new reality.

I could still hide myself in dreams, and a favorite one was the Lake of Mirrors, for as one walks by and sees if they just stop long enough, not one reflection remains the same. Maybe it is a thousand mirrors or enough for those who can see further out so much so they cannot count. The Lake of Mirrors by which I walked and where I have been able to bring some of you—this magnificent sight only exists when one is alone. Each wave is soft, but the mirrors easily move in the breeze, and you and I can tell that each view of ourselves changes in the breath of the moment. We want to capture the ones that are the loveliest and hang them from a wall to see ourselves at our very best. Some are so horrid and distorted that we want to throw a rock on the water and crush that glass letting the rock sink to the bottom to become hidden in the sediment that comes from the land above it.

Once I had seen the mirrored lake I had come to a time of choosing, and I began first in my choice of how I could find friends, for much that I had thought about before had sunk like a boat. Once more I was moving in to a group a little older and sometimes wiser than me. The prettiest mirror that came of the water seemed to resemble me at a wonderful moment, all ready to smile, and the more stern ones brought me the message that thinking rather than reacting so quickly might be a better way of opening doors. The sad mirrors—those I was beginning to let go of, too, for the new friends coming in to my life had been to other places and came from other places as most Washingtonians did then. It was so important to find the right the friends who had some influence on me, my new guides, and the ones years would not take away. Maybe it would be my luck that they knew of lakes with mirrors, and earth with scent, and how the full moon seemed to take us all out, as that great event each month rolled around. Once you have found this place where you feel enough strength to begin something breathe deeply, for the chance has come to glue the broken places.

Choose well, so very well, and in your happy hours, I hope that you will meet friends like Jim and Diane Pierce, a real married couple, the first well-functioning apartment I had been in that was treated as a home, and where I could go to figure out something of myself. Soon I would realize that both of them had come from different places. Diane was a West Virginian, and she and Jim were excellent chefs just for fun. This was something I would be influenced by for the rest of my life, and on the lake of silver where my photograph broke apart, the person who I was began evolving. The heartbreak of Kathy, Carol, and Natalie's departure had gone away, and new VISTA and Peace Corps people would come in. I could never say good-bye without tears, and I did not want to have the friends who were planning on leaving immediately, so Jim and Diane's place was such a refuge to me that I took an apartment in the same building.

I met another Jewish boy who had gotten out of the Israeli Army and who was breaking the stress of education and Army years with a year's reprieve at the Embassy of Israel. Amazingly, his name was Shimon, and he brought to me the gift of learning that there were extremely appealing and wonderful Jewish guys in Washington after all, and I would spend time at his place one floor up. Yes, half the time he was after the girl and the body which I was then, but most of the time he was just a very affectionate friend, and I told him it was going to be nothing more. I was not going to be involved with another person who was going back most probably to an old girlfriend. Note that I made the decision, and he even congratulated me the last time he saw me for bearing up under all of his sexual harassment. But it had been generally pleasant, and we were able to say fond farewells. This leaving and moving from relationship to relationship was in no manner how I pictured my life. Jim and Diane told me, "It is time for you to meet a nice guy for a change." Those were the exact words, and not really knowing what a nice boy was, I was very curious.

If I felt alone now there were other places to go, but I protected all of them from my Lake of Mirrors, and I would not let the secret out that I understood. Wisdom of the water, your abiding soul, and the wonderful vessels we are. How others see us. unfortunately does matter. This reflection of me had said, "Something marvelous may come, like new friends who will wipe the tears away from your time of mourning, for you are about to make a passage with them and will awaken to the new memories who will open your heart once more to relationships which move on like the moon across the marsh near the tiny lakeshore."

Chapter Thirty Nine

I see the importance of telling you about my first city friend of Appalachia, for most of my life my world had been spent within a 100-mile radius of my home. How can I possibly explain to you that when my world was that small and when each day was more than a twelve-mile journey to a small town for school or supplies and then a trip back to the farm on which I was raised. Seven brothers and sisters would come to the home with the address of Belvidere, Tennessee, for that was our nearest post office, but we never considered the Fandrick's Feed Store, Burial Insurance Business, General Store, and the post office to be a town, for that was basically all that was there, but I would be the only child who spent all of my school years in the Tennessee valley. Going back and forth to the mountain out in Alabama was the farthest world that I knew, until I was about twelve years old, and I went with my parents to Nashville, Tennessee, for the first time. That was where the country ended as far as I could see, except for that other America on television, the perfect America.

I came to know about Chicago and surrounding environs when Daddy went to work there, but even though I had geography and had to learn all of the state capitals, none of it existed, but in books, and I thought the cowboy westerns like Gene Autry and Roy Rogers were for real. The United States had only had cowboys, weathered storefronts, cheeky ladies, and horses that could sail like the wind when the Native American tribes would strike out and make war. I had history books, too, and I loved history. I could envision the Oregon Trail which really opened up the country. The belief of peoples and cities existing even bigger than Nashville or Atlanta of the sixties was simply too much to comprehend.

It was greatly important, for there were Appalachian cities bigger than my towns, bigger than Nashville back then, for they were usually older. No one told me that cities such as Portsmouth, Ohio, Wheeling, West

Virginia, and places like Pittsburgh were really a people not too different from my own and that these were great cities, all built on the rivers, and generations of people grew up eating the country food that I ate and learning early American and Celtic Folk songs and hymns. Probably the biggest difference of all was black coal which came from the earth and spewed from these towns' factories, and city life could be hard just like life in my land off the main roads. It was true, though, that more Europeans would find coal country, especially Eastern Europeans, for they came from lands where mining had begun centuries before, and the towns needed their know-how.

I will confess that I am, to this day, absolutely dyslexic when it comes to directions, and I believed that one road existed in the whole darned country, and that was Highway 64. And if you got on that highway and went far enough on a Trailways or Greyhound, or lucked out and got to travel by passenger train, which was dying out almost completely for most of the country then, then I was fairly certain that you could get anywhere. I remember Daddy and the farmers who went to work at the factories used some highway that was route 41 that got them from north to south, and by this time you understand that mountain cities and Appalachian cities were just not in my vocabulary. And to think that Europeans had pretty much built things which reminded them of "The Old World" as we called it.

Of course we knew about Washington, D.C. The seniors from most high schools in our region sold candy, held bake sales, picked cotton, and stripped tobacco for processing—whatever it took to save for the trip to Washington, D.C., which they could take as a graduating senior, but I had this idea since my sisters and a brother had gone there that it would have been a waste of money to go on that trip, that I would make it there someday. It did not have the "Old Country" second- and third-generation German and Polish immigrants who left their stamp so beautifully on the cities of Appalachia. It also did not talk much about the coal mines where men died early from black lung disease, from the coal dust day in and day out, or the not infrequent explosions within the mines when safety was lax and walls would collapse, so we began talking about the other Appalachia, with these wonderful cities, not so much farm country, but one whole heck of a lot of folks being used to get to the "black gold," the kinder name for deep and dark coal.

It was a scratch-out living, a little more communal than dirt farming, and the companies in the first third of the century pretty much owned what my Bohemian Club friend called "The Patch." Joseph Smiell, a San Francisco fixture and musician, taught me later on about his life in this area. The patch had a general store, a telephone for the town, maybe a doctor, and houses built in close proximity with little if any plumbing just like those of us in the non-mining Appalachia. But many of us had fathers who would do share-cropping in which you and your family worked and slaved and planted and harvested the crop and then your share of money usually went to someone who you owed money to for planting the crop in the first place, and then you might could make it through the winter if you had enough fruit jars of food plus a pig to slaughter. Were you a part of the patch, the company owned everything, and the land wasn't that good for growing food, so the scratched-out living from mining went back to the company that owned the mines and before winter was over and hungry kids were fed while your Daddy was killing himself or being killed in the mine from a misplaced "Fire in the Hole," you would need to work another year just to keep even. Only the rare soul made a living.

In both areas moonshine helped to ease the bite of the pain, so once again there was family abuse, particularly wife abuse, a destiny that there was about no way out of unless a son left the family to go into the United States Armed Services, and meanwhile the few who had or owned something had houses on the main roads that you were never invited to, and money from the mines kept building mine towns.

Some folks would run off to the towns and find factory jobs, just like the southern farmer went to the northern cities to factories. We were still a nation of manufacturers well into the mid-50s and early 1960s, so the miners added their brand of Appalachian flavors to larger cities which sprang up on the backs of miners. Wherever we went, we took a part of us. My friend, Diane, and her best friend Elsa had come to Washington some years before me, and Diane and I, not knowing that we were actually two mountain babies, just from two different areas, became very good friends as we worked together, enjoyed one another's company, and took our walks home from work together. She was a Wheeling, West Virginia, girl and not from wealth, but being a city girl of my heritage she became my mentor in all things. She was married to a guy who was great fun, a good guy, though he had probably done a few too many drugs in Vietnam, and he was another city kid to my memory. He and Diane had developed a taste for classical music, having a few more school privileges than me, and they had made a new life of learning to be great home chefs.

I'd never seen an eggplant, an artichoke, or prepared a Thanksgiving goose with chestnut dressing, or taken a voice lesson until I met Diane and Jim and Elsa. They knew Wheeling; they knew about West Virginia and what coal mines had done to the land, and they were about eight and nine years older than me, so I absorbed everything they began to share with me from the new 1960s rock and roll music to listening to opera with Maria Callas and some Italian tenor who I would learn was the great Pavarotti. Jim was a flute player and Diane desperately wanted to sing operatic music, and they had a friend who I am certain has passed on to better hands, but he was a connoisseur of their wonderful cooking, dressed like a British dandy. He had a music school with some other folks in Washington, and his name should have been in a Dickens Novel: Wendell Margrave

So we would gather around the table, Wendell regaling us with his knowledge as a Doctor of Musical Arts, his appreciation for fine cigars and drink, all the while, taking shots of bourbon, then moving on to Courvoisier, which I decided was an amazingly wonderful brandy. Our Captain of table conversation loaded with a couple of shots of whiskey began stroking my legs under the table, and I just had no patience with this anymore. I sort of felt like saying, "For God's sake, would you guys just keep your wandering hands to yourself?" It never occurred to me that he was probably doing the same thing to Diane or Elsa, or would have had his rotund body not been holding a brandy snifter in one hand, and after I would carefully remove his hands from my legs, he would decide food had some appeal once more

This was when I would learn to make things like rice pilaf—Greek foods I had become somewhat familiar with Mehale—and the novel soufflé. Or as I might call it, "a lot of work for not much food." We were beginning the years of making crepes of all kinds—basic Julia Child recipes that worked one to death, but we could switch it off and do the corn bread and pinto beans and feel just as happy. That was a summer to remember, but as autumn approached Diane took her own advice and decided that Thanksgiving I was going to meet a nice guy.

His name was Frank Heintz, and he was from San Francisco, California. He was in Washington because he was lucky enough to have escaped being sent to Vietnam by auditioning after his graduation from The Curtis Institute of Music and being accepted into "The President's Own:" The United States Marine Band. He was a bassoon player, and as with most new college graduates, he really wanted to be back in Philadelphia where he had received a degree because he combined studies at University of Pennsylvania with his music classes all through Curtis which was fully endowed by The Curtis Publishing Company. New York had its Julliard, but people paid money to go to Julliard if they were accepted in by audition. But at Curtis you were admitted on full scholarship, so that audition was among the most coveted to be won.

Chapter Forty

I do not mean to compare schools, but I can reassure you that most of the classically trained musicians, could they, would go to Curtis to this day for it is the jewel of classical music arts whether you play an instrument, sing opera, or desire to have among you the most elite musician teachers in this country. You would go to Curtis were you accepted. The great Philadelphia Orchestra was often home for many of the inspiring instructors. I would learn that Curtis was the incubator of world-renowned musicians. Disagree if you must, but that is just the way it is, and, of course, I knew none of this. Frank Heintz's education meant college to me, and that was about it. I may have been more impressed when I learned that he had been valedictorian of his graduating class at San Francisco's Polytechnic High School where he went for the music teacher there.

I learned that he had played at the Music Academy of the West before he graduated high school, and he played music festivals from California to the Grand Tetons in Wyoming in the summertime, but I was not impressed still, and that Bassoon—"Clown of the Orchestra" meant even less to me in meeting him. He had been known to tell people like me that he played violin just because the bassoon was not all that common, but I was willing to meet him. I think the thing that impressed him most about me was that I could sing a cappella all the words to "Come to Jesus." It is a musicians' joke, and I will tell you to this day, I am not so certain how it got to be so humorous in the musical community. In the Protestant churches, especially, it is a song which is used when the altar call or the invitation to be baptized is given. I would later sing in a quite good church choir, but my shyness prevented me from ever going forward with any voice training. Though I can sing relatively on key and have a good ear for sound, if I endeavored to sing anything to anyone by myself I develop the terror of a performer, and thus I would sing for no one but myself and, strangely, for this Frank Heintz person.

"Come to Jesus. He will save you, though your sins as crimson glow." That impressed this young man that Diane and Jim were fixing me up with. It is good not to know some things, for then you do not make such an idiot out of yourself trying to impress someone with your keen knowledge of what is their life's work, and for me just singing to myself was enough, and Frank Timothy Heintz, his mother's beloved only son, happened to have had a mom who grew up on a farm in Petaluma, California. Being myself and having fun with Diane and Jim, not to mention Wendall Margrave, I had all of that, and no one told me that that being five-seven with dark hair to my waist and the British complexion of my ancestors had their own way of impressing. I have possessed many faults and many qualities in my life, but vanity when I was younger would be the least among them. Thus through the love of an Appalachian sister who took me under her wing, again, life was about to change. And this time, the autumn leaves had a brighter color.

I believe that if you grow up in Tennessee and the southern states that you learn from an early age to be amazed at the glorious scent of fresh rain upon the earth. The woods fill with the redbuds first, then come the dogwoods, and no explanation outside of something holy is going to convince you that a dogwood has not had a holy past. It comes with Easter and is usually hearty enough to withstand a little cold. Throughout most of the woodlands where they grow, you may gather them, peek at the flowers, and marvel that you are holding a sign that there is a promised land and that heaven is that moment while you stand under those wild and majestic trees and watch the old earth and woodland floor become a carpet of blooms, from wild violets to mountain laurel and the pink honeysuckle. It is almost springtime again, and there may be ice on the mountains, but the warm days are coming. You can still find refreshing spring waters if you know the right place to look. There are houses with porches and swings in the hollows even now and to swing on a front porch and to watch the winter world fade and to see bunnies scampering from some playful dog are the simple gifts I remember.

I could tell Diane and Jim about these things, but in Wheeling, where Diane had come from, something happened to the beautiful mountains which did not happen so much in Tennessee at that time and for that matter, never, for all states learned the serious damage brought on by blasting away mountain forests to get at the black coal. Only for those who got the money did it make any sense. Fortunately, some of the patches remained wild enough to hold the same blessing we in Tennessee and northern Alabama experienced, so even though the coal fields ripped the land to shreds, places like Wheeling and the little coal valleys and mountain towns were able to keep some semblance of the woodlands' past glory.

The first time I came through West Virginia, I looked out from a bus and, being the polite Southern girl, these words did not leave my mouth: "What the hell?" I am telling you that it was shocking to see bald mountains, the great erosion, the coal-dark streams. It would be pleasant to go back there later when finally the United States Government got some sense and joined with the West Virginians to stop the clear-blasting without a plan for reforestation. Diane also knew about the discrimination of poor white folks just like poor blacks, because she had lived it like me in a different way.

We would share our sameness, and we would share simple everyday life most of 1968, but I was not certain about this boyfriend that she was cooking up for me, having already met a few of their friends, but she was convinced that this boy, Frank Heintz—the Californian, as I thought of him—was going to fit perfectly in my life. I have told you that I learned all of these life experiences he'd had as a musician and as an honor student and I had learned he played his music for presidential inaugurations, funerals, weddings, you name it. The President's Own United States Marine Band and the classical musicians who played in it were news to me. He played for both the Johnson and into the Nixon administration, and he had strange friends. One of them had put a pipe that he smoked stuck into his Marine band coat still lit and this was not a good thing to do when you were performing at The White House. I learned everything I could about Frank and their group of friends from Diane and so Thanksgiving of 1968 was the planned date for our meeting.

When November came to the mountains, to the valleys, and to Washington, D.C, I often felt so happy and hardly understood why. After finding ourselves "pulling bolls," as we called the last of the cotton harvest someone would suddenly mention that it was Thanksgiving. We might all look around and wonder, "What is so special about this day?" For here we would not even know that people were sitting around a table with food from the harvest flowing over every bowl they had taken from the pantry. Some of us as children thought it was a holy day, for Thanksgiving must have something to do with Almighty God. We had read about the pilgrims gathered with the Indians to celebrate making it through a year and how they all bowed in prayers of thanks over this great feast, but that was in a schoolbook in a pretty picture. As I mentioned before, I had no idea that people really took a day off from work, that this was not a biblical feast. For some reason I felt very touched by the image of those big roasted birds on the tables and pilgrims sitting around what appeared to be a picnic table. For many years I liked to think of it in my dreams.

I liked to see the Indians standing with colorful corn, a table that seriously looked like something one could order from the Sears and Roebuck catalogue. There were usually bowls of potatoes, big pumpkin pies, what appeared to be hearth-baked bread, and a jug of cider. All the Puritans of that seventeenth-century storybook tale dressed alike, white bonnets for the ladies who had on gray to black dresses all so beautiful with hands held in prayer. The men dressed in black with nice hats and black britches and nice vests. If the Indians got lucky for the pictures, they might have animal furs draped over what appeared to be boxer shorts in many of our schoolbooks. But I felt somewhat cynical about Thanksgiving dragging a cotton sack on my knees just like the brothers, sisters, and Daddy. I had some hope for a nice pot of beans and some bread had Mama been able to get some supper on with three babies, for we were hungry when we came in from work. If I wanted to be really cynical, then I would picture

Daddy with those nice buckled shoes all the pilgrim men wore, and that was my way with coping with the first chilling winds which were moving in. In Washington, the leaves were golden, red, and all sorts of colors in between for the real Thanksgiving Day that I had been invited to. I had to be careful not to zone out in one of my imaginary gatherings while there eating with these good people.

During my last years at home, turkey was introduced to our table, for Dad won one. After that, we all sure had a taste for turkey. But that Thanksgiving in D.C., Diane and Jim got out the European flavors. They were cooking a goose that smelled wonderful. There was a roasted chestnut dressing, pumpkin pies Diane baked, which were cookbook pictorial, and there was hot cider with rum and Jack Daniels black label whiskey to have with early prepared eggnog. Also there was again Courvoisier, and Frank, the man I was to meet.

Jim had found a source for a 1944 Hooper's Port over at some liquor store that did not have any more sense than to sell it for ten dollars to two fools who were going to crack it for dessert not knowing they were holding a treasure in their hand. I loved shopping along Connecticut Avenue then and I brought something Diane had asked me to for the festivities. I think I took a suggested wine that was all the rage then that was white, sweet, and apt to give one a hangover for the next month.

I was not a drinker, but on this day I wanted to be grown-up like the rest of the folks, so maybe they started me out with the port. Of course the guest of honor was Wendell, or Margrave as they chose to call him. and Diane's friend Elsa who had a job in the district after summering in San Francisco. In 1968 that meant she had probably shacked up in The Haight Ashbury, met a Guru, smoked pot, and danced around naked somewhere. She had lost her boyfriend Tony to a New England college graduate sort, and she had vowed not to spend another winter in San Francisco where it had rained solid the year before from September through February. She had been chilled straight through to the bone. She was blond and pretty, almost thirty, though—which made her seem more refined than the rest of us, and her old love Tony and she could exist in D.C. again without her falling back into a broken heart.

A time was coming when I, too, would learn that if you do not like cold and rain, take Elsa's advice and head back to the east coast, for people on the east coast and throughout most of America had learned the beauty of central heat, warm clothes, and electric blankets. The more pretentious might have one of those bed-warming devices from Victorian England, but coats were the real magic, and I had the one my sister had helped me get. I had not heard of Frank's summer cold season in San Francisco.

Pot was inevitably a part of the conversation if not a part of dinner, but I was not a pot smoker either. I was one of the few religious people at the table, and I hoped that I could impress them maybe with my knowledge about Thanksgiving Day from scripture, but after looking through the Bible pictures and going to the concordance, I could find no mention of such a special gathering in the Bible, so I kept my mouth shut about that one. I also sort of wondered if Elsa was going to be interested in this guy who was coming, the Curtis Institute Guy who I was there to meet. But at 30, she was getting over a broken heart from her guitar and artistic guy and as she was in graphic design. I think she was still hooked on the Beatles, and we all wanted to be either Judy Collins, Joan Baez, or Joni Mitchell. Odetta was kind of big, too, but she was big as a mountain and she was more the black New Orleans or Deep South folk/blues which was a little unfamiliar to us. A hippy with a military hair cut wasn't her idea of a good time.

He was a little late, but soon this guy with really dark hair, huge blue eyes, of thin build, and about six-one came in, and Diane must have read him the riot act, for he immediately turned his attention to me in my purple madras mini-dress and hair that was so straight it made me sort of look like a cousin of another folk goddess Buffy Saint Marie. He took my hand and seemed very pleased to meet me. They were all friends already, but graciously everyone drew me in to the conversation, and dinner was great fun except for Wendell's ever-probing hands. We ate in courses, and somehow I was not a stranger. That table felt better than the pictures of Thanksgiving flowing through my brain.

It did help that everyone was adding to the cider this or that other beverage which I had been told was evil, and by the end of dinner I was letting this fellow Frank Heintz hold my hand. By the end of the evening, I felt warm and content. I was not certain what to say or do, though, when Frank decided to sit with his back to me sort of resting his head in my lap. It was not in a rude way, just sort of sweet and affectionate, and he did not seem to be going beyond that sweet affection. By midnight we were all in a state between lying down on a table or chairs, but I had the option of going to my apartment across the hall, and since I was sort of his date, he walked me home. I let him come in, for no one was fit to drive. On my pathetic little bed, we just lay down. We were so tired and so warm that we were dozing off to sleep.

I heard him say, "I guess you do not want to have relations with me on the first date," After which he gave a sinister and sleepy laugh. And I finally was able to say, "You are absolutely right." But I also heard myself say, "Maybe sometime," to which he gave an enthusiastic, "Can I call you in a week or two?"

He and I slept on my little bed, his arms over my shoulders, and we slept as if we had been married for twenty years. The next morning I let him get cleaned up and out. Something about needing to be at a White House ceremony, but the National Christmas Tree Lighting didn't mean too much to me other than that I knew he had to play afterwards, something about a pre-dinner concert afterwards, and that was it. Thanksgiving was over and I thought, "He will call. Or he will not." I felt so peaceful to have been with him and saying that we spent the night together might sound pretty awful, except we both had slept in our clothes. I rushed to tell Diane all of the news and to see someone happy for me and so proud of herself was not a feeling I'd gotten too often.

Again, we southern girls got the bad news mainly for it was presumed that was worth telling. I helped clean up, and I learned about cooking a goose. It is a novel idea if you need a can of goose lard, but for the ordinary meal it is like cleaning the vat after lard-making day on the farm and forget about after-Thanksgiving sandwiches. Diane and I were of the same mind, though. Let's get this grease out of here and contemplate if the call will ever happen. But we were pleased, so pleased that it had been about my first really Happy Thanksgiving. I started writing poems again.

Maybe I had about given up on having this new man in my life call, and I felt it disconcerting though maybe not so disappointing. I'd had so many bad boyfriends before, some still coming around hoping "to get lucky." But if an old boyfriend came in the door, usually they were definitely interested in intimacy over whatever new conversation I might share. I was hearing about "The Sexual Revolution" and how it got started in San Francisco and swept across the country like wildfire. Drums, tambourines, the first of disco dancing of a sort—not particularly dance but a great deal of body movement which had the "come hither" message. For the first time music was definitely feeding the frenzy toward sexual gratification, and were you not dense, you got the message that it was often about getting naked. However, Dupont Circle in D.C. had the same atmosphere.

I have wondered what great mind came up with the idea of a "Sexual Revolution," for basically nothing was particularly new, except women were definitely requested to take the lead in starting these trysts. My friends, I do not hesitate to tell you that I personally do not believe there was a "Revolution" at all. Perhaps there was a revelation of sorts, but having sex before marriage did not begin in San Francisco among a bunch of freak kids dressed as if they just came out of an East Indian brothel, for fathers through the ages knew that their daughters were capable of the act of sex, and I have talked about all the "premature" seven-pound babies over back from the days of my mothers and theirs.

From the mountains to the prairies, from Jackson County, Alabama, at Sand Mountain's peak and on out to elite places like the eastern United States to the wealthy of Marin County, California, people were pretty much the same as always about premarital sex. It happened, and if anything changed, it was more the attitude that parents had begun to reveal. Appalachian mountain dads and moms and parents across the country were no longer so interested in the the shotgun weddings of their time and of their generations. For they had seen too often the sorrow and the misery girls were placed in for having let their bodies respond to what they thought was love, find themselves pregnant, and having marriages that were disasters and school lives fully interrupted. . Many of these parents had their own memories of leaving home as children trying to be parents when they were hardly old enough to wear grown-up clothing.

Mothers were fed up with having their daughters sent to "the home," as most regions referred to a girl's place where she would be kept in hiding until a baby was born. Some mothers used to go so far as to pretend the newborn was their own, just hiding out for a time and keeping the daughters in and telling them the misery they were about to suffer. I remember an aunt telling me how having a baby was the only pain that could be compared to the pain of cancer, and I thought that was horrendous, for one diagnosed with cancer in the middle years before any decent treatment was available usually went into a hospital and died a horrible death. I thought having a baby must be about the worst thing that could ever happen to a girl after that. Parents were also asking questions such as, "Why are we staying in marriages where we are both miserable and unhappy?" Or they, like my parents in the days of the big fights would say, "I'm stayin' with you because of these kids," and that was a very heavy burden on children.

Studies were going on all across the country about how sex could be pleasant for women, as well as men, and obviously a lot of the girls with whom I went to school knew that a long time before I did. My Daddy would have no need for a shotgun wedding, because he had probably murdered any of the girls in our family if we came up in that "P. G." state of being. When my father spoke, you never doubted him for a moment. It is entirely feasible that birth control advances increased risk-taking, but if you had my parents, then you were not going to take any risks. I really believed that it was far more normal to be celibate until marriage. But with the threat of death hanging over your head, not that I recommend such, the revolution did happen in how our elders had begun to think of babies and marriage as not uniquely an ideal that had worked very well for them. And we were in a war in Vietnam. There simply seemed to be other considerations beyond the strict moral code of the sexuality any of us had known. Pope John would call for Vatican II where birth control would be reaffirmed as a moral and social evil, but even a large percentage of Catholics were no longer willing to accept his warnings and ultimatums. It was a confusing time, so we began to want color in our world without all of the black and white. If our elders had become so discontented with their lot, then what about us?

Here they were, though, the old boyfriends. I began to be the one to tell them that they might want to meet a friend of mine, and meanwhile the sheer friendship of people like my Catholic friend George and my friend Stan were beginning to accept me just for the companionship, the love of friends. They were there for me as ones whose name I could call upon. They respected me for having some wisdom and did not condemn me for standing on the sidelines and for hoping that someday, maybe, someone was going to love me.

Thus I was visiting a few old VISTA friends, spending even more time with my friends the Pierces, and a full two weeks, if not more, passed before I heard from Frank and he finally called as he said he would. He sounded a little anxious on the phone, told me how he had enjoyed Thanksgiving and said one reason he had not called was he wanted to think of some place special to take me for a date. Now let's be clear, date was not a word used that often around that time, for people liked to hang out and drink. More than a few did drugs for recreation and we tended to gather in groups and then pair off, so a date was a concept that I had hardly heard of in my entire life. This young man from San Francisco, where all cool people were heading to play hippie for at least a week or so, was asking me for a date! How could anyone care about me enough to ask me to just go out and to relate that they had to plan something really special?

He said he wasn't very good at such things, and when he told me that he wanted to take me to a Textile Museum that had a special exhibit and then we could share dinner, I was all but speechless. I wanted to say, "You are from California where the sexual revolution is going on and you want to take me to a Textile Museum and to have dinner?" Instead I delightedly accepted the invitation.

It came on a day when he was free from his Marine Band duties and the November rain had begun, just begun, and I smelt earth and leaves and I felt happy. He held my hand, something David would do when we walked the old town of Murfreesboro, and it placed a little fear in my heart, but somehow we chatted easily as if we had known each other for a very long time. Our hands warmed the chilly afternoon when the last of Washington, D.C.'s, beautiful autumn leaves could be crushed one last time before the wind and the chill of our nation's capital would blow them somewhere afar. where they would settle and become a new tree or new earth. I liked being with this person very much.

We went to the textile museum that I had never visited before. It was close to the Corcoran Gallery of Art, where Tom and I had gone one of the times he'd visited me before he went to Barbados, so a little nostalgia reigned there for me. With Frank, though, I could lay it to rest. He knew of a wonderful Greek restaurant near Dupont Circle and fortunately, because of Diane and Jim, the menu did not leave me totally lost. For the first time in my life, a man was telling me about things on the menu that he liked and that maybe we should try the dolma, the eggplant moussaka, and he said that the hummus was really good. I wanted to know about him and he wanted to know about me. Who could ever really want to know about me? That was the sadness of relationships with older men and flaky young guys with girlfriends back home had left me with, but I would share none of this. I would take the day and remember it all of my life.

Yes, we had a little wine and we bought some Metaxa, a strong Greek brandy, to take to my place. The rain began to turn into the earliest of snowflakes, as if everything of beauty had been painted into one day and we would have that one day to remember. As we walked along the quieter area of Connecticut Avenue back to my place, he placed his arms around my shoulders to keep me warm. The wool of his coat had absorbed the scents of fading autumn, and I leaned my head in to his arm. My face can still sense those moments and that day. I had so much more to tell him, and we had so much more to talk about. We ended our day with a visit to Diane and Jim's place, shared the Metaxa, and listened to some group called The Rolling Stones.

I think Jim and Frank shared the evil weed of the ages, marijuana, then they started passing the joint around the room, and I think that I will quote President Clinton who was about our age then: "I did not inhale." What is amusing is that I probably didn't, because I was not a smoker as most girls were then and I did not know how to inhale; however, I do remember that things just seemed perfect and that the man with the blue eyes that were large and intellectual had somehow bonded with a girl from Lexie Crossroads.

The intimacies we shared would probably be more than some kindred of mine could bear, but I never felt pressured into a relationship with Frank, He wasn't very suave, admittedly, when he showed me how his passenger seat in the Peugeot which he was driving would recline, but that was not the place for me. Within another couple of weeks, he would take me to his apartment in Arlington, Virginia. It was smaller than mine, really an efficiency. He would go and play whatever President Johnson's family desired for a state dinner with the smaller concert group for the Marine Band, and I would stay at his place for those hours. He had a horrid kitchen, and I thought of making something special for him, but he had told me that he was going to make the dinner on this night, and I remember it well, because from somewhere the Post Exchange had gotten in cantaloupe. He made me hummus and chickpea dal, my introduction to curry, and he had it planned this all as a surprise for me.

I loved dinner, and there was a communication going on at a level which I had not known before, something lasting and something poems are made of—that feeling of permanency that I knew little of. I think that I downplayed a lot of my old fears to him, but I could show him a picture of Mama in her kitchen and the one of Daddy that had been taken for the local paper. He was holding the largest rattlesnake anyone had seen, and the news got out about the six-foot-long rattler. That was Frank's first introduction to my family. I had school pictures of my little brothers and sister, some old pictures of the older kids, and a lot of my prize certificates that I had won during my school years. He shared his photographs, and we talked about our homes and families. I would learn that his father was older when Frank was born and that his dad had died the previous summer. He talked about the house in San Francisco and painted a most picturesque childhood growing up in that city by the bay before its Haight-Ashbury became infamous for the hippies. We were all hearing about this wild and crazy town where anything goes. His San Francisco was a family town about to blast open as the desired spot of younger people who weren't hell-bent back-east souls, and I found myself knowing that the television Frisco existed—a name the natives despised—but it was not of big city status in his world. It was home.

He had a desk for making the reeds for his bassoon, and I would learn about the cane that came from one district in France. I was mesmerized by the making of the reed from a simple piece of something which looked like ordinary dried and wide cane. He did almost precision surgery to cut his reeds and to wrap them, and they turned into the mouthpiece for the bassoon. He would tell me about the instrument, the high keys, the low keys, the woodwind family of orchestral instruments, and he never spoke down to me. He was a good teacher.

A table, a couple of chairs, the reed desk, and some bookshelves and a bed were conveniently placed, and that was about the whole of his apartment. It was all he needed and then it became all we needed, for as if I were reading a novel I could not have pictured how we ever found each other. This Appalachian girl, this San Francisco man one generation removed from Alsace Lorraine and from a town called Wyk off the coast of Denmark.

We began to share our days and our nights and was innocence being lost once more for this girl who was raised to be a celibate until the time of marriage and even then to be petrified, for it was going to wind up leading me to childbirth which aunt said hurt as much as cancer. But I remembered back to our meeting at Thanksgiving when an inner voice was saying to me, "You will marry this man." Before two months had passed my friend George had told me he cherished me, and all of this was leaving me as confused as I had ever been when all of the sudden ones, I cared for, were saying such with abounding intimacy words so sacred I felt as if they were gifts from women in my life just showing me how rapidly life could change from emotional scars to a face flushed with the thought that finally I was meeting genuine Love, and it was stabbing my heart with good things.

What did I have other than words, and where was the proof that any of this existed beyond girlish imagination that I was mature enough to make a sound judgment? I had no large diamond to prove it. Frank just said it, and I trusted with my heart that my judgment was sound, so I said goodbye to George with great difficulty, for I loved that Ohio man, born with the Great Lakes at his city's edge and someone who had wanted me to teach him how to make love even though he was about twelve years older, and I think I got his point about this request, and it was a shared innocence for the most part. George knew that we could have grown in that regard together. I could have been that wife of the teacher he became, a solid Catholic mother, and I would have been cherished for his and my life, for that was the core of how kind this wonderful man had to be in giving up his life's journey to find how love and marriage actually were a higher calling than the Priesthood for which he gave all of his youth for. I could have been making the worst mistake of my life on that Thanksgiving Day and I was definitely needing some angels again to show me the way. It would finally have to be me making a choice, and no one had a "Marriage Guaranteed" flashing from Frank's heart, but this time it appeared that a "Love At First Sight," appeared to be mutual and he was just about the perfect age plus he was courting me showing no sign of needing time to, "Find himself," the over used mantra of many of our mutual friends. He also continued his pronouncement; "I will marry you, yes, I will marry you, along with the love he expressed and shared so early and so willingly hinted with no doubt that I was the something he now needed in his life. For once my doubts were placed within a place where I felt no need to explore them.

It was good that all of the cotton was in and Dad was in public works and Mama had taken a job, but I would wait to tell them. That winter began with stars falling around me, brilliant and bright stars, and though I was not the untouched girl, and Frank had had other loves as well, I think the stars falling were making us light up like the moonbeams over Ocean Beach. I wanted to call other young girls to showers of stars and to let them know that it is when you allow yourself some peace and place false intimacy on hold that, you like me, may find that when love becomes real, you will hear its voice. Innocence can be a remarkably beautiful way of living. Because I cherish my sisters of the mountains and valleys, I am sharing these truths and the best news that I may offer is that to be cherished and to have known love is a pilgrim journey with a little divine wisdom.

Chapter Forty One

Oh Glory, we went to the Washington Mall, because sad things happened down in Memphis in 1968, and the United States of America was blazing with the fires probably not seen since the Civil War. Martin Luther King had been slain and some said he was a martyr and maybe a saint. Sister Coretta King was going to carry the lamplight for the poor, risking herself for the poverty-stricken areas of our great country where we were told there is plenty. I am going to take you down to Memphis and I'll tell you a few stories, telling them sweet and low. They are as I remember and your views may not be the same. There was camping on the Washington Mall and the poor were mad and asking for help. Poor blacks mainly came to Washington, and a whole lot of idealistic kids took up the mantle, for "poor" was a beautiful word.

I am going to need Father Abraham and sacred Jesus to help me tell this story. LBJ's War on Poverty was at hand and the times were changing and the folk singers came and the little rich kids pounded on tambourines and marched around in a circle. Back home, the cotton and tobacco crops were gone and a new creation of white poor was being created, the likes of which had not been seen since The Great Depression. It seems somehow something to laugh about that sometimes mothers could get blocks of cheese, for the cartoons always showed rats scurrying for cheese and somehow a point was being missed that if we labor and toil and we learn how to take care of ourselves, then we are apt to rise up. Better still, if we toil with all men regardless of color, then perhaps we rise up like leavened bread, so soft and pleasant to the taste and easier to break. So I need you, Blessed Lord, to help me with this story which will focus on 1968, but it is going to talk about the problem of giving away jars and cans and food stamps instead of helping people to plant the grain, take it to the mill, and to feed a hungry family with the pride and the work of one's labors.

We are going to talk about white folks, too, Appalachian folks, like my family and the people on the mountains who would begin to get a taste of government's saving grace instead of "The Grace," which the fathers and mothers had known, the knowledge of how to labor and toil and to seek a better world. I saw very few pictures of little white kids from the mid- to lower-South, or the coal mine patches of the north. Heck, no one even thought we were good enough to have pictures made on our porch steps. Instead they showed men and women acting ugly, saying that word known as the "N-word" now, and called us a bunch of ignorant hillbillies—we who lived in harmony with our black brothers and sisters when given a chance. The southern heart has generally been great big all along, but those folks who acted out got on TV and painted a picture that would not change for another generation when Atlanta started charging forth as the next Los Angeles, where there were no building boundaries in spite of the fact there were pine forests mowed down in the name of progress. Atlanta was becoming the megapolis that stretched almost as far as the eye can see. People in the north saw the new industry and a reverse migration was to begin southward.

I want to do a little teaching and preaching, for I used to tell Miss Nell Baker that I might like to preach, and my beloved and I would join the beautiful and widowed Coretta Scott King as she carried on the Poor People's March in Washington where people, for the most part, needed to learn how to use their hands instead of the hand-outs. Dr. King did not want for anyone to be left out, and that is what made him different from those to come. It is a pretty sad state when the coal miners and the farmers lost their will to make the next generation better, because there wasn't much reason to work for minimum wage when it wouldn't feed the dogs, much less a family. My mother was so happy when she finally got two dollars and fifty cents an hour as a school cook, for we could have white bread from the day-old bread store then.

We're going down to Memphis and hear the shot that changed the world one evening and we're going to Atlanta to Ebenezer Baptist Church, and we are going to cry that another peacemaker had to die. It is time to tell the truth about food lines, food stamps, drugs hitting the streets, and the first whisper of gangs, which young people wanted as a badge of pride. Being poor makes you want a sign or symbol of something someone else does not have. I agree fully that hungry bellies should be immediately filled, but so should hungry spirits, and there are a whole lot of hungry people running around here right now.

I am no expert on any of the decisions that came about after we lost President Kennedy, his brother Bobby, and the most eloquent speaker and teacher of the time, Dr. Martin Luther King. "Come together my poor little children." That was his call, but in some ways we went the other direction. Why? I do not know, but having lived as a daughter of Appalachian poor, I am going to tell you what I believe, and you must come to your own conclusions. My daddy thought he was a rich man when he died, and Mama agreed, for she said, "We had it all and what we didn't have, you kids gave it to us." They were humble and did what they heard preached. They shared the table.

So get ready, for pink honeysuckle is about to grow, and I was growing and going someplace then, too. I heard there was wrong in the world, and I wanted to know why it wasn't made right. I wanted to know why fields went fallow and people forgot how to plant the gardens and smoke the meat. Yes I wanted to know, so help me out here, for what I write may not be textbook pure, but I have some ideas and some ideals. It is hard work to stretch dollars, to build churches and schools. It is hard to change language and it is especially hard when you are left naked and invisible.

Be ready, my friend, for the story is coming, the story which I will tell the grandchildren, and I want to see some wrongs made right for all men. "Oh gracious Lord, through the storms, wrong or right, take my hand, blessed Lord and lead me home." I will type singing it softly and sweetly, and I will know that John, Bobby, and Martin made it to the Promised Land, because no one can murder human spirit, and Frank learned from me about the kind of poverty of which Dr. King preached.

I like to linger within my dreams at the end of 1968 when my world seemed to fill incredibly with love—a true love—one that meant his words had come in to my life. I was so unaccustomed to the very idea that anyone actually could care that much about me so quickly and that my personal life could be taking a turn toward what most girls from my high school had already done: getting married sometime the next year. The year was filled with so many goodbyes as the VISTA and Peace Corps classes went on back to college or stayed and organized grassroots campaigns against the War in Vietnam. We liked to talk about the importance of ending the war, for it seemed as if there was no other way out of a conflict where we were not winning at almost any time, but our boys were still coming home maimed, or dead, and the enemy was difficult to recognize from the friend.

As always, a disproportionate number of young men from our hills and valleys from home would sign up instead of wait to be drafted, for that was The Appalachian Way. Either they kept the home fires burning or they would make their mothers and fathers weep, ready to sign up for military service as had all generations before them because it was noble, it was good pay, and there was some opportunity for education and military benefits after they got out. Was it the way to leave the farms and mines for good?

I think that the entire concept of sending one's children off to fight jungle warfare was poorly understood by many of us, because usually wars had more to do with the needs of allies we had developed after World War II. Even the Korean war was a mystery to most of us, for we were not taught the peculiar differences between the South and North Koreas. We were taught this about Communism: they do not believe in God, they do not have the same values as American people in that you are not allowed freedom of speech, religion, or press, and that we were in something called a Cold War, helping the good Koreans who valued democracy.

Castro's Cuban Missile Crisis during President Kennedy's short term as president left us all scared to death, because where we lived beneath the Appalachians and everywhere else in this country teachers had us jumping under our desks in case a bomb struck. That gave us the knowledge that we better not look straight into the mushroom cloud flash without dark glasses on, and there was a lot of information about how to build and to stock our fallout shelters. We'd heard this since we were in grade school that the Russians and now the Cubans could slam us at any time. I for one worried to death that we could not dig a fallout shelter, and I would think that maybe Mama's old root vegetables in the root cellar along with the snakes which like to cool off in there might could share some space. There might be a few jars of last year's tomatoes to live on in there, and we had heard about how POWs ate rats and worms if they had to. Well we had vermin of all varieties that liked to move in to the root cellar back at the old house. My prayers were left back there that NASA in Huntsville, Alabama, would not take a dead hit, for I knew darned well the fall-out was headed straight in line for our school and for our homes.

War had something to do with communism and the atomic bomb preventing the Soviet Union from taking over our right to believe in God and a whole lot of killing and injury for which there may be no pardon. I knew the Great Commandments handed down by God himself, and among them was Thou Shalt Not Kill. I had no idea where Vietnam was or why my best elder friend in Murfreesboro, Tennessee, had to lose her only son there until I got the picture that the communists were going to take it over, then all of the Asian countries were going to fall like matchsticks, and thus we had to once again nip it in the bud. I did not know for certain that we were in a real war there until I went to Washington, and I heard about boys from my senior class signing up and getting sent there. But by 1968 the television news was flooded with the news of the day about the Viet Cong, about people running from Napalm fires, and that our boys were coming back wondering why in heck they had gone in the first place.

My Frank was one of the lucky fellows. Having seen his draft number come up, he had hustled off to Washington as most young men did to endeavor to play their finest hour, the most meaningful hour they would ever play, for if they were lucky then they might get sent to a service band somewhere in the nation. Only the best of the best got to stay in Washington to play with one of the United States Service Bands, but the Marine Band was the ultimate goal, for you had to be so good to get into it since you were going to play for presidential functions. The Marines certainly did not think you would ever be a warrior in that case, so why waste money on basic training? The Marines were very smart in this regard, for most bandsmen were not from ordinary families, and they would have lost a lot of good players, because these were mainly the more privileged men. My future husband, along with most of the younger people who had music and arts training in the great academies, across the United States, were taught what we back home would have called "the finer arts of life;" like music and art appreciation, and most of them were from homes where being a boy scout was about as close as they would ever get to learning basic life-saving skills.

I do not condemn them for this, because there were other subgroups who would fall under the same genre, and it was a known fact that the college boys who really did not want to go off to war were apt to be able to get some type of deferment. One of my best straight male friends did decide that he would get out by convincing the service boards that he was both gay and crazy as a loon and had me spend some time reading the letters which he wrote to endeavor to prove such. The gay part was a fallacy, but his upbringing in Los Angeles had left him fairly messed up, so I had no problem editing his "I'm crazy" letters.

The point I am endeavoring to make is that sometime after I left high school I heard there was a war going on, and then I sort of filled a heart space that had gone empty within this woman in Murfreesboro after losing her only boy. She would take me to church, and for the first time in my life, I would know what it was like to leave church and to have my dinner bought for me, and I was there for her to remember her William who went off to Vietnam and who never set foot on the soil, but was picked off by a sniper as he got off the boat. She had even endeavored to fix me up with one of her son's friends, but we had a drink together, and that was about it. So you tell me how it took me until 1968 to realize that we were a nation at war, that there were all kinds of anti-war sentiments, and that this woman had lost her son without an official war ever having been declared.

But by 1968, the United States of America and its people were wanting out, for it seemed that there was more loss than gain, and if you wanted to go to an anti-war rally. then all you had to do was to be in the nation's capital, and next thing you knew you were marching with someone and singing, "There ain't gonna be no war, no more." I found myself following the anti-mantra, since I did not believe in killing in the first place, and I would have to take a lot of classes to this day to understand how we got in to this one called the War in Vietnam. It was the first that I had heard of guerrilla warfare, but once they said "communist" enough I had mixed feelings. When boys were coming back drug-addicted, dysfunctional, and without a clue as to what they had fought for, then I wanted to see this war end, and I knew about the times for "all things under heaven," and things were going very poorly at home.

We had all grieved our hearts out some years earlier when John Fitzgerald Kennedy left us in sorrow after his assassination. He was the first president we got to really know through television who could make us laugh, made us feel like we were regal citizens in a glamorous country, and who promised us something better than we had known before. "Johnny, we hardly knew ya" would stay deep with our conscience as something deplorable, this younger, vital, Catholic president of Irish heritage with the most beautiful wife and charming small children who served in World War II was president from 1961 to 1963 before he was assassinated, and the whole country was in mourning except for those who did not want a democrat or a Catholic as our president. And there were many. Maybe we thought assassinations were something from another age, not 1968. That would open us to knowing that even the most protected was not safe.

We would watch rioting and burning in every city, especially in Washington when in April of 1968, a good and decent black man by the name of Martin Luther King would fall to another assassin's bullet, something I want to go into great depth about, for southern people were so maligned by the activities of the ugly few who shamed us so after the death of Dr. King. We were shown as a bunch of illiterate and ignorant hopeless mouthfuls of venom toward the black people which made for hell in our days to endeavor to diffuse such imagery. Southern whites and blacks of intellect knew that poverty was the breeding ground of a new form of unspoken slavery.

The embers of this fire had no more than been put out until we were fixed on our television sets to both see and to hear the events which surrounded the murder, another planned assassination of Robert Kennedy, the brother of John, and an emptiness settled over the land, for no one else could carry this peacemaker's torch. We did not know what we were in the middle of. Dr. King had won the Nobel Peace Prize, and Robert Kennedy seemed to be our best hope to get our nation out of the war in Vietnam, so we became anxious and confused. Poor people seemed poorer, and there was no end in sight in Asia to the killing, so we were at about the hundred-year anniversary of the end of the Civil War, and the South was draped with darkness and hatred not seen since the time before the end of the disaster of brother against brother and fathers against sons. There was a new war, and it was at our doorstep. We had the war on poverty at home and an unwinnable war in Asia.

1968 was a deep and dark year in the history of not just this nation, but of mankind. We were feeling as if we could accomplish so much, and yet we learned that all accomplishments were fragile. And we, the sons and daughters of the God's new creation, had to ask some serious questions about ourselves and all that we had been taught. We were no longer children playing in the cotton fields with the little black children that ate lunch with poor little white children, but we were divided worse than ever. The boys coming home from Vietnam had a big hunger for another kind of gold they had learned to get by on, not unlike the bad alcohol that was so pervasive among the World War II veterans, only this time it was even more costly and expensive. We had new kings, and they were called "Drug Lords," and we would know innocence lost as perhaps never before, for when one drug wasn't big and bad enough a tweak here and a stir there brought up another one.

I told Frank once about how my daddy said that he and his brothers knew what hemp was out in the field, but the early 1960s marijuana battles would seem like nothing compared to the carnage which heroin, cocaine, and their latter manufactured cousins would bring to this society. I found a lot of kindness and love at the end of 1968, but there was a rage in this country that was a lightning bolt. White people and black people were supposedly building bridges, but winding up with moats, and mothers were still grieving the lost sons. Poor babies, poor mothers, beloved sons. When would we actually be seeing that dawning of peace? Our New Jerusalem and mankind celebrating the bell's toll for a generation of peacemakers?

I do not want to leave this place or this time of 1968 without telling some truth about white southerners, poverty, and our relationship to people of color. These are the kind of things that I could talk to Frank about as the year drew to a close, and I wanted to tell someone that "one cannot hate the brother and sister they do not know." So how is it that southern farmers got to be the poster derelicts of hatred for black people?

Farmers did not go to those cities with shovels and pitchforks. I never knew a farmer who belonged to the clan. But any old fool they could film in a pair of overalls and ladies sneering about the "colored people" were the evening news fodder during freedom marches. The real proprietors and purveyors of such hatred were called out from ghetto white America to take the heat off the land owners and businesses. The back home folks had too much work to do and too much pride to go looking for trouble. Again poor whites were made to look as if they were disagreeing that we were poverty-stricken and needed help. Why would we want to destroy our own voices?

Dr. Martin Luther King would refer to us along the way as "All of God's Poor Little Children." Only when it came to white kids no one wanted to hear us put in the same wagon which was being led by an underground movement of black people called The Southern Christian Leadership Conference, or as it was best know when Dr. King headed it the "SCLC." Any white person connected to it had to keep their mouths shut, for if you were sympathetic to the cause, then you and your household were apt to be in danger.

Dr. King, a graduate of Morehouse College in Atlanta, did preside over the SCLC until it wanted to become focused less on non-violence. Many black people, and certainly a whole lot of white folks, wanted to make his life's work something different from what he liked to speak about most, the poor. He meant the poor anywhere and any color, but the poor he was most familiar with were the poor southern blacks and whites who did not have a seat at anyone's table. Before he died in 1968 from James Earl Ray's assassin's bullet, he was talking about something poor whites were not prepared to hear: "Black and White Together." Blacks and whites walking hand in hand, and what a political force that would be, and I can remember to this day that people who knew about the poor people's marches did not want a thing to do with it because it brought up the issue of a nation which would not predominantly be a white person's nation. You can still find Aryan Nation sympathizers, but the Kennedys and Dr. and Mrs. King would ask us to pray for those folks to experience a change of heart. Non-violence will ever be the legacy left by Dr. Martin Luther King and the call to solve issues of poverty and civil rights.

Chapter Forty Two

I grew up only knowing that "Black Joe's" house was near us, and I would hear N-word jokes, but I did not understand them. For the most part, God as my witness, not much of anyone talked about any issues which involved black people, and rarely did we see a person of color, because they had begun the migration to the northern cities long before the southern white farmers gave up on the land. I am the great-granddaughter of a Confederate soldier and uncle on my father's side, and my memory is that on Mother's side the family had some that went off to the Union in the Civil War. I really knew almost nothing about black people.

I began to endeavor to understand why Washington, D.C., and every other city across the nation had black people burning mainly their own communities, and when I saw the National Guard posted outside our apartment building that April after Dr. King's murder, I remember thinking this: "Well, if you have nothing but a voice, and the voice is silenced, then maybe your buildings do not seem to have much value anymore." My year to find love was probably one of the most hateful years since the Civil War. A different feeling fell over Washington, and I began to be afraid, because Dr. King's voice of peace had become one taken over by a lot of racist whites and blacks as a call to arms. You just felt edgy, as if people wanted to fight about anything.

Rosa Parks 1955 decision to keep a white person only assigned seat on a bus in Montgomery was playing on every television as if it were yesterday, after a beautiful speech that would forever be remembered as the "I Have A Dream" speech which this man, Martin Luther King, gave in Washington in 1963 during what was called the Poor People's March On Washington. I thought that was one divine speech, and so much of it was taken straight from the messages I had read that Jesus taught us. Grown-up white folks were complaining about it, and I began to hear rumblings that this Dr.

King was a communist and that J. Edgar Hoover, who headed the FBI, was going to out him any day, but that speech moved me, for someone was talking about me, kids that I grew up with, Black Joe and his family, and he called us so sweetly "my poor little children." He told us better times were coming and I really hoped so. Watching the fires getting closer to the White House, I wondered how this man had gotten a war started, "the war within" some called it, leading the fires and devastation of 1968 when the embers of homes and villages covered the cities from east to west.

I told Frank one story about racial prejudice and it would leave him saying he felt chilled inside, for he had grown up where devious oppression of races prevailed, and he got a tooth knocked out one day coming home from school because he was white and a few black boys decided to show him the kind of justice common in their community. I did remember that we had finally gotten a car after Dad worked up north for some years, and we went to Winchester one Saturday, and Mama wanted us to just keep driving around the courthouse square, for on Saturdays folks would walk down Keith Springs Mountain to Winchester to get supplies and to sell what little they had, but this Saturday, there was a black woman dressed just like Aunt Jemima on the pancake syrup, and she was sitting in the sun, all beautiful with chubby little children sitting around her, and she was nursing her baby. It may as well have been the arrival of the circus in town, for folks could not get enough of driving around and looking at this mama feeding her baby. I had seen my aunts nurse their babies, and Mama did not nurse her last babies, so this was better than a copy of *National Geographic*, which at that time seemed to photograph more naked black people than seemed to be necessary, but I would read the magazines at Aunt Ruth's place and felt a little surprised that blacks and whites had the same body parts. I fear that it took some geography through the years to learn that people who were native to hotter climates were not all like my pale-faced uncle who used to winter in Florida. After Dad drove around twice, he told Mama just to forget about it, but years later I would understand that the white dress and the headscarf probably meant that this poor

Mama was taking care of some white folks' kids most of the rest of the time.

Sometimes it is almost as if some of us got stuck in a time warp after the Civil War, for the white farmers came home to the land they left behind, got behind a mule, and stayed there through the period called Reconstruction, which saw the old southern cities get rebuilt. Those who'd had before. still had for the most part and those who lived a self-sustaining lifestyle just simply endeavored to get back to their little spot of the Mountain or Valley from the South where they came from. I would learn that my relatives never owned slaves, that only about five percent of the white folks of America had such immoral property. Some, just like some of us whites, did not believe in earthly masters. Why am I bothering telling you all any of this? For maybe it should not be a part of my story. But I claim it, for poverty never has come in color, and still in 1968 while black people were searching for another voice, poor whites after all, were just trash.

Integration would come to my high school the fall after I graduated, and the boys who threatened to bring guns to school just behaved like they were supposed to because this Martin Luther King had touched some hearts.

Was he a communist? He had associates who had interest in the Communist Party, but as hard as Mr. Hoover tried, he never could paint this great man as a communist. Dr. Ralph Abernathy and Reverends Andrew Young and Jesse Jackson, along with Julian Bond would carry on the mission of helping poor blacks make inroads toward integration and better lives for all Americans. In fact for many years to be poor and white began to be about the worst thing you could be in this country, because we became the rednecks, the hillbillies, and the crackers. To other whites, we were the ones left over to do the hard labor and to the blacks we were part of the crowd spitting on them in Selma. Oh how some of us still wanted to be somebody's poor little children. Yes, we could use the water fountains, the same toilets, ride the city buses, but this did not mean a thing to us, since we never got to these places in the first place. My new boyfriend got the picture, and he held my hand.

Beautiful Mrs. Coretta Scott King who would carry on her husband's call for justice would lead the Poor People's March in Washington that next Spring of 1969, and somehow Frank and I got there early, and we were only a few rows back from her and her Reverend escorts and children, and a lot of young white folks were out with us marching the streets of Washington from the Capitol grounds where it had all begun, and I remember feeling so happy because we were singing hymns and holding hands, and the spring was so beautiful. But for a second I felt a chill run down my spine. I realized that we were making ourselves visible in a world where hate still abounded. The same hate had killed President Kennedy, Robert Kennedy, and Martin Luther King, and we were just kids, not really understanding how vulnerable we really were. The cities would recover, but a deeper gulch was pervasive, for it was going to take several more decades before the N word would no longer be tolerated in language, and the years have not come for white brothers and sisters of the South to shake off the routine jokes.

Mrs. King made her mark by getting Antioch College in Yellow Springs, Ohio, to open its doors to her, and she was a classically trained singer from the New England Conservatory of Music. The Kings' friend Mrs. Mahalia Jackson would sing the funeral song Dr. King had requested, sweet and slow, as he liked it, and it was a song that touched the ears of every poor kid black or white, for it was from our old Hymnals: "Precious Lord, Lead Me Home." We all can remember at least one verse, so if I have raised you to mayhem over something, just hear these words of this beloved song:

Lord, I am a child,
And You care for me
On the storm of the night
Lead me on wrong or right
Take my hand

Precious Lord
and lead me home.

But sing it soft, and sing it sweetly, so that the saints before us can light the lanterns to show all of us the way.

In this year of hell's ire, my personal life, unlike the country, seemed to grow into a genuine love story. After our second or third meeting Frank and I became inseparable, and sometimes, much to my amusement, my apartment seemed to be a gathering place for a few old boyfriends and whomever of my friends I had fixed them up with. This was a new role for me entirely. I had always been my old friends' best bet for boyfriends that they were finished with, something called "casual relationships" that I was most unacquainted with, for if you gave your heart, body, and soul over to someone that meant marriage where I had come from.

As 1968 came to a close, though our country seemed to be in peril, my personal life had taken a turn for the very best, because now I had placed my body, soul, and spirit into my California boy. A new and exhilarating comfort began to sail over my life. Much to my amusement, some of my old boyfriends would still come around, and it was most pleasant to let them know that I was not available. So my cadre of women friends had quite a few eligible young men they could get to know through me. Almost every hour I was not working was now spent with Frank, Diane, and Jim, as if we had all known each other for a very long time. I believe that I suddenly understood something, and that is, when it is the right person, you are not going to be surprised that love is shared, and it is kind. There is no longer just waiting for a person to call you but a mutual understanding that you will be there when they do call, or they will know where you are. At least that is how it was for Frank and for me.

Chapter Forty Three

I had grown up with the belief that a woman never approached a man, but the times had changed to a new reality when women could lead a relationship. For Frank Heintz and for me there was no leader or follower. The same head that rested in my arms after the beautiful Thanksgiving usually had called me as soon as I came home from work, and admittedly I got upset if he did not, for there was that old and lingering doubt that I had about myself which cried out in raw seconds saying this was too good to be true! His place was becoming my place very quickly, and it all felt like a natural way of our being, as if all of our lives these moments had been planned, and we had nothing to add but to surrender our fear of them. I have remarked that marriage was on our tongues in the brief and early weeks, and Frank was significantly older than me so I realized that I was taking a genuine risk leaving behind other boys who wanted an open relationship and commitment only later on.

Frank simply seemed to adore me, and the adoration flowed both ways. It seemed almost scripted, as if we were part of a never-ending play, and it took little to entertain either of us. We would begin sharing our life stories which was imperative, because Frank seemed interested in the real me, not a character without baggage. He was accepting the whole package. He did begin to introduce me to some vice which I had never been tempted in to before, some appreciation for good wines and ports and the 1960s version of marijuana that was absolutely not in the ballpark with the drugs that would come later to our younger generations. What can I say? Frank was a Californian, and he knew way more about any of these subjects than did I, and by then it was like having a sloe gin at a speakeasy had been well before we were born. It was also illegal and not a good idea to have it around, but it was everywhere then, and I will profess to you that when I hear about younger people doing alcohol in shots now, chasing those by a few beers, and then waiting until the buzz wears off and driving, I tremble. I want to scream at them and say, "You idiots! That has to be metabolized in some way, and it is going to take hours, not a couple of hits of caffeine to burn it off." As the years would move along, old field marijuana would become equally as deadly, so we, as did most of our old friends, gave up on that, especially around children.

I remembered the three effects: laughter, hunger, and love-making, a nice sleep, and one was ready to go. What Dad could point out growing wild in the fields was available for a larger sum of money than he would have ever dreamt, and the next thing we knew Tennessee, Alabama, and the whole South joined the rest of the country in endeavoring to rid ourselves of the evil weed of our forefathers. It came under attack by way of chemical sprays as if it was as dangerous as Agent Orange and as if it was what had brought a change in decency to our homeland. No one liked to talk much about what really was the problem, the taste for hardcore drugs the boys brought back from Vietnam and the rush to keep making bigger, badder, gorked-out drugs that would somehow ease the pain of a crew of young men and women who had not been rewarded as homecoming heroes by anyone.

As Christmas 1968 rolled around, it was almost news to me that it was Christmas. I had sent presents home, had gotten a card from Mama, and I had not much of an idea what the families nearby were doing, though I believe that brother and his wife had invited us out to Silver Springs, Maryland, for Christmas dinner. Frank had done his White House duties with the Marine Band, and I stayed over at his place. I was so excited for I had his favorite Courvoisier wrapped up, but when I awoke he was near me with packages in his hand, and I thought that they were presents from home. Instead, he handed them to me, and one by one I opened them tearfully, for never before in my entire life had I had this many Christmas packages to open. He had wrapped up German cookies, a kind he liked, a little silver bracelet, a string of bells woven into macramé, and a little amber-colored vase, all for me along with an ornament or two. What kind of person was this who had gone out and shopped for me? I felt as if I had been given an engagement ring, and I knew that it was premature for that, but I felt very tacky when all I had to offer was a bottle of brandy. He felt guilty because he had a whole box of packages from home, and I marveled as he opened one package after the other, and I did imagine what a pretty ring on Christmas day would have meant.

Soon I would learn that he had made a list of things which were of ordinary use, like a stapler, small tools, books, and such things, so his mom had gone to find the silliest and funniest of things she could find to meet his request and his needs, so he enjoyed his animal-themed presents, his silly things stuck in by his sister, and I just sat in awe that a Christmas morning could be so incredibly pleasant—just Frank and me and our small gifts and a love story of our own that we were writing on our hearts. The year was ending with my Christmas bells clanging against a Washington, D.C., wind, and there was a song being sung that was being composed just for us. Only wind on ice could play it, and this lover alone could hear it and it was kept safely in my heart's secret place. It was simple and it was sweeter than most, for it said that we were merely beginning our Christmas days together, but this one would remain over time the one that would remain for us the dearest and kindness, for rarely does the word become brand new. Isn't that what we are looking for at Christmas? Something which changes us, something lasting, and to feel the love of something quaint and marvelous unveiling before our eyes. The virgin's child was the miracle of the ancients. How could we match or even come close to such depth? Maybe, because we cannot, for often there is an after Christmas down feeling many experience. But 1968 left me with no such pain.

I thanked God for these perfect moments and I wondered what we would be doing when Christmas came once more. I had no doubt that we would be sharing it together, somehow and somewhere. This was my second year away from Tennessee, and I would wonder what they had up for decoration, and I knew there were apples and oranges these days aplenty which they could now afford, with both parents working. Maybe some elder brother or sister had gone home, and perchance they did, Mama and my little sister would have made chocolate, coconut, and perhaps Mama's stacked apple cakes, for it was a measure of a fine Christmas just how many desserts one had to choose from.

It would no longer be the time of standing around the fire at the old house while Daddy cut the fresh coconut he had shelled with his pocket knife to see that we all got a slice, nor the one bag of candy shared. The yule fire burned in some distant hollows, but now Mom and Dad had electric heat, and they would close the back of the house off to save on the bill, but they would declare that the new brick house the FHA loan had helped them to build was tight and warm and kept the winds of winter out.

I felt so incredibly blessed for my younger brothers and sister that they would not have to awaken to a kettle of water that had frozen over night on our wood-fired Franklin stove, that maybe they were still young enough to look for Santa Claus, and that somehow they would know just how good they were, for there might be presents to open. Mama had finally learned to make turkey and dressing at her school-cooking job, so Mom and Dad would get the biggest turkey they could, and it would go in the oven in time to fall off the bones around twelve noon on Christmas day. They would gather with a few at the old church which once was a school where Mr. Jeff or Mr. Collins would have a fire roaring doing little good as the chill broke through, and everybody would want to sing the Christmas carols just like they had heard at the school play. It would become apparent though, that the songs in the hymnal were written for the generations and trying to follow them would not send out the melodious singing of the school glee clubs.

Frank and I would have opened our gifts, and each of us would be having some home thoughts, for his mother was in her second year without his dad, and his world had changed also. So for a while we just rested quietly and let our thoughts go to those other times and places. There was nostalgia always, but we spoke briefly of our different worlds, held on to each other, and carried our Christmas gifts to share again later that morning. Again, it was so comfortable, and no matter what was going on around us that day we were each other's—the San Francisco boy and the country girl from Tennessee felt no desire to be anywhere else. Yes, Mr. Dylan, our time was changing, moving on like the finicky wind, and what the new year would bring was left to chance, but this time it seemed as if better days were ahead. I went home to my winter woods that night, Frank's hand in mine, and the last of autumn acorns fell, so there was a faint crackle. I found the persimmon tree as I dreamt, and one was left, shriveled, but so soft and very sweet, and I told the woods that I would have a surprise to tell the forest on my return, and I would be free of the loneliness which I'd left behind. Hear me, little spring, where I played with tadpoles and got the drinking water for a small falls which fed it--hear me and share my dreams. "It is all right," I told the angels of nature. Hear me, for I will not return alone.

Chapter Forty Four

I did not think much about it until a few weeks had passed that I had not met many of Frank's friends, but as the New Year of 1969 approached, I was able to ask him a little about the kind of people he enjoyed spending his time with before me, and this must have got him to thinking that maybe if he was going to see fit to talk to a girl about marriage after a few weeks of seeing her then there must be some need to commit to her through friendship, and I believe this had him a little frightened. That is the glorious thing about being young and enjoying holidays, though, for New Year's Eve arrived, and my new love invited me to one of the Marine Band parties where I would first learn that musicians tend to band with the people who play similar instruments, and in Frank's case it would be wind instruments, and specifically, the double reed appreciation group.

A double reed instrument was something I had begun to know something about, for I would watch Frank soak the cane, take lessons, and work hours and hours to get the perfect reed which he could feel by blowing into the reed itself. I think that if it was the absolute best reed if it would sound somewhat like a duck's quack, and he could feel it against his lips as having a little vibration as well as the ability to stay in one piece. Understand this, I never endeavored to act as if I were a knowledgeable musician of any sort, and what he told me of bassoon playing and the other instruments, I would learn because I asked.

In fact early on in our relationship I would start having these dreams that he had an audition, but I had to take the audition for him, and I would suddenly be sitting on a stage somewhere and realize that I did not know how to play bassoon, but I would endeavor to play because I did not want him to be embarrassed for lack of my ability to help him out with the audition. I was either selfish or grandiose in this though because playing symphonic-level bassoon had taken him the better part of a decade of work before that just to play other school band instruments. He had started out on saxophone in early junior high school having studied with this delightful man, Joseph Smiell, who would come back to San Francisco and teach in the public schools where Frank met him.

This was the same Joseph Smiell who would teach me about "The Patch," the coal towns many years later. After education at Peabody and Johns Hopkins, he decided to teach in San Francisco Public Schools. He had a natural kindness toward children playing musical instruments, for it was his accordion, the polkas, and waltzes that had gotten him into Peabody as a lark to see if he and his buddy could take such an audition. He would play a great role in Frank's youth as well as in Frank's adult life when Joseph Smiell, Jr., also a gifted musician, and Frank would become good friends through the Bohemian Club of San Francisco, a haven for geniuses and artists of all walks of life regardless of what they had chosen as a profession. They could still excel at their first love, the arts. Maybe it was from the influence of Joseph Smiell that Frank would learn that good people could come from humble places, and I want this to be a legacy we both pass on to those who fail to understand this.

Friends are extremely important to a relationship, and Frank had met mine, and I was ready to meet his. Thus came the New Year's Eve of my life, 1969. One of the people from another service band, a wind player, was having a party, and Frank asked me for a real date to this one. I had explained to him that my usual New Years had been spent in fear of what all was going to get broken within our house after Dad got with the uncles and drank too much, and he seemed to somehow understand, but he reassured me of the nice people that I would meet, so I did what a 1960s girl would do. I threw on my best pink mini dress, brushed my then long dark hair, and though everything within me was aching with anxiety and fear that no one would like me, I accepted my boyfriend's love, and I went to the first New Year's party I had been to in my entire life!

It became very apparent that everyone there was service band-related, but it was from all branches of the United States bands who were stationed in Washington at the time, and I would also learn that most of them were married already either with a first baby or one on the way, so when it came to women I became a little bit of a distraction for single guys endeavoring to connect with a single lady. As the evening wore on, I knew that Frank was giving me the sweet punch, and I began to feel a warmth taking over which I did not relate to alcohol. Frank was making certain that I was well introduced as his date for the evening to which now and then I would here an "Oh Man!" There was disappointment from some that I was not out there and available, and the more admiration which I received I noticed in Frank's face that he needed reassurance that I was not going to just walk out with someone else.

I met married couples including Isabella and Steven, who would become lifelong friends, Kathy and Eric, Linda and Bill, and so many others, but most wives were musicians also. I think that it was a curiosity to meet someone who had come from a pre-med program and who had just taken off from a town in Tennessee to work toward going back to school, so I spent a lot of time answering questions about me. I thought these people were so incredibly beautiful and kind to ask about my life, and some of my answers were probably a little shocking, because I had lived with "never tell a lie" as the mantra of a sacred life. I also found that even those schooled in arts and music adore their babies, so I immediately took to the couples with children and who were planning on having children.

I found my face full of tears to hear that Isabella and Steven had lost a little girl to Down Syndrome, because I did not know how people were able to go on after such a loss, though this was a very well adjusted couple. I enjoyed hearing all of the birth stories, about the different military hospital experiences, and of how these couples had met and wound up in Washington together, and what was going on I would understand later. My new boyfriend had enough married friends that he wanted to see how they felt about me. It was probably the equivalent of passing the board affiliates of Future Homemakers of America, but it seems that such a night in my life opened up to me the friends we would spend the better part of 1969 with. One of his unmarried friends Bob, who was an oboe player, kept us laughing most of the evening as the raconteur of the group from

Philadelphia. It seems that when he had moved to Washington, his cat whose name was Lassie had jumped on the moving truck after they had unloaded his stuff in Arlington, and he had never met her again. He, too, would become part of our group of friends, and by the end of the evening Frank was so pleased to be with me that he made certain that he was near me as the New Year rang in.

I left with the usual uncertainty about myself, but just like with the VISTA Volunteers and Peace Corps group, I suddenly had a lot of new friends. I had received gold stars from all of Frank's friends, and he took a great deal of pride as young men would walk by and ask him where in the heck he had found me. We would just say that we had met over Thanksgiving, and that things were moving along for us rapidly, meaning we had used the M word. I do not think that I had ever experienced such flattery nor did I think that I deserved it, but that was the self-deprecating way in which I would approach much of my life. Undeserving is what you are taught to feel in so many places to this day if you come from the reality of poverty. By this time I was losing the full southern accent, not that I really meant to, but when one is away from it you almost have to work at keeping it, for the phrasing is very different. The dialects in the South differ from area to area, and I happen to think that Tennessee has one of the sweeter dialects, for it is a little softer being more of a borderline state to the North. If you get up around Bristol, Tennessee, then those of us from the Southern border of the state can get a little confused as the people from Bristol sound almost kissed by the North in their manner of speech.

Not a one of us should have been driving after that party, and I would later agree as a mom with full purpose that there should be zero tolerance for alcohol and driving, but somehow we all got back home safely. Had Frank had more room in Arlington, I would have moved in at the time, but we were happy with one comfortable bed, his desk, the dining table, and what was becoming "our music." Frank enjoyed the rock musicians way more than I did, and somewhere between Mick Jagger and Grace Slick I got him fully hooked on Judy Collins's *Wildflowers* and anything else she sang. I loved the folk singers of the time, and because of my old friend from

Murfreesboro, Tom, I still enjoyed the master of words Bob Dylan. Thus with new friends, a most loving welcome to the new year, and the simplicity of just being together, whatever would happen in the world or around us was put away. Frank's friends had shown him that if he wasn't interested, they were, but that was just a compliment to the fact that we had already discovered that we were a pair. It did not occur to me that he might have doubt and just not be there, and when he would visit old friends back in Philadelphia I would feel some angst and wish that I could have gone with him, but in our own way, we were each letting go of past loves and perceived ideas that we might be moving far too quickly, so I let him go through the early year, and as luck would have it, he seemed so happy to get back to me.

Chapter Forty Five

Suddenly in 1969, I would find myself turning the age of twenty, and that was becoming an age where most of my old friends had left college, gotten married, had a baby, and all of the grown-up things their families relied on. I kept my apartment, and Frank kept his, but the fact that we were cohabiting most of the time made it seem useless other than my folks would never hear these words from me, "Mom and Dad, I am living with a young man, and we plan to be married…sometime." For that was a statement which they would think so shameful as to call all friends, neighbors and kin to observe a prayer service for my damned soul.. The new reality that few virgins ever made it to the altar had not kicked in back in Middle Tennessee, the cradle of the Bible Belt, even though it had become apparent to me a couple of years earlier that I had blossomed later than most of my friends.

I called home as often as I felt that I could afford these calls, reserved for birth, death, sins, illness, and "Hello" on rare occasions. A marriage announcement might be excusable. The cost was per minute and it was seen as very stupid to rack up phone bills over the ten-dollar mark. I also hated calling home, for my mother had decided in her youth that what you wanted to hear was all of the bad news, and so I would get the details of all of the old friends and loved ones who had passed on, the new babies born to the cousins complete with how hard the labor was compared to the multitude of womanhood over the earth who had given birth before. Or a good tornado ripping the side off of a barn or sadly carrying away a family was worth her repeating over the next months of conversation for Mama liked to repeat chaos. I once asked her why when she was older and she remarked that she just liked hearing the stories again herself. Most southerners, of her age especially, were given a natural gift of story-telling and there was a grain of truth to most things, though from person to person the story might keep being enhanced or fizzle out like a spilled cola can.

It was difficult when she would put Daddy on the phone, for Daddy liked talking on the phone about as much as he liked the idea of cooking for himself. I would usually say about the same thing and it might be that I was going to come home soon, and I would try to tell him one interesting thing about my work, because Dad had shown himself as someone who did enjoy sharing the strength and accomplishments of his children. Had I told him about Frank, other than I was going out with a Marine and that we were discussing marriage, then he might say something enthusiastic such as, "Well." That was about as much enthusiasm as one was going to get out of him. He would have listened though, and you would soon learn Daddy had been bragging to his friends, "Yeah, Barbara Ellen is going out with a Marine movie star who got drafted."

Mother would usually report that the younger children were ill in one way or another, from bad colds to being half dead with the flu, but it was unusual for her ask, "How are you doing?" or "How are you feeling?" You had called her for the news and that was what you were going to get. I was sad when I heard that Mrs. Jesse's house had burned down with all of her beautiful homemade quilts, for I used to long for one of them. She was among the finest quilters in the county. People who have been poor have a very hard time parting with anything, so it broke my heart to hear that her stack of about a hundred quilts had become embers, and no one could save anything. Mama called her the flower lady, too, for every patch of her yard was covered with one flowering plant or the other, and often Mama would get cuttings from her. She and Mr. Charlie were about the first of the neighbors to die off, and I had to agree with Mom's "Lord have mercy," for death was a community event held in high esteem, and it brought neighbors together.

Sometimes I just wanted to listen and listen, because I enjoyed the stories for the most part. I may have gotten in somewhere the news that I was taking a new job with the American Society of International Law, and I did tell her at some point that I might have some news to share by the springtime to which I got the usual, "Are you gettin' married?" which really meant, "Are you gettin' married fast enough if you're pregnant?" It was nobody else's business. But I would not make it official until later on that year. I now spent so much time at Frank's place because on his way to the Marine barracks he could drop me off a few blocks away from the Massachusetts Avenue and Embassy Row area where the International Society of Law was located. Most of the few people to whom I would write about my life with Frank were accepting, but my old church friend from The Church of Christ in Murfreesboro basically told me that I was going straight to hell. It was made much worse by the fact that I had become Catholic, but she would also, want to know what kind of young man was going to want his wife to be living with him? And what kind of "amoral person" had I become to be "living with this man who was not my husband?" I did not take kindly to the wording, so I did write her back, thanked her for all that she had done for me, and I told her that I was the same girl that I always was. I just saw no reason to lie to myself, my friends, or to God that I had chosen to be in a relationship that seemed to have permanency written all over it. Sometimes I wish that I had lied.

Everyone we knew lived with their husbands and wives-to-be, and I knew the scriptures which the elder folks referred to, but I thought maybe God was telling us divorce rates were going so high that we had better see how it was going to work before we walked in the middle of marriage. I had lived in a world where I did not see good marriages, but I believed then and even now that marriage requires much of us to make them meet the context of "lasting." I wanted to enter such a state well informed that we had a chance of making it something other than the phrase "I'd be leaving you were it not for the kids." That was a refrain I heard in every other household either from the children or the parents themselves. I even wondered about marriage sometimes—if it was appropriate anymore, but I was a strong enough believer that a wedding was a sacrament, and I would not be whole unless Frank and I shared marriage vows. Some folks we knew were talking about everything from trading partners for the sake of heightened sexuality, and some were wishing they were out of the marriage before the ink dried on the official documents. But others like Isabella and Steven and Kathy and Eric were my idols, for they appeared to love their closeness, to adore the idea of having children together, and they shared dinners with Frank and me, so I was getting good pictures from them and from other couples that marriage could be a good thing.

I would like to have shared it with my mother, but I had to keep it relatively quiet in my family, for I still felt that I was letting down my Christian vows, and Frank and I could not be whole until we met at an altar. To make matters worse, I was beginning to question God and found myself in a period of agnosticism because I saw no way that anyone could be good enough to be considered a Christian, and all of the books on alienation from society and alienation from a nation had begun to take a toll. I would hold on to something of my upbringing, but a search which I was not prepared for had begun: Where are you, God? I kept waiting for a eureka moment only to find that such brought up other questions. Friends were leaving their churches, and Frank could take it or leave it, but he did not appear to be strongly spiritual, so I would join in conversations about the reality or the unreality of God.

It seemed so improbable when I thought about it, but I would later pick up the pieces of the puzzle to place God back in my life—our lives. If you live long enough and you look hard enough, you are going to feel and know the difference when some divine intervention has taken place. It has got to come from within, and if you do not question, then you are probably missing something that is as other-worldly as a voice in the dark calling, "This way." Encounters with the Divine often change the course of your life. Waiting for the eureka moment is apt to leave you wanting, but some intense study in Judeo-Christian history might be a good starting point to begin the search. The best of people are apt to lose directions over and over again. For if we are so incredibly wise, the search of a deity gets suffocated by our self-aggrandizement.

"Have you met this Frank Heintz's family?" Mama would ask, and I would say, "I will, soon, Mama." Those were not the words she wanted, for she wanted me to climb to the mountain top as she had, pay the preacher for the license and for his work, have a witness, and then be called "wed." She wanted that news, and time would tell whether my judgment was sound about a man about whom I would tell everyone but my folks that I knew that we were meant to be together, and was that love? I think it was about as close as one was going to get to knowing true love, for your heart bursts at the thought of losing any portion of it. Only years would hold the reality of whether I had chosen correctly and whether Frank and I had a lifetime to share. I wanted so to tell my mother that I thought I had found such a special being, but instead I would reflect on Mrs. Jesse's beautiful quilts and wonder if they soared into the cosmos there for the angels to rest.

Chapter Forty Six

To experience a Washington, D. C., winter was now becoming more normal to me, but it was vastly more wonderful, because I had a new love to share it with. The Potomac valley of Washington has steaming heat in the summertime, but it has a remarkable chill in the winter to be as far south as it genuinely is. The nearness to the cold east Atlantic coast and the Chesapeake Bay seem to combine to bring in just enough wind that the chill is heightened intensely, especially in January. When I look back I can see icicles from houses trickling little bits of water on the winter porches of homes, for we often would have sun on snow, and when a Nor'easter as we called the northeast storms, moved up the east coast oftentimes Washington was that perfect dumping ground for fluffy and deep ice and snow. The snow-covered monuments and the little frozen ponds and fountain areas were so beautiful to look at. At that time one could go to Lafayette Park and see the White House all white itself, made so much whiter by new-fallen snow which would sometimes come to a foot or more during the day.

We could walk all around the capitol area in the snow and sometimes the government would almost be closed down, because most of the government employees could not get in to work from Virginia and Maryland. Snow plowing was not one of the nation's Capital's strong suit at that time. The city became ours then to run around Dupont Circle and to walk on up to the Capitol area all around the government buildings and the monuments. It was all achievable, because I always opted to live in the city after I moved in. I loved having Frank's warm gloved hand to reach for as we walked or ran, and I have such special memories of just standing under street lamps and holding each other as if we were in some Hollywood scene where two lovers kiss for a long moment, the picture moving, but the warmth of that moment radiating throughout one's body.

I think it was that winter that I finally developed a feeling that I belonged somewhere. The two of us required an extremely small amount of entertainment. I rarely went anywhere the Marine Band played. Obviously I was not invited to State dinners, but Frank would begin to take me to concerts which were easily found around Washington, and I would fall in love with classical music, so much so that I could hardly bear to listen to anything else. At that time, too, Frank was fascinated with electronic music and fun shows like Peter Schicklele and his group. Most of his friends, like him, were using their Washington period as a time and place to further their musical training, so we would go to graduate recitals from Catholic and Georgetown Universities so there was always more beautiful music to hear. One great night was a night we went to a concert by the well-known black folk and blues singer Odetta.

I loved the choral concerts at both the Catholic and the Episcopal cathedrals, for the choirs there could have all been professional singers down to the last person. Sitting in the chapels with the sunlight streaming through stained glass during the day or all lit up at night we could lose ourselves in the most beautiful singing that I had ever heard in my entire life. We could be entertained constantly if we desired such, but we chose our concerts and we chose our evenings out, for we also were equally content to stay in. That is when we would listen to records from the likes of The Beatles and the Rolling Stones, make some good food, and share it with Diane and Jim, Isabella and Stephen with their new baby, or with Kathy and Eric who had a new baby as well. I kept feeling as if I was lost in some kind of wonderful story and when I woke up, I would feel the pages of a chapter in a book closing and I would somehow be transported back in time.

My world was real, and the Appalachian child was feeling as if heaven had arrived somewhat early, for I had so adapted to Washington life that I knew something of the old me was being lost. I had things to share with Frank also, though. For instance, we loved a Greek restaurant called The Astor, and I got hold of some Greek recipes. I was no stranger to making food. My boyfriend loved for me to cook and I could make it all within a short period of time. Moussaka, eggplant parmesan, more Greek than Italian, hummus, and baklava. If Frank liked it, I learned to make it.

I'd been trained in the kitchen of "God help me! What does Mama want me to do with all of this stuff she pulled out of the garden and left me to fix?" I knew the nature of food preparation and I'd had a home economics teacher who taught us to make the right sauces to "please your man!" Southern women were sealed before birth with a hidden mark that delineated them as women who would learn to feed a family, for was that not what we were all living for? The South also, simply due to climate and our ability to forage, also gave us an upper hand when it came to the kitchen. We all enjoyed sharing meals and holding other's babies. Frank and I only got nailed once for our cooking when a couple from another band came to dinner, took one look at the beautiful eggplant parmesan and said, "We can't eat anything that looks like that." Fortunately they ate salad and dessert, but never in my life had I heard such a statement. Southern manners dictate that you act overjoyed about what is placed in front of you even if it looks like dirt, so I sat with my heart overwhelmed that anyone had the nerve to be so callous.

I introduced Frank to my cultural tastes as well, which included my continued love for my mother's style of pinto beans, potatoes, cornbread, and onions, and it proved to be another feather in my bouquet of exotic events, because Frank immediately loved it all. He began to listen to a little country music and found the lyrics to be amusing, but also somewhat tender. So being with a fellow from California turned out to be not distant at all from all of the things I loved, and I never had to pretend that my life was something different. Frank enjoyed watching me grow as a person and he was fascinated by my ability to adapt. That I was well read and continued to add to that did seem to be important, because education in his family was not a choice so much as a right, and he liked that I could keep up with conversation when needed. He also seemed to think that I was special just as I was. I did not have to be a musician, change any facts about my history, or hide behind any shell. It was alright to be me, Barbara Ellen Everett, born on a mountain top in Alabama and raised on a dirt farm in

Tennessee. Even to this day, I would tell any girl that if she is having to remake herself because she thinks she is in love, then it is a false love, for the very word involves the essence of all that separates us from lower species—that love is a natural feeling. Love does not mean that you stop where you are, but it does mean that you can grow with the person and if sharing your basic self is not good enough, you are with the wrong person. Let them get a piece of clay and mold it, but you are not a thing to be molded. You are flesh and bone and someone will love you as you are.

My confidence had so grown that winter that I will keep it forever as a treasure trove of wonderful. I can almost feel my lungs fill with the fresh cold air, see us walking on winter streets and skimming over icy sidewalks.

Chapter Forty Seven

The year 1969, with its howling winds and ever-present wintry storms and ice, would be a ferocious year, not only from the perspective of winter, but from all across America. In every city, the people were calling for an end to the war in Vietnam, and as the boys came home from service, I cannot imagine what they felt like after having been out there fighting every conceivable sniper the jungle hid, seeing Agent Orange dropped everywhere to kill the foliage and knowing that it was apt to affect not just the people of Vietnam, but they were going to bring it home, their nostrils flaring and filled with the burning, the stench of death, and looking back at villages they'd helped burn and knowing that in that fire were children and grandmothers and parents who did not have one darned thing to do with the carnage nor Communism but who were among the glowing embers.

The March wind would bring in a march on the Pentagon to end the war, another time when the streets of Washington would overflow with busloads of college kids and citizens from all over the country who were calling for an end to the killing fields. I remember how naive it was in some regards that it was applauded that young men were burning their draft cards right there in Washington and more parents were encouraging their kids to hit the road for Canada, anything but fight this Vietnam War, which was draining the federal coffers and causing the country to have an increase in poverty across the nation. We were not the manufacturing hub that we'd been in World War II, and fuel prices were going up. The concept of alternative sources of energy was in the back of people's minds, but oil was still the golden liquid the country ran on, so more and more women were coming in to the work force, as my folks might say, "to make ends meet."

From Detroit to Washington on out to San Francisco, it had become a national cry, especially among the young, to end the war and it was not done thoughtfully. Had we not been taught that communism was the enemy from the day we left our mother's breast? To this day we, as a nation, owe these young men and women who served a collective thank you. Their sacrifice wasn't their choice. They had been drafted and they could not hide behind the hardships of home or college degrees. To be a conscientious objector still carried with it a negative connotation that suggested cowardice. The home boys did not know to look for all of the ways of not going, but they kissed their families goodbye, and so many would return less than the sons who had left, because the painkillers available on the battlefield this time, could be bought for a price were things like heroin and cocaine and per every war, the alcohol flowed like honey.

How easy it was to be young know-it-alls when you had the blessing of a home to hide in and had no experience with jungle rot. Never in the known history of this country, had soldiers ever been treated this way. Later on I would run into them when I worked in a V.A. hospital, and I can honestly say that I could pick out a Vietnam vet from the minute they opened their mouth, for usually the voice was angry, impatient, and something which resembled arrogance, but which I would learn later was their sense of betrayal. I was taking care of them by the time the alcohol and drug addiction had turned their livers into non-functioning organs or when they were in kidney failure. They were leaving this world as sons and husbands lost to a country that had not recognized them as heroes. When we were marching for peace, we should have all been carrying banners just for the boys and not those that said, "I don't give a damn, we gotta' get out of Vietnam."

The ones who came home have probably let us get off too easy, for they have not asked for more apologies, and we haven't found a way to make up for our own stupidity. When we are able to simply admit that there are leaders, wealthy and influential individuals, with zero conscience, then we can finally conclude that there are some situations we cannot fix and we can take our time, our national funds, the lives of service men and women, but no matter what we do, we cannot give such rulers a heart. Some wise woman once said this and I have remembered it: nations often wind up with the rulers for whom they have asked as well as the lifestyle in which they feel comfortable. Though it is hard for us to conceive, there are some societies that request a dominant government and who are willing to keep their people enslaved, but can we change such a society? Our 20th century history shows how difficult it is, and the World War II victory remains our military's finest hour.

Frank and I had other things to think about also, and as we talked marriage, I suppose that I should have been concerned that opportune times would come and go. I would not be offered an engagement ring, but I did not feel afraid, because for all the world, Frank was becoming what appeared to be a full partner to me and we were rarely apart. His sister would be the first of his family that I would meet, and I thought that she was exquisitely beautiful because she was generally blond of hair and had the same large blue eyes Frank had—the wonderful Irish blue eyes of their one Irish grandmother and I would find her to be absolutely fascinating. because she had just gotten her master's degree and a fellowship in computer science to the University of Wisconsin in Madison after completing her bachelors degree at U.C. Berkeley. She had managed to have a wonderful trip to Europe and was coming back knowing full well that she was unique in the new world of computer science and then she came to Tim's place—as she and the other Californians called him so as to not confuse him with his father who was also called Frank.

I have little memory of what all that we did together, but Frank Timothy had managed to get his sister a place to stay or he may have decided that she could just have my place, but during her short stay she was going to learn the truth of her brother. He had a serious girlfriend, a very serious girlfriend, and I do not know how much they knew out in California at the time, but when she returned home, she was apt to know that her brother's relationship was not to be taken lightly. I marveled at how natural it seemed that her life should have such a pleasant order as to go to college, to have one brother and an adoring mother, and I would learn that she was probably one of the smartest girls in San Francisco, having graduated not only Summa Cum Laude from Berkeley, but also having graduated from her high school—known for its academics—Lowell High

School of San Francisco as a valedictorian, just as her brother had done from another high school there. I thought that this must be some kind of brilliant family and I had good conversations with her while Frank played a concert on one of her few evenings there. She had kindly lugged her brother a pasta machine from Italy and that was in the days before rolling luggage, so that was quite a sacrificial gift.

We were very impressed with it, though at the time none of our friends had gotten into pasta-making, and we had no earthly idea of what to do with it. For the time being it would become decoration. I let them have time alone, because I did not wish to be invasive, and they had lost their father the year before, so I believed that they should have private time to discuss their mother, how everyone was coping, and what Roberta would be doing once she got back out to the west coast. In some regards they were very similar, but at seventeen months his junior, Frank's sibling was probably a little more shy. I think that even though she had a wonderful time in Europe, she expressed gratitude in going home, finally, to the most "beautiful place on earth." It would be some time before I knew what that really meant. It was fairly apparent that Frank and I were staying together. Either that, or the hand-washing in his bathroom was for cross-dressing, but we did not endeavor in any manner to cover up that we were a pair.

I did not know that this was probably my first hurdle to cross in becoming a family member and that before summer's end, I would be meeting not just his sister, but also his mother. By this time Frank was going to my family's places, the homes my siblings had established in Virginia and Maryland. Though they had seen little of me, he was welcomed right from the start. My brother's new twin daughters thought my husband was a wonderful toy, and on the good spring days, he would lie on the lawn and they would take turns jumping on him. I became aware of a man that I had never met before, one who played games with children, who let them use him like a trampoline, and I began to think about the television families of my youth where the fathers were kind and they always knew just the right words to say to children who needed discipline. So here he was, that man.

It was true. California fathers really existed, and this man, my chosen love, had already become a *Father Knows Best* or *Leave It to Beaver* kind of dad.

I then, at the ripe old age of twenty, knew that this was the man I longed to marry. We would have the most wonderful summer riding bikes along the C and O Canal Bike Path that ran through Georgetown, walking through Rock Creek Park, and taking a trip out to my relatives' now and again. We would begin to have visits from people that he had known in Philadelphia and in California growing up and I never thought of being in a position where they needed to like me, for I felt it was all about how we felt about each other. We were pleased to do everything under the sun in Washington that didn't cost much money. There was constant entertainment. Then more and more we were like a couple as we visited the military friends he had made from all of the bands. As the time passed, we were solidly connected. When you got one of us, then you got the other. It never occurred to me that had any of these people found me less than desirable they had a lot of influence on this man and I could have been left out in the cold dawn of aloneness.

My naiveté to this was probably my salvation, because I had developed a confidence and comfort about me for the very first time in my life. I felt that it was almost preordained that we would find each other in our worlds, which could have not been further apart without something divine separating the landmasses and creating another ocean between us. Somehow things just happen to me, and without an engagement ring, I took it on faith that come the next spring we would go out to California and be married as it came nearer his time to depart from the Marine Band. Fear of losing him was not even something that occurred to me, because I trusted him with my life. Was I as dumb as the college girl that I'd been to have placed such trust or was I finally just knowing that things were going to be all right? Was I waiting with a sense of awaiting the next disappointment? Absolutely not. We had begun to introduce ourselves as engaged, and when the wedding conversation would come up, we would both answer, "next spring," without a hint of questioning from either of us. These moments were golden, as golden as I would find the summer hills of California one day. I will not live my life asking, "What were my happiest moments?" but somewhere if I did, then these would be as high as the mountain where I was born, as high as the mountain my mama had walked up to marry my father so many autumns ago.

By 1969 most of the group whom I had loved so very much, the VISTA and Peace Corps volunteers, the young men who were my first insight in to the relationships of men and women, so many people from the governing body of downtown Washington, D.C., and friends from George Washington University Hospital and University Research Corporation had all somehow gone on to other jobs and other things. I had made new work friends at the Society of International Law, a most wonderful place to work and to have international figures, heads of universities, and people of national and international importance to pass through. They are still having the famed moot court competitions that brought the nation's best and most talented law students to Washington to participate in life-like experiences of international law. I was a private secretary there, and I was chosen to be the one who would meet and greet people as they came in. I also served tea to the head of ASIL each afternoon and had the uncanny ability to make this man smile even when he seemed rather dark and was feared by most of the staff.

I loved my job, and that got me selected to meet people of influence world-wide. I wanted to think that it was all my brain power, but as I have aged I am loathe to admit that I know now that they placed someone at the front desk who had some poise and maybe a glimmer of youthful beauty. If you came to our place off Massachusetts Avenue in late 1968-69 you would have been greeted by me, and I would have made you feel comfortable, important, and wonderful. In-so-far as Washingtonians go, I did have a deep respect for the lawyers, especially those in international law, and for those members of a future or then present Supreme Court. They were on my list of the world's smartest people to whom I did not mind showing some respect. I usually did not bring bad days to work, and even later in life I endeavored to make that a rule—if something was wrong in my heart, people to whom I was responsible were going to have to be mind readers to know it.

Personal issues got left on the doorstep, except I did befriend the law librarian whose family made the Marlborough Music Festival a summer's tradition, and they knew about my betrothed's school, the Curtis Institute of Music. The Marlborough lovers were impressed with the credentials of the young man who would pick me up many days. Suddenly I was in another world with all of these folks and I did not apologize for my not completing my own education, but I merely told the truth, that I was going to pick up school again when it was a time that I did not need to work so hard. . I learned everything I could from these good people, and my salary remained fairly high by Washington standards, so I had something to write home about now and then. Once again I found it very easy to marginalize what I had taken on, and the job was sometimes very hard. Try typing up International Law Statistics on an old IBM Selectric, greet a senator or two, and then escorting them to the famed conference room I might have prepared during my downtime.

Chapter Forty Eight

Kathy and Carole still kept some presence around for a little while, but their big adventure was to hit the road and do what people did back then—hitchhiking out west. Carole had a car as well, so a time or two they headed for the happening place: California. If you were just released from state prison it was not unusual to hitchhike back in those days, and now and then I wondered if I was missing out on the time of my life by learning about music and planning to marry my boyfriend, for a lot of people made hitchhiking west sound as if it were the best time they ever lived. After the hitchhiking days were over, most went home and married the boy left behind in Ohio or California that they had known all of their lives.

Our circle of friends kept growing in the service bands, and we always had company or we were company in our spare time. Disappointedly though, Jim and Dianne made a decision as a couple and when they told us they had an announcement to make, I thought that a baby might be in the picture. But it was one of those 1960s decisions; they were going to sell all they owned, move to Ireland, and roam around the country making their living with Jim playing flute and Diane singing vocals. I had no idea what Wendell and Frank and I would ever do for the next Thanksgiving.

I felt broken, for Diane had been my best friend for well over a year, and Jim, Frank, and other theater-types all hung out together doing such things as improvisational theater now and then with a friend they called "Hobbs." One night we paid to go lie in the darkness of a warehouse sort of theater, and I think that we were all supposed to go into some state of alternative being. I lay my body next to Frank's and we held hands, and I have no idea what other people did, but you would hear such statements like, "Man, that was so real," and "Nothing has hit me like that before." I am telling you, Hobbs was a master of organizing theater about nothing, but later I think I would learn that he was the source for a lot of the younger guys to buy marijuana and hashish. So at this very moment you are forgetting that I mentioned the name Hobbs.

The United States felt hostile then from our perspective. Crime on the streets was abysmal at best in most American cities. Everyone was leaving churches, especially Catholics before the efforts of Vatican II had begun to settle in, and suddenly the northern people were looking southward again. War staggered on, and about the most joy people experienced was the space program, going to the moon, and hoping the stars were next. Hope was hard to find, so "start over" was one mantra people were taking seriously. Our friends Jim and Diane had made their decision to leave the country and to search for a mythical land of peace on an emerald Isle. They, as did others, felt our country was headed in a downward spiral. I hate to look back and say that Richard Nixon, not a very pleasant man, would be the person who would change national policy for the better in that regard, but I am going to have to say that he was better at international affairs than those who preceded him after President Kennedy was murdered and that part of our dream of a new day dawning had descended into the prolonged and grievous loss of more mother's sons in Vietnam.

Fortunately, our great friends put off Ireland at least through the late autumn, and Frank's four years in Washington would be ending in 1970. Selfishly, I somehow thought that real friends were for a lifetime, for that is how you think when you come from a world that does not change with time. I had known continuity, even if part of it was savage; one good part I could keep was that most of the home folks were just as present at home as they'd remained ever-present in my memories.

Mom and Dad's life was staying pretty much the same. I would hear news from home that my disabled brother was having grand mal seizures so horribly that we were not going to have him for long, and Mama started having a string of surgeries that would last for about fifteen more years. That is what happens when medical care is so marginal that a sponge gets sewn up in a poor woman after she has her gallbladder out, so after I left it was Mama or James, and if they told me my Grandfather Hood was at death's door; I felt no remorse for him. Had he slipped on a boulder and fallen into the river and the feared clan of water moccasins killed him, then maybe I would have known he got his life's reward.

I never could even begin to tell Mama that I was really sad, because my friends of all friends were leaving, the ones who had introduced me to Frank. No one back home seemed too interested in what I was doing, so I wrestled with a gnawing pain that I, too, had news, and I had problems to share, for the problems at home always seemed bigger than mine. Who would know what it was like to be from a land where development meant that you gave up your know-how in order to work for minimum wage and get to buy day-old white bread, ten loaves for a dollar now and then? Diane and I understood each other's worlds, though being from an old area like Wheeling, West Virginia, she had more culture than I did. Still, she knew what it was like to swing on a front porch swing sipping your RC cola and eating the salted peanuts which made the RC all foamy and left us to eat sweet and salty nuts. Only an old friend understood that kind of being lucky and someone's mother saying, "Come on in."

Mid-summer brought a new event in my and Frank's life, for his mother and sister came to town and stayed at a southeast Washington house where Frank sometimes house-sat for the people. So for the first time, I would be invited to meet Frank's mother. We had an understanding that during that week I would meet her, but we would each stay in our own places, and he would do as much sightseeing with them as possible. I had to work anyway, but I so dreaded a whole week without my friend and love of my life, and I worried what it was going to be like to meet the mother of my future husband, something I somehow realized he had not made as clear to her yet.

I was invited for lunch for their first Sunday in town, and what they offered seemed peculiar to me, for they had made sandwiches from cold meatloaf, and we had a favorite of Frank's mother, something similar to what we called 7 & 7, and then there was some small dessert and coffee. They would have laughed for a month had they known what an unusual luncheon this was for a southern girl on a Sunday afternoon. On a summer Sunday at our house with company, even when things were harder, there was going to be at least one dead chicken killed and fried, vegetables of all kinds, and one cake was never enough, for your hens were laying eggs, and your cows were giving milk and some old banny rooster was about to get the chopping block. No southern summer Sunday would be complete without the prerequisite iced tea made from real tea, and I knew that I would never have too much of a problem entertaining these people, or so I thought. I would become aware that this was one of my husband's favorite treats though, these meatloaf sandwiches, so I left armed with something more that he loved.

Being apart for a week seemed like a long sacrifice, but the first night after he settled them in, I had already started resting under my covers and watching some television, and I reluctantly peeked out the window—having had my purse snatched twice already that summer, one as a gun hold up—and from the corner of my window I could see that there stood Frank. And each night of their visit he continued to return, and I would see him off in the morning before I went to work. I had not expected this from him at all, not before cell phones, and I worried that his mother might find out and think less of me, but he reassured me that the days were planned, and we had our evenings, and it was so wonderful and encouraging that he did not want to be away from me even through the family's stay.

My place was cool compared to the heat of those Potomac River basin steamy nights, and somehow that he cared that much again reassured me that the days ahead were ours. I turned twenty in 1969, and Mother and the aunts were curious, because I had not married, so I told Mama that week that I was certain of a wedding, but I did not know when, and I was so afraid of alarming Frank and sending him away by a request that we somehow make it all more official. As the band wives kept having little ones something else was beginning to stir deep within me, that I would like to have a baby.

Even as late as 1969 an abandoned pregnant girl could depend on the mercy of some Catholic girl's home, so I was repressing what was already the pride and joy of our military friends who tended to be somewhat older than me. I was also so fearful of losing this man who loved me and said so regularly, so I would just tell Mama, "Frank said that we will marry in the springtime in San Francisco." She would reply that she knew that I had always been a good girl, and I would know that my mama saw me as the pure girl who left home so terrified of being with a man that I had to lock myself in the bathroom, because Mama would not send them away knowing what they were probably really there for.

She wrote me a letter, and after the illnesses at home and the, "When are you coming home?" question, she said so out of character, "Then I am gettin' old. My little Barbara getting married." I wept, for I felt unsure of what next spring would bring; I was beginning to want to see Lexie Crossroads, most of our family, and I could not for one minute tell Mama that I really wanted a baby like the other cousins. It would not happen, and it could not happen. All of the band member husbands even showed despair when their wives announced pregnancy, and I had grown up in a world where a new baby was the first thing that happened in a marriage.

The notion of a pregnancy before marriage left a girl with little choice unless she married and the husband could act as a provider. Another option was to allow your baby to be placed in a proper home or have the shotgun wedding of old, but worst of all, homes for unwed mothers still existed in 1969. Some women went to Vietnam to take care of men with faces burned or shot off, but if they came home pregnant then everyone was concerned about everything except for the life of that young woman who would be that baby's mother. Forget the stupid bra-burning and the women's love-ins as far as I was concerned and start making women proud that their bodies could produce such a wonderful gift instead.

The strength of the new birth control pills was so great a mare could probably not ovulate, but it was only the women who got sick from them and the husbands who put their hands over their heads when they learned of their wives' pregnancies. Most men by now knew that one could prevent pregnancy with pills, but they did not want to hear that you were getting sick every month just by taking these hormones. Prophylactics did not have great names like "Monster" or "Burly Man's Finest," nor were they ribbed and flavored so the women were supposed to be ready to lie down at a moment's notice in this new paradise for sexually active young men, and that was about every mother's son, even then. Praise God that my generation would begin to say that such indignities had to end and young women, look at us and thank us, for we are still fighting that war for you, and that sanctuary that is your womb deserves to be treated like the spiritual house it is. Bless the babies that were given away and bless the moms who had no choice other than to hear that child's first cry and see it whisked away from her young arms because she had no right to make informed consent. Her parents were the last word on whether or not she would get to keep her baby and once she had it whether or not they would help her. Some did not help just to punish their daughters. Then she would have to make it on grace wherever she could find it.

How many pink little hands would never feel their mother's breast, nor take her milk, much less just lie in her arms, solely because pregnancy was still seen as a woman's shame. I praised some of the old country preachers who were making some waves in churches by suggesting to fathers that they might have had a hand in creating a child, and the younger pastors were picking up some of this as sermon and passing it on. It would still take another decade if not two before women would be able to dream of themselves as equal partners, and whether out of necessity of loss learned from lessons of enslavement, black women seemed to huddle around far earlier than the white women to take care of their pregnant girls. People of color recognized first that a little child was a gift and a reason for celebration. White poor women, well into the late 1970s, would still see the burden of a newborn as something to be shared only when the equation of perfect family model was met. A mother and father and other children got big points for a job well done, but the sharing, the gathering, and the grace of celebrating that mother to be was still awkward were it an unwed white mother. Oh, I ache for the children and the mothers who had to part; know this, sweet mothers, that someone, and many of us, still grieve for your loss, and we will not forget you. And those of you who were the babies, your mother had little choice, so mourn for her, and she will be mourning for you in the afterglow.

Chapter Forty Nine

When I would go with Frank to the Marine barracks for the program which was available to all of the visiting public gathered in Washington, I would sometimes remember when my old roommate and I went to a concert at the Capitol on those same kind of summer nights, and the young men in uniform walked by us, and I wondered what their lives were like. As I grew to know Frank more and more and would accompany him on such outings I would learn that most of them were either fellows not unlike Frank, only some were married and had a family, and most were just living in Washington because they were talented enough to get into one of the most prestigious bands and stationed near the President. Never did I see myself as being engaged to one of them, because I wanted to be a doctor, and that was what I had set out to become, because I was meant to be a healer, the earth mother who could strike out disease like a lightning bolt, but I waited until the majestic display of rifle exchanges, swords, marches, and all such gallantry pleased the crowds of people from all over the United States. Now I was walking out with one of those men on my arm. Frank could not march with the bassoon, so he had some old hollowed-out trumpet or something they gave to him which he could make obnoxious sounds with—which he did at one parade to my memory. A distorted noise equated with passing gas in the perfect situation granted such laughs that fellow marchers could hardly keep from falling over if he blew in to the darned thing, but he had the marching down and whatever else he needed to do for the Marine Corps.

By then our friends Isabella and Stephen had become close friends along with Kathy and Eric, all musicians, so I was sort of the odd person out. I got to hold their new babies closely and we all seemed to share dinner at one house or the other at every given chance, so my fear of loneliness was disappearing. I had been taught by my mother to get up and wash dishes after ever meal so I think that made me a welcome guest, particularly at Isabella and Steve's place, for these people had a handle on recreational activities and way before any of us ever knew, they had found that housekeeping was a futile effort. It is entirely feasible that dishes might not have been thoroughly washed for a week or so when I would begin. But sometimes I liked to work in their kitchen by myself, for I escaped conversation about the more technical aspects of the music, and I could just think about moments that I loved, the pleasant conversation over dinner, and I would hope that a little one might wake up for me to hold in my arms.

Our favorite subject was politics, and we were all rooting for Hubert Humphrey to become our new president. Our Kennedy enthusiasm over public office would return, and if you lived in and love Washington you talk a lot of politics, because *The Washington Post* was your daily read, at least for all of us. Still trading spaces by then, Frank and I began looking for a place to live together and share our limited resources, and with my desire to garden organically, have my children naturally, and live the San Francisco experience of a natural woman; we decided we could only take a place outside Washington—to my heart's greatest pain. With no units in Frank's building we found a place in Arlington, gathered up all of our junk, and without asking anyone we moved in that early autumn thinking that spring would come soon enough for me to become a bride.

One phone call to Frank's mom put urgency to the situation when she told her son much to his surprise and mine, "You know your father would not have approved of this and neither do I." Her problem was not with me as Frank's girlfriend, but we were living together unwed, so on that warm early autumn night Frank finally showed me where the power was: not in an engagement ring but in his mother.

He finally said, "I guess this means I should honestly ask you. Will you marry me?"

I thought that was what we were planning all along, but he meant within a month or two, so the next day I was on the phone to a disenchanted priest at St. Matthew's Cathedral from whence had come President Kennedy's funeral when I was in the seventh grade, and I explained to the priest that we really needed to get married—fast—not realizing that I had not explained why. He was less than thrilled when I told him when and explained to me that we had not allowed enough time for marriage preparation classes, much less the publishing of our banns of marriage, another way of saying to the world, "We will marry on such a date, and if you've got a good reason to stop this wedding, then you better spill it now, or forever hold your peace." By the time I had finished talking to him I was a disenchanted Catholic again, so I wound up calling a Unitarian Church friends knew about on 16th Street, and thus a disenchanted Episcopalian priest who had become Unitarian looked at his calendar, and a wedding date was set for November 23rd, 1969, which to most people would have seemed impossible. But big weddings were out then as well as the trappings of all the finery associated with weddings.

I will admit that I was nervous, excited, and even a little conflicted, for I had a couple of other people who were most interested in me at the time, and one was a very attractive Pentagon lawyer that stayed with us sometimes, but I knew that after all of this time I chose Frank, and he chose me. So everything began to happen so rapidly that I hardly knew what to do. I had never been to a wedding before, but I had seen pictures of my sister's wedding at St. Matthew's some years before. I never thought to ask to see if her dress would fit, for she was several inches shorter than me, and it was a formal gown. I had read how the California brides were just going for regular mini dresses—at least that is what the magazine said, so I chose a short sage green dress and had a small hair piece made to go with it. I did not know anything about bridal showers particularly, and when Sister said that she would give me a reception after the wedding I thought that was a very nice thing to do, because usually women of my world either got a night in the Smokies and went home the next day to take care of the cows, or they just went home, took care of the cows, did the evening chores, and they had experienced becoming a bride. This reception idea was just overwhelmingly generous, for left up to me we would have gone to that church, gotten married, and maybe we would go to our favorite Italian restaurant on Constitution Avenue and called it a day.

Chapter Fifty

Frank dropped me off at Sister's house the night before the wedding, and when asked what I was doing for flowers I said that I was going to make my own bouquets. Having chosen Diane as my bridesmaid, we would just sort of coordinate our dresses. Frank planned the music with my favorite canon from *Appalachian Spring* and a couple of pieces that he had arranged for a woodwind quintet, and he honored my request that they play the traditional wedding march. By the time I had planned the entire thing, and after I bought the flowers for the bouquets at some K-store kind of place, we had spent less than four hundred dollars and fifty cents, and I could hardly look Frank straight in the face to say that we had spent that much which he thought was somewhat hilarious. Our friend Merlin was to photograph the entire thing for us for free being a photographer as a hobby. The poor guy and his wife had had their cars tripped up twice, because Merlin did amateur radio, and having chosen to live in a trailer park had gotten labeled as communists because of the antennas on their house and because Merlin had a Russian name, but I was so appreciative that he was voluntarily taking his time to do our wedding pictures.

Mama had sent me a little box that had, as she put it, "Just a little something to wear on my wedding night." Without opening her package I knew that it was "baby doll pajamas," and I told Frank so. I was surprised that he had never heard of such a thing, so I was feeling extremely amused that I was going to have "baby dolls" to spice up my wedding night. My mother had climbed up the darned side of Sand Mountain, met Daddy, her preacher, and an older brother at age sixteen, then she had to walk all the way to Pisgah to Uncle Weaver's home place where Uncle Weaver informed her he—not even Daddy—would be expecting three meals a day beginning the next morning. So those pajamas meant a whole lot to me when my mother probably had one change of underwear and a slip at best having run off while her mother and brother were doing the milking, and the last words she heard heading up the mountain being her brother's "I hope the old heifer never comes back." So I called home on my wedding day just to check in and to hear Mama say, "I sure wish we could be there." But we had no place to keep them and certainly not the money to fly them up. And it was rare that girls down my way needed a mama at their weddings. Really, weddings did not get a lot of attention, but for the few in the county who knew the ways of the land outside and away from our mountain and valley floor.

I was invited to a lunch with the lawyer for whom I was secretary at a very fancy French bistro along Connecticut Avenue one day before everyone at work got the news. I thought that it was just because I had been working so hard and that he wanted to treat me. Instead, he was seeing if I wanted to date him, so that was when everyone at work would learn that I had a wedding coming up, and I thought they seemed rather shocked about the brevity of the formal engagement, and I once again just did not get the expectations that they seemed to have about weddings. They brought me a most beautiful package, and there before me was a casserole with the most beautiful silver band and lid to make everything look beautiful when I served my guests and a wonderful card with all of their names on it.

No one had to do anything for me to get ready the day of the wedding, but I pieced together my bouquets in sister's bathroom sink and endeavored to clean up the colossal mess that I had made. A telegram arrived from my boss, Jim Nafzieger, wishing me all the happiness in the world, and I have it to this day stashed away in the tiniest memory box the kids will ever find some day. Mama called me back to tell me there was an emergency, that I owed my college another two hundred dollars which I'd thought was paid for with my library work, but since I had quit school it was left for me to pay. I fell into tears about my over-spending ways again and made certain that Mama and Daddy did not have to worry about it, so I borrowed some from Frank.

My brother-in-law and sister had been at each other's throats all morning, and I would learn why later, but it got on my nerves so much after the phone call that I told them to just cut it out.

"This is my wedding day," I said, finally getting the drift that weddings were bigger deals than I had imagined. Fortunately I had written our wedding vows because as it turns out our former Episcopal priest was questioning the reality of God, and I wanted a spiritual tone to my wedding if nothing else. People were going to hear the Word that day one way or the other. So I had already dropped the vows off at the pastor's office, and on that warmer than usual day for November my family was taking me to the church, and my brother-in-law sweetly had a little Kodak which he shot some pictures with. Suddenly, as we got closer to the church, my heart was racing, and I felt terror cross over me, and I knew that I should feel happy, so happy. Was this not what every twenty-year-old longed for? And the aunts wouldn't have to give up on me catching up with their girls, but I was in panic mode.

I got to the church, and Frank had something to tell me, a last-minute message about walking down the aisle, because the pastor was feeling more Episcopal that day, and I could hear all of the prelude music as Diane hugged me trying to calm me down as only Diane could do, and then it came—the wedding march. I undoubtedly almost ran down the aisle. My relatives were there who lived in the nearby District communities, those who had settled because of the good work, and all of the military friends, the musicians who played, wives, a few children, and on the groom's side there were our newest friends Jack and Pam from the Bay Area who had come up to Westinghouse near Annapolis, Maryland. I could feel the fire in my face burning, tears streaming, panic attack still in progress, but Frank left the quintet, came down from the altar, took my hand, and I began to collect myself as my eldest brother responded to the, "Who giveth this woman to be married," and Brother gave the, "I do, in the name of her father who cannot be here today."

I was getting married, the brainiac who was supposed to be the "brain surgeon" according to our high school year book, and all seemed to go well enough until I realized that Merlin, the photographer, had not shown up, and the only pictures we would ever have would be the few made with my brother-in-law's little Kodak. I was very sad about that, though I think had my mother and father seen me get married in a green mini dress in a state of sin they would have been horrified. Later I would learn that my teenaged niece was heartbroken about the dress I wore and I thought we were bidding everyone for the most part farewell at the wedding, but when they got me back to my older sister's place, I walked into her home, and almost the entire wedding party had come. There was food for everyone, beautiful punch, and the prettiest wedding cake under the heavens. Kathy and Carole had bought me a white dove, the peace symbol which I loved, as a gift as the centerpiece for my cake, and I was unprepared for just how beautiful it all looked.

Next, Sister asked me to come to the family room, and there was a stack of packages in pretty papers with bows long before everybody stuck things in bags, and I asked, because I was curious, "Who are these presents for?"

And my sister sort of whispered, "They are for you, dummy. It is your wedding day." Now give me a break here, because remember, I never looked at bridal magazines, and I thought my sister got presents because she got married in St. Matthew's like a proper Catholic girl, so what made me worthy of this stack of presents? Most girls I knew started out with their mother's few things that could be spared and then increased their basic needs around Christmas if there was money available. Were all of these gifts for me and for us just for getting married? I did not count on this, for certain! I got a mixer from Jack and Pam, a real electric mixer, and for some reason that alone took my attention away from everything else so beautiful. There were linens and a real flower vase, and someone gave me a set of bibs—just in case, but no soul there other than Sister, Diane, and me ever knew that I had no earthly idea that presents and a wedding reception were part of a wedding day. I was overwhelmed at the generosity, and when it was over and time to go back to our place in Arlington, I had even sort of put aside that our neighbors were going to figure out that we had just come from our own wedding. We were afraid we could not get this choice house so near Fort Myers if they'd known that we were not married when we moved in, for at that time it was not an everyday thing.

We returned home, and I was so worried, because Frank was quiet all the way, and I somehow felt that all worries were on hold at that moment, but something was wrong. We had some champagne, and I just knew that taking out Mama's present would bring him around to the joy of the moment, and I had even read a small book on surprises for your lover on a wedding night. So I put on Mama's blue baby doll, laid my head onto his back, and told him that he had to see Mama's present, and when that did not work, I used whispers I had read in the *Make Your Man Happy* book, and he and I alone will go to our graves with those words—our own to remember.

And then all of the sudden a rattlesnake came from under the pink honeysuckles, and the wind whipped all of the trees like a tornado had hit, and my mind was spinning, for I was not there. I had to be someplace else, because I heard these words from him: "I feel like I am getting sick and that I have a bad cold. In fact, I felt so bad that I thought about not even showing up at that wedding today, and right now I am wishing that I hadn't."

He was sick, but undoubtedly he had a case of great misgiving, and when he drove through Rock Creek Parkway on the way to the church he had considered bolting on me. I was bitten by the snake; it had come out of nowhere. Blood was dripping from my every pore, and I wanted to die then and there, and I wanted to run. I wanted help, and instead I tried to ask for forgiveness, because I had used language that was taunting and sexual and any other day were we not married he would have gone through the threat of mortal wounds to come to me, but not on this our wedding day.

Chapter Fifty One

I wish that I could say that all was just fine the next morning, but the truth is the next morning came, and he still seemed remorseful and told me the sensual words had just made it all worse. Through the years I would learn that apologies were among his weaker points. During the next few days things seemed tense, because he had come out of the forest, but I went in big time, and I had pulled the black curtain around me tightly, for I was experiencing every pain that I had suffered at the hands of men as a young girl. We did not have a honeymoon, and I did not balk when he decided to keep his usual Monday appointment of all-day bridge or chess down at the Marine barracks. I was so ashamed, and I could tell no one. Look girls, the rain is falling. We have to get home with these flowers for Mama, for we will get a whipping if we don't go now. My mind would go into a full state of waiting for the next axe to fall.

What possibly could ever make one remark that they had thought of not showing up for the wedding which a couple who seemed inseparable would share; and why to me did such inexplicably painful words been said, for we know someone after a year do we not? That night I would think of many things including packing my bags and just leaving, running anywhere. I would ask God what kind of hideous dream was I in, and I would stare at the light on the wall where the street lamp glowed. It usually was consoling, but tonight my shadow would be cast on it; and with no answers, I asked the silent shadow; what must I do to ease this hurt, and shadow just lay there looking back.

My mother's wonderful surprise would make me feel like a giraffe in cheap garments, so I dust them off, for I wanted to feel clothed and pure somehow. If I clothed myself, then perhaps I could be the girl that all seemed well with 48 hours ago. Was a cold and fever that devastating that a new wife could not just be told; "You are beautiful, and I am an idiot." But daybreak came and no such words were said, not even on Frank's awakening.

I hoped for just the right words to be said, but they did not come forth; thus I did what any rational newlywed would do from my background. I cried, and I asked what "I" had done wrong. I would learn of my new husband that there is no perfect being, not I, not him, and he would through the years avoid the expression of remorse. His upbringing was to place remorse in some hiding place, and to leave it hidden, for one was to keep such deep emotions rarely expressed. He could not deal with fixing hearts, and the tragic result of all of this hiding also left him with similar problems showing deep affection but my choice was to accept that he was responsible, giving in other ways, and that with him I felt safe and no longer without. I found my love and comfort there.

The powerhouse in his family was a mother, and in mine, I would always look to a father. I had to learn that from his childhood he was the perfect son. I became aware that he could not be the perfect son and the perfect husband, and he had been raised by a father easily old enough to be a grandfather. He was overwhelmed to be perfect in all things, so to experience doubt one day, he could not view it as that serious. He wanted me to just leave the whole thing where we were happiest and forget such a day. That was his apology to just let it go. I tried really hard, but there would be another flaw from someone I trusted to have to patch up on my heart, and it would come out years later in a psycho therapist office.

Frank would even benefit from the whole event, because I would raid every book coming out on being better at what folks in my area considered to just come naturally. From that Kinsey reports to, "Everything you wanted to know about sex." I read it, and I was out to make my man a happy one.

I did draw the line at wrapping myself in cellophane, and I decided not to tell Daddy that my new husband should be peppered with buck shot for being stupid on our wedding night.

I have found that forgiveness for destroying some of life's moments has no words, and the recall of these events are more than some can bear, but I placed them where I endeavoured not to go. His apologies were most sincere as we grew up and older. I wound up rewarding him with warm oil massages, incense, Victorian night gowns, and whatever else I could think of or read about to redeem whatever I was lacking. He never knew where or when he would be surprised; I endeavored to fix me in so many ways that I think I would have gone to Nevada to learn from prostitutes what their secrets were to making men happy, and I think the more that I did, gave him the idea that one bad night was just passed over and we were in some what of a marital bliss. It never occurred to me that a man who had been so romantic before marriage could have not given his bride the most beautiful of wedding nights. It was not in his nature. The hardest thing you will first have to do if you are going to save a marriage is to accept that each of you are imperfect, and that gives no one license to hurt out of stupidity, but for the brighter souls, it is apt to mean you stand a chance of making a wrong right before a disaster has been created. I needed the strength of a very few words: My husband had a cold, and he was scared, nervous, and he felt bad one night, and you both lived through it. I was having such a hard time finding the kind of humor I was going to have to find to make this all to leave though, so I admit it to this day that on that cold November night I needed to have given out some country justice, probably beginning with a mop handle and having one of The United State's own Marine Band player dancing on our front porch on that freezing night of November, because the fever would have come down he was experiencing, and his brain would have gotten a firm and unforgotten message that it is alright to be thoughtless maybe, but stupid and thoughtless will never fly.

But his angry words on a wedding night would equal one great big score board of secrets and whispers that were ours, that healed, that sustained us through the most difficult times. That I grieved was not the answer though, and that I would think I was worthy of being hurt just went back to bad habits I would have to break through the years where I always questioned my worth. Books were once in short supply that helped one to understand that men just do not have the general potential to over think raw emotion as do women, and Frank had the bad luck of marrying on a day when he needed his mother's chicken soup, but instead he got a wife, so the somewhat spoiled child would change with the days and years, become a better man, but he also got the benefit of my thinking I needed to hone womanly skills, and was he fortunate that I endeavored to become the best lover he could have known. No one polite would ever ask, and we would never tell, but we kept our marriage interesting, the two of us, and neither us have suffered from lack of intimacy along the way. I could never have divulged my hurt to any of the family then, and had I told my folks, then Frank would have known the same manly suffering of the farm cats. That is not a beautiful thought.

We had picked up the pieces for all practical purposes within the week, or so I would make it seem. The fact was that I wanted company around us almost around the clock, for that was protection from all of the hurt. I could not look at things and just take them for what they were, a bad day—a day that he could share with none of his family except in phone calls, and the fact, too, that he was that callous, for on such critical days of your life even the most well-refined young woman would have had the same problems. Only they would have gone home to Mother the very next day. I did my very best to let it pass over me, to use my new mixer, and to begin becoming a housewife, but I was in trouble, serious trouble, and I had to pretend that all was well. He would manage an apology of sorts, admitting years later that what I said was actually quite an aphrodisiac, but I would begin to understand that no one was perfect, even the most perfect person that I'd ever known, my new husband. I thought of old ballads that warned women of such trial and scorn, and I did take it to Diane before she and Jim got away.

Probably the thing that happened that helped the most was that Diane and Jim had us there for Thanksgiving once more, and having married on a Saturday with that next Thursday as Thanksgiving I could see my husband in the same light in which I had met him, and I would take him in my arms when we got home. The bad memory would just fade, and it would be paradise from then on. It was a foolish thought if I ever had one, but it seemed to be the balm that covered the wound, that sealed it up enough that I could be his lover once more and not just an estranged new wife who was terrified that I had walked into a chamber of horrors. We would be well again and the two of us once more, because contrary to love meaning that you are never going to have to say you are sorry, a theme from a movie we would see later, it means you apologize as if it is a prayer. It cannot take a day or two or five; it must be done when needed. Then it occurred to me that in my parents' life neither of them could ever say to each other the simple "I am sorry that I hurt you so," and they would end their days calculating the normalcy of husbands and wives and how it is so normal to "fuss and fight sometimes." I wish that my mother could have heard those words once, could have said them once, but the power of conversation was not in their tool kit for taking care of themselves or their children, and it would be years before I would learn to use conversation instead of packing sorrows in like dead wood melding to a forest floor. Oh my happy day had come and gone, but a new me was already beginning to emerge, and I was going to need some help along the way, so my dear ones, remember these words: "I need help." And find a place where someone hears your voice clearly.

Marriage, according to how I was brought up, included "keeping house," "serving your man," "coming to know your neighbors," and making certain that you took every suggestion your mother-in-law had to offer, because by doing these things, you automatically became a good wife. I kept getting called back to the American Society of International Law because they had not found a suitable replacement, and I worried about money. Oh how I worried about money. There was always this gnawing fear that I would be without it again, and I did not know how to ask my husband for help. He did kindly and voluntarily pay off my two-hundred-dollar student loan that I'd so worried about on my wedding day. In my heart, I was caught between a new order where women were expected to have a career and the old model of the wife as homemaker. Most of my Appalachian sisters were not faced with that dilemma yet, but I was in D.C. and I knew that something more was expected of me.

Patching up my wedding night fiasco was still something I struggled with, for I would dream about the "not showing up" part. I did not know how to keep that terrifying prospect from entering my thoughts, though for our ordinary life, we went back to friends per usual, dinners out at our two favorite restaurants, Ninos and the Astor, and I continued to experiment with the Greek cooking we had come to love. The vegetarian part especially seemed to be more inclined to help keep Frank's tradition as a non-meat eater back in the days before we had such enjoyable spreads such as tofurkey and fake seafood to round out the cuisine. Since he was not a vegan, I got such dishes as cheese soufflés, dolmas, frittatas, and hummus with my own homemade bread down. I was becoming a doyenne of sorts in my own world, because somehow I could have a meal at a restaurant, go home, and recreate most of it. My new husband was most appreciative.

Our old college and service band friends would turn us on to the joy of Boone's Farm, Cold Duck, and other cheap and intoxicating alcoholic beverages, so that and the food that I could cook up made for quite a party. I was so afraid of losing my husband that I wanted our house to be filled with guests at a moment's notice, for therein I felt secure. Having other people around made the feeling of abandonment disappear. Diane and Jim had left us with a stash of kitchen tools when they took off for Ireland. The kitchen was a sanctuary and the rest of our place was pretty pathetic, though little by little we were finding things to make it more homey. Frank built us a bed and a parson's table early on and we had moved my comfortable couch and his music entertainment center. In those days, that could be all a home needed. One day a most joyful event occurred when Frank found an abandoned old spool that had been used for electric or telephone lines and—voila—a coffee table was added to the pathetic decor.

His mother gave us a thousand dollars for a wedding present, and with that we bought a vacuum cleaner, a miniature wringer-washer, and a sewing machine because I knew that if we were in absolute poverty, I could sew something just like Aunt Ruth had back home. I made myself a dress or two as well as a pair of pajamas for my husband that looked like something he could do tricks in when the circus came in to town, because I had chosen an orange and black-striped fabric. The 1970s would usher in an age where we were probably color blind and fabrics looked as if they were meant for creatures from another planet, but I was out to save us money because I had to prove my worth—or so I thought.

Chapter Fifty Two

I endeavored to take transcriptions for a court reporter and that was disastrous. He was accustomed to doing his own typing and after one court case where I tried to do it for him with little success, I threw my hands up in the air and quit. The last day I would work for ASIL was on a March 17th, a date that will continue in my memory, for the snow was seventeen inches deep. I made it to Massachusetts Avenue by bus then almost broke my neck on the ice-covered streets. As I was coming down from the upper offices along the beautiful staircase I had a strange feeling. I was sick, a little nauseous, and streaks of what appeared to be "my friend," as we called it, appeared on my underclothes, but then the bleeding stopped and I decided that maybe I should see a doctor. Everything else had gone wrong around my wedding day, so it was likely that I had cervical cancer as far as I was concerned. So on a day in late March I went to my first military doctor, and I had my very first woman's check-up, my knees trembling, for I figured the cancer would have advanced significantly. Instead, words floated over my head that sounded something like, "Congratulations, you are pregnant. Do you want a boy or a girl?"

I absolutely wept, not because I was so happy, but because I was afraid that once more Frank would decide to shake his head and to think about not coming along for the journey. As it was, he took it pretty well, and I made the phone call home to Mama. By then, she and Daddy had enough grandchildren that I got words such as, "Ain't that nice." And the most important question they wanted answered was when it was due, figuring that the marriage had a reason behind it after all. I think Mama was a little disappointed that the baby was not due until November, because there went her fun of nodding heads with her sisters and being able to say, "We should have known when that girl got married," but my angel's had given me the grace of keeping me out of that storm. Their Barbara Ellen was going to have a baby almost a year to the day after she got married. Mama always said the same thing to every daughter, knowing that it would not be asked of her, "Well I will be there if you need me." Mama was still at home with three young kids herself and not even taking care of the babies as the years went along since the older children did. I hated to even go through the charade of her saying, "I'll come and help you if you need me." Frank's mother, being more pragmatic, just said that the family would be really excited for us.

Military doctors then treated women like cattle. "Rustle 'em up, bring 'em in, check 'em over, and let 'em go home again." I decided on Walter Reed because my friend Isabella had said they were so wonderful when she had given birth to her little baby Carla who had died early on and especially wonderful a year later when she had a live and healthy birth of her son Matthew. By this time Isabella and Stephen were our main guides, along with our beloved Kathy and Eric, who would wind up leaving and going for a symphony job in Dallas. They helped me get through five months of unending nausea and vomiting. "It's just your nerves," the male doctors would say, but for my first five months I gained not a pound and lay in bed day and night endeavoring not to move, for movement made the need to be sick worse. One day Frank came home from work and in the fashion of most men at the time, he said that he was tired of me being sick and that was about the time my friend Isabella decided to give me the lecture.

"Barbara, these men have got to learn that they cannot get away with this kind of behavior and I want you to start now advocating for yourself. because no one else is going to do it for you." I took these words to heart as the last days of sickness began to fade. I had to advocate for myself. There was a new power coming and it was from inside women.

I next became preeclamptic, which meant my blood pressure shot up and I swelled like a balloon. The male physician's take on that was, "You are eating all of that salt and that is what is wrong with you. Do you want to spend the rest of your pregnancy in the hospital?" Again, I was crushed, because I could eat again. Mainly I craved sweet things, as if my body knew the baby needed some sweets and fat to make up for lost time, but I wallowed in the "I am sick. I am going to have to leave Frank alone. This is all my doing," because the doctors said it was. So hanging on marginally with the blood pressure just below the hospitalization line and my legs and feet swollen like tree trunks for the rest of the pregnancy, I made in until November 8th, when this earth mama was going to give birth naturally to the little baby that was about to come! I was in a hard labor from 10:30 in the morning until about 8:30 in the evening, though they would shoot me up with Demerol every so often, which made me sick and did little for the pain. Instead of what should have been a C-Section, the learned physicians decided at that point that the head was there, so if they did a nice cut like a cross all the way back to the rectum, they could do a forceps delivery of the baby—I just sort of passed out then.

About two hours later, I woke up in recovery. Steve and Frank were there and I would find out that the dream that I was dreaming, that a baby boy was being born, had not been a dream but reality. He weighed in at a whopping nine pounds, and I had failed or the books had lied about this labor stuff. One in my situation in the old days would have probably died along with a fine healthy baby, but that November 8th Frank and I had our first-born son, and we named him Jacob Frank to honor his Grandfather Heintz who had gone on before. His hair was fully blond, and his eyes were even more blue than his father's, the prettiest baby in the nursery the nurses would tell me, for large babies often did not have the pinched look of other newborns. Jacob looked as if he should have been delivered about a week earlier even though I'd had to walk myself into labor by walking the Roosevelt Island the day before hoping that he would just fall out then. He was so beautiful that I could hardly believe that he came from me.

We would go home on the coldest of November days and there were a few presents from our friends, the usual call to Mama and Daddy, and it would be six weeks before a family member of mine would come even though they lived in easy driving distance. It just was not seen as necessary. But that one day in December, my middle sister, Violet, visited me, held my baby, and gave him a little bear. I did not expect her, so I worried more that she would see that my house needed to be cleaned, and I could still hardly sit down because of the big laceration the doctors had made. I do not know why my family did not come, but I think that each of us were still in self-preservation mode, and I would see them all again around my nephew's baptism. In the valley or on the mountain, the entire clan would have shown up, but we had left that behind us, and were carving out tunnels of lives of our own. That they could not come will remain somewhat of a mystery. I got through it though the same way we did most things as children, on our own. I only could imagine how wonderful it would have been to show him off as a newborn back at home with all of the families, for that is when people gathered and were at their best: births, illness, and death. I longed for them to show me how to ease my cracking breast, to hold my baby, and to share with the cousins.

All of those gifts of Appalachian culture were lost to me in the city, even though three families now lived within less than an hour from me. We were like the mother cats on the farm, hiding out in our own places and afraid to leave what we had perchance it would disappear. Self-preservation was deep in our psyche, and though the drums beat and called for us to come together, a lead drummer had not emerged to see that such happened. As a result our distances included something far beyond miles.

Maybe the best part of Jacob's birth was that it made the marriage bond quickly stronger. Frank, Jacob, and I would now be three, and the little baby that kicked his feet so early to make his butterfly mobile swirl with pretty colors made us much better for each other. The labor from hell gave Mama something to share with her sisters for the better part of a year, and when I took Jacob home to Tennessee for the first time, I made certain that he had a pair of Duck Head overalls just like Grandpa, who was beginning to show affection with little grandchildren in a manner he had been unable to do with all of us.

Barbara at College (MTSU) – Murfreesboro

Barbara at US Capitol 1967

The Capitol, 1967

Barbara and Frank, Wedding Day – November 23, 1969

Barbara with 4 month old Jacob, 1971

Chapter Fifty Three

We would take Jacob to California the very next springtime, our honeymoon, if we could still call it that, and the family was so thrilled for that line of Heintzs was dying out, so having a boy named for a father, brother, and husband just lost a couple of years before made my coming into California for the first time quite an event. It would be the only and last time that I would get the meet the Heintzs all together, because their family had grown older and there were not many children to gloat over except for neighborhood kids Aunt Mary would sort of adopt. But Jacob was the prize, and this body, this girl from a valley they would never see but in pictures, became generally of high value early on. I was no princess, but when they gave me their mother's wedding bowl, I felt like it. Jacob was a little prince in every sense of the word. He would become the symbolic torchbearer for a family line that had almost died out. Oh my baby, my sweet baby. You made me real.

We stayed an entire month in San Francisco, and my mother-in-law would fall fully in love with our first-born, Jacob, and he would not know it, but it would be a life-long bond with her. She was fit and full of energy and ready to drop anything for the grandchildren as they came along, but she would have the most quality time with her husband's namesake. San Francisco was "The Magical City," and I would see it while the cherry blossoms swept over Golden Gate Park and while bougainvillea, roses, camellias, and all of the flowers of a tropical spring were in bloom, and nowhere outside of Washington had I seen more beautiful parks and gardens. The hill the Heintz family dwelt up on still had the old neighbors, the kind you wanted to stay around for all of your years, and they would bring fresh produce that was popping out in their gardens in and out of the city. I would see the movies of Frank's idyllic childhood when the vegetable man would come up the hill loaded to bear with all the gifts of golden California, and when Edison School was the heart of the community, and when he would take Sunday walks with his father in an area known as The Mission, for then the Mission Delores community was one of family. The things that would remain through the years were Dianda's, a wonderful bakery offering cakes for every Italian and American taste of holiday seasons and Lucca's, the Italian deli which to this day puts out the freshest and most wonderful ravioli freshly made on the premises and washed with the scents of sweet olive oils, pungent vinegars, and cheap but wonderful red wine, and baguettes.

Once, having experienced the city, I just knew that we belonged there, and our goal would be for Frank to win an audition which he took with the San Francisco Symphony at the time. His grandmother's advice to "stay in the Marine Band" would haunt us through the years; for the SFO job found Frank with nerves so tangled from all of the family hope that playing just did not come naturally to him. The second audition he would take would be in Cincinnati, Ohio, which I knew one thing about and that was that on Saturday nights when we returned from Grandma Hood's place a voice would begin on the radio: "This is your radio Bible program live and direct from Cincinnati, Ohio." That was all that I had ever heard about Cincinnati except that a girl I went to school with used to come up in the summer time to visit her cousins, and the neighborhood had a swimming pool, but it was to this place, Cincinnati, where Frank would win the audition and where we would be headed.

I read about it trying to get excited about what I read was that it had one of everything: a fine arts museum, a symphony orchestra that had remained intact while others in similar cities had died during the Depression years, and it was said to have a world-renowned zoo, as well as among the finest police forces in the nation. I paid some attention to a place called The University of Cincinnati, for I figured that was where I would probably go to school. Frank, knowing the slim chances of getting another symphony job soon, signed the contract the day he auditioned for Thomas Schippers, one of many conductors in the Cincinnati Symphony's pool of fine conductors.

I had gathered presents for every family member back home and wrapped them in boxes as souvenirs for the family in Tennessee, for going to California seemed like a privilege I should not keep to myself. Frank's mother helped me pack them approvingly, for I had been overwhelmed at the offerings of the old Cost Plus in San Francisco. I had never seen such wonderful foreign imports as one could find there or in Chinatown, and to this day, I know that there is no other place that would hold the shopping fun of going through all of the little things those places had to offer. It was the first time in my life that I would learn there were teas not known as Lipton and about wok cookery that I would never master well because I was terrified of the flames which had to come from the wok if one was cooking properly, but San Francisco was the place of goods you could sort through bins for and that were not covered with plastic when you bought them. My mother got the gifts and would say the same thing year after year: "We'll be seeing San Francisco sometime." The years would move along, and it would become apparent to me that San Francisco would be out of my parents' comfort zone, though I hold a huge pain in my heart that I never got them there. How could I explain that we knew what hills were in Tennessee, but the kind of walking one had to do in San Francisco was all too similar to the mountain Mama had climbed on her wedding day. Maybe I console myself with that as a reason that I never brought them out.

I think my folks were glad that I would be closer in Ohio though, so they showed no disappointment compared to the disappointment that began to encircle about me as I sat on the moving boxes in the summer of 1970 while the movers picked up our belongings and baby Jacob and I sat waiting to have it all loaded up. Frank had gone on ahead to an apartment we had found in a last-minute run through Cincinnati, when we had paid a visit to Tennessee after his winning the audition. I held my baby, and I cried until I could cry no more, and for the first time in my life had there been an escape chute on that lifeline, I would have bailed. As difficult as things had been changing from a young girl to a mom in Washington, I did not want to leave there, even for Frank. I wanted to stay with the family that I had created even though everyone, one by one, was leaving as their time ended in the service bands—everyone but Stephen and Isabella who had decided to stay in the area getting pick-up jobs in their fields of music. "Oh please, God, may lightning strike this box that I am sitting on, but do not send me to Cincinnati."

During our first trip I had seen the better sights like Music Hall and the Taft Museum, Union Terminal, and the wonderful downtown right out of a Christmas miracle story where families gathered and shopped and ate having fun, but the parks looked then like big open fields or the woods behind my places of early childhood. I knew not one soul, and I had no job or money of my own, and I did not understand why we had to leave Washington. It seemed as if everything important that would ever happen to me had happened there, and though my marriage had undergone a rocky start, things had settled into a pattern of generally joyful days as Frank's Marine band days ended. "Please, God, you can take me to San Francisco again. I will pick up trash off the streets if need be. Leave us in Washington or send all of what seemed like a dream away. I would even choose Murfreesboro for I know what to expect there, but do not let this day end in Cincinnati."

My ride to the airport came after all of the boxes were loaded, and I was so distraught that I did not realize that I had signed papers that said that everything we owned was bent, broken, or smashed to bits, so the movers had packed everything as if it was junk not even worthy of starting a household, and maybe it wasn't, but it was our junk. What kind of sick minds would do that to a mother and little baby? But they did. Frank had cheaped out and rented military cots for our homecoming. The upstairs neighbor's demented kids had let their rabbit loose in our apartment, and it had left small pellet gifts all over the floor, so even after Frank picked us up, I was aching so much inside that arsenic would not have been poison strong enough to relieve the pain, but before I knew it we would be settled in to our place in Cincinnati.

A few symphony members would start coming around. Ice was broken as we were invited to dinners by the good people in my husband's section, and, much to my surprise, it turned out that our neighbors seemed to think that coming into the symphony orchestra was somewhat like coming into the Promised Land. When I saw Music Hall for the first time, a hall that had been built in the nineteenth century when Porkopolis, as Cincinnati was known then, was being considered as a candidate for the permanent capital of the United States, I would have to catch my breath because it was among the most beautiful places that I had ever been. A prominent couple well known within Cincinnati had just seen that the entire Music Hall was refurbished, and little by little, I would begin to put away pre-conceived notions that I was in a place to be reminded that my soul was in jeopardy of hell at all times as the Bible program often times warned.

Chapter Fifty Four

The new life would begin to seem to have some possibilities, though the Cincinnati crowd then was not quite used to outsiders. Strangely enough we could go to breakfast in certain areas of town like the old East End, and I would hear these voices, voices that took me some four hundred miles southward, for in clusters people from Appalachia had settled along the river banks where the property was cheaper then, and every little hamlet seemed to have its own cluster of what I called back home people. So I found something that was consoling and disturbing at the same time, for the people whose dialect I caught on to well were usually poor, were often times screaming at one or two little kids, and they looked weathered like the mothers and fathers of old. Later I would learn that they had come from Kentucky and that Appalachian area, and that being in the city had brought a great liking for the cheapest beers still being produced in Cincinnati by the local braumeisters whose family names were dying even as we came, and national brands were taking over. All seemed to love one Cincinnati creation, the Cincinnati chili, and what it had to do with chili other than ground beef was very peculiar to me, because it sort of tasted like a Greek spaghetti.

It turns out that a Greek family started the whole love for these concoctions of addictive fast and cheap chili, and instead of some bar on every city corner there was a chili parlor, and we, like the rest of the people, would fall in love with it. Another local taste was something the German immigrants brought called Goetta, and it was a mixture of spring oat tips with pork analogs, as they were called. Later we would learn that analogues meant basically favouring, and it was boiled until thickened, rolled in to some kind of logs, and fried up like the east coast scrapple, only it had a lot more texture, and I found it to be much more pleasing. Here and there some semblance of a German restaurant was still in town, more similar to the Eastern European and Danish places with plenty of noodles and beef and wonderful cakes with cream-filled pastry. Outside of the Cincinnati area, one would have to go far to get a more traditional schneken, for the Germans had brought it to this city with its central hub called Over the Rhine.

By 1981, I had become a citizen of Cincinnati, and I would have put it up against any metro area in the country for great living standards. I had two more little boys, Isaac and Matthew, and I graduated from The University of Cincinnati College of Nursing and Health. I should have had a second degree in literature, for between the semesters in Murfreesboro and the years in Cincinnati I had loaded myself down with literature, for it was my great escape from the reality of learning that I could not be a brain surgeon, have three children, and be a good wife to my husband. Once again I made friends of a lifetime with names like Emmaly, Roberta, Marilyn, and all of my nursing college cohorts who were older students like me. I do not advise that anyone follow my path, because I became a sacramental object in some ways, so tired at times that I would have out-of-body experiences where exhaustion was so overwhelming that my body would be soaring over me in my half sleep, and in my thought processes. But I did it; I finished college, and I brought most of my family together for the celebration.

As in all lives, disappointments, anguish, joy, and sorrows would mix like vinegar and water, something you just had to sip to get through it, and down the path twin daughters would be born like the highest and most joyful answer to a prayer life which I never completely stopped believing in. I would make a few psychotherapists richer for having passed their way endeavoring to sort through all that had happened to me and all that would lie before me, but I would somehow be alright. "Walk a little faster," Daddy might have said, "but keep going." And I would do just that through the most difficult of those times.

My favorite story from a children's reader which I read over and over again in the classroom as a five and six-year-old was about a tug boat that went through an idyllic little town, and as with the magic of children's books, the tugboat could talk, and so many times when I was a child I would close my eyes and endeavor to go to that little town, because it was such a wonderful place to dream and to hide. Washington and San Francisco were the ideals, but in some ways I think that story of long ago was my fate, for where happier could one be than in a town where a river runs through it as it does in Cincinnati, and where for celebrations, patriotic or otherwise, people gathered at the river. Even now and then if you go up or downstream, you may pass a little town where you hear the sounds of a cappella singing, look out upon the water, and the voices ringing out so clearly, "Come home, come home, ye who are weary, come home." Softly and with tender touch a minister will lay the wounded soul down through the symbolic death of sins with the cleansing water. And something of yesterday will make you want to linger on the river's banks.

The Appalachian soul where I began exists all over the mountains and in the valleys still. Maybe we need more calling to the water and there leave the burdens and clear our paths. Everyone of us, no matter who we are or where we came from, are a part of our yesterdays. We cannot separate one from the other, and no matter how difficult was the journey, there is an echo that makes us long for a time and for a place. A sweet river, the Ohio, is now my homecoming, but something of me is left in the woods, within the pines, where the pink honeysuckle grows and the dogwoods bloom. Save them for the next mother of the child willing to find them there.

Barbara, Frank, Jacob, Matthew and Isaac

The Ohio River

Made in the USA
Charleston, SC
25 April 2015